The Good Plant Guide

Brian Davis

PENGUIN BOOKS

PENGUIN BOOKS

Published by the Penguin Group
27 Wrights Lane, London W8 5TZ, England
Viking Penguin Inc., 375 Hudson Street, New York, New York 10014, USA
Penguin Books Australia Ltd, Ringwood, Victoria, Australia
Penguin Books Canada Ltd, 10 Alcorn Avenue, Toronto, Ontario, Canada M4V 3B2
Penguin Books (NZ) Ltd, 182–190 Wairau Road, Auckland 10, New Zealand

Penguin Books Ltd, Registered Offices: Harmondsworth, Middlesex, England

First published 1991

Filmset in Lasercomp Melior
Printed in England by Clays Ltd, St Ives plc

Contents

List of Illustrations

All photographs were taken by the author.

List of Abbreviations

cm	centimetre(s)
c	Centigrade
(D)	Deciduous
dia.	diameter
(E)	Evergreen
F	Fahrenheit
(F)	Female
fl. oz.	fluid ounces
ft	feet
g(s)	gram(s)
in	inch(es)
k	kilo(s)
l	litre(s)
lb(s)	pound(s)
m	metre(s)
(M)	Male
oz.	ounce(s)
(S-E)	Semi-evergreen
sq.	square
syn.	synonym

Introduction

On the whole nurseries and garden centres supply plant material in the best size, form and condition for the individual plant. *The Good Plant Guide* has been written to help the buyer ensure that plants adhere to these specifications.

To fully understand the traditional methods of producing and supplying plant material as bare-rooted and root-balled, we need to look into the history of the supply of plant material. Today, what is used is a mixture of old and new supply systems. These traditional methods of supplying material are still of merit and are practised by many nurseries and garden centres. Plants prepared by these means should not be ignored when purchasing.

Some plants were always grown in pots, owing to their reluctance to transplant and establish from bare-rooted or root-balled material. Today this method is being extended, and pot-grown stock is coming to the fore, but it will be some time before the transition is completed.

To the range of bare-rooted, root-balled and pot-grown plants, root-wrapped and pre-packed plants have been added for greater convenience. The former is a very acceptable method of purchasing, but the latter carries many hidden problems.

Before the 1970s, and the birth of the modern garden centre, the industry supplied the majority of its trees, shrubs, roses, fruit and hedging as bare-rooted or root-balled, as well as a limited number of specific plants in pots. The majority were supplied in the autumn (October to mid-December) and a few in the spring.

In the spring, conifers were offered root-balled, the bulk of the perennials as bare-rooted, and alpines were grown in pots.

Formerly, nurseries were specialist or consisted of specialist units within the overall framework of a company. Staff were knowledgeable within their own individual fields. They could offer advice and assistance and ensure that the plant material was dispatched at the correct planting time. Particular groups such as bulbs, the roots of Asparagus and some of the more choice perennials such as Scabious and Agapanthus were dispatched at very precise times. Orders could be dispatched in three or four consignments throughout the growing year, as and when the time was right.

Dispatch was by mail order or rail with orders placed by post or telephone, after referring to a catalogue. Plants were larger than they are today, and pound for pound they were more expensive, because of the cost of postage and packing.

Staff became very expert in the range of plants they grew and handled, which was relatively small compared with that of today's garden centre. They had served an apprenticeship often in excess of seven or eight years, working with a limited range of plants.

Sadly today, when nurseries and garden centres offer the full range of plant material, the staff do not receive the same apprenticeship training. Coupled with this, the skill of the professional and amateur gardeners has been lost and the traditional Head Gardener and his team of undergardeners do not exist today, as a rule. The garden owner is the Head Gardener of today, employing extra labour as it is required.

This lack of knowledge must be put into context. There is a vast range of plants available. In the past, the information on requirements, performance, general management and techniques would rarely have been available from one source. It would have been gathered from a whole plethora of different suppliers. So today it is not surprising that all one needs to know is not available on request.

Garden books make a very bold effort, offering advice on design, plant selection, plant cultivation and general gardening techniques, but they rarely offer advice on plant purchasing because, in the main, the authors take for granted their own knowledge and experience of the production and supply of the plants they write about.

The Good Plant Guide has been written to fill this gap. It sets out to assist the purchaser, whether private or commercial, to select plant material of an acceptable standard from which the best performance and establishment can be achieved.

Horticulture is always changing and there may well be different formats in the future. However, the rules that inform this *Guide* have been in existence for a hundred years or more, and are well-proven. They have been amended to take into account today's retailing conditions, while still maintaining good plant purchasing practices.

Explanation of Entries

1. The group
At the beginning of each section the plants being discussed are placed in a plant group: Trees, Shrubs, Fruit, etc. This may not be a botanical classification; rather it is the grouping under which the plant will be found in both nurseries and garden centres.

2. The botanical name
The botanical name given is that which is most used and universally accepted at time of writing. If a synonymous name exists, this is also shown. In many cases the botanical name will be the same as the 'common name'. (See also 11.)

3. The common name
Wherever a recognized common name is known it is given, but in many cases it will be the same as the botanical name.

4. Time to buy
The way a plant is sold, that is, bare-rooted, pot-grown, and so on, is shown first, followed by the planting time that will achieve the best establishment and growth. Adverse weather conditions, such as hard frost, waterlogging and drought should be avoided and planting delayed. In some cases it is important to plant at one specific time; in others, plants may fall into more than one category; but in all cases a correct planting time should be planned for each specific plant.

5. Where to find
This section suggests the primary area where the plants may be found displayed in nurseries and garden centres. At times of seasonal interest, plants may be on special promotion and so be on display elsewhere. This may be misleading when you are trying to find what you want, but the nursery or garden centre staff should be able to guide you to the right area.

6. Size
Purchasing the right size of plant is important and the sizes shown are those which are most reliable. Many of the sizes are well-founded on a historical basis reaching back over the last 100 years or more.

Where appropriate the girth of stem at 3 ft (1 m) above ground level is shown for trees. This measurement is normally only shown in centimetres, for example, 6–8 cm, within the industry. With all other sizes, both imperial and metric may be used at present. Where applicable, stem heights, number of branches and branch size are also shown.

Some plants may be offered by the supplier correctly, but smaller than desired, for example *Acer pseudoplatanus* 'Brilliantissimum'. The need for this smaller size is due to the propagation and production method required together with the natural growth of the individual plant concerned.

Terms such as 'bush' or 'standard' are used to describe a specific pre-trained growth pattern for specific plants. Where applicable they should adhere to the British Standard formula for nursery stock, but with such a wide range of plant material available, there are some plants that are not covered by this formula, and the sizes shown are those recommended by the author.

The imperial and metric measurements given throughout are those commonly used in the nursery and garden centre industry. They do not represent exact conversions.

7. Foliage

Evergreen or deciduous is indicated and the leaf colour is given. Any deterioration that may be expected naturally and premature defoliation which is not normally detrimental are mentioned.

Many evergreens experience leaf-drop in spring and this is indicated where applicable, for example, Ilex (Holly) or Cedrus (Cedar).

8. Roots

Recommendation is given on whether to purchase plants bare-rooted, root-wrapped, root-balled or pot-grown.

Where the plant is pot-grown, the top diameter of the pot is shown as a guide, but this may vary considerably. It may be regarded as a reasonable minimum, but plants in larger sizes are of course an advantage as long as this does not affect the price adversely. In all cases they must be well-established.

No distinction has been made between container-grown and containerized plants, as both methods are used in plant production and the difference is of little consequence to the purchaser.

Roots of bare-rooted, root-wrapped, root-balled and pre-packed plants should be moist with good fibrous root systems and stored in such a way as to maintain this condition.

9. Hints

Special points that relate to purchasing, establishment, soil, hardiness or planting. Notes in this section are often most important to the success or failure of the plant's establishment.

10. Most widely available
Here an attempt has been made to list those forms that may most readily be found, but availability will always be influenced by such factors as crop failures, market supply and demand, geographical location and so on.

11. Naming
Throughout this book I have attempted to use the acceptable format for presenting plant names. You may find many other different styles used in nurseries and garden centres, both in catalogues and lists and on labels and display boards. Many names may be shortened, or only the common names used rather than the full accepted botanical name. I have only deviated from this principle with plants where both the purchasing public and the plant retailers and producers use the common names, as in Herbs, Fruit, Vegetables and Wild Flowers.

How to get the best from your nursery or garden centre

Retail nurseries and garden centres offer skilled advice but this may not be available at all times. It is not always practicable to have a skilled person on duty every hour of the trading week. So it is a good idea to check on the name and availability of the person you need to talk to in advance of your visit.

Garden centres also have very high peaks and low troughs of activity. In the months of March, April, May and June, they are normally so busy, particularly at weekends, that the staff are stretched to the very limit.

Of course you will need to visit them in these months, so always attempt to go on a weekday. If you are forced to visit at the weekends, then the best times to go are early in the morning just after opening times, lunchtime between 12–2 p.m. or after 4 p.m. These periods are often the quietest and the staff will be able to give you their full attention.

If you have a specific need or are attempting to solve a particular problem, always go armed with the full details of what you have in mind. Simple sketch plans and photographs will make it far easier for the staff to advise you correctly.

Their only aim is to fulfil your needs, but if you don't give them the correct information, they may not be able to do so.

Nursery and garden centre staff will always advise you of the correct planting distance; believe what they say, and don't overplant. If there is any major problem today in gardening, it is that of overplanting, which is not only expensive as far as you are concerned, but also a waste of plant material and nearly always leads to disappointment with the final result.

You may have had your garden designed by a garden architect or designer. This is a sensible approach if you are not sure of your own expertise, or not sure of exactly what you want to achieve. They can produce a plan that contains all the plant material you will need, which will be available from your local nursery or garden centre.

Plants are seasonal in availability. Gardens are a combination of different plant material and each item should be purchased at the best time.

You may have to search a number of outlets or use mail-order companies to find what you want. This may mean waiting a whole year or part of a year before what you want is available. Do not substitute another plant unless there is no other alternative, and if you do, take advice to be sure that it is suitable. So many groups of plants have different characteristics, and the wrong substitute can put a whole planting scheme out of balance, not only by colour but in size and stature.

Purchasing Tips
1. Check that the skilled advice you require is available, and at what time.
2. Try to visit the nursery or garden centre when they are at their least busy.
3. Have all the information with you in the form of sketches/photographs, to aid the staff in giving you the best possible advice and service.
4. If you use a garden architect or designer, listen to their advice and be wary of accepting substitutes; be prepared to shop around to find what you require.
5. If possible, always prepare the soil in advance of visiting the nursery or garden centre, and have materials such as stakes, ties and planting compost to hand.
6. If you are planting in large numbers, make sure you have the labour available that you will need.
7. If you are buying large numbers of plants, make sure that your vehicle is suitable for transporting them.
8. Never carry plants on the roof-rack, particularly when they are in leaf, unless protected with a plastic sheet or bag; even then avoid if possible.
9. Never allow roots to dry out in transit. If you are purchasing delicate plants for the conservatory or greenhouse, never leave them in the vehicle when it is frosty or very cold, particularly overnight.

Pots
Today in horticulture a wide range of materials is used for pots.

These consist of polybags, rigid or semi-rigid plastic pots. In addition to professional containers, there may be others such as fertilizer bags, tin cans, waste plastic pots from other industries, peat pots – in fact over the years almost every type of container has been used. Many of these are acceptable as long as the plants reach the other specifications required.

In the horticultural industry, plants are described as being grown in the following pot sizes – 70 mm (2¾ in), 90 mm (3½ in), 1 litre (4–5 in), 2 litre (5–6 in), 3 litre (6–8 in), 5 litre (8–12 in), 10 litre (12–15 in), 15 litre (15–18 in), 20 litre (18–21 in), 30 litre (21–4 in) – but for easy reference the sizes are shown in inches per top diameter. Plants are also sold in multiple trays, where this is acceptable.

Trees

Trees offer not only interest, height and form but are also beneficial to the environment. Whether a tree is to be used for foliage, flowers or fruit, the range available is wide, but choice will be dictated by space, and research into height and spread is important to avoid overcrowding.

Not all trees will be available from one outlet, and some varieties will need searching for.

Trees are offered in a range of sizes and pre-trained shapes. The sizes indicated are the minimum that should be accepted. Larger specimens may be available, but care must be taken not to purchase material that is too large as it rarely establishes quickly, if at all. This, of course, does not apply to Extra Heavy Trees, which have been suitably prepared for the purpose.

Some trees are not supplied pre-trained in half-standard or standard shapes and so these will require further work – but this should not be seen as a disadvantage.

Transporting trees is often difficult due to their size, but particularly in severe cold or when they are in leaf, they must not be carried on a roof-rack or in open vans. If they are, stem and leaf damage will be caused and in some cases this will be terminal or, at the very least, set establishment back.

Once selection has been made it is important to follow correct planting procedures especially in the case of trees where a rapid increase in the height and spread of the tree is required.

A hole at least 3 ft (1 m) in diameter should be dug to a depth of 18 in (50 cm), keeping the top-soil at the top throughout the operation. Adequate organic material must be added to aid root development.

Bare-rooted trees should be 'heeled in' in soil to keep roots moist until they can be planted.

If pot-grown, root-balled and root-wrapped trees are purchased or delivered at difficult planting times, the roots can be protected with straw, old carpet or similar material.

Correct staking and tying is important to aid the establishment of the root-systems and subsequent growth. Stakes and ties will often be needed for not less than five years, and with some trees, for life.

ACACIA
Wattle

Time to buy Pot-grown, April–July. Avoid adverse weather conditions.

Where to find Outside in Trees. Inside in House Plants, or under protection in winter.

Size MAIDEN Height 3–4 ft (1–1.2 m) min. Limited side branches. FEATHERED Height 2–6 ft (60 cm–2 m) min. Single stem. Minimum three side branches.

Foliage Evergreen. Light grey/green. Yellowing to basal leaves July onwards.

Roots Pots 6 in (15 cm) min. dia.

Hints Any well-prepared soil. Light stake and ties – five years. Maiden and feathered, further training for five years. Fast-growing evergreen, but hardiness suspect. Permanent containers, use a soil-based potting compost. In conservatory or greenhouse, often exceeds space allowed.

Most widely available *Acacia armata. A. dealbata.*

ACER (medium to fast growing)
Time to buy Pot-grown, any time. Root-wrapped and bare-rooted, October–March. Avoid adverse weather conditions.

Where to find Outside in Trees.

Size MAIDEN Height 3–5 ft (1–1.5 m) min. Limited side branches. FEATHERED Height 4–5 ft (1.2–2.5 m) min. Minimum four 9 in (23 cm) long side branches. HALF-STANDARD Height 10 ft (3 m) min. Clear stem of 4 ft (1.2 m). Minimum three 1½ ft (50 cm) long branches. Stem girth at 3 ft (1 m) from ground, 2½–3 in (6–8 cm) min. SEMI-MATURE Specialist nurseries supply a range of sizes.

Foliage Deciduous. Spring/summer, green, purple, gold or variegated. Premature autumn colour and leaf drop.

Roots Maiden and feathered, pots 6 in (15 cm) min. dia. Half-standard and standard, pots 12 in (30 cm) min. dia.

Hints Any well-prepared soil. Stake and ties – five years. Maiden and feathered, further training for five years.

Most widely available

Acer platanoides (Norway Maple): *Acer platanoides. A. p.* 'Crimson King' ('Goldsworth Purple'). *A. p.* 'Drummondii'. *A. p.* 'Royal Red'. *A. p.* 'Schwedleri'.

Acer pseudoplatanus (Sycamore): *Acer pseudoplatanus. A. p.* 'Leopoldii'. *A. p.* 'Simon-Louis Frères.' *A. p.* 'Worleei' (Golden Sycamore).

OTHERS *A. campestre* (Field Maple). *A. cappadocicum* forms. *A. saccharinum* (Silver Maple) forms.

ACER GRISEUM
Paperbark Maple

Time to buy Pot-grown, any time. Balled, October–March. Avoid adverse weather conditions.

Where to find Outside in Trees.

Size WHIP Height 1½–2½ ft (50–80 cm). Limited side branches. MAIDEN Height 1½–2½ ft (50–80 cm). Limited side branches. Larger may be available.

Foliage Deciduous. Light to mid green. Premature autumn colour and leaf drop.

Roots Pots 6 in (15 cm) min. dia. Balled, good fibrous root system.

Hints Any well-prepared soil, except alkaline. Scarce. Staking not normally required. Whip and maiden, further training for five years. May have bent stems. Takes time to mature.

ACER NEGUNDO
Ash-leaved Maple, Box Maple

Time to buy Pot-grown, any time. Root-wrapped and bare-rooted, October–March. Avoid adverse weather conditions.

Where to find Outside in Trees.

Size WHIP Height 1½–2½ ft (50–70 cm) min. Limited side branches. FEATHERED Height 3–6 ft (1–2 m) min. Minimum four 9 in (23 cm) long side branches. BUSH Height 6 ft (2 m). Clear stem of 3 ft (1 m). Minimum three 12 in (30 cm) long branches.

HALF-STANDARD Height 8 ft (2.5 m) min. Clear stem of 5 ft (1.5 m). Minimum three 15 in (40 cm) long branches. Stem girth at 3 ft (1 m) from ground, $1\frac{1}{2}$–$2\frac{1}{2}$ in (4–6 cm) min. STANDARD Height 10 ft (3 m) min. Clear stem of 8 ft (2.5 m). Minimum three 15 in (40 cm) long branches. Stem girth at 3 ft (1 m) from ground, $1\frac{1}{2}$–$2\frac{1}{2}$ in. (4–6 cm) min. SEMI-MATURE Specialist nurseries supply a range of sizes.

For training as walkways, tunnels, arches, pleached or fan-trained, use whip or feathered.

Foliage Deciduous. Spring/summer, green, silver or golden variegated with pink tips. Premature autumn colour and leaf drop.

Roots Maiden and feathered, pots 6 in (15 cm) min. dia. Bush, half-standard and standard, pots 10 in (25 cm) min. dia. Root-wrapped and bare-rooted, good fibrous root system.

Hints Any well-prepared soil. Scarce. Stake and ties – five years. Maiden and feathered, further training for five years. Top-worked – short lived, poor shape.

Most widely available Acer negundo. A. n. 'Auratum'. A. n. 'Elegantissimum'. A. n. 'Flamingo'. A. n. 'Variegatum' ('Argenteovariegatum').

ACER PSEUDOPLATANUS 'BRILLIANTISSIMUM'

Shrimp-leaved Maple

Time to buy Pot-grown, any time. Balled, October–March. Avoid adverse weather conditions.

Where to find Outside in Trees.

Size BUSH Height 4 ft (1.2 m) min. Minimum three 9 in (23 cm) long branches. HALF-STANDARD Height 6 ft (2 m) min. Clear stem of 4 ft (1.2 m). Minimum two short branches. Stem girth at 3 ft (1 m) from ground, $1\frac{1}{2}$–$2\frac{1}{2}$ in (4–6 cm) min. STANDARD Height 7 ft (2.2 m) min. Clear stem of 6 ft (2 m). Minimum two short branches. Stem girth at 3 ft (1 m) from

ground, $1\frac{1}{2}$–$2\frac{1}{2}$ in (4–6 cm) min. Acer pseudoplatanus 'Prinz Handjery' less attractive but offered as (A. p. 'Brilliantissimum'.)

Foliage Deciduous. Spring, shirmp-pink. Summer, green. May show black blotches and premature autumn colour and leaf drop.

Roots Pots 10 in (25 cm) min. dia. Balled, good fibrous root system.

Hints Any well-prepared soil. Half-standard and standard need stake and ties for five years min. Slow growth. Must be budded or grafted.

Most widely available Acer pseudoplatanus 'Brilliantissimum'. A. p. 'Prinz Handjery'.

ACER RUBRUM

Red Maple, Scarlet Maple

Time to buy Pot-grown, any time. Root-wrapped and bare-rooted, October–March. Avoid adverse weather conditions.

Where to find Outside in Trees.

Size WHIP Height $1\frac{1}{2}$–$2\frac{1}{2}$ ft (50–80 cm) min. Limited side branches. MAIDEN Height 3–5 ft (1–1.5 m) min. Limited side branches. FEATHERED Height 4–7 ft (1.2–2.2 m) min. Minimum four 9 in (23 cm) long side branches. HALF-STANDARD Height 8 ft (2.5 m) min. Clear stem of 4 ft (1.2 m). Minimum three $1\frac{1}{2}$ ft (50 cm) long branches. Stem girth at 3 ft (1 m) from ground, $1\frac{1}{2}$–$2\frac{1}{2}$ in (4–6 cm) min. SEMI-MATURE Specialist nurseries supply a range of sizes.

Foliage Deciduous. Spring, light to mid green. Summer, reddish shading around edges. Premature orange/red autumn colours and leaf drop.

Roots Whip and maiden, pots 6 in (15 cm) min. dia. Half-standard and standard pots 12 in (30 cm) min. dia. Balled, root-wrapped and bare-rooted, good fibrous system.

Hints Well-prepared acid soil. Stake and ties – five years. Whip, maiden and feathered further training for five years.

ACER, SNAKE-BARKED

Snake-barked Maple

Time to buy Pot-grown, any time. Balled, October–March. Avoid adverse weather conditions.

Where to find Outside in Trees.

Size WHIP Height 1½–2½ ft (50–80 cm) min. Limited side branches. MAIDEN Height 3–4 ft (1–1.2 m) min. Limited side branches. FEATHERED Height 4–6 ft (1.2–2 m) min. Minimum three short side branches. HALF-STANDARD Height 7 ft (2.2 m) min. Clear stem of 4 ft (1.2 m). Minimum three 2 ft (60 cm) long branches. Stem girth at 3 ft (1 m) from ground, 1½–2½ in (4–6 cm) min. STANDARD Height 9 ft (2.7 m) min. Clear stem of 6 ft (2 m). Minimum three 2 ft (60 cm) long branches. Stem girth at 3 ft (1 m) from ground 1½–2½ in (4–6 cm) min.

Foliage Deciduous. Spring/summer, light to mid green. Premature autumn colour and leaf drop.

Roots Maiden and feathered, pots 6 in (15 cm) min. dia. Half-standard and standard, pots 10 in (25 cm) min. dia. Balled, good fibrous root system.

Hints Well-prepared neutral or acid soil, plus extra organic material. Scarce. Stake and ties – five years. Whip, maiden and feathered, further training for five years. Smaller in size than other young trees. Stem markings may not show for three years.

Most widely available *Acer capillipes. A. davidii* and forms. *A. grosseri. A. pennsylvanicum. A. rufinerve.*

AESCULUS

Buckeye, Horse Chestnut, Red Chestnut

Time to buy Pot-grown, any time. Balled, root-wrapped and bare-rooted, October–March. Avoid adverse weather conditions.

Where to find Outside in Trees.

Size WHIP Height 1–3 ft (30 cm–1 m) min. Limited side branches. MAIDEN Height 3–5 ft (1–1.5 m) min. Limited side branches. BUSH Height 5 ft (1.5 m) min. Clear stem of 3 ft (1 m). Minimum three 1½ ft (50 cm) long branches. HALF-STANDARD Height 8 ft (2.5 m) min. Clear stem of 5 ft (1.5 m). Minimum three 1½ ft (50 cm) long branches. Stem girth at 3 ft (1 m) from ground, 1½–2½ in (4–6 cm) min. STANDARD Height 10 ft (3 m) min. Clear stem of 5 ft (1.5 m). Minimum three 2 ft (60 cm) long branches. Stem girth at 3 ft (1 m) from ground, 2½–3½ in (6–8 cm) min. SEMI-MATURE Specialist nurseries supply a range of sizes.

Foliage Deciduous. Spring/summer, light to mid green. Premature autumn colour and leaf drop.

Roots Whip, pots 4 in (10 cm) min. dia. Maiden, pots 6 in (15 cm) min. dia. Half-standard and standard, pots 12 in (30 cm) min. dia. Balled, root-wrapped and bare-rooted, good fibrous root system.

Hints Any well-prepared soil. Stake and ties – five years. Whip and maiden, further training for five years. Roots open and coarse. Limited number of branches *Aesculus × carnea* 'Briotii', stems bent. *Aesculus flava, A. indica* and *A. pavia* normally only as whip, maiden and bushes.

Most widely available *Aesculus × carnea* 'Briotii' (Red Chestnut). *A. flava* (*octandra*) (Yellow Flowered Chestnut). *A. hippocastanun* (Common Horse Chestnut). *A. h.* Baumannii' ('Flore Pleno'). *A. indica* (Indian Chestnut) *A. pavia* (Flesh-coloured Chestnut, Red Buckeye). *A. × plantierensis* (Sterile Chestnut).

AILANTHUS ALTISSIMA

Tree of Heaven

Time to buy Pot-grown, any time. Balled, root-wrapped and bare-rooted, October–March. Avoid adverse weather conditions.

Where to find Outside in Trees.

Size WHIP Height 1½–2½ ft (50–80 cm)

min. No side branches. MAIDEN Height
3–4 ft (1–1.2 m) min. No side branches.
STANDARD Height 9 ft (2.7 m) min. Clear
stem of 7 ft (2.2 m). No side branches.
Stem girth at 3 ft (1 m) from ground, 2½–
3 in (6–8 cm) min. SEMI-MATURE Specialist
nurseries supply a range of sizes.
Foliage Spring/summer, light green. Premature autumn colour and leaf drop.
Roots Whip and maiden, pots 6 in
(15 cm) min. dia. Standard, pots 12 in
(30 cm) min. dia. Balled, root-wrapped
and bare-rooted, good fibrous root
system.
Hints Any well-prepared soil. Stake and
ties – five years. Whip and maiden further
training for five years. Limited branching. Gaunt appearance. Reduced growth
rate and ultimate size.

ALBIZIA
Pink Mimosa, Pink Siris, Silk Tree
Time to buy Pot-grown, April–July. Con-
servatory or greenhouse, any time.
Where to find Outside in Trees. Inside
in Conservatory or House-Plants.
Size 9 in–3 ft (23 cm–1 m) min. Single
stem. Limited branches.
Foliage Deciduous. Spring/summer, dark
green. Premature autumn colour and leaf
drop.
Roots Pots 4 in (10 cm) min. dia.
Hints Any well-prepared soil. Scarce.
Cane or other light support – five years
min. Hardiness in doubt.

ALNUS
Alder
Time to buy Pot-grown, any time. Root-
wrapped and bare-rooted, October–
March. Avoid adverse weather con-
ditions.
Where to find Outside in Trees.
Size WHIP Height 1–2 ft (30–60 cm) min.
Limited side branches. MAIDEN Height
1½–5 ft (50 cm–1.5 m) min. Limited side
branches. FEATHERED Height 3–9 ft (1–
2.7 m) min. Minimum five 1½ ft (50 cm)

long branches. STANDARD Height 8 ft
(2.5 m) min. Clear stem of 5 ft (1.5 m).
Minimum five 1½–2½ ft (50–80 cm) long
branches. Stem girth at 3 ft (1 m) from
ground 1½–2½ in (4–6 cm) min. SEMI-
MATURE Specialist nurseries supply a
range of sizes.
Foliage Deciduous. Spring/summer, mid
to dark green or gold. Premature autumn
colour and leaf drop.
Roots Whip and maiden, pots 6 in
(15 cm) min. dia. Feathered and standard,
pots 10 in (25 cm) min. dia. Root-wrapped
and bare-rooted, good fibrous root
system.
Hints Well-prepared, moist soil. Scarce
in garden centres. Obtain from nurseries
and forestry. Stake and ties – five years.
Whip, maiden and feathered, further
training for five years.
Most widely available *Alnus cordata*
(Italian Alder). *A. glutinosa* (Common
Alder). *A. g.* 'Imperalis'. *A. g. incisa*
(Thorn-leaved Alder). *A. incana* (Grey
Alder). *A. i.* 'Aurea' (Golden-leaved
Alder). *A. i.* 'Laciniata' (Cut-leaved
Alder). *A. i.* 'Pendula' (Weeping Alder).

AMELANCHIER (grown as trees)
Snowy Mespilus
Time to buy Pot-grown, any time. Balled,
root-wrapped and bare-rooted, October–
March. Avoid adverse weather conditions.
Where to find Outside in Trees and
Shrubs.
Size MAIDEN Height 2–5 ft (60 cm–1.5 m)
min. Some short side branches.
FEATHERED Height 4–9 ft (1.2–2.7 m)
min. Minimum five 1½ ft (50 cm) long
side branches. HALF-STANDARD Height
9 ft (2.7 m) min. Clear stem of 4 ft (1.2 m).
Minimum three 2 ft (60 cm) long branches. Stem girth at 3 ft (1 m) from ground
1½–2½ in (4–6 cm) min. SEMI-MATURE
Specialist nurseries supply a range of
sizes. Shrub-grown can be trained as
trees.

Foliage Deciduous. Spring/summer, light green. Premature autumn colour and leaf drop.

Roots Whip and maiden, pots 8 in (20 cm) min. dia. Half-standard, 10 in (25 cm) min. dia. Balled, root-wrapped and bare-rooted, good fibrous roots.

Hints Any well-prepared soil. Half-standards may be scarce. Stake and ties – five years. Maiden and feathered, further training for five years.

Most widely available Amelanchier canadensis (*A. lamarckii*). *A. laevis. A. lamarckii* 'Ballerina'.

ARBUTUS
Strawberry Tree

Time to buy Pot-grown, any time. Balled, October–March. Avoid adverse weather conditions.

Where to find Outside in Trees or Shrubs.

Size 9 in–2½ ft (23–80 cm). Bushy habit. No leading shoot.

Foliage Evergreen. Dark green. Basal leaf drop, February–March.

Roots Pots 6 in (15 cm) min. dia. or larger. Balled, good fibrous root system.

Hints Well-prepared soil except alkaline, plus extra organic material. Stake and ties – five years. Needs protection from cold and winds. Technically a shrub, but thought of as a tree. Slow-growing.

Most widely available Arbutus unedo (Killarney Strawberry Tree). *A. u.* 'Rubra'.

BETULA
Birch

Time to buy Pot-grown, any time. Root-wrapped and bare-rooted, October–March. Avoid adverse weather conditions.

Where to find Outside in Trees.

Size WHIP Height 1½–2½ ft (50–80 cm) min. Limited side branches. MAIDEN Height 3–5 ft (1–1.5 m). min. Limited side branches. FEATHERED Height 3–10 ft (1–

3 m) min. Minimum five side branches. More for 7–10 ft (2.2–3 m). Stem girth at 3 ft (1 m) from ground 1½–2½ in (4–6 cm) min. STANDARD Height 9 ft (2.7 m) min. Clear stem of 4 ft (1.2 m) Minimum seven 1½ ft (50 cm) long branches. Stem girth at 3 ft (1 m) from ground, 2½–3 in (6–8 cm) min. SEMI-MATURE Specialist nurseries supply a range of sizes. MULTI-STEMMED (*Betula pendula*) only from specialist nurseries. *B. p.* 'Youngii' weeping habit.

Foliage Deciduous. Spring, light to mid green. Premature autumn colour and leaf drop.

Roots Whip, maiden and short feathered, pots 6 in (15 cm) min. dia. Taller feathered and standard, 10 in (25 cm) min. dia. Balled, root-wrapped and bare-rooted, good fibrous root system.

Hints Any well-prepared soil, except extremely alkaline. Light stake and ties – five years. Whip, maiden and feathered further training for five years. Wide range available. Not always sold as 'named'.

Most widely available Betula ermanii. *B. jacquemontii. B. nigra* (River Birch, Black Birch). *B. papyrifera* (Paper Birch). *B. pendula B. alba, B. verrucosa* (Silver, White or Common Birch). *B. p.* 'Dalecarlica' (Swedish Birch). *B. p.* 'Fastigiata'. *B. p.* 'Purpurea' (Purple Leaf Birch). *B. p.* 'Tristis'. *B. p.* 'Youngii' (Young's Weeping Birch). *B. utilis*.

BUDDLEIA (grown as tree)
Butterfly Bush

Time to buy Pot-grown, any time. Avoid adverse weather conditions.

Where to find Outside in Shrubs or Trees.

Size SHRUB Height 1½ in (50 cm) min. Single or multiple stems. STANDARD Height 9 ft (2.7 m) min.

Foliage Deciduous. Spring/summer, light to mid green or grey to grey-green, depending on form. Premature autumn colour and leaf drop.

Roots Pots 5 in (12 cm) min. dia.

Hints Any well-prepared soil. Best grown in situ from a shrub. Requires further training. *Buddleia alternifolia* possibly available as standard tree. Stake and ties required. Shoots are fragile.

Mostly widely available *Buddleia alternifolia* and forms. *B. davidii* 'Harlequin'. *B. d.* 'Pink Delight'. *B. d.* 'Royal Red'. *B. d.* 'White Bouquet'. *B. globosa*. *B.* × *weyerana*.

CARAGANA
Salt Tree

Time to buy Pot-grown, any time. Balled, root-wrapped and bare-rooted, October–March. Avoid adverse weather conditions.

Where to find Outside in Trees or Shrubs.

Size MAIDEN Height 3–5 ft (1–1.5 m) min. Limited side branches. FEATHERED Height 7 ft (2.2 m) min. Minimum five 9 in (23 cm) long side branches. HALF-STANDARD Height 8 ft (2.5 m) min. Clear stem of 5 ft (1.5 m). Minimum three 15 in (40 cm) long branches. Stem girth at 3 ft (1 m) from ground, 1½–2½ in (4–6 cm) min. STANDARD Height 10 ft (3 m) min. Clear stem of 6 ft (2 m). Minimum three 1½ ft (50 cm) long branches. Stem girth at 3 ft (1 m) from ground, 1½–2½ in. (4–6 cm) min. SEMI-MATURE Specialist nurseries supply a range of sizes. ORNAMENTAL Top-worked onto stems of *Caragana arborescens*. Minimum height 3 ft (1 m), 4 ft (1.2 m), 5 ft (1.5 m) or 6 ft (2 m). Minimum three 12 in (30 cm) weeping or upright branches.

Foliage Deciduous. Spring/summer, light green. Premature autumn colour and leaf drop.

Roots Maiden, pots 5 in (12 cm) min. dia. Feathered, half-standard and standard, pots 10 in (25 cm) min. dia. Balled, root-wrapped and bare-rooted, good fibrous root system.

Hints Any well-prepared soil. Ornamental may be scarce in all sizes and sometimes looks unsightly. *Caragana arborescens* from specialist nurseries. Light stake and ties – five years. Maiden and feathered, further training for five years.

Most widely available *Caragana arborescens* (Pea Tree, Siberian Pea Tree).

ORNAMENTAL *Caragana arborescens* 'Lorbergii'. *C. a.* 'Pendula'. *C. a.* 'Walker'. *C. pygmaea* (standard).

CARPINUS
Hornbeam

Time to buy Pot-grown, any time. Balled, root-wrapped and bare-rooted, October–March. Avoid adverse weather conditions.

Where to find Outside in Trees.

Size WHIP Height (1½–2½ ft (50–80 cm) min. Limited side branches. MAIDEN Height 2–3 ft (60 cm–1 m) min. Limited side branches. FEATHERED Height 3–5 ft (1–1.5 m) min. Minimum five short side branches. HALF-STANDARD Height 8 ft (2.5 m) min. Clear stem of 4 ft (1.2 m). Minimum three 1½ ft (50 cm) long branches. Stem girth at 3 ft (1 m) from ground 1½–2½ in (4–6 cm) min. STANDARD Height 10 ft (3 m) min. Clear stem of 6 ft (2 m). Minimum three 1½ ft (50 cm) long branches. Stem girth at 3 ft (1 m) from ground, 1½–2½ in (4–6 m) min. SEMI-MATURE Specialist nurseries supply a range of sizes. *Carpinus betulus* offered as hedging, can be trained as trees.

Foliage Deciduous. Spring, light to mid green. Premature autumn colour and leaf drop.

Roots Whip and maiden, pots 6 in (15 cm) min. dia. Feathered, half-standard and standard, pots 10 in (25 cm) min. dia. Balled, root-wrapped and bare-rooted, good fibrous root system.

Hints Any well-prepared soil. May be scarce. Stake and ties – five years. Whip, maiden and feathered, further training for five years.

Most widely available *Carpinus betulus* (Common Hornbeam). *C. b.* 'Fastigiata'

(Fastigiated Hornbeam). *C. b.* 'Pendula'
(Weeping Hornbeam). *C. b.* 'Pyramidalis'
(Pyramid Hornbeam).

CASTANEA SATIVA
Spanish Chestnut, Sweet Chestnut
Time to buy Pot-grown, any time. Balled,
root-wrapped and bare-rooted, October–
March. Avoid adverse weather conditions.
Where to find Outside in Trees, Fruit
Trees or Forestry.
Size WHIP Height 1½–2½ ft (50–80 cm)
min. Limited side branches. MAIDEN
Height 2–4 ft (60 cm–1.2 m) min. Limited
side branches. HALF-STANDARD Height
6–8 ft (2–2.5 m) min. Clear stem of 4 ft
(1.2 m). Minimum three 1½ ft (50 cm) long
branches. Stem girth at 3 ft (1 m) from
ground, 1½–2½ in (4–6 cm) min. STAN-
DARD Height 9 ft (2.7 m) min. Clear stem
of 6 ft (2 m) Minimum three 2 ft (60 cm)
long branches. Stem girth at 3 ft (1 m)
from ground, 1½–2½ in (4–6 cm) min. SEMI-
MATURE Specialist nurseries supply a
range of sizes.
Foliage Deciduous. Spring, mid green or
variegated. Premature autumn colour and
leaf drop.
Roots Whip and maiden, pots 6 in
(15 cm) min. dia. Feathered, half-standard
and standard, pots 12 in (30 cm) min. dia.
Balled, root-wrapped and bare-rooted,
good fibrous root system.
Hints Any well-prepared soil, plus extra
organic material. May be scarce. Stake
and ties – five years. Whip and maiden,
further training for five years. Poorly
rooted.
Most widely available *Castanea sativa.*
C. s. 'Albomarginata'. *C. s.* 'Aureomarginata'. *C. s.* 'Heterophylla'.

CATALPA
Indian Bean Tree
Time to buy Pot-grown, any time. Balled,
October–March. Avoid adverse weather
conditions.

Where to find Outside in Trees or
Shrubs.
Size MAIDEN Height 3–4 ft (1–1.2 m) min.
Limited side branches. BUSH Height 4 ft
(1.2 m) min. Normally no stem. Minimum
three 1½ ft (50 cm) long branches. *Catalpa
bignonioides* 'Aurea' height 2 ft (60 cm)
min. HALF-STANDARD Height 8 ft (2.5 m)
min. Clear stem of 4 ft (1.2 m), with or
without side branches. Stem girth at 3 ft
(1 m) from ground, 1½–2½ in (4–6 cm) min.
STANDARD Height 10 ft (3 m) min. Clear
stem of 6 ft (2 m). Minimum three 2 ft
(60 cm) long branches. Stem girth at 3 ft
(1 m) from ground, 1½–2½ in (4–6 cm) min.
SEMI-MATURE Specialist nurseries supply
range of sizes. *Catalpa × erubescens* 'Purpurea', only Bush. *C. bignonioides* 'Aurea'
grafted bush and half-standard.
Foliage Deciduous. Spring/summer, light
to mid green, golden or purple. Premature
autumn colour and leaf drop.
Roots Maiden, pots 6 in (15 cm) min. dia.
Bush, half-standard and standard, pots
10 in (25 cm) min. dia. Balled, good
fibrous root system.
Hints Any well-prepared soil, plus extra
organic material. Scarce. Stake and ties –
five years. Stem bent. Die-back of main
stem and branches with hollow centres
is normal.
Most widely available *Catalpa bignonioides. C. b.* 'Aurea'. *C. × erubescens*
'Purpurea' (*C. × hybrida* 'Purpurea').

CERCIDIPHYLLUM
Katsura Tree
Time to buy Pot-grown, any time. Balled,
October–March. Avoid adverse weather
conditions.
Where to find Outside in Trees or
Shrubs.
Size BUSH Height 2–6 ft (60 cm–2 m) min.
Minimum five 12 in (30 cm) long side
branches. HALF-STANDARD Top-worked
on to 5–6 ft (1.5–2 m) stem. Minimum
three 2 ft (60 cm) long weeping or upright
branches. *Cercidiphyllum japonicum*

'Pendulum' only as half-standard top-worked.

Foliage Deciduous. Spring/summer, mid green with reddish hue. Premature autumn colour and leaf drop.

Roots Pots 10 in (25 cm) min. dia. Balled, good fibrous root system.

Hints Any well-prepared soil, except alkaline, plus extra organic material. *Cercidiphyllum japonicum* 'Pendulum' needs staking and tying for life. Avoid planting all in frost pockets. A tree, often offered as a shrub.

Most widely available *Cercidiphyllum japonicum. C. j.* 'Pendulum'.

CERCIS SILIQUASTRUM
Judas Tree, Red Bud

Time to buy Pot-grown, any time. Balled, October–March. Avoid adverse weather conditions.

Where to find Outside in Trees or Shrubs.

Size 9 in–3 ft (23 cm–1 m).

Foliage Deciduous. Spring/summer, olive-green. Premature autumn colour and leaf drop.

Roots Pots 6 in (15 cm) min. dia. Balled, good fibrous root system.

Hints Any well-prepared soil, except extremely alkaline. After two years, single or multi-stemmed may be trained as trees or left as bushes. Takes a number of years to achieve tree proportions.

CORNUS (grown as tree)
North American, Chinese and American Dogwood

Time to buy Pot-grown, any time. Balled, October–March. Avoid adverse weather conditions.

Where to find Outside in Trees or Shrubs.

Size Shrubs, 2–6 ft (60 cm–2 m) min. In excess of 5 ft (1.5 m), minimum two 9 in (23 cm) long branches.

Foliage Deciduous. Spring/summer, mid green. Premature autumn colour and leaf drop.

Roots Pots 6 in (15 cm) min. dia. Larger, in pots 10 in (23 cm) min. dia. Balled, good fibrous root system.

Hints Any well-prepared soil, except alkaline, plus extra organic material. *Cornus florida* acid soil only. Scarce. Stake and ties – five years. Normally as shrubs, 1–3 ft (30 cm–1 m) min. which requires training.

Most widely available *Cornus florida* forms (American Dogwood). *C. kousa* forms (Chinese Dogwood). *C. nuttallii* (North American Dogwood). *C.* 'Eddie's White Wonder'. *C.* 'Norman Haddon'.

CORYLUS COLURNA
Turkish Hazel

Time to buy Pot-grown, any time. Balled, October–March. Avoid adverse weather conditions.

Where to find Outside in Trees.

Size MAIDEN Height 1–4 ft (30 cm–1.2 m) min. Limited side branches. FEATHERED Height 3–6 ft (1–2 m) min. Minimum four 9 in (23 cm) long side branches. HALF-STANDARD Height 8 ft (2.5 m) min. Clear stem of 4 ft (1.2 m). Minimum three $1\frac{1}{2}$ ft (50 cm) long branches. Stem girth at 3 ft (1 m) from ground, $1\frac{1}{2}$–$2\frac{1}{2}$ in (4–6 cm) min. SEMI-MATURE Specialist nurseries supply a range of sizes.

Foliage Deciduous. Spring/summer, light green. Premature autumn colour and leaf drop.

Roots Maiden, pots 6 in (15 cm) min. dia. Feathered, half-standard and standard, pots 10 in (25 cm) min. dia.

Hints Any well-prepared soil. Scarce. Stake and ties – five years. Maiden and feathered, further training for five years.

COTONEASTER (grown as tree)

Time to buy Pot-grown, any time. Balled, October–March. Avoid adverse weather conditions.

Where to find Outside in Trees or Shrubs.

Size MOP-HEADED SMALL-LEAVED FORMS:

Top worked 3 ft (1 m) to 6 ft (2 m) min. with minimum three branches, normally weeping. UPRIGHT GROWING LARGE-LEAVED FORMS: MAIDEN Height 4–7 ft (1.2–2.2 m) min. Limited side branches. FEATHERED Height 4–9 ft (1.2–2.7 m) min. Minimum five 1½ ft (50 cm) long side branches. STANDARD Height 7 ft (2.2 m) min. Clear stem of 7 ft (2.2 m). Minimum three 2 ft (60 m) long branches. Stem girth at 3 ft (1 m) from ground, 1½–2½ in (4–6 cm) min.

Foliage Deciduous, semi-evergreen or evergreen. Dark green. Evergreen may show leaf drop, February–March.

Roots Pots 10 in (35 cm) min. dia. Balled good fibrous root system.

Hints Any well-prepared soil. Stake and ties – five years. Whip, maiden and feathered further training for five years. Large-leaved susceptible to Fire Blight and should be avoided.

Most widely available

MOP-HEADED *Cotoneaster* 'Coral Beauty' (D). *C. dammeri* (E). *C. horizontalis* (Fishbone Cotoneaster) (E). *C. microphylla* (E). *C.* 'Skogholm' (D).

LARGE-LEAVED *Cotoneaster* 'Cornubia' (E). *C.* 'Exburiensis' (E). *C.* 'Hybridus Pendulus' (Weeping Cotoneaster) (E). *C. franchetii* (E). *C.* 'Rothschildianus' (E). *C. salicifolius (Willow-leaved Cotoneaster)* (E). *C. s.* var. *floccosus* (E). *C.* 'St Monica' (E). *C.* × *wateri* (E).

CRATAEGUS
Thorn, May

Time to buy Pot-grown, any time. Balled, root-wrapped and bare-rooted, October–March. Avoid adverse weather conditions.

Where to find Outside in Trees.

Size WHIP Height 1½–2½ ft (50–80 cm) min. Limited side branches.

MAIDEN Height 1–4 ft (30 cm–1.2 m) min. Limited side branches. FEATHERED Height 3–6 ft (1–2 m) min. Minimum four side branches. BUSH Height 6 ft (2 m) min.

Clear stem of 2 ft (60 cm). Minimum three short branches. HALF-STANDARD Height 8 ft (2.5 m) min. Clear stem of 4 ft (1.2 m). Minimum three 1 ft (30 cm) long branches. Stem girth at 3 ft (1 m) from ground, 1½–2½ in (4–6 cm) min. STANDARD Height 10 ft (3 m) min. Clear stem of 6 ft (2 m). Minimum three 1½ ft (50 cm) long branches. Stem girth at 3 ft (1 m) from ground, 1½–2½ in (4–6 cm) min.

Foliage Deciduous. Spring/summer, dark green. Premature autumn colour and leaf drop.

Roots Whip and maiden, pots 6 in (15 cm) min. dia. Bush, half-standard and standard, pots 12 in (30 cm) min. dia. Balled, root-wrapped and bare-rooted, good fibrous root system.

Hints Any well-prepared soil. May be scarce. Stake and ties – five years. Whip and maiden, further training for five years.

Most widely available *Crataegus* 'Autumn Glory'. *C. crus-galli* (Cockspur Thorn): *C.* × *grignonensis*. *C.* × *lavallei* (*C. carrierei*) *C. oxycantha* 'Alba Plena'. *C. o.* 'Fastigiata'. *C. o.* 'Paul's Scarlet'. *C. prunifolia*. *C.* 'Rosea Plena'.

CYSTISUS BATTANDIERI (grown as tree)
Pineapple Broom

Time to buy Pot-grown, any time. Balled, October–March. Avoid adverse weather conditions.

Where to find Outside in Trees.

Size STANDARD Height 9 ft (2.7 m) min. Clear stem of 4 ft (1.2 m). Minimum three 2 ft (60 cm) long branches. Stem girth at 3 ft (1 m) from ground, 1½–2½ in (4–6 cm). Shrubs can be trained as trees.

Foliage Deciduous. Spring/summer, silver-grey. Premature autumn colour and leaf drop.

Roots Pots 10 in (25 cm) min. dia. Balled, good fibrous root system.

Hints Any well-prepared soil. May be scarce and only found in mild, coastal areas. Not successful more than thirty-five miles inland as standards. Stake and ties for life.

CYTISUS (grown as mop-headed tree)
Broom
Time to buy Pot-grown, any time. Balled October–March. Avoid adverse weather conditions.
Where to find Outside in Trees and Shrubs.
Size Grafted as top-worked mop-headed trees onto stems of *Laburnum vulgaris*. Clear stem 2 ft (60 cm) min. 3 ft (1 m) or 4 ft (1.2 m). Minimum three 1–2 ft (30–60 cm) long branches.
Foliage Deciduous. Few apparent leaves. Stems green to grey/green. Avoid yellowing.
Roots Pots 6 in (15 cm) min. dia. Balled, good fibrous root system.
Hints Any well-prepared soil. Full range may be scarce and normally only sold when in flower. Stake and ties for life. Graft unsightly.
Most widely available *Cytisus* × *praecox* 'Albus'. *C.* × *p.* 'Allgold'. *C. scoparius* 'Andreanus'. *C. s.* 'Burkwoodii'. *C. s.* 'Windlesham Ruby'. Others may be available.

DAVIDIA INVOLUCRATA
Handkerchief Tree, Ghost Tree, Dove Tree
Time to buy Pot-grown, any time. Balled, October–March. Avoid adverse weather conditions.
Where to find Outside in Trees.
Size Single or multi-stemmed root clumps. Shoots up to 3 ft (1 m) high. Taller do not establish well.
Foliage Deciduous. Spring/summer, mid green. Premature autumn colour and leaf drop.
Roots Pots 6 in (15 cm) min. dia. Balled, good fibrous root system.
Hints Any well-prepared soil, plus extra organic material. Normally scarce. New

shoot in second spring after planting needs light stake and ties. Strongest shoot is normally selected, all others removed. Further training by removal of side branches for five years. Looks stunted. Plant and allow to grow *in situ*.

EUCALYPTUS
Gum Tree
Time to buy Pot-grown, April–August. Avoid adverse weather conditions.
Where to find Outside in Trees or Shrubs.
Size 2–4 ft (60 cm–1.2 m) min. Single stem. Limited side branches.
Foliage Evergreen. Green-grey.
Roots Pots 4 in (10 cm) min. dia.
Hints Any well-prepared soil. Stake and ties – five years. Hardiness in doubt *Eucalyptus gunnii* most reliable. Beware purchasing coastal areas, or planting more than thirty-five miles inland.
Most widely available *Eucalyptus coccifera. E. dalrympleana. E. gunnii* (Cider Gum). *E. niphophila* (Snow Gum). *E. parvifolia.*

FAGUS
Beech
Time to buy Pot-grown, any time. Balled, root-wrapped and bare-rooted October–March. Avoid adverse weather conditions.
Where to find Outside in Trees.
Size WHIP Height $1\frac{1}{2}$–$2\frac{1}{2}$ ft (50–80 cm) min. Limited side branches. MAIDEN Height 1–4 ft (30 cm–1.2 m) min. Limited side branches. FEATHERED Height 3–6 ft (1–3 m) min. Minimum four side branches. BUSH Height 6 ft (2 m) min. Clear stem of 3 ft (1 m). Minimum three $1\frac{1}{2}$ ft (50 cm) long branches. HALF-STANDARD Height 8 ft (2.5 m) min. Clear stem of 4 ft (1.2 m). Minimum three $1\frac{1}{2}$ ft (50 cm) long branches. Stem girth at 3 ft (1 m) from ground $1\frac{1}{2}$–$2\frac{1}{2}$ in (4–6 cm) min. STANDARD Height 10 ft (3 m) min. Clear stem of 6 ft (2 m). Minimum three $1\frac{1}{2}$ ft (50 cm) long branches. Stem

girth at 3 ft (1 m) from ground 2½–3 in (6–
8 cm) min. SEMI-MATURE Specialist nurseries supply a range of sizes. *Fagus sylvatica*
sold as hedging can be trained as trees.
Foliage Deciduous. Spring/summer, light
green or coloured. Premature autumn
colour and leaf drop.
Roots Maiden and feathered, pots 6 in
(15 cm) min. dia. Bush, half-standard, standard, pots 10 in (25 cm) min. dia. Root-
wrapped or bare-rooted, good fibrous root
system.
Hints Any well-prepared soil, plus extra
organic material. May be scarce. Stake and
ties – five years. Whip, maiden, and
feathered, further training for five years.
Bent stems. Do not allow roots to dry out.
Most widely available *Fagus sylvatica*
(Common Beech). *F. s.* 'Dawyck' (Fastigiated Beech). *F. s. heterophylla* (Cut-
leaved Beech). *F. s.* 'Pendula' (Green-
leaved Weeping Beech). *F. s.* 'Purpurea'
(Copper or Purple Beech). *F. s.* 'Purpurea
Pendula' (Purple-leaved Weeping Beech).
F. s. 'Riversii' (Rivers Purple or Copper-
leaved Beech) *F. s.* 'Rohanii'. *F. s.* 'Roseo-
marginata'; *F. s.* 'Zlatia' (Golden Beech).

FORSYTHIA (grown as tree)
Golden Ball
Time to buy Pot-grown, any time. Balled,
root-wrapped and bare-rooted, October–
March. Avoid adverse weather conditions.
Where to find Outside in Shrubs or Trees.
Size STANDARD Clear stem 4 ft (1.2 m)
min. Minimum three 2 ft (60 cm) long
branches. SHRUB Clear stem 1½ ft (50 cm),
single or multi-stemmed.
Foliage Deciduous. Spring/summer, light
green. Premature autumn colour and leaf
drop.
Roots Pots 10 in (25 cm) min. dia. Balled,
root-wrapped and bare-rooted, good
fibrous root system.
Hints Any well-prepared soil. Normally
offered when in flower. Stake and ties for
life.

Most widely available *Forsythia* 'Lynwood' (*F. intermedia*). *F.* 'Lynwood Gold'.
F. 'Spring Glory'.

FRAXINUS
Ash
Time to buy Pot-grown, any time. Balled,
root-wrapped and bare-rooted, October–
March. Avoid adverse weather conditions.
Where to find Outside in Trees.
Size WHIP Height 1½–2½ ft (50–80 cm)
min. Limited side branches. MAIDEN
Height 1–4 ft (30 cm–1.2 m) min. Limited
side branches. FEATHERED Height 3–6 ft
(1–2 m) min. Minimum four short side
branches. HALF-STANDARD Height 8 ft
(2.5 m) min. Clear stem of 4 ft (1.2 m).
Minimum three 1½ ft (50 cm) long
branches. Stem girth at 3 ft (1 m) from
ground 1½–2½ in (4–6 cm) min. STANDARD
Height 10 ft (3 m) min. Clear stem of 6 ft
(2 m). Minimum three 2 ft (60 cm) long
branches. Stem girth at 3 ft (1 m) from
ground 2½–3 in (6–8 cm) min. *Fraxinus
excelsior* 'Pendula' feathered or top-
worked. Clear stem 6 ft (2 m) min. Minimum two 2½ ft (80 cm) long weeping
branches. SEMI-MATURE Specialist nurseries supply a range of sizes.
Foliage Deciduous. Spring/summer, light
green. Premature autumn colour and leaf
drop.
Roots Whip, maiden and feathered, pots
6 in (15 cm) min. dia. Half-standard and
standard, pots 10 in (25 cm) min. dia.
Balled, root-wrapped and bare-rooted,
good fibrous root system.
Hints Any well-prepared soil. May be
scarce. Stake and ties – five years.
Whip, maiden and feathered, further
training for five years. Research ultimate
overall size.
Most widely available *Fraxinus americana* (White Ash). *F. excelsior*
(Common Ash). *F. e.* 'Diversifolia'. *F. e.*
'Jaspidea (Golden-stemmed Ash). *F. e.*
'Pendula' (Weeping Ash). *F. e.* 'West-

hof's Glory'. *F. ornus* (Manna Ash). *F. oxycarpa* 'Flame'.

GLEDITSIA
Honeylocust
Time to buy Pot-grown, any time. Balled, root-wrapped and bare-rooted, October–March. Avoid adverse weather conditions.
Where to find Outside in Trees.
Size MAIDEN Height 2–4 ft (60cm–1.2 m) min. Normally single stem. FEATHERED Height 4–6 ft (1.2–2 m) min. Minimum three short side branches. STANDARD Height 9 ft (2.7 m) min. Clear stem of 6 ft (2 m). Minimum three 1 ft (30 cm) long branches. Stem girth at 3 ft (1 m) from the ground 1½–2½ in (4–6 cm) min. *Gleditsia triacanthos inermis* top-worked onto clear stem. *Gleditsia triacanthos* 6–8 ft (2.2–2.5 m) min. Minimum four 1 ft (30 cm) long branches. *Gleditsia triacanthos* 'Ruby Lace' and *G. t.* 'Sunburst' normally only as maiden and feathered.
Foliage Deciduous. Spring/summer, green, gold or purple. Premature autumn colour and leaf drop.
Roots Whip and maiden, pots 6 in (15 cm) min. dia. Half-standard and standard, pots 12 in (30 cm) min. dia. Balled, root-wrapped and bare-rooted, good fibrous root system.
Hints Any well-prepared soil. May be scarce. Stake and ties – five years. Maiden and feathered, further training for five years. Young trees look fragile and bent.
Most widely available *Gleditsia triacanthos* (Honeylocust). *G. t. inermis* (Thornless Honeylocust). *G. t.* 'Ruby Lace'. *G. t.* 'Sunburst'.

GYMNOCLADUS DIOICUS
Kentucky Coffee Tree
Time to buy Pot-grown, any time. Balled, October–March. Avoid adverse weather conditions.
Where to find Outside in Trees.

Size WHIP Height 1½–4 ft (50 cm–1.2 m) min. Normally single stem.
Foliage Deciduous. Spring/summer, light green. Premature autumn colour and leaf drop.
Roots Pots 6 in (15 cm) min. dia. Balled, good fibrous root system.
Hints Any well-prepared soil, plus extra organic material. May be scarce. Light stake and ties for life. Small. Will need further training.

HYDRANGEA PANICULATA 'GRANDIFLORA' (grown as tree)
Time to buy Pot-grown, any time. Balled, October–March. Avoid adverse weather conditions.
Where to find Outside in Trees or Shrubs.
Size Clear stem of 3–3½ ft (1–1.1 m) min. Minimum three 18 in (50 cm) long main branches. Overall height 5 ft (1.5 m).
Foliage Deciduous. Spring/summer, mid green. Premature autumn colour and leaf drop.
Roots Pots 8 in (20 cm) min. dia. Balled, good fibrous root system.
Hints Any well-prepared soil, except alkaline or dry. May be scarce. Stake and ties for life. Cut back all previous season's growth within two buds of origin in April. Repeated annually. Looks 'dead' February–March. Branches fragile.

IDESIA POLYCARPA
Igiri Tree
Time to buy Pot-grown, any time. Avoid adverse weather conditions.
Where to find Outside in Trees and Shrubs.
Size WHIP 1–3 ft (30 cm–1 m) min. Single stem.
Foliage Deciduous. Spring/summer, light to mid green. Premature autumn colour and leaf drop.
Roots Pots 6 in (15 cm) min. dia.
Hints Any well-prepared soil, plus extra

organic material. Scarce. Hardiness in doubt. Stakes and ties – five years.

JUGLANS
Walnut

Time to buy Pot-grown, any time. Balled, root-wrapped and bare-rooted, October–March. Avoid adverse weather conditions.
Where to find Outside in Trees or Fruit Trees.
Size WHIP Height 1½–2½ ft (50–80 cm) min. Limited side branches. MAIDEN Height 3 ft (1 m) min. Limited side branches. FEATHERED Height 4 ft (1.2 m) min. Minimum four short side branches. BUSH Height 3 ft (1 m) min. Clear stem of 2 ft (60 cm) min. Minimum three 1½ ft (50 cm) long branches. HALF-STANDARD Height 7 ft (2.2 m) min. Clear stem of 4 ft (1.2 m). Minimum three 1½ ft (50 cm) long branches. Stem girth at 3 ft (1 m) from ground, 1½–2½ in (4–6 cm) min. STANDARD Height 10 ft (3 m) min. Clear stem of 6 ft (2 m). Minimum three 2 ft (60 cm) long branches. Stem girth at 3 ft (1 m) from ground, 1½–2½ in (4–6 cm) min. SEMIMATURE Specialist nurseries supply a range of sizes.
Foliage Deciduous. Spring, light to mid green. Early autumn colour and leaf drop.
Roots Whip and maiden, pots 6 in (15 cm) min. dia. Feathered, bush, half-standard, and standard, pots 10 in (25 cm) min. dia. Balled, root-wrapped and bare-rooted, good fibrous root system.
Hints Any well-prepared soil, plus extra organic material. Scarce. Often only maiden, feathered, half-standard or standard, with limited branches. Stake and ties – five years. Whip, maiden and feathered, further training for five years. Poor rooting system in pots.

KALOPANAX PICTUS
Time to buy Pot-grown, any time. Rootballed October–March. Avoid adverse weather conditions.

Where to find Outside in Trees.
Size 2–5 ft (60 cm–1.5 m). Single stem. Limited side branches.
Foliage Deciduous. Spring/summer, mid green. Premature autumn colour and leaf drop.
Roots Pots 10 in (25 cm) min. dia. Rootballed, good fibrous root system.
Hints Any well-prepared soil, plus extra organic material. Scarce. Stake, ties and training – five years. Gaunt and uninteresting when young.

KOELREUTERIA PANICULATA
Golden Rain Tree

Time to buy Pot-grown, any time. Rootballed, October–March. Avoid adverse weather conditions.
Where to find Outside in Trees.
Size MAIDEN 2–4 ft (60 cm–1.2 m). Single stem. Limited side branches. STANDARD Height 8 ft (2.5 m) min. Clear stem of 4 ft (1.2 m). Minimum three 18 in (50 cm) long branches. Stem girth at 3 ft (1 m) from ground, ¾–1½ in (2–4 cm) min.
Foliage Deciduous. Spring/summer, light green. Premature autumn colour and leaf drop.
Roots Pots 10 in (25 cm) min. dia. Rootballed, good fibrous root system.
Hints Any well-prepared soil, plus extra organic material. Scarce. Stake and ties – five years. Maiden, further training for five years. Stems bent.

LABURNOCYTISUS ADAMII
Pink Laburnum

Time to buy Pot-grown, any time. Balled, root-wrapped and bare-rooted, October–March. Avoid adverse weather conditions.
Where to find Outside in Trees.
Size MAIDEN Height 2–4 ft (60 cm–1.4 m) min. No side branches. BUSH Height 3–5 ft (1–1.5 m) min. Minimum three 2 ft (60 cm) long side branches. HALF-STANDARD Height 9 ft (2.7 m) min. Clear stem of 4 ft (1.2 m) Minimum three 2½ ft

(80 cm) long branches. Stem girth at 3 ft (1 m) from ground, $\frac{3}{4}$–$1\frac{1}{2}$ in (2–4 cm) min.

Foliage Deciduous, Spring/summer, mid green. Premature autumn colour and leaf drop.

Roots Maiden, pots 6 in (15 cm) min. dia. Bush and half-standard, pots 10 in (25 cm) min. dia. Balled, root-wrapped and bare-rooted, good fibrous root system.

Hints Any well-prepared soil. Scarce. Stake and ties – five years. Maiden, further training for five years. First flowers pink, yellow not shown for some years.

LABURNUM
Golden Rain Tree

Time to buy Pot-grown, any time. Balled, root-wrapped, and bare-rooted, October– March. Avoid adverse weather conditions.

Where to find Outside in Trees.

Size MAIDEN Height 1–4 ft (30 cm–1.2 m) min. Limited side branches. FEATHERED Height 3–6 ft (1–2 m) min. Minimum four 9 in (23 cm) long side branches. BUSH Height 6 ft (2 m) min. Minimum three 1 ft (30 cm) long branches. HALF-STANDARD Height 8 ft (2.5 m) Clear stem of 4 ft (1.2 m). Minimum three 15 in (40 cm) long branches. Stem girth at 3 ft (1 m) from ground, $1\frac{1}{2}$–$2\frac{1}{2}$ in (4–6 cm) min. STANDARD Height 10 ft (3 m) min. Clear stem of 6 ft (2 m). Minimum three 15 in (40 cm) long branches. Stem girth at 3 ft (1 m) from ground, $1\frac{1}{2}$–$2\frac{1}{2}$ in (4–6 cm) min. TOP-WORKED GRAFTED *Laburnum* 'Pendulum', clear stem of 4 ft (1.2 m) min. Minimum two 2 ft (60 cm) long weeping branches. SEMI-MATURE Specialist nurseries supply a range of sizes. For walkways, tunnels, arches, pleaching or fan-training, use whip or feathered.

Foliage Deciduous. Spring/summer, mid green. Premature autumn colour and leaf drop.

Roots Maiden, pots 6 in (15 cm) min. dia. Feathered, bush, half-standard and standard, pots 10 in (25 cm) min. dia. Balled, root-wrapped and bare-rooted, good fibrous root system.

Hints Any well-prepared soil. Stake and ties – five years. Maiden and feathered, further training for five years. Poor root system. FRUITS POISONOUS.

Most widely available *L.* × *watereri* 'Vossii'. *L. alpinum* 'Pendulum' (Weeping Scots Laburnum).

LIQUIDAMBAR
Sweet Gum

Time to buy Pot-grown, any time. Root-balled, October–March. Avoid adverse weather conditions.

Where to find Outside in Trees.

Size WHIP Height $1\frac{1}{2}$–$2\frac{1}{2}$ ft (50–80 cm) min. Limited side branches. FEATHERED Height $3\frac{1}{2}$–9 ft (1.1 m–2.7 m) min. Minimum five 12 in (30 cm) long side branches. HALF-STANDARD Height 7 ft (2.2 m) min. Clear stem of $3\frac{1}{2}$ ft (1.1 m). Minimum five $1\frac{1}{2}$ ft (50 cm) long branches. Stem girth at 3 ft (1 m) from ground, $\frac{3}{4}$–$1\frac{1}{2}$ in (2–4 cm) min. SEMI-MATURE Specialist nurseries supply a range of sizes.

Foliage Deciduous. Spring/summer, mid green. Premature autumn colour and leaf drop.

Roots Whip, pots 6 in (15 cm) min. dia. Feathered and half-standard, pots 10 in (25 cm) min. dia. Root-balled, good fibrous root system.

Hints Any well-prepared soil, except severe alkaline, plus extra organic material. Stake and ties – five years. Whip and feathered, further training for five years. European stock has poor root system and may fail. Careful planting may overcome this disadvantage.

LIRIODENDRON
Tulip Tree

Time to buy Pot-grown, any time. Root-balled, October–March. Avoid adverse weather conditions.

Where to find Outside in Trees.

Size WHIP $1\frac{1}{2}$–$2\frac{1}{2}$ ft (50–80 cm) min. Limited side branches. MAIDEN 2–5 ft (60 cm–1.5 m) min. Some short side branches. STANDARD Height 8 ft (2.5 m) min. Clear stem of 4 ft (1.2 m). Minimum three $1\frac{1}{2}$ ft (50 cm) long branches. Stem girth at 3 ft (1 m) from ground, $\frac{3}{4}$–$1\frac{1}{2}$ in (2–4 cm) min. SEMI-MATURE Specialist nurseries supply a range of sizes.
Foliage Deciduous. Spring/summer, mid green. Premature autumn colour and leaf drop.
Roots Whip and maiden, pots 6 in (15 cm) min. dia. Root-balled, good fibrous root system.
Hints Any well-prepared soil, except alkaline, plus extra organic material. Stake and ties – five years. Whip and maiden, further training for five years.
Most widely available Liriodendron tulipifera. L. t. 'Aureomarginata'.

MALUS
Crab Apple
Time to buy Pot-grown, any time. Balled, root-wrapped and bare-rooted, October–March. Avoid adverse weather conditions.
Where to find Outside in Trees.
Size MAIDEN Height 1–4 ft (30 cm–1.2 m) min. Limited side branches. FEATHERED Height 3–6 ft (1–3 m) min. Minimum four 9 in (23 cm) long side branches. BUSH Height 6 ft (2 m) min. Clear stem of 3 ft (1 m). Minimum three 12 in (30 cm) long branches. HALF-STANDARD Height 8 ft (2.5 m) min. Clear stem of 5 ft (1.5 m). Minimum three 15 in (40 cm) long branches. Stem girth at 3 ft (1 m) from ground, $1\frac{1}{2}$–$2\frac{1}{2}$ in (4–6 cm) min. STANDARD Height 10 ft (3 m) min. Clear stem of 8 ft (2.5 m) Minimum three 15 in (40 cm) long branches. Stem girth at 3 ft (1 m) from ground, $1\frac{1}{2}$–$2\frac{1}{2}$ in (4–6 cm) min. TOP-WORKED HALF-STANDARD AND STANDARD, Malus 'Echtermeyer' only. Grafted on clear stem of 4 ft (1.2 m) min. Minimum four 2 ft (60 cm)

long branches. Stem girth at 3 ft (1 m) from ground, $1\frac{1}{2}$–$2\frac{1}{2}$ in (4–6 cm) min. SEMI-MATURE Specialist nurseries supply a range of sizes. For walkways, tunnels, arches, pleaching or fan-training, use whip or feathered.
Foliage Deciduous. Spring/summer, light green or purple. Premature autumn colour and leaf drop.
Roots Maiden and feathered, pots 6 in (15 cm) min. dia. Bush, half-standard and standard, pots 10 in (25 cm) min. dia. Balled, root-wrapped and bare-rooted, good fibrous root system.
Hints Any well-prepared soil. May be scarce. Stake and ties – five years. Maiden and feathered, further training for five years. Research overall size.
Most widely available
GREEN-LEAVED Malus 'Dolgo'*. M. floribunda. M. 'Golden Hornet'*. M. 'Hillieri'. M. hupehensis. M. 'John Downie'*. M. 'Professor Sprenger'*. M. 'Red Sentinel'*. M. × robusta*. (Siberian Crab). M. r. 'Red Siberian'*. M. r. 'Yellow Siberian'*. M. tschonoskii. M. 'Wintergold'*. M. 'Royalty'*. M. 'Wisely'*.
PURPLE-LEAVED Malus 'Eleyi'. M. 'Lemoinei'. M. 'Lizet'. M. 'Profusion'.
WEEPING Malus 'Echtermeyer'*. M. 'Red Jade'*.
Other forms are worth consideration, and new forms are being introduced.

* Best fruiting forms.

NOTHOFAGUS
Southern Beech
Time to buy Pot-grown, any time. Balled, root-wrapped and bare-rooted, October–March. Avoid adverse weather conditions.
Where to find Outside in Trees.
Size WHIP Height 1–2 ft (30–60 cm) min. Limited side branches. MAIDEN Height $1\frac{1}{2}$–5 ft (50 cm–1.5 m) min. Some short side branches. FEATHERED Height 2–7 ft (60 cm–2.2 m) min. Minimum three 1 ft

(30 cm) long side branches. HALF-STANDARD Height 7 ft (2.2 m) min. Clear stem of 3½ ft (1.1 m). Minimum three 1 ft (30 cm) long branches. Stem girth at 3 ft (1 m) from ground, ¾–1½ in (2–4 cm) min. STANDARD Height 9 ft (2.7 m) min. Clear stem of 5 ft (1.5 m). Minimum three 12 in (30 cm) long branches. Stem girth at 3 ft (1 m) from ground, ¾–1½ in (2–4 cm) min. SEMI-MATURE Specialist nurseries supply a range of sizes.

Foliage Deciduous. Spring/summer, light green. Premature autumn colour and leaf drop.

Roots Whip, maiden, and feathered, pots 6 in (15 cm) min. dia. Half-standard and standard, pots 10 in (25 cm) min. dia. Balled, root-wrapped and bare-rooted, good fibrous root system.

Hints Any well-prepared soil. Scarce. Stake and ties – five years. Whip, maiden and feathered, further training for five years. Stems bent.

Most widely available Nothofagus antarctica. N. obliqua. N. procera.

NYSSA SYLVATICA
Nyssa, Black Gum, Sour Gum, Tupelo

Time to buy Pot-grown, any time. Balled, October–March. Avoid adverse weather conditions.

Where to find Outside in Trees or Shrubs.

Size Height 2–4 ft (60 cm–1.2 m) min. Taller may be available.

Foliage Deciduous. Spring/summer, light green. Premature autumn colour and leaf drop.

Roots Pots 5 in (12 cm) min. dia. Balled, good fibrous root system.

Hints Acid, well-prepared soil, plus extra organic material. Scarce. Rarely found as pre-trained tree. Stake, ties and training – ten years.

OSTRYA CARPINIFOLIA
European Hop Hornbeam

Time to buy Pot-grown only, any time.

Avoid adverse weather conditions.

Where to find Outside in Trees or Shrubs.

Size Height 2–4 ft (60 cm–1.2 m) min. Taller may be available.

Foliage Deciduous. Spring/summer, light to mid green. Premature autumn colour and leaf drop.

Roots Pots 5 in (12 cm) min. dia.

Hints Any well-prepared soil, except very dry. Scarce. Stake, ties and training – ten years.

PARROTIA PERSICA
Persian Parrotia

Time to buy Pot-grown, any time. Balled, October–March. Avoid adverse weather conditions.

Where to find Outside in Trees or Shrubs.

Size WHIP Height 1½–2½ ft (50–80 cm) min. Limited side branches. FEATHERED Height 5 ft (1.5 m) min. Numerous side branches.

Foliage Deciduous. Spring/summer, mid green. Premature autumn colour and leaf drop.

Roots Whip, pots 6 in, (15 cm) min. dia. Feathered, pots 10 in (25 cm) min. dia. Balled, good fibrous root system.

Hints Any well-prepared soil, plus extra organic material. Scarce. Looks one-sided, but grows symmetrical in time.

PARROTIOPSIS JACQUEMONTIANA

Time to buy Pot-grown, any time. Balled, October–March. Avoid adverse weather conditions.

Where to find Outside in Trees or Shrubs.

Size Height 1½–4 ft (50 cm–1.2 m) single stem. Limited side branches or multi-stemmed bushes.

Foliage Deciduous. Spring/summer, mid green. Premature autumn colour and leaf drop.

Roots Pots 6 in (15 cm) min. dia. Balled, good fibrous root system.

Hints Any well-prepared soil, plus extra organic material. Scarce. Stake, ties and training – five years.

PAULOWNIA TOMENTOSA
Foxglove Tree

Time to buy Pot-grown, any time. Balled, October–March. Avoid adverse weather conditions.

Where to find Outside in Trees or Shrubs.

Size MAIDEN Height 2–6 ft (60 cm–2 m) min. Normally no side branches.

Foliage Deciduous. Spring/summer, light to mid green. Premature autumn colour and leaf drop.

Roots Pots 6 in (15 cm) min. dia. Balled, good fibrous root system.

Hints Any well-prepared soil, plus extra organic material. Scarce. Stake and ties – five years. New stem emerges from base as a 'sucker' and should be trained to form tree. May be late in foliage, often not until early summer.

PHELLODENDRON AMURENSE
Amur Cork Tree

Time to buy Pot-grown, any time. Balled, root-wrapped and bare-rooted, October–March. Avoid adverse weather conditions.

Where to find Outside in Trees.

Size WHIP Height $1\frac{1}{2}$–$2\frac{1}{2}$ ft (50–80 cm) min. Limited side branches. MAIDEN Height 2–4 ft (60 cm–1.2 m) min. No side branches. FEATHERED Height 3–7 ft (1.2–2 m) min. Minimum three 12 in (30 cm) long side branches. HALF-STANDARD Height 7 ft (2.2 m) min. Clear stem of $3\frac{1}{2}$ ft (1.1 m). Minimum three $1\frac{1}{2}$ ft (60 cm) long branches. Stem girth at 3 ft (1 m) from ground $1\frac{1}{2}$–$2\frac{1}{2}$ in (4–6 cm) min. STANDARD Height 9 ft (2.7 m) min. Clear stem of $4\frac{1}{2}$ ft (1.4 m). Minimum three $1\frac{1}{2}$ ft (50 cm) long branches. Stem girth at 3 ft (1 m) from ground $1\frac{1}{2}$–$2\frac{1}{2}$ in (4–6 cm) min.

Foliage Deciduous. Spring/summer, mid green. Premature autumn colour and leaf drop.

Roots Maiden, pots 6 in (15 cm) min. dia. Half-standard and standard pots 10 in (25 cm) min. dia. Balled, root-wrapped and bare-rooted, good fibrous root system.

Hints Any well-prepared soil. Scarce. Stake and ties – five years. Whip, maiden and feathered, further training for five years. Protect from spring frosts until established.

PHOTINIA VILLOSA

Time to buy Pot-grown, any time. Avoid adverse weather conditions.

Where to find Outside in Trees or Shrubs.

Size Height 2–4 ft (60 cm–1.2 m) min. Taller may be available, but growth rate reduced and establishment less easy.

Foliage Deciduous. Spring/summer, light green. Premature autumn colour and leaf drop.

Roots Pots 5 in (12 cm) min. dia.

Hints Well-prepared acid soil, plus extra organic material. Scarce. Stake, ties and training – ten years.

POPULUS
Poplar

Time to buy Pot-grown, any time. Balled, root-wrapped, and bare-rooted, October–March. Avoid adverse weather conditions.

Where to find Outside in Trees or Forestry.

Size WHIP Height $1\frac{1}{2}$–$2\frac{1}{2}$ ft (50–80 cm) min. Limited side branches. MAIDEN Height 2–4 ft (60 cm–1.2 m) min. Limited side branches. FEATHERED Height 3–5 ft (1–1.5 m) min. Minimum five $1\frac{1}{2}$–2 ft (50–60 cm) long side branches. HALF-STANDARD Height 8 ft (2.5 m) min. Clear stem of $3\frac{1}{2}$ ft (1.1 m). Minimum three 2 ft (60 cm) long branches. Stem girth at 3 ft (1 m) from ground $1\frac{1}{2}$–$2\frac{1}{2}$ in (4–6 cm) min. STANDARD Height 10 ft

(2.7 m) min. Clear stem of 6 ft (2 m). Minimum three 2 ft (60 cm) long branches. Stem girth at 3 ft (1 m) from ground 1½–2½ in (4–6 cm) min. SEMI-MATURE Specialist nurseries supply a range of sizes.

Foliage Deciduous. Spring/summer, mid green. Premature autumn colour and leaf drop.

Roots Whip and maiden, pots 6 in (15 cm) min. dia. Feathered, half-standard and standard, pots 10 in (25 cm) min. dia. Balled, root-wrapped and bare-rooted, good fibrous root system.

Hints Any well-prepared soil. Trees for screening from specialist nurseries or forestry. Stake and ties – five years. Whip, maiden and feathered, further training for five years. Requires space, plant away from foundations and underground services. Poor root system. Avoid those that have dried out.

Most widely available

WHITE-LEAVED *Populus alba. P. a.* 'Pyramidalis'. *P. a.* 'Richardii'.

BALSAM *Populus × candicans. P. × c.* 'Aurora'. *P. trichocarpa. P. t.* 'Fritzi Pauley'.

TIMBER *Populus nigra. P.* 'Robusta'.

ORNAMENTAL *Populus lasiocarpa*. P. nigra* 'Italica'*. *P. n.* 'Italica Aurea'*. *P. serotina* 'Aurea'. *P. tremula. P. t.* 'Pendula'*. *P. t.* 'Erecta'*.

*Normally only found as whip, maiden and feathered.

PRUNUS CERASIFERA
Purple-leaved Plum, Purple Plum

Time to buy Pot-grown, any time. Root-wrapped and bare-rooted, October–March. Avoid adverse weather conditions.

Where to find Outside in Trees.

Size FEATHERED Height 3–6 ft (1–3 m) min. Minimum four 9 in (23 cm) long side branches. BUSH Height 6 ft (2 m) min. Clear stem of 3 ft (1 m). Minimum three 12 in (30 cm) long branches. HALF-STAND-

ARD Height 8 ft (2.5 m) min. Clear stem of 5 ft (1.5 m) Minimum three 2 ft (60 cm) long branches. Stem girth at 3 ft (1 m) from the ground, 1½–2½ in (4–6 cm) min. STANDARD Height 10 ft (3 m) min. Clear stem of 6 ft (2 m). Minimum three 2 ft (60 cm) long branches. Stem girth at 3 ft (1 m) from ground, 1½–2½ in (4–6 cm) min. SEMI-MATURE Specialist nurseries supply a range of sizes.

Foliage Deciduous. Spring/summer, dark green, purple to purple-black. Premature autumn colour and leaf drop.

Roots Pots 10 in (25 cm) min. dia. Root-wrapped and bare-rooted, good fibrous root system.

Hints Any well-prepared soil. Stake and ties – five years. Feathered, further training for five years. Stems thin.

PRUNUS (flowering forms)
Flowering Cherries, Peaches and Apricots

Time to buy Pot-grown, any time. Root-wrapped and bare-rooted, October–March. Avoid adverse weather conditions.

Where to find Outside in Trees.

Size FEATHERED Height 3–8 ft (1–2.5 m) min. Minimum five 9 in. (23 cm) long side branches. BUSH Height 6 ft (2 m) min. Clear stem of 3 ft (1 m). Minimum three 1½ ft (50 cm) long branches. HALF-STANDARD Height 8 ft (2.5 m) min. Clear stem of 4 ft (1.2 m). Minimum three 2 ft (60 cm) long branches. Stem girth at 3 ft (1 m) from ground, 1½–2½ in (4–6 cm) min. STANDARD Height 10 ft (3 m) min. Clear stem of 6 ft (2 m). Minimum three 2 ft (60 cm) long branches. Stem girth at 3 ft (1 m) from ground, 1½–2½ in (4–6 cm) min. TOP-WORKED Half-standard and standard grafted on to stems of *Prunus avium*. SEMI-MATURE Specialist nurseries supply a range of sizes.

Foliage Deciduous. Spring/summer, mid green. Premature autumn colour and leaf drop.

Roots Feathered and bush, pots 6 in (15 cm) min. dia. Half-standard and standard, pots 10 in (25 cm) min. dia. Root-wrapped and bare-rooted, good fibrous root system.

Hints Any well-prepared soil. May be scarce in particular years, due to poor propagation results. Stake and ties – five years. Feathered, further training for five years. Gum-bleeding may be seen. Research overall size.

Most widely available

JAPANESE FLOWERING CHERRIES *Prunus* 'Ichiyo'. *P.* 'Kanzan'. *P.* 'Pink Perfection'. *P.* 'Shimidsu Sakura' (*P. serrulata var. longpipes*). *P.* 'Shirofugen'. *P.* 'Shirotae' (*P.* 'Mount Fuji'). *P.* 'Tai Haku' (Great White Cherry). *P.* 'Ukon' (Green-flowering Cherry).

WILD CHERRIES (Gean, Mazzard, Sweet Cherry) *Prunus avium. P. a.* 'Flore Pleno'.

EARLY-FLOWERING *Prunus* 'Accolade'. *P.* 'Hally Jolivette'. *P.* × *hillieri* 'Spire'. *P. incisa. P. i.* 'February Pink'. *P.* 'Kurear'. *P.* 'Okame'. *P.* 'Pandora'. *P. sargentii* (Sargents Cherry). *P. s.* 'Rancho'. *P.* 'Shosar'. *P. subhirtella* 'Fukubana'. *P.* 'Umineko'. *P.* × *yedoensis* (Yoshino Cherry).

UPRIGHT (Lombary Cherry, Flagpole Cherry) *Prunus serrulata* 'Amanagawa'.

AUTUMN-FLOWERING (Winter-flowering Cherry, Higan Cherry) *Prunus subhirtella* 'Autumnalis'. *P. s.* 'Autumnalis Rosea'.

WEEPING *Prunus* 'Hillings Weeping'. *P.* 'Kiku-shidare Sakura' (*P.* 'Cheals Weeping') (Weeping Cherry). *P. subhirtella* 'Pendula'. *P. s.* 'Pendula Rosea'. *P. s.* 'Pendula Rubra'. *P.* × *yedoensis* 'Ivensii' *P.* × *y.* 'Shidare Yoshino' *P.* × *y. purpendens*).

BIRD CHERRIES (European Bird Cherry) *Prunus padus. P. d.* 'Albertii'. *P. p. var. colorata. P. p.* 'Purple Queen'. *P. p.* 'Watereri'.

FLOWERING ORNAMENTAL PEACHES *Prunus persica* 'Klara Mayer' plus all fruiting forms.

FLOWERING ALMONDS *Prunus* × *amygdalo-persica* (*P. amygdalo* 'Pollardii') plus all fruiting forms.

PEELING BARK CHERRY *Prunus serrula* (*P. s.* 'Tibetica').

PRUNUS TRILOBA (*Prunus triloba multiplex*)

Double-flowering Almond

Time to buy Pot-grown, any time. Balled, October–March. Avoid adverse weather conditions.

Where to find Outside in Trees or Shrubs.

Size BUSH Budded or grafted. Height 1½ ft (50 cm) min. Minimum three 1½ ft (50 cm) long branches.

HALF-STANDARD Budded or grafted top-worked on to *Prunus avium*. Height 8 ft (2.5 m) min. Clear stem of 4 ft (1.2 m). Minimum four 2 ft (60 cm) long branches. Stem girth at 3 ft (1 m) from ground, 1½–2½ in (4–6 cm) min.

Foliage Deciduous. Spring/summer, mid green. Early autumn colour and leaf drop.

Roots Pots 10 in (25 cm) min. dia. Balled, good fibrous root system.

Hints Any well-prepared soil. May be scarce out of flowering time. Stake and ties – five years. Check two of the three buds are growing. Avoid any showing signs of brown foliage.

PTELEA

The Hop Tree

Time to buy Pot-grown, any time. Balled, October–March. Avoid adverse weather conditions.

Where to find Outside in Trees or Shrubs.

Size BUSH Height 2 ft (60 cm) min. Minimum two upright stems. Limited side branches.

Foliage Deciduous. Spring/summer, light green or golden. Premature autumn colour and leaf drop.

Roots Pots 8 in (20 cm) min. dia. Balled, good fibrous root system.

Hints Any well-prepared soil. May be scarce. Stake and ties – five years in windy locations. Only found multi-stemmed. Research ultimate overall size.

PYRUS
Ornamental Pear

Time to buy Pot-grown, any time. Root-wrapped and bare-rooted, October–March. Avoid adverse weather conditions.

Where to find Outside in Trees.

Size MAIDEN Height 1–2 ft (30 cm–1.2 m) min. Limited side branches. FEATHERED Height 3–6 ft (1–3 m) min. Minimum four 9 in (23 cm) long side branches. BUSH Height 6 ft (2 m) min. Clear stem of 3 ft (1 m). Minimum three 2 ft (60 cm) long branches. HALF-STANDARD Height 8 ft (2.5 m) min. Clear stem of 5 ft (1.5 m). Minimum three 2 ft (60 cm) long branches. Stem girth at 3 ft (1 m) from ground, $1\frac{1}{2}$–$2\frac{1}{2}$ in (4–6 cm) min. STANDARD Height 10 ft (3 m) min. Clear stem of 8 ft (2.5 m). Minimum three 2 ft (60 cm) long branches. Stem girth at 3 ft (1 m) from ground, $2\frac{1}{2}$–3 in (6–8 cm) min. TOP-WORKED Half-standard and standard offered. Not long-lived, and do not form such good shapes. SEMI-MATURE Specialist nurseries supply a range of sizes.

Foliage Deciduous. Spring/summer, light green or silver. May show brown scorching. Premature autumn colour and leaf drop.

Roots Maiden and feathered, pots 6 in (15 cm) min. dia. Bush, half-standard and standard, pots 10 in (25 cm) min. dia. Root-wrapped and bare-rooted, good fibrous root system.

Hints Any well-prepared soil, plus extra organic material. Scarce. Stake and ties – five years. Whip and feathered, further training for five years. Poor fibrous root system. Late to show leaf in spring. Flowering is not a sign of establishment unless accompanied by foliage.

Most widely available

UPRIGHT *Pyrus calleryana* 'Chanticleer'. *P. communis* (Common Pear). *P. c.* 'Beech Hill'. *P. nivalis* (Silver Pear).

WEEPING *Pyrus salicifolis* (*P. s.* 'Pendula') (Weeping Silver-leaved Pear).

QUERCUS
Oak

Time to buy Pot-grown, any time. Balled, root-wrapped and bare-rooted, October–March. Avoid bad weather conditions.

Where to find Outside in Trees.

Size WHIP Height $1\frac{1}{2}$–3 ft (50 cm–1 m) min. Limited side branches. MAIDEN Height 2–4 ft (60 cm–1.2 m) min. Limited side branches. FEATHERED Height 6 ft (2 m) min. Minimum three 9 in (23 cm) long side branches. HALF-STANDARD Height 8 ft (2.5 m) min. Clear stem of 5 ft (1.5 m). Minimum three 1 ft (30 cm) long branches. Stem girth at 3 ft (1 m) from ground, $1\frac{1}{2}$–$2\frac{1}{2}$ in (4–6 cm) min. STANDARD Height 10 ft (3 m) min. Clear stem of 8 ft (2.5 m). Minimum three $1\frac{1}{2}$ ft (50 cm) long branches. Stem girth at 3 ft (1 m) from ground, $2\frac{1}{2}$–3 in. (6–8 cm) min.

Half-standard and standard in short supply. *Quercus robur* 'Concordia' found as whip and maiden. *Quercus frainetto* and *Quercus robur* 'Fastigiata' found as maiden and feathered. *Quercus robur* 'Pendula', weeping habit, should be purchased as grafted top-worked standard with clear stem 6 ft (2 m) min. and minimum two 2 ft (60 cm) long weeping branches, evenly arranged. Stem girth at 3 ft (1 m) from ground $1\frac{1}{2}$–$2\frac{1}{2}$ in (4–6 cm) min.

Foliage Evergreen, dark green, silver reverse. Deciduous, spring/summer, green, golden or variegated. Premature autumn colour and leaf drop.

Roots Whip and maiden, pots 6 in (15 cm) min. dia. Feathered, half-standard and standard, pots 12 in (30 cm) min. dia. Balled, root-wrapped and bare-rooted, good fibrous root system.

Hints Any well-prepared soil, plus extra organic material. Scarce. Stake and ties – five years. Whip, maiden and feathered, further training for five years. Poor root system. Smaller trees establish better.

Most widely available

ENGLISH (COMMON) *Quercus robur* (English Oak). *Q. r.* 'Concordia'. *Q. r.* 'Fastigiata' (Cyprus Oak). *Q. r.* 'Pendula' (Weeping English Oak).

SCARLET OAKS *Quercus coccinea* (Scarlet Oak). *Q. c.* 'Splendens'. *Q. frainetto* (Hungarian Oak). *Q. palustris. Q. petraea. Q. rubra (Quercus borealis maxima)* (Red Oak). *Q. r.* 'Aurea' (Golden-leaved Red Oak).

EVERGREEN *Quercus ilex* (Holm Oak). *Q. × kewensis Q. suber* (Cork Oak). *Q. turneri* (Turner's Oak). Normally only as whip and maiden, balled or pot-grown.

OTHER INTERESTING OAKS *Quercus canariensis* (Algerian Oak). *Q. castaneifolia* (Spanish Chestnut-Leaved Oak). *Q. cerris* (Turkey Oak). *Q. c.* 'Variegata' (Variegated Turkey Oak). *Q. phellos* (Willow Oak). Normally only as whip and maiden.

RHUS

Sumac, Sumach

Time to buy Pot-grown, any time. Avoid adverse weather conditions.

Where to find Outside in Trees or Shrubs.

Size WHIP Height 1½–3 ft (50 cm–1 m) min. No side branches. MAIDEN Height 2–4 ft (60 cm–1.2 m) min. Limited short side branches. BUSH Height 4 ft (1.2 m) min. Minimum three 12 in–3 ft (30 cm–1 m) long, irregular side branches.

Foliage Deciduous. Spring/summer, light to mid green. Premature autumn colour and leaf drop.

Roots Whip and maiden, pots 6 in (15 cm) min. dia. Bush, pots 8 in. (20 cm) min. dia.

Hints Any well-prepared soil. Stake and ties in windy areas – five years. Whip and maiden, further training for five years. Always misshapen, except *Rhus typhina* and *R. t.* 'Laciniata'.

ROBINIA

Acacia, False Acacia, Black Locust, Golden Acacia

Time to buy Pot-grown, any time. Balled, October–March. Avoid adverse weather conditions.

Where to find Outside in Trees.

Size MAIDEN Height 2–4 ft (60 cm–1.2 m) min. Limited side branches. FEATHERED Height 8 ft (2.5 m) min. Minimum four 9 in (23 cm) long side branches. BUSH Height 6 ft (2 m) min. Clear stem of 2–3 ft (60 cm–1 m). Minimum three 1½ ft (50 cm) long branches. HALF-STANDARD Height 8 ft (2.5 m) min. Clear stem of 4–5 ft (1.2–1.5 m). Minimum three 1½ ft (50 cm) long branches. Stem girth at 3 ft (1 m) from ground, 1½–2½ in (4–6 cm) min. STANDARD Height 10 ft (3 m) min. Clear stem of 6 ft (2 m). Minimum three 1½ ft (50 cm) long branches. Stem girth at 3 ft (1 m) from ground, 1½–2½ in (4–6 cm) min. TOP-WORKED Half-standard and standard may be offered, but these are not as long-lived and do not form such good shapes. *Robinia pseudoacacia* 'Inermis' top-worked. Clear stem 6 ft (2 m) min. Minimum three 1 ft (30 cm) long branches. *Robinia pseudoacacia* 'Pyramidalis' feathered. Height 3–5 ft (1–1.5 m) min. Limited side branches. *Robinia pseudoacacia* 'Tortuosa' bushes. Height 2–4 ft (60 cm–1.2 m) min. Contorted appearance. Limited side branches. *Robinia hispida* 'Macrophylla' found as maiden, bush or top-worked half-standards.

SEMI-MATURE Specialist nurseries supply a range of sizes. For walkways, tunnels, arches, pleaching and fan-training use whip or feathered.

Foliage Deciduous. Spring/summer, light grey-green or gold. Premature autumn colour and leaf drop.

Roots Maiden, pots 6 in (15 cm) min. dia. Feathered, bush, half-standard and standard, pots 12 in (30 cm) min. dia. Balled, good fibrous root system.

Hints Any well-prepared soil, except wet, plus extra organic material. Scarce. Stake and ties – ten years. Maiden and feathered, further training for five years. Root system poor; maiden and feathered establish better. Branches brittle and protection needed when transporting and from wind damage. In spring, overall appearance dead and late to show leaf. Tips of branches may die.

Most widely available
WHITE FLOWERING *Robinia pseudoacacia*. *R. p.* 'Bessoniana'. *R. p.* 'Inermis' (Mop-headed Acacia), (Thornless Black Locust). *R. p.* 'Pyramidalis' (*R. p.* 'Fastigiata') (Fastigiated Acacia). *R. p.* 'Tortuosa' (Contorted Acacia).
PINK FLOWERING *Robinia × ambigua*. *R.* 'Casque Rouge'. *R. fertilia* 'Monument'. *R. × hillieri*. *R. hispida*. *R. h.* 'Macrophylla' (Rose Acacia. Bristly Locust). *R. kelseyi. R. luxurians.*
GOLDEN-LEAVED *Robinis pseudoacacia* 'Frisia' (Golden Acacia).

SALIX (grown as mop-headed standard)
Mop-headed Willow
Time to buy Pot-grown, any time. Balled, October–March. Avoid adverse weather conditions.
Where to find Outside in Trees or Shrubs.
Size TOP-WORKED GRAFTED OR BUDDED Understocks of *Salix caprea* or *Salix daphnoides*: height 5 ft or 7 ft (1.5 m) (2.2 m) min. Clear stem of 4 ft (1.2 m) min., not more than 6 ft (2 m). Minimum three 9 in (23 cm) long branches. Stem girth at 3 ft (1 m) from ground, $\frac{3}{4}$–$1\frac{1}{2}$ in (2–4 cm) min. Non top-worked cannot be trained as standards.
Foliage Deciduous. Spring/summer, mid green to silver. Premature autumn colour and leaf drop.

Roots Pots 8 in (20 cm) min. dia. Balled, good fibrous root system.
Hints Any well-prepared soil. May be scarce. Stake and ties for life.
Most widely available *Salix hastata* 'Wehrhahnii'. *S. helvetica. S. alba integra maculata. S. lanata. S. lapponum. S. repens argentea.*

SALIX (grown as tree)
Willow
Time to buy Pot-grown, any time. Balled, root-wrapped and bare-rooted, October–March. Hardwood cuttings, December–March, normally mail order. Avoid adverse weather conditions.
Where to find Outside in Trees or Shrubs.
Size HARDWOOD CUTTINGS 9–12 in (23–30 cm). WHIP Height 1–3 ft (30 cm–1 m) min. Limited side branches. MAIDEN Height 2–5 ft (60 cm–1.45 m) min. Limited side branches. FEATHERED Height 3–8 ft (1–2.5 m) min. Minimum three $1\frac{1}{2}$ ft (50 cm) long side branches. HALF-STANDARD Height 8 ft (2.5 m) min. Clear stem of 4 ft (1.2 m). Minimum three 2 ft (60 cm) long branches. Stem girth at 3 ft (1 m) from ground $1\frac{1}{2}$–2 $\frac{1}{2}$ in (4–6 cm) min. STANDARD Height 10 ft (3 m) min. Clear stem of 6 ft (2 m). Minimum three 2 ft (60 cm) long branches. Stem girth 3 ft (1 m) from ground $1\frac{1}{2}$–$2\frac{1}{2}$ in (4–6 cm) min. SEMI-MATURE Specialist nurseries supply a range of sizes.
Salix Matsudana 'Tortuosa' only as maiden and feathered. For training as walkways, tunnels, arches, pleaching or fan-training use whip or feathered.
Foliage Deciduous. Spring/summer, grey-green or green. Premature autumn colour and leaf drop.
Roots Whip and maiden, pots 4 in (10 cm) min. dia. Feathered, pots 8 in. (20 cm) min. dia. Half-standard and standard, pots 10 in. (25 cm) min. dia. Balled, root-wrapped and bare-rooted, good fibrous root system. Hardwood cuttings, no roots.

Hints Any well-prepared soil, including moist and wet areas. May be scarce. Stake and ties – five years. Whip, maiden and feathered, further training for five years. Poor root system compensated by rapid growth. Maiden and bush purchased and trained as standard.

Most widely available

SILVER AND WHITE FOLIAGED *Salix alba* 'White Willow'. *S. a.* 'Liempde' (Silver White Willow). *S. a.* 'Sericea' (*S. a.* 'Argentea') (Silver Willow).

RED OR YELLOW WINTER STEMMED *Salix alba* 'Chermesina' (*S. a.* 'Britzensis') (Red Stem). *S. a.* 'Vitellina' (Yellow or Golden-stemmed Willow).

VIOLET WINTER STEMMED *Salix daphnoides*. *S. d.* 'Aglaia'. *S. acutifolia* 'Blue Streak'. *S. a.* 'Pendulifolia'.

CONTORTED STEMMED *Salix matsudana* 'Tortuosa'.

GOOD CATKIN PRODUCING *Salix aegyptiaca* (*S. medemii*) (Egyptian Musk Willow). *S.* 'Coerulea' (Cricket-bat Willow). *S. caprea* (Goat Willow, Great Willow, Pussy Willow). *S. smithiana*. *S.* 'The Hague'.

TIMBER PRODUCING *Salix* 'Coerulea' (Cricket-bat Willow).

SASSAFRAS ALBIDUM

Time to buy Pot-grown, any time. Balled, October–March. Avoid adverse weather conditions.

Where to find Outside in Trees.

Size WHIP Height 1½–3 ft (50 cm–1 m) min. Limited side branches. MAIDEN Height 2–5 ft (60 cm–1.5 m) min. Limited side branches.

Foliage Deciduous. Spring/summer, grey-green. Early autumn colour and leaf drop.

Roots Pots 5 in (12 cm) min. dia. Balled, good fibrous root system.

Hints Well-prepared acid to neutral soil, plus extra organic material. Scarce. Stake and ties – five years. Whip and maiden, further training for five years. Thin and weak in constitution, but worth persevering with.

SOPHORA

Japanese Pagoda Tree, Scholar Tree

Time to buy Pot-grown, any time. Balled, October– March. Avoid adverse weather conditions.

Where to find Outside in Trees.

Size WHIP Height 1½–3 ft (50 cm–1 m) min. Limited side branches. MAIDEN Height 2–4 ft (60 cm–1.2 m) min. Limited side branches. FEATHERED Height 4–9 ft (1.2–2.7 m). Minimum three 12 in (30 cm) long side branches. HALF-STANDARD Height 8 ft (2.5 m) min. Clear stem of 4 ft (1.2 m). Minimum three 1½ ft (50 cm) long branches. Stem girth at 3 ft (1 m) from ground, 1½–2½ in (4–6 cm) min. STANDARD Height 1 ft (30 cm) min. Clear stem of 6 ft (2 m). Minimum three 2 ft (60 cm) long branches. Stem girth at 3 ft (1 m) from ground, 1½–2½ in. (4–6 cm) min. TOP-WORKED Half-standard and standard also offered, but these are not long-lived and do not form such good shapes.

Sophora japonica 'Pendula' normally as top-worked grafted on to stem of *Sophora japonica*. Clear stem 6–8 ft (2–2.5 m) Minimum two 2 ft (60 cm) long branches. Stem girth at 3 ft (1 m) from ground 1½–2½ in (4–6 cm) min.

Foliage Deciduous. Spring/summer, grey-green to dark green. Premature autumn colour and leaf drop.

Roots Whip and maiden, pots 5 in (12 cm) min. dia. Feathered, half-standard and standard, 10 in (25 cm) min. dia. Balled, good fibrous root system.

Hints Any well-prepared soil, plus extra organic material. Scarce. Stake and ties – five years. Whip, maiden and feathered, further training for five years. May be late to show leaf in spring. *Sophora japonica* 'Pendula', irregular in shape when young. Will need care when transporting.

Most widely available *Sophora japonica* (Japanese Pagoda Tree). *S. j.* 'Pendula' (Weeping Sophora).

SORBUS
Whitebeam
Time to buy Pot-grown, any time. Balled, root-wrapped and bare-rooted, October–March. Avoid adverse weather conditions.
Where to find Outside in Trees.
Size MAIDEN Height 2–4 ft (60 cm–1.2 m) min. Limited side branches. FEATHERED Height 6 ft (2 m) min. Minimum three 1½ ft (50 cm) long side branches. BUSH Height 6 ft (2 m) min. Clear stem of 3 ft (1 m). Minimum three 12 in (30 cm) long branches. HALF-STANDARD Height 8 ft (2.5 m) min. Clear stem of 5 ft (1.5 m). Minimum three 2 ft (60 cm) long branches. Stem girth at 3 ft (1 m) from ground 1½–2½ in (4–6 cm) min. STANDARD Height 10 ft (3 m) min. Clear stem of 6 ft (2 m). Minimum three 2 ft (60 cm) long branches. Stem girth at 3 ft (1 m) from ground 1½–2½ in (4–6 cm) min.
Sorbus cashmiriana, S. sargentiana and *S. vilmorinii* normally as whip and maiden. *S. vilmorinii* also as bush. *Sorbus aria* 'Fastigiata' best as feathered. *Sorbus aria* 'Pendula' normally as topworked grafted onto stems of *Sorbus aucuparia'*. Clear stem 6–8 ft (2–2.5 m). Minimum two 2 ft (60 cm) long branches. Stem girth at 3 ft (1 m) from ground, 1½–2½ in (4–6 cm) min.
Foliage Deciduous. Spring/summer, light green or silver. Premature autumn colour and leaf drop.
Roots Maiden and feathered, pots 6 in (15 cm) min. dia. Bush, half-standard and standard, pots 10 in (25 cm) min. dia. Balled, root-wrapped and bare-rooted, good fibrous root system.
Hints Any well-prepared soil, particularly alkaline. May be scarce. Stake and ties – five years. Maiden and feathered, further training for five years.
Most widely available *Sorbus aria. S. a.* 'Chrysophylla'. *S. a.* 'Decaisneana'. *S. folgneri. S. a.* 'Lutescens' *S. a.* 'Magnifica'. *S. a.* 'Majestica' *S.* 'Mitchellii'

ROWAN OR MOUNTAIN ASH *Sorbus aucuparia. S. a.* 'Asplenifolia'. *S. a.* 'Beissneri' (Orange-stemmed Mountain Ash). *S. a.* 'Fastigiata' (Upright Mountain Ash). *S. a.* 'Pendula' (Weeping Mountain Ash). *S. a.* 'Sheerwater Seedling'. *S. a.* 'Xanthocarpa'.
OTHER GOOD FRUITING FORMS *Sorbus* 'Apricot Queen'. *S. cashmiriana* (The Kashmir Mountain Ash). *S. domestica* (The Service Tree). *S. torminalis* (Wild Service Tree). *S. decora. S. esserteauana. S. e.* 'Flava'. *S.* 'Golden Wonder' *S. huphensis. S. h. obtusa. S.* 'Joseph Rock' (Rock's Variety). *S.* 'Kirsten Pink'. *S. matsumurana* (Japanese Mountain Ash). *S. pohuashanensis. S.* 'McClaren D84' (*S. poterifolia*). *S. pratti. S. scalaris. S.* × *thuringiaca* 'Fastigiata'. *S. vilmorinii.*
AUTUMN FOLIAGE *Sorbus* 'Embley' (*S. discolour*). *S. sargentiana.*

STEWARTIA PSEUDOCAMELLIA
Time to buy Pot-grown, any time. Balled, October–March. Avoid adverse weather conditions.
Where to find Outside in Trees or Shrubs.
Size WHIP Height 1–2 ft (30–60 cm) min. Limited side branches. MAIDEN Height 2–3½ ft (60 cm–1.1 m) min. Limited side branches. FEATHERED Height 3–5 ft (1–1.5 m) min. Minimum three 9 in (23 cm) short side branches.
Foliage Deciduous. Spring/summer, light to mid green. Premature autumn colour and leaf drop.
Roots Whip and maiden, pots 6 in (15 cm) min. dia. Feathered, pots 10 in (25 cm) min. dia. Balled, good fibrous root system.
Hints Well-prepared acid to neutral soil, plus extra organic material. Scarce. Stake, ties and training – five years. Always small. Not found as half-standard or standard. Ten years to establish as tree.

STYRAX JAPONICA
Japanese Snowball

Time to buy Pot-grown, any time. Balled, October–March. Avoid adverse weather conditions.

Size WHIP Height 1–2 ft (30–60 cm) min. Limited side branches. MAIDEN Height 2–5 ft (60 cm–1.5 m) min. Limited side branches. FEATHERED Height 3–6 ft (1–2 m) min. Minimum three short side branches.

Foliage Deciduous. Spring/summer, dark green. Early autumn colour and leaf drop.

Roots Whip and maiden, pots 6 in (15 cm) min. Feathered, pots 10 in (25 cm) min. Balled, good fibrous root system.

Hints Well-prepared acid to neutral soil, plus extra organic material. Scarce. Stake, ties and training – five years. Always small. Not found as half-standard or standard. Takes ten years to establish as tree.

SYRINGA (grown as tree)
Lilac

Time to buy Pot-grown, any time. Balled, October–March. Avoid adverse weather conditions.

Where to find Outside in Trees or Shrubs.

Size PRE-TRAINED STANDARD grafted onto *Syringa vulgaris* or *Ligustrum vulgaris* (common privet) and *Ligustrum ovalifolium* (oval-leaved privet). Clear stem 4 ft (1.2 m) min. and not more than 6 ft (2 m). Height, $5\frac{1}{2}$–$7\frac{1}{2}$ ft (1.8–2.3 m) min. Minimum three $1\frac{1}{2}$ ft (50 cm) long branches.

An exception to this is *Syringa meyeri var. Palibin* which has a clear stem of 3 ft (1 m) min. Height 4 ft (1.2 m) min. Minimum three 6 in (15 cm) long branches.

Syringa microphylla 'Superba' and *S. m.* 'Palibin' have thinner branches. Shrub-grown, cannot be trained successfully.

Foliage Deciduous. Spring/summer, mid to dark green. Premature autumn colour and leaf drop.

Roots Pots 8 in (20 cm) min. dia. Balled, good fibrous root system.

Hints Any well-prepared soil. May be scarce. Stake and ties for life. Remove suckers of *Syringa vulgaris*. *Ligustrum ovalifolium* or *Ligustrum vulgare*, side growths below graft or budded union are normally suckers.

TILIA
Lime

Time to buy Pot-grown, any time. Balled, root-wrapped and bare-rooted, October–March. Avoid adverse weather conditions.

Where to find Outside in Trees.

Size MAIDEN Height 1–4 ft (30 cm–1.2 m) min. Limited side branches. FEATHERED Height 3–6 ft (1–2 m) min. Minimum four 1 ft (30 cm) long side branches. HALF-STANDARD Height $1\frac{1}{2}$ ft (50 cm) min. Clear stem 5 ft (1.5 m). Minimum three $1\frac{1}{2}$ ft (50 cm) long branches. Stem girth at 3 ft (1 m) from ground $1\frac{1}{2}$–$2\frac{1}{2}$ in (4–6 cm) min. STANDARD Height 10 ft (3 m) min. Clear stem 6 ft (2 m). Minimum three 2 ft (60 cm) long branches. Stem girth at 3 ft (1 m) from ground, $2\frac{1}{2}$–3 in (6–8 cm) min. TOP-WORKED Height 8 ft (2.5 m) min. Clear stem 6 ft (2 m) min., not more than 9 ft (2.7 m). Minimum three 2 ft (60 cm) long branches. Stem girth at 3 ft (1 m) from ground, $2\frac{1}{2}$–3 in (6–8 cm) min. SEMI-MATURE Specialist nurseries supply a range of sizes. PLEACHING OR FAN-TRAINING Request information from supplier or choose trees with flat, one-sided growth.

For walkways or arches, use feathered.

Foliage Deciduous. Spring/summer, light green or silver. Premature autumn colour and leaf drop.

Roots Maiden, pots 6 in (15 cm) min. dia. Feathered, pots 8 in (20 cm) min. dia. Half-standard and standard, pots 12 in (30 cm) min. dia. Balled, root-wrapped and bare-rooted, good fibrous root system.

Hints Any well-prepared soil. May be scarce. Stake and ties – five years. Maiden and feathered, further training for five years.

Most widely available *Tilia americana* (American Lime or Linden Basswood). *T. a.* 'Erecta'. *T. cordata* (Small-leaved Lime. Littleleaf Linden). *T. c.* 'Erecta'. *T. c.* 'Gold Spire'. *T. × euchlora* (Yellow-twigged Lime. Crimson Linden). *T. × europaea* (Common Lime, European Linden). *T henryana. T. petiolaris* (Weeping Silver Lime, Pendent Silver Linden). *T. platyphyllos. T. p.* 'Erecta' *T. p.* 'Rubra' (Red-Twigged Lime). *T. tomentosa* (Silver Lime or Linden).

ULMUS
Elm

Time to buy Pot-grown, any time. Root-wrapped and bare-rooted, October–March. Avoid adverse weather conditions.

Where to find Outside in Trees.

Size MAIDEN Height 1–4 ft (30 cm–1.2 m) min. Limited side branches. FEATHERED Height 3–6 ft (1–2 m) min. Minimum four $1\frac{1}{4}$ ft (40 cm) long side branches. HALF-STANDARD Height 8 ft (2.5 m) min. Clear stem 4 ft (1.2 m). Minimum three 2 ft (60 cm) long branches. Stem girth at 3 ft (1 m) from ground, $1\frac{1}{2}$–$2\frac{1}{2}$ in (4–6 cm) min. STANDARD Height 9 ft (2.7 m) min. Clear stem 6 ft (2 m). Minimum three 2 ft (60 cm) long branches. Stem girth at 3 ft (1 m) from ground, $2\frac{1}{2}$–3 in (6–8 cm) min. TOP-WORKED *Ulmus glabra* 'Pendula' and *Ulmus* 'Camperdownii', height 8 ft (2.5 m) min. Clear stem 6 ft (2 m) min, not more than 9 ft (2.7 m). Minimum three 2 ft (60 cm) long branches. Stem girth at 3 ft (1 m) from ground, $2\frac{1}{2}$–3 in (6–8 cm) min.

Foliage Deciduous. Spring/summer, mid green or golden. Premature autumn colour and leaf drop.

Roots Maiden, pots 6 in (15 cm) min. dia. Feathered 8 in (20 cm) min. dia. Half-stand-

ard and standard, pots 12 in (30 cm) min. dia. Root-wrapped and bare-rooted, good fibrous root system.

Hints Any well-prepared soil. Stake and ties – five years. Maiden and feathered, further training for five years. Can be susceptible to Dutch Elm disease when stems form a bark. Some partially immune forms, such as *Ulmus hollandica* 'Groeneveld', *U* 'Dodoens', *U.* 'Lobel' and *U.* 'Platijn' exist, but are scarce.

Most widely available *Ulmus angustifolia* (*cornubiensis*) (Cornish Elm). *U.* 'Camperdownii' (Weeping Elm). *U. carpinifolia* (Smooth-leaved Elm). *U. glabra* (Witch or Scotch Elm). *U. g.* 'Lutescens'. *U. g.* 'Pendula' (Weeping Witch Elm). *U. × hollandica* 'Wredei' (*U. × h.* 'Wredei Aurea'). *U. procera* (English Elm).

VIBURNUM (grown as tree)
Spring-flowered Viburnum, Standard Viburnum

Time to buy Pot-grown, any time. Balled, October–March. Avoid adverse weather conditions.

Where to find Outside in Trees or Shrubs.

Size Top-worked pre-trained mop-headed standard, height 6 ft (2 m) min. Clear stem 4 ft (1.2 m). Minimum three 1 ft (30 cm) long branches.

Only *Viburnum opulus* can be trained well as a standard from a shrub-grown plant.

Foliage Deciduous. Spring/summer, mid green. Premature autumn colour and leaf drop.

Roots Pots 8 in (20 cm) min. dia. Balled, good fibrous root system.

Hints Any well-prepared soil. Scarce. Stake and ties – five years. Small and unattractive when young. Command a high price, due to work entailed in production.

Most widely available *Viburnum × carlcephalum. V. carlesii. V. × juddii. V. opulus* 'Sterile'.

WEIGELA (grown as tree)
Time to buy Pot-grown, anytime. Balled root-wrapped and bare-rooted, October–March. Avoid adverse weather conditions.
Where to find Outside in Trees or Shrubs.
Size Pre-trained mop-headed standard, clear stem 4 ft (1.2 m) min. Minimum three 2 ft (60 cm) branches.
Foliage Deciduous. Spring/summer, light to mid green. Premature autumn colour and leaf drop.
Roots Pots 8 in (20 cm) min. dia. Balled, root-wrapped and bare-rooted, good fibrous root system.
Hints Any well-prepared soil. May be scarce. Stake and ties for life. If kept too long in nursery or garden centre can become weak.
Most widely available *Weigela* 'Bristol Ruby' is mainly pre-trained, but others may be available.

WISTERIA (grown as tree)
Time to buy Pot-grown, any time. Balled, October–March. Avoid adverse weather conditions.
Where to find Outside in Trees, Shrubs or Climbing Plants.
Size Clear stem of 4 ft (1.2 m) min., not more than 8 ft (2.5 m). Two 1 ft (30 cm) min. branches at top. If grown as climber, can be trained as mop-headed standard.
Foliage Deciduous. Spring/summer, light green. Premature autumn colour and leaf drop.
Roots Pots 8 in (20 cm) min. dia. Balled, good fibrous root system.
Hints Any well-prepared soil, plus extra organic material. Scarce. Stake and ties

for life. Command a high price, due to work entailed in production. In time, plants grown for climbing can be trained as standards.
Most widely available *Wisteria sinensis*. *W. s.* 'Alba'. *W. s.* 'Rosea'.

ZELKOVA
Elm Zelkova
Time to buy Pot-grown, any time. Balled, root-wrapped and bare-rooted, October–March. Avoid adverse weather conditions.
Where to find Outside in Trees.
Size MAIDEN Height 1–4 ft (30 cm–1.2 m) min. Limited side branches. FEATHERED Height 3–6 ft (1–2 m) min. Minimum four short side branches. HALF-STANDARD Height 8 ft (2.5 m) min. Clear stem 4 ft (1.2 m). Minimum three 2 ft (60 cm) long branches. Stem girth at 3 ft (1 m) from ground, $1\frac{1}{2}$–$2\frac{1}{2}$ in (4–6 cm) min. STANDARD Height 10 ft (3 m) min. Clear stem 8 ft (2.5 m). Minimum three 2 ft (60 cm) long branches. Stem girth at 3 ft (1 m) from ground $2\frac{1}{2}$–3 in (6–8 cm) min. SEMI-MATURE Specialist nurseries supply a range of sizes.
Foliage Deciduous. Spring/summer, light green. Premature autumn colour and leaf drop.
Roots Maiden and feathered, pots 6 in (15 cm) min. dia. Half-standard and standard, pots 10 in (25 cm) min. dia. Balled, root-wrapped and bare-rooted, good fibrous root system.
Hints Any well-prepared soil. May be scarce. Stake and ties – five years. Maiden and feathered, further training for five years. Always looks one-sided.

Shrubs

The wide range of shrubs available makes selection difficult. With so many variations of leaf, flower, size and shape, it is important to research all these points. To find what is required, it will inevitably be necessary to use a number of garden centres and nurseries.

Some shrubs will be found presented as semi-mature (extra large), and if an instant effect is required, they are worth the extra expenditure. Hardiness and soil requirements are also important considerations for the overall well-being of the chosen shrubs, and in ensuring their successful establishment.

One of the most dangerous times for many young shrubs is from mid to late spring, when they are taken from their protected production areas and offered for sale. Plants can be purchased during this period, but must be kept under frost-free protection until safe to plant out.

The opposite applies to those that are grown without protection: they should not be protected. If planting is not possible at time of purchase, they should be kept outdoors in a sheltered corner.

Shrubs will be predominantly container-grown, although the use of root-balled, root-wrapped and bare-rooted material should always be considered, as long as it is purchased in the correct planting season. Prepacks can also be considered, but select with care and check the condition of roots and stems. Avoid any showing signs of premature growth due to incorrect storage.

Correct planting preparation is important. A hole at least 3 ft (1 m) in diameter should be dug to a depth of 18 in (50 cm), keeping the top-soil at the top throughout the operation. Adequate organic material must be added to aid root development. If a large area is to be planted, then the soil should be double-dug in advance of purchasing the shrubs, again adding organic material.

Many shrubs require pruning in order to establish, and for their long-term well-being and research is needed to discover the correct procedure to use in each case.

Bare-rooted plants purchased during unfavourable planting conditions should be 'heeled in' so their roots are covered, and left until safe to plant.

Root-balled and root-wrapped plants should be stored with some form of insulating material such as straw, newspaper or old carpet placed around and between the root-balls to protect them from hard frosts.

ABELIA
Time to buy Pot-grown, any time. Avoid adverse weather conditions.
Where to find Outside in Shrubs.
Size Height 1 ft (30 cm) min., single or multi-stemmed.
Foliage Semi-evergreen. Mid green to red-green. Some premature autumn colour and leaf drop.
Roots Pots 4 in (10 cm) min. dia. Larger for preference.
Hints Any well-prepared soil. If kept under cover in winter, avoid planting until spring frosts have finished. Fragile. Take care when transporting. Avoid soft, leafy plants, March–April. *Abelia grandiflora* 'Francis Mason' benefits from light shade.
Most widely available *Abelia* 'Edward Goucher'. *A. × grandiflora. A. g.* 'Francis Mason'. *A. schumannii.*

ABELIOPHYLLUM DISTICHUM
Korean Abelia Leaf, White Forsythia
Time to buy Pot-grown, any time except January. Avoid adverse weather conditions.
Where to find Outside in Shrubs.
Size Height 1 ft (30 cm) min., single or multi-stemmed.
Foliage Deciduous. Spring/summer, light green. Premature autumn colour and leaf drop.
Roots Pots 4 in (10 cm) min. dia. Larger for preference.
Hints Any well-prepared soil. If kept under cover in winter, avoid planting until spring frosts have finished. Looks unattractive, apart from its flower. May be scarce.

ABUTILON
Trailing Abutilon
Time to buy Pot-grown, May–July. Avoid adverse weather conditions.
Where to find Outside in Shrubs.
Size Height 1½ ft (50 cm) min., single or multi-stemmed.

Foliage Deciduous. Spring/summer, dark to mid green or golden variegated. Premature autumn colour and leaf drop.
Roots Pots 4 in (10 cm) min. dia. Larger for preference.
Hints Any well-prepared soil. If kept under cover in winter, avoid planting until spring frosts have finished. May be scarce. Hardiness in doubt. For wall use, plant 15–18 in (40–50 cm) away. Open and straggly when young.
Most widely available *Abutilon megapotamicum. A. m.* 'Kentish Belle'. *A. m.* 'Variegatum'.

ACANTHOPANAX
Fiveleaf Aralia
Time to buy Pot-grown, any time except January. Avoid adverse weather conditions.
Where to find Outside in Shrubs.
Size Height 1½ ft (50 cm) min., single or multi-stemmed.
Foliage Deciduous. Spring/summer, green or variegated. Premature autumn colour and leaf drop.
Roots Pots 5 in (12 cm) min. dia. Larger for preference.
Hints Any well-prepared soil. If kept under cover in winter, avoid planting until spring frosts have finished. May be scarce. Signs of leaf scorching may be due to improper storage. European stock potted in winter may not be established by spring. Requires light, dappled shade.
Most widely available *Acanthopanax sieboldianus. A. s.* 'Argentea Variegatus'.

ACER GINNALA
Amur Maple
Time to buy Pot-grown, any time except January. Balled, root-wrapped and bare-rooted, October–May. Avoid adverse weather conditions.
Where to find Outside in Shrubs or Trees.
Size Height 2½ ft (60 cm) min., single or multi-stemmed. Shrubs up to 5 ft (1.5 m)

are successful. May be found as feathered tree.
Foliage Deciduous. Spring/summer, mid green. Premature autumn colour and leaf drop.
Roots Pots 6 in (15 cm) min. dia. Balled, root-wrapped and bare-rooted, good fibrous root system.
Hints Any well-prepared soil. Scarce. Over 3 ft (1 m) requires stake and ties for five years. Should be more widely planted.

ACER JAPONICUM
Japanese Maple, Full-moon Maple
Time to buy Pot-grown, any time except January. Balled, October–May. Avoid adverse weather conditions.
Where to find Outside in Shrubs.
Size Height, 1½ ft (50 cm) min. One or more central shoots. *Acer japonicum* 'Aureum', height 6 in (15 cm) min. Limited side branches. Wide range of sizes.
Foliage Deciduous. Spring/summer, light to mid green or golden. Premature autumn colour and leaf drop.
Roots Pots 8 in (20 cm) min. dia. Larger for preference. Balled, good fibrous root system.
Hints Any well-prepared soil, plus extra organic material. If kept under cover in winter, avoid planting until spring frosts have passed. *Acer japonicum* 'Aureum' smaller and more expensive due to slow rate of growth and propagation difficulty. Requires light shade.
Most widely available *Acer japonicum.* A. j. 'Aconitifolium' (A. j. 'Laciniatum'). A. j. 'Aureum'. A. j. 'Filicifolium'. A. j. 'Vitifolium'.

ACER PALMATUM
Japanese Maple
Time to buy Pot-grown, any time except January. Balled, October–May. Avoid adverse weather conditions.
Where to find Outside in Shrubs.
Size Height 1½ ft (50 cm) min. Single or

multi-stemmed. *Acer palmatum* 'Dissectum' types, height 1 ft (30 cm) min. Minimum two shoots. Wide range of sizes.
Foliage Deciduous. Spring/summer, mid to dark green, purple, golden or pink. Premature autumn colour and leaf drop.
Roots Pots 8 in (20 cm) min. dia. Larger for preference. Balled, good fibrous root system.
Hints Any well-prepared soil, except alkaline or dry, plus extra organic material. If kept under cover in winter, avoid planting until spring frosts have finished. May show leaf scorching. Plant in light, dappled shade. European stock potted in winter may not be established by spring.
Most widely available *Acer palmatum.* A. p. 'Atropurpureum'. A. p. 'Bloodgood'. A. p. 'Butterfly'. A. p. 'Chitoseyama'. A. p. 'Dissectum' (cut-leaved Japanese Maple). A. p. 'Dissectum Atropurpureum'. A. p. 'Dissectum Garnet'. A. p. 'Dissectum Inabashidare'. A. p. 'Dissectum Nigrum'. A. p. 'Dissectum Ornatum'. A. p. 'Dissectum Rubrifolium'. A. p. 'Linearilobum'. A. p. 'Senkaki' (Coral-barked Maple). A. p. 'Shishio'. A. p. var. *Heptalobum*. A. p. h. 'Elegans Purpureum'. A. p. h. 'Osakazuki'. A. p. 'Versicolor'.

AESCULUS PARVIFLORA
Buckeye, Bottlebrush Buckeye
Time to buy Pot-grown, any time except January. Balled, October–May. Avoid adverse weather conditions.
Where to find Outside in Shrubs.
Size Height 1½ ft (50 cm) min. Minimum two main shoots.
Foliage Deciduous. Spring/summer, mid green. Premature autumn colour and leaf drop.
Roots Pots 10 in (25 cm) min. dia. Balled, good fibrous root system.
Hints Any well-prepared soil. May be scarce. Must be allowed space for development. European stock potted in winter may not be established by spring.

AMELANCHIER
Allegheny Serviceberry, Snowy Mespilus,
June Berry, Service Bush
Time to buy Pot-grown, any time except
January. Balled, root-wrapped and bare-
rooted, October–May. Avoid adverse wea-
ther conditions.
Where to find Outside in Shrubs.
Size Height 2 ft (60 cm) min. Minimum
two main shoots.
Foliage Deciduous. Spring/summer, mid
green. Early autumn colour and leaf drop.
Roots Pots 8 in (20 cm) min. dia. Larger
for preference. Balled, root-wrapped and
bare-rooted, good fibrous root system.
Hints Any well-prepared soil. Allow adequate space for development. Often looks
bent. European stock potted in winter
may not be established by spring.
Most widely available *Amelanchier* 'Ballerina'. *A. lamarckii* (*Amelanchier canadensis*). *A. laevis*.

AMORPHA
False Indigo, Indigo Bush Amorpha,
Bastard Indigo
Time to buy Pot-grown, any time except
January. Balled, October–May. Avoid ad-
verse weather conditions.
Where to find Outside in Shrubs.
Size *Amorpha fruticosa*, height 2 ft
(60 cm) min. Minimum two main shoots.
Amorpha canescens, height 6 in (15 cm)
min. Minimum two main shoots.
Foliage Deciduous. Spring/summer, light
green. Premature autumn colour and leaf
drop.
Roots Pots 5 in (12 cm) min. dia. Balled,
good fibrous root system.
Hints Any well-prepared soil. If kept
under cover in winter, avoid planting
until spring frosts have finished. Scarce.
Always misshapen and ungainly. *Amorpha fruticosa* poor root system, short
stake and ties for life.
Most widely available *Amorpha canescens* (Lead Plant). *A. fruticosa* (Indigo
Bush).

ANDROMEDA
Bog Rosemary
Time to buy Pot-grown, any time except
January. Balled, October–May. Avoid ad-
verse weather conditions.
Where to find Outside in Shrubs or
Acid-loving Plants.
Size *Andromeda glaucophylla* and *An-
dromeda polifolia*, height 1 ft (30 cm) min.
Andromeda polifolia 'Compacta', height
6 in (15 cm) min. Both single or multi-
stemmed. Limited side shoots.
Foliage Evergreen. Olive to grey-green.
Premature basal leaf drop.
Roots Pots 4 in (10 cm) min. dia. Balled,
good fibrous root system.
Hints Well-prepared acid soil, plus extra
organic material. Scarce.
Most widely available *Andromeda poli-
folia* (Bog Rosemary). *A. p.* 'Compacta'.
A. glaucophylla.

ARALIA
Japanese Angelica Tree, Japanese Aralia
Time to buy Pot-grown, any time except
January. Balled, October–May. Avoid ad-
verse weather conditions.
Where to find Outside in Shrubs.
Size *Aralia eleta*, height 1½ ft (50 cm) min.
Single-stemmed. No side shoots. *Aralia
elata* 'Aureovariegata' and *A. e.* 'Variegata', height 5 in (12 cm) min. Single-
stemmed. No side shoots.
Foliage Deciduous. Spring/summer, light
green or variegated. Premature autumn
colour and leaf drop.
Roots Pots 6 in (15 cm) min. dia. Balled,
good fibrous root system.
Hints Any well-prepared soil, plus extra
organic material. If kept under cover in
winter, avoid planting until spring frosts
have finished. *Aralia elata* 'Aureovariegata' and *A. e.* 'Variegata' command
high price due to difficulty in propagation.
Most widely available *Aralia elata; A. e.*
'Aureovariegata'. *A. e.* 'Variegata'.

ARCTOSTAPHYLOS UVA-URSI
Red Bearberry, Kinnikinick
Time to buy Pot-grown, any time except January. Balled, October–May. Avoid adverse weather conditions.
Where to find Outside in Shrubs or Acid-loving Plants.
Size Height 4 in (10 cm) min. Single or multi-stemmed.
Foliage Evergreen. Grey-green. Premature basal leaf drop.
Roots Pots 4 in (10 cm) min. dia. Balled, good fibrous root system.
Hints Well-prepared acid soil, plus extra organic material. Scarce.

ARONIA
Chokeberry
Time to buy Pot-grown, any time except January. Balled, October–May. Avoid adverse weather conditions.
Where to find Outside in Shrubs or Acid-loving Plants.
Size Height 1½ ft (50 cm) min. Single or multi-stemmed.
Foliage Deciduous. Spring/summer, mid green. Premature autumn colour and leaf drop.
Roots Pots 4 in (10 cm) min. dia. Balled, good fibrous root system.
Hints Well-prepared acid soil, plus extra organic material. Scarce.
Most widely available Aronia Arbutifolia (Red Chokeberry). A. 'Erecta'. A. melanocarpa (Black Chokeberry). A. m. 'Brilliant'. A. prunifolia (Purple Chokeberry).

ARTEMISIA (shrubby forms)
Southernwood, Lad's Love
Time to buy Pot-grown, any time except January. Balled, October–May. Avoid adverse weather conditions.
Where to find Outside in Shrubs or Acid-loving Plants.
Size Height 9 in (23 cm) min. Single or multi-stemmed.
Foliage Deciduous. Spring/summer, grey-green. Premature autumn colour and leaf drop.
Roots Pots 4 in (10 cm) min. dia. Balled, good fibrous root system.
Hints Any well-prepared soil. Plants more than two years old not recommended.
Most widely available Artemisia abrotanum. A. arborescens.

ATRIPLEX HALIMUS
Tree Purslane, Salt Bush
Time to buy Pot-grown, any time except January. Balled, October–May. Avoid adverse weather conditions.
Where to find Outside in Shrubs.
Size Height 1 ft (30 cm) min. Single or multi-stemmed.
Foliage Semi-evergreen. Spring/summer, silver-grey. Some premature autumn colour and leaf drop.
Roots Pots 5 in (12 cm) min. dia. Balled, good fibrous root system.
Hints Any well-prepared soil. Scarce. Avoid plants heavily cut back.

AUCUBA
Japanese Aucuba, Spotted Laurel, Himalayan Laurel, Japanese Laurel
Time to buy Pot-grown, any time except January. Balled, October–May. Avoid adverse weather conditions.
Where to find Outside in Shrubs.
Size Height 9 in (23 cm) min. Single or multi-stemmed.
Foliage Evergreen. Green or golden variegated. Some premature basal leaf drop.
Roots Pots 4 in (10 cm) min. dia. Balled, good fibrous root system.
Hints Any well-prepared soil. May be scarce. For fruiting, select one male to any number of female forms.
Most widely available Aucuba japonica. A. j. 'Crotonifolia' (M). A. j. 'Mr Goldstrike' (F). A. j. 'Picturata' (M). A. j. 'Salicifolia' (F). A. j. 'Variegata' (F). A. j. 'Variegated Gold Dust' (F).

AZALEAS
Time to buy Pot-grown, any time except
January. Balled, October–May. Avoid adverse weather conditions.
Where to find Outside in Shrubs, Acid-
loving Plants or specific Rhododendron/
Azalea area. (Azaleas are a sub species
of the Rhododendron family.)
Size DWARF Height 5 in (12 cm) min.
Single or multi-stemmed. TALL Height
1½ ft (30 cm) min. Single or multi-
stemmed. Seedling forms may be available, flowering performance and colour
not always known.
Foliage EVERGREEN Dark green. Prema-
ture basal leaf drop TALL DECIDUOUS
Spring/summer, mid green. Premature
autumn colour and leaf drop.
Roots DWARF Pots 5 in (12 cm) min. dia.
TALL Pots 10 in (25 cm) min. dia. Balled,
good fibrous root system.
Hints Well-prepared acid soil, plus extra
organic material. Wide range offered in
flower. Outside of this time may be
scarce. Research overall size.
Most widely available
DWARF EVERGREEN **Kurume** types
Azalea 'Addy Wery'. A. 'Blaauw's Pink'.
A. 'Hatsugirl'. A. 'Hinodegirl'. A. 'Hinom-
ayo'. A. 'Imashojo' (Christmas cheer). A.
'Kure-no-yuki'. A. 'Rosebud'. **Vuyk**
hybrids Azalea 'Beethoven'. A. 'Blue
Danube'. A. 'Palestrina'. A. 'Vuyks
Rosy Red'. A. 'Vuyks Scarlet'. **Dwarf**
hybrid crosses Azalea 'Favorite'. A. 'John
Cairns'. A. 'Leo'. A. 'Mother's Day'. A.
'Naomi'. A. 'Orange Beauty'. A. 'Sil-
vester'.
TALL-GROWING DECIDUOUS **Knaphill**
hybrids Azalea 'Balzac'. A. 'Berryrose'; A.
'Brazil'. A. 'Cecile'. A. 'Fireball'. A. 'Gal-
lipoli'. A. 'Gibraltar'. A. 'Homebush'. A.
'Hotspur'. A. 'Hugh Wormald'. A.
'Klondyke'. A. 'Satan'. A. 'Strawberry
Ice'. A. 'Tunis'. **Mollis** hybrids Azalea
'Apple Blossom'. A. 'Chevalier de Reali'.
A. 'Christopher Wren'. A. 'Dr. M. Oost-
hoek'. A. 'Golden Sunlight'. A. 'Kosters

Brilliant Red'. **Ghent** hybrids Azalea coccinea speciosa. A. 'Daviesii'. A. 'Narcissi-
florum'; A. 'Pallas'. A. pontica (Rhododendron luteum). Many other forms available.

AZARA
Time to buy Pot-grown, any time except
January. Avoid adverse weather conditions.
Where to find Outside in Shrubs.
Size Height 1 ft (30 cm) min. Single stem
with numerous short side shoots.
Foliage Evergreen. Mid, dark green or variegated. Premature basal leaf drop.
Roots Pots 6 in (15 cm) min. dia.
Hints Any well-prepared soil, plus extra
organic material. Scarce. If kept under
cover in winter, avoid planting out until
spring frosts have finished. Hardiness in
doubt.
Most widely available Azara dentata. A.
lanceolata. A. microphylla, A. m. 'Variegata'. A. serrata.

BALLOTA PSEUDODICTAMNUS
Time to buy Pot-grown, May–June. Avoid
adverse weather conditions.
Where to find Outside in Shrubs or
Summer Bedding.
Size Height 4 in (10 cm) min. Numerous
short side shoots.
Foliage Evergreen. Grey-green. May show
signs of damage in severe winters.
Roots Pots 3 in (8 cm) min. dia.
Hints Any well-prepared soil. If kept
under cover in winter, avoid planting
until spring frosts have finished. Hardi-
ness in doubt. Avoid old, woody plants.

BERBERIS
Barberry
Time to buy Pot-grown, any time except
January. Balled, root-wrapped and bare-
footed, October–May. Avoid adverse wea-
ther conditions.
Where to find Outside in Shrubs.

Size DECIDUOUS AND EVERGREEN Low-growing: Height 6 in (15 cm) min. Tall-growing: Height 1½ ft (50 cm) min. DECIDU-OUS Medium-growing: Height 1 ft (30 cm) min. All single or multi-stemmed.

Foliage DECIDUOUS: Spring/summer, green, purple, pink or variegated. Premature autumn colour and leaf drop. EVER-GREEN: Dark green or purple. Some premature basal leaf drop.

Roots Pots 5 in (12 cm) min. dia. Balled, root-wrapped and bare-rooted, good fibrous root system.

Hints Any well-prepared soil. Thorns make handling difficult. Signs of leaf scorch if not correctly stored in garden centres. *Berberis thunbergii* 'Nana', *B. t.* 'Bagatelle' and *B. t.* 'Kobold' very brittle, handle with care.

Most widely available
DECIDUOUS Low-growing: *Berberis sieboldii. B. thunbergii* 'Aurea'. *B. t.* 'Bagatelle'. *B. t.* 'Green Carpet', *B. t.* 'Green Ornament', *B. t. atropurpurea* 'Nana' ('Little Favourite'), *B. t.* 'Kobold'. Medium growing: *Berberis rubrostilla. B. thunbergii* 'Erecta'. *B. t.* 'Gold Ring'. *B. t.* 'Halmond's Pillar'. *B. t.* 'Harlequin'. *B. t.* 'Kelleriis'. *B. t.* 'Lombarts Purple'. *B. t.* 'Red Chief'. *B. t.* 'Red Pillar'. *B. wilsoniae*. Tall growing: *Berberia aggregata. B.* 'Buccaneer'. *B. dictophylla* (*B. d.* 'Albicaulis'). *B. jamesiana. B. koreana. B.* 'Pirate King'. *B. temolaica. B. thunbergii var. atropurpurea. B. t.* 'Golden Ring'. *B. t. × ottawensis* 'Purpurea'. *B. t.* 'Rose Glow'. *B. vulgaris* 'Atropurpurea' (Purple-leaved barberry).
EVERGREEN Low-growing: *Berberis × bristolensis. B. buxifolia* 'Nana'. *B. calliantha. B. candidula* (Paleleaf Barberry). *B. c.* 'Amstelveen'. *B. c.* 'Telstar'. *B.* 'Chanaultii' (Chenault Barberry). *B. panlanensis. B.* 'Parkjuweel'. *B. × stenophylla* 'Corallina Compacta'. *B. × s.* 'Crawley Beauty'. *B. × s.* 'Irwinii'. *B. × s.* 'Pink Pearl'. *B. verruculosa*. Tall-growing: *Berberia atrocarpa. B. darwinii* (Darwin's

Barberry). *B. gagnepainii. B. julianae* (Wintergreen Barberry). *B. knightii. B. linearifolia. B. l.* 'Orange King'. *B. × lologensis. B. × l.* 'Apricot Queen'. *B. × l.* 'Gertrude Hardyzerii'. *B. sargentiana. B. stenophylla. B. s.* 'Autumnalis'. *B.* 'Walitch Purple'.

BETULA NANA
Dwarf Birch, Rock Birch

Time to buy Pot-grown, any time except January. Balled, October–May. Avoid adverse weather conditions.

Where to find Outside in Shrubs.

Size Height 6 in (15 cm) min. Single or multi-stemmed.

Foliage Deciduous. Spring/summer, mid green. Premature autumn colour and leaf drop.

Roots Pots 5 in (12 cm) min. dia. Balled, good fibrous root system.

Hints Any well-prepared soil. May be scarce. Looks small and insipid when young.

BUDDLEIA
Butterfly Bush, Summer Lilac

Time to buy Pot-grown, any time. Avoid adverse weather conditions.

Where to find Outside in Shrubs.

Size Height 1½ ft (50 cm) min. Single or multi-stemmed.

Foliage Deciduous. Spring/summer, mid green, grey or variegated. Premature autumn colour and leaf drop.

Roots Pots 5 in (12 cm) min. dia.

Hints Any well-prepared soil. Except *Buddleia alternifolia*, cut back all previous season's growth within two buds of origin in April. Repeat annually. If kept under cover in winter, avoid planting until spring frosts have finished.

Most widely available *Buddleia alternifolia* (Alternate-Leaf Butterfly Bush). *B. davidii* 'Black Knight'. *B. d.* 'Empire Blue'. *B. d.* 'Fascinating'. *B. d.* 'Fortune'. *B. d.* 'Harlequin'. *B. d.* 'Ile de France'. *B. d.* 'Nanho Alba'. *B. d.* 'Nanho Blue'. *B. d.*

'Nanho Purple'. *B. d.* 'Opera'. *B. d.*
'Orchid Beauty'. *B. d.* 'Peace'. *B. d.* 'Pink
Delight'. *B. d.* 'Purple Prince'. *B. d.* 'White
Profusion'. *B. globosa. B.* 'Lochinch' (*Bud-
dleia × fallowiana* 'Lochinch'). *B. × wey-
riana. B. × w.* 'Golden Glow'. *B. × w.*
'Sun Gold'.

BUPLEURUM FRUTICOSUM
Time to buy Pot-grown, April–July. Avoid
adverse weather conditions.
Where to find Outside in Shrubs.
Size Height 6 in (15 cm) min. Single or
multi-stemmed.
Foliage Evergreen. Dark green. Premature
basal leaf drop.
Roots Pots 4 in (10 cm) min. dia.
Hints Any well-prepared soil. Scarce. If
kept under cover in winter, avoid planting until spring frosts have finished. May
need protection first winter after planting. Straggly and gaunt when young.

BUXUS
Box
Time to buy Pot-grown, any time, except
January. Balled, October–May. Avoid adverse weather conditions.
Where to find Outside in Shrubs. *Buxus
sempervirens* and *Buxus* 'Suffruticosa'
may also be found in Hedging.
Size Height 6 in (15 cm) min. *Buxus* 'Suffruticosa' 2 in (5 cm) min. Central stem
with short side shoots.
Size PRE-TRAINED SHAPED TREES Box
balls, 8 in (20 cm) min. dia. Pyramids,
12 in (30 cm) min. Minimum basal spread,
6 in (15 cm). Specific trained shapes,
good full branch system and solid shape.
Mop-headed standard scarce.
Foliage Evergreen. Dark green or variegated. Premature basal leaf drop.
Roots *Buxus* 'Suffruticosa' pots 3 in
(8 cm) min. dia. Other forms, excluding
pre-trained, pots 5 in (12 cm) min. dia. Pre-
trained as pyramids, balls, mop-headed
standards, shaped and spirals, pots 10 in

(20 cm) min. dia. Balled, good fibrous root
system.
Hints Any well-prepared soil. Height is
often less than described. Research overall ultimate size. Buxus can be used as
hedging, see p. 144 for details.
Most widely available *Buxus sempervirens* (Hedging Box). *B. s.* 'Aurea Pendula' (*B. s.* 'Aurea Maculata Pendula').
B. s. 'Elegantissima'. *B. s.* 'Handsworthensis' (*B. s.* 'Handsworthii'). *B. s.* 'Latifolia Maculata' (*B. s* 'Japonica Aurea'). *B. s.*
'Suffruticosa' (Edging Box).

CALLICARPA
Beauty Berry
Time to buy Pot-grown, any time except
January. Balled, October–May. Avoid adverse weather conditions.
Where to find Outside in Shrubs.
Size Height 1¼ ft (40 cm) min. Single or
multi-stemmed.
Foliage Deciduous. Spring/summer, mid
green. Premature autumn colour and leaf
drop.
Roots Pots 5 in (12 cm) min. dia. Balled,
good fibrous root system.
Hints Any well-prepared soil. Look uninteresting outside of fruiting season. For
good pollination of fruit, more than one
shrub must be planted.
Most widely available *Callicarpa bodi-
nieri var. giraldii. C. b.* 'Profusion'. *C.
japonica* 'Leucocarpa' (Japanese Beauty
Berry).

CALLISTEMON
Australian Bottle Brush
Time to buy Pot-grown, April–July. Avoid
adverse weather conditions.
Where to find Outside in Shrubs.
Size Height 1½ ft (50 cm) min. Single or
multi-stemmed.
Foliage Evergreen. Mid green. Premature
basal leaf drop.
Roots Pots 5 in (12 cm) min. dia.
Hints Well-prepared acid soil, plus extra
organic material. May be scarce. Har-

diness in doubt. May need protection by pot-growing and bringing into greenhouse in winter. In pots, use good quality lime-free potting compost. If kept under cover in winter, avoid planting until spring frosts have finished.
Most widely available *Callistemon citrinus. C. c.* 'Splendens'.

CALLUNA
Scotch Heather, Ling
Time to buy Pot-grown, any time, except January. Avoid adverse weather conditions.
Where to find Outside in Heathers.
Size Year-old plants, height and spread 2 in (5 cm) min. Two-years-old, height and spread 3 in (8 cm) min. Both with multiple shoots.
Foliage Evergreen. Mid green, gold or purple. Premature basal leaf drop.
Roots One-year-old, pots 3 in (8 cm) min. dia. Two-years-old, pots 4 in (10 cm) min. dia.
Hints Well-prepared acid soil. Avoid old and woody plants. It is not always explained that *Calluna vulgaris* requires acid soil.
Most widely available *Calluna vulgaris, C. v. alba* (White Heather). *C. v.* 'Alba Plena' (*C. v.* 'Alba Flore Pleno'). *C. v.* 'Aurea' *C. v.* 'Cuprea'. *C. v.* 'Golden Feather'. *C. v.* 'Gold Haze'. *C. v.* 'Goldsworth Crimson'. *C. v.* 'H. E. Beale'. *C. v.* 'Joan Sparkes'. *C. v.* 'Joy Vanstone'. *C. v.* 'Kinlochruel'. *C. v.* 'Mullion'. *C. v.* 'Orange Queen'. *C. v.* 'Peter Sparkes'. *C. v.* 'Red Haze'. *C. v.* 'Robert Chapman'. *C. v.* 'Silver Night'. *C. v.* 'Silver Queen'. *C. v.* 'Spring Torch'. *C. v.* 'Spitfire'. *C. v.* 'Sunset'. *C. v.* 'Tib'. *C. v.* 'Tricolorifolia'. *C. v.* 'Winter Chocolate'. Many others of interest.

CALYCANTHUS
Allspice, Pale Sweetshrub
Time to buy Pot-grown, any time except January. Balled, October–May. Avoid adverse weather conditions.
Where to find Outside in Shrubs or Acid-loving Plants.
Size Height 1½ ft (50 cm) min. Single or multi-stemmed. Minimum three short side branches.
Foliage Deciduous. Spring/summer, mid green. Premature autumn colour and leaf drop.
Roots Pots 5 in (12 cm) min. dia. Balled, good fibrous root system.
Hints Well-prepared acid soil, plus extra organic material. May be scarce.

CAMELLIA
Time to buy Pot-grown, any time except January. Balled, October–May. Avoid adverse weather conditions.
Where to find Outside in Shrubs or Acid-loving Plants.
Size Height 1 ft (30 cm) min. Short side shoots.
Foliage Evergreen. Dark green. Premature basal leaf drop.
Roots Pots 5 in (12 cm) min. dia. Balled, good fibrous root system.
Hints Well-prepared acid soil. Wide range of forms.
Most widely available *Camellia* 'Cornish Snow'. *C. japonica* 'Adolphe Audusson'. *C. j.* 'Apollo'. *C. j.* 'Arejishi'. *C. j.* 'Better Sheffield Supreme'. *C. j.* 'Contessa Lavinia Maggi'. *C. j.* 'Elegans'. *C. j.* 'Madame Victor de Bisschop'. *C. j* 'Mars'. *C. j.* 'Mathotiana Alba'. *C. j.* 'Mathotiana Rosea'. *C. j.* 'Mercury'. *C. j.* 'Nagasaki'. *C. j.* 'Tricolor'. *C. × 'Mary Christian'. C. × williamsii* 'Donation'.

CARAGANA
Dwarf Salt Tree, Pygmy Peashrub
Time to buy Pot-grown, any time except January. Balled, October–May. Avoid adverse weather conditions.
Where to find Outside in Shrubs.
Size Height 8 in (20 cm) min. Single or multi-stemmed.
Foliage Deciduous. Spring/summer, light green. Premature autumn colour and leaf drop.

Roots Pots 5 in (12 cm) min. dia. Balled, good fibrous root system.

Hints Any well-prepared soil. May be scarce. Insipid and uninteresting when small.

Most widely available *Caragana arborescens* 'Nana'. *C. frutex globosa*. *C. pygmaea*.

CARPENTERIA CALIFORNICA

Time to buy Pot-grown, March–July. Balled, March–May. Avoid adverse weather conditions.

Where to find Outside in Shrubs.

Size Height 1 ft (30 cm) min. Single or multi-stemmed.

Foliage Evergreen. Mid green. Premature basal leaf drop.

Roots Pots 5 in (12 cm) min. dia. Balled, good fibrous root system.

Hints Any well-prepared soil. May be scarce. If kept under cover in winter, avoid planting until spring frosts have finished. May need protection first winter after planting.

CARYOPTERIS

Blue Spiraea, Bluebeard, Blue-mist Shrub

Time to buy Pot-grown, any time except January. Avoid adverse weather conditions.

Where to find Outside in Shrubs.

Size Height 6 in (15 cm) min. Multi-stemmed.

Foliage Deciduous. Spring/summer, grey-green. Premature autumn colour and leaf drop.

Roots Pots 4 in (10 cm) min. dia.

Hints Any well-prepared soil. If kept under cover in winter, avoid planting until spring frosts have finished. Hard prune within 2 in (5 cm) of ground level in April. Repeat annually.

Most widely available *Caryopteris incana × mastacanthus* 'Ferndown'. *C. i. × m.* 'Heavenly Blue'. *C. i. × m.* 'Kew Blue'. *C. i. × mongolica* 'Arthur Simmonds' (*Caryopteris × clandonensis*).

CASSINIA FULVIDA syn.
Diplopappus chrysophyllus
Golden Heather

Time to buy Pot-grown, any time except January. Avoid adverse weather conditions.

Where to find Outside in Shrubs.

Size Height 1 ft (30 cm) min. Single-stemmed. Numerous side shoots.

Foliage Evergreen. Grey or golden-green. Premature basal leaf drop.

Roots Pots 5 in (12 cm) min. dia.

Hints Well-prepared acid soil, plus extra organic material. Scarce. If kept under cover in winter, avoid planting until spring frosts have finished. May need protection first winter after planting. Insipid looking when young.

CEANOTHUS
Callifornia Lilac

Time to buy Pot-grown, April–August. Avoid adverse weather conditions.

Where to find Outside in Shrubs.

Size Height 1½ ft (50 cm) min. Single or multi-stemmed.

Foliage DECIDUOUS Spring/summer, mid green. Premature autumn colour and leaf drop. EVERGREEN Dark green. Premature basal leaf drop.

Roots Pots 5 in (12 cm) min. dia.

Hints Any well-prepared soil. May be scarce. If kept under cover in winter, avoid planting until spring frosts have finished. With deciduous forms cut back all previous season's growth within two buds of origin in April. Repeat annually. Evergreen forms, no pruning. May need protection for 1–2 years. Open and straggly.

Most widely available

DECIDUOUS *Ceanothus* 'Gloire de Versailles'. *C.* 'Henri Defosse'. *C.* 'Marie Simon'. *C.* 'Perle Rose'.

EVERGREEN *Ceanothus arboreus* 'Trewithen Blue'. *C.* 'A. T. Johnson'. *C.* 'Autumnal Blue'. *C.* 'Burkwoodii'. *C.* 'Cascade'. *C.* 'Delight'. *C. dentatus* 'Sant Barbara

Ceanothus'. *C.* 'Dignity'. *C. impressus.*
C. i. 'Puget Blue'. *C.* 'Italian Skies'.
C. × lobbianus 'Russellianus'. *C. rigidus.*
C. 'Southmead'. *C. thyrsiflorus C. t.* 'Blue
Mound'. *C. t. var. repens* (Creeping Blue
Blossom). *C.* 'Topaz'. *C. × veitchianus. C.*
'Yankee Point'.

CERATOSTIGMA
Shrubby Plumbago
Time to buy Pot-grown, April–August.
Avoid adverse weather conditions.
Where to find Outside in Shrubs.
Size Height 6 in (15 cm) min. Single or
multi-stemmed. Minimum four side shoots.
Foliage Deciduous. Spring/summer mid-
green. Premature autumn colour and leaf
drop.
Roots Pots 4 in (10 cm) min. dia.
Hints Any well-prepared soil. If kept
under cover in winter, avoid planting
until spring frosts have finished. Hardiness in doubt. Cut back to 2 in (5 cm)
from ground level in April. Repeat
annually. Open and straggly.
Most widely available *Ceratostigma grif-
fithii. C. willmottianum.*

CHAENOMELES
Cydonis, Ornamental Quince, Japonica,
Japanese Flowering Quince
Time to buy Pot-grown, any time except
January. Avoid adverse weather condi-
tions.
Where to find Outside in Shrubs.
Size Height 1 ft (30 cm) min. Single or
multi-stemmed.
Foliage Deciduous. Spring/summer, mid
green. Premature autumn colour and leaf
drop.
Roots Pots 5 in (12 cm) min. dia.
Hints Any well-prepared soil. May be
scarce. Often one-sided and gaunt. For
wall use, plant 15–18 in (40–50 cm) away
from wall.
Most widely available *Chaenomeles
japonica. C. j. var. alpina. C. speciosa* 'At-
rococcinea'. *C. s..* 'Brilliant'. *C. s.* 'Car-

dinalis'. *C. s.* 'Geisha Girl'. *C. s.* 'Moer-
loosii' (Apple Blossom). *C. s.* 'Nivalis'.
C. s. 'Simonii'. *C. s.* 'Snow'. *C. s.* 'Um-
bilicata'. *C. × superba* 'Chosan'. *C. × s.*
'Coral Sea'. *C. × s.* 'Crimson and Gold'.
C. × s. 'Elly Mossel'. *C. × s.* 'Fire Dance'.
C. × s. 'Knap Hill Scarlet'. *C. × s.* 'Hollan-
dia'. *C. × s.* 'Nicoline'. *C. × s.* 'Pink Lady'.
C. × s. 'Rowallane'.

CHIMONANTHUS PRAECOX
Fragrant Wintersweet
Time to buy Pot-grown, any time except
January. Balled, October–May. Avoid adverse weather conditions.
Where to find Outside in Shrubs.
Size Height 1½ ft (50 cm) min. Single or
multi-stemmed.
Foliage Deciduous. Spring/summer, mid
green. Premature autumn colour and leaf
drop.
Roots Pots 5 in (12 cm) min. dia. Balled,
good fibrous root system.
Hints Well-prepared acid soil. May be
scarce. Uninteresting in appearance
when not in flower. Research ultimate
overall size.

CHIONANTHUS VIRGINICUS
White Fringetree, North American
Fringetree
Time to buy Pot-grown, any time except
January. Balled, October–May. Avoid ad-
verse weather conditions.
Where to find Outside in Shrubs.
Size Height 1 ft (30 cm) min. Single or
multi-stemmed.
Foliage Deciduous. Spring/summer, olive-
green. Premature autumn colour and leaf
drop.
Roots Pots 5 in (12 cm) min. dia. Balled,
good fibrous root system.
Hints Any well-prepared soil. Scarce. Un-
interesting until established.

CHOISYA
Mexican Orange Blossom
Time to buy Pot-grown, any time except

January. Avoid adverse weather conditions.
Where to find Outside in Shrubs.
Size Height 6 in (23 cm) min. Single or multi-stemmed.
Foliage Evergreen. Dark green or gold. Premature basal leaf drop.
Roots Pots 4 in (10 cm) min. dia.
Hints Any well-prepared soil. If kept under cover in winter, avoid planting until spring frosts have finished.
Most widely available *Choisya ternata. C. t.* 'Sundance'. *C. t.* 'Aztec'.

CISTUS
Rock Rose
Time to buy Pot-grown, any time except January. Avoid adverse weather conditions.
Where to find Outside in Shrubs.
Size Height 9 in (23 cm) min. Single or multi-stemmed.
Foliage Evergreen. Mid green to grey. Premature basal leaf drop.
Roots Pots 5 in (12 cm) min. dia.
Hints Any well-prepared soil. May be scarce. If kept under cover in winter, avoid planting until spring frosts have finished. Hardiness in doubt in northern locations. Small-leaved forms hardiest.
Most widely available *Cistus × aiguilari. C. × a.* 'Maculatus'. *C. × corbariensis. C. × cyprius. C. × c.* 'Albiflorus'. *C.* 'Greyswood Pink'. *C. ladanifer* (Gum Cistus). *C. × l.* 'Albiflorus'. *C. laurifolius. C. × lusitanicus. C. × l.* 'Decumbens'. *C.* 'Peggy Sannons'. *C. populifolius. C. × pulverulentus (C. albidus × crispus). C.* 'Warley Rose'. *C. × purpureus. C. salvifolius. C.* 'Silver Pink'. *C. × skanbergii. C.* 'Sunset'.

CLERODENDRUM
Time to buy Pot-grown, any time except January. Balled, October–May. Avoid adverse weather conditions.
Where to find Outside in Shrubs.
Size Height 1½ ft (50 cm) min. Single or multi-stemmed.

Foliage Deciduous. Spring/summer, purple-green. Premature autumn colours and leaf drop.
Roots Pots 5 in (12 cm) min. dia. Balled, good fibrous root system.
Hints Any well-prepared soil, plus extra organic material. Scarce. If kept under cover in winter, avoid planting until spring frosts have finished. Late to produce leaves in spring. Can take up to two years to establish.
Most widely available *Clerodendrum trichotomum. C. t. var. fargesii.*

CLERODENDRUM BUNGEI
Time to buy Pot-grown, any time except January. Balled, October–May. Avoid adverse weather conditions.
Where to find Outside in Shrubs.
Size Dies to ground in winter. Spring onwards, height 1 ft (30 cm) min. Single-stemmed.
Foliage Deciduous. Spring/summer purple-green. Premature autumn colour and leaf drop.
Roots Pots 5 in (12 cm) min. dia. Balled, good fibrous root system.
Hints Any well-prepared soil, plus extra organic material. Scarce. If kept under cover in winter, avoid planting until spring frosts have finished. Plants look insipid, and are of weak constitution. Can become invasive.

CLETHRA
Summersweet Clethra, Sweet Pepper Bush, White Alder
Time to buy Pot-grown, any time except January. Balled, October–May. Avoid adverse weather conditions.
Where to find Outside in Shrubs or Acid-loving Plants.
Size Height 1½ ft (50 cm) min. Single or multi-stemmed.
Foliage Deciduous. Spring/summer, light green. Premature autumn colour and leaf drop.

Roots Pots 5 in (12 cm) min. dia. Balled, good fibrous root system.
Hints Well-prepared acid soil, plus extra organic material. Scarce. Its need for acid soil is not always explained.
Most widely available *Clethra alnifolia. C. a.* 'Paniculata'. *C. a.* 'Rosea'. *C. a.* 'Pink Spire'. *C. acuminata* (White Alder). *C. tomentosa.*

COLLETIA
Anchor Plant
Time to buy Pot-grown, any time except January. Avoid adverse weather conditions.
Where to find Outside in Shrubs.
Size Height 6 in (15 cm) min. Irregular-shaped small side shoots.
Foliage No foliage. Spiny grey-green stems.
Roots Pots 4 in (10 cm) min. dia.
Hints Any well-prepared soil. If kept under cover in winter, avoid planting until spring frosts have finished. May need protection in first few years after planting. Careful siting important. Spiny and difficult to handle. Avoid plants with yellowing of stem. Unstable root system in pots.
Most widely available *Colletia armata. C. cruciata.*

COLUTEA
Bladder Senna
Time to buy Pot-grown, any time except January. Avoid adverse weather conditions.
Where to find Outside in Shrubs.
Size Height 1½ ft (50 cm) min. Single or multi-stemmed.
Foliage Deciduous. Spring/summer, light green. Premature autumn colour and leaf drop.
Roots Pots 5 in (12 cm) min. dia.
Hints Any well-prepared soil. May be scarce. Always look gaunt and sparse in growth. Avoid plants hard pruned back.
Most widely available *Colutea arbore-*

scens. *C. a.* 'Copper Beauty'. *C. × media. C. orientalis.*

CONVOLVULUS CNEORUM
Time to buy Pot-grown, May–June. Avoid adverse weather conditions.
Where to find Outside in Shrubs.
Size Height 5 in (12 cm) min. Single or multi-stemmed.
Foliage Evergreen. Light grey-green. Premature basal leaf drop.
Roots Pots 3 in (8 cm) min. dia.
Hints Any well-prepared soil. If kept under cover in winter, avoid planting until spring frosts have finished. Straggly and open in habit.

CORDYLINE
Cabbage Tree of New Zealand, Cabbage Palm
Time to buy Pot-grown, May–June. Avoid adverse weather conditions.
Where to find Outside in Shrubs.
Size Height 15 in (40 cm) min. Minimum five upright spear-shaped leaves originating from central point.
Foliage Evergreen. Dark green or purple. Premature basal leaf drop.
Roots Pots 5 in (12 cm) min. dia.
Hints Any well-prepared soil. If kept under cover in winter, avoid planting until spring frosts have finished. Hardiness in doubt. Take care regarding planting position.
Most widely available *Cordyline australis. C. a.* 'Atropurpurea'.

CORNUS ALBA
Red-barked Dogwood, Tatarian Dogwood
Time to buy Pot-grown, any time except January. Balled, root-wrapped and bare-rooted, October–May. Avoid adverse weather conditions.
Where to find Outside in Shrubs.
Size Height 2 ft (60 cm) min. Single or multi-stemmed.
Foliage Deciduous. Spring/summer, dark

to olive-green, gold or silver. Premature autumn colour and leaf drop.

Roots Pots 5 in (12 cm) min. dia. Balled, root-wrapped and bare-rooted, good fibrous root system.

Hints Any well-prepared soil. May be scarce. Research overall size.

Most widely available Cornus alba. C. a. 'Aurea'. C. a. 'Elegantissima' (C. a. 'Sibirica Variegata'). C. a. 'Gouchaltii'. C. a. 'Kesselringii'. C. a. 'Sibirica' (C. a. 'Atrosanguinea') (C. a. 'Westonbirt') (Westonbirt Dogwood). C. a. 'Variegata'.

CORNUS ALTERNIFOLIA
Pagoda Cornus, Pagoda Dogwood, Pagoda Tree

Time to buy Pot-grown, any time except January. Balled, October–May. Avoid adverse weather conditions.

Where to find Outside in Shrubs.

Size Height 10 in (25 cm) min. Short sideshoots. Wispy growth.

Foliage Deciduous. Spring/summer, mid green. Premature autumn colour and leaf drop.

Roots Pots 4 in (10 cm) min. dia. Balled, good fibrous root system.

Hints Any well-prepared soil, plus extra organic material. Scarce. If purchasing by mail-order, use full name.

Most widely available Cornus alternifolia. C. a. 'Argentea'.

CORNUS CANADENSIS
Bunch Berry, Creeping Dogwood

Time to buy Pot-grown, any time except January. Avoid adverse weather conditions.

Where to find Outside in Shrubs or Acid-loving Plants.

Size Height 3 in (8 cm) min. from May–September. Limited growth through winter.

Foliage Semi-evergreen. Mid green. Leaf drop from October–April. May show brown at ends of leaves from July onwards.

Roots Pots 5 in (12 cm) min. dia.

Hints Well-prepared acid soil, plus extra organic material. Scarce. Rarely looks good from July onwards, as it dislikes being grown in pot.

CORNUS CONTROVERSA
Wedding Cake Tree

Time to buy Pot-grown, any time except January. Balled, October–May. Avoid adverse weather conditions.

Where to find Outside in Shrubs.

Size Height 10 in (25 cm) min. Limited side branches.

Foliage Deciduous. Spring/summer, mid green or white. Premature autumn colour and leaf drop.

Roots Pots 5 in (12 cm) min. dia. Balled, good fibrous root system.

Hints Any well-prepared soil, plus extra organic material. Scarce. If kept under cover in winter, avoid planting until spring frosts have finished. Requires protection in spring for first three years after planting. Slow to form large shrub.

Most widely available Cornus controversa. C. c. 'Variegata'.

CORNUS FLORIDA syn. *Benthamidia florida*
North American Flowering Dogwood

Time to buy Pot-grown, any time except January. Balled, October–May. Avoid adverse weather conditions.

Where to find Outside in Shrubs.

Size Height 1½ ft (50 cm) min. Single or multi-stemmed. Minimum three short sideshoots.

Foliage Deciduous. Spring/summer, mid-green with purple hue or golden variegated. Premature autumn colour and leaf drop.

Roots Pots 5 in (12 cm) min. dia. Balled, good fibrous root system.

Hints Well-prepared acid soil, plus extra organic material. May be scarce. If kept under cover in winter, avoid planting until spring frosts have finished.

Most widely available *Cornus florida.*
C. f. 'Apple Blossom'. *C. f.* 'Cherokee
Chief'. *C. f.* 'Cherokee Princess'. *C. f.* 'Pen-
dula'. *C. f.* 'Rainbow'. *C. f.* 'Rubra'. *C. f.*
'Spring Song'. *C. f.* 'Tricolor'. *C. f.* 'White
Cloud'.

CORNUS KOUSA
Chinese Dogwood, Japanese Dogwood,
Kousa Dogwood
Time to buy Pot-grown, any time except
January. Balled, October–May. Avoid adverse weather conditions.
Where to find Outside in Shrubs.
Size Height 1½ ft (50 cm) min. Single or
multi-stemmed. Minimum three short side
shoots.
Foliage Deciduous. Spring/summer, mid
green. Premature autumn colour and leaf
drop.
Roots Pots 5 in (12 cm) min. dia. Balled,
good fibrous root system.
Hints Neutral to acid, well-prepared soil,
plus extra organic material. *Cornus
kousa* often sold as *Cornus kousa chinensis,* which has larger flowers. Balled European stock slow to establish.
Most widely available *Cornus capitata*
(*Benthamia fragifera*). *C. Kousa. C. k. chinensis. C. k.* 'Milky Way'. *C.* 'Norman
Haddon'.

CORNUS MAS
Cornelian Cherry, Cornel
Time to buy Pot-grown, any time except
January. Balled, October–May. Avoid ad-
verse weather conditions.
Where to find Outside in Shrubs.
Size Height 1½ ft (50 cm) min. green-
leaved forms, 1 ft (30 cm) variegated.
Single or multi-stemmed. Minimum three
side shoots.
Foliage Deciduous. Spring/summer mid
green, white or gold variegated. Prema-
ture autumn colour and leaf drop.
Roots Pots 5 in (12 cm) min. dia. Balled,
good fibrous root system.
Hints Any well-prepared soil, plus extra

organic material. Coloured and variegated may be scarce. 3–4 years to come
into full flower. Research ultimate overall
size.
Most widely available *Cornus mas. C. m.*
'Aurea'. *C. m.* 'Elegantissima' (*C. m.* 'Tricolor'). *C. m.* 'Variegata'.

CORNUS NUTTALLII
Pacific Dogwood, Pacific Cornel
Time to buy Pot-grown, any time except
January. Balled, good fibrous root system.
Avoid adverse weather conditions.
Where to find Outside in Shrubs.
Size Height 1½ ft (50 cm) min. Single or
multi-stemmed. Minimum three side
shoots.
Foliage Deciduous. Spring/summer, mid
green or golden variegated. Premature
autumn colour and leaf drop.
Roots Pots 5 in (12 cm) min. dia. Balled,
good fibrous root system.
Hints Neutral to acid, well-prepared soil,
plus extra organic material. Variegated
and named forms scarce. Research over-
all size.
Most widely available *Cornus* 'Eddie's
White Wonder'. *C. nuttallii. C. n.* 'Gold
Spot'.

CORNUS STOLONIFERA
'FLAVIRAMEA'
Yellow-stemmed Dogwood, Golden-twig
Dogwood
Time to buy Pot-grown, any time except
January. Balled, root-wrapped and bare-
rooted, October–May. Avoid adverse wea-
ther conditions.
Where to find Outside in Shrubs.
Size *Cornus stolonifera* 'Flaviramea':
height 1½ ft (50 cm) min. Single or multi-
stemmed. Minimum five short side
shoots. *Cornus stolonifera* 'Kelsey's
Dwarf': height 6 in (15 cm) min. Multi-
stemmed. Limited side shoots.
Foliage Deciduous. Spring/summer, mid
to light green. Premature autumn colour
and leaf drop.

Roots Pots 5 in (12 cm) min. dia. Balled, root-wrapped and bare-rooted, good fibrous root system.

Hints Any well-prepared soil. Research overall ultimate size.

Most widely available *Cornus stolonifera* 'Flaviramea'. *C. s.* 'Kelsey's Dwarf'.

COROKIA
Wire Netting Bush

Time to buy Pot-grown, April–July. Avoid adverse weather conditions.

Where to find Outside in Shrubs.

Size Height 1 ft (30 cm) min., except *Corokia cotoneaster*, height 3 in (8 cm) min. Single or multi-stemmed. Minimum five short side shoots.

Foliage Evergreen. Grey-green to purple-green. Sparse. Premature basal leaf drop.

Roots Pots 4 in (10 cm) min. dia.

Hints Any well-prepared soil. Scarce. If kept under cover in winter, avoid planting until spring frosts have finished. Hardiness in doubt. Requires sheltered position. Small when young and takes time to develop.

Most widely available

MEDIUM   HEIGHT   *Corokia × virgata*; *C. × v.* 'Red King'; *C. × v.* 'Red Wonder'; *C. × v.* 'Yellow Wonder'.

DWARF *Corokia cotoneaster*.

CORONILLA

Time to buy Pot-grown, any time except January. Avoid adverse weather conditions.

Where to find Outside in Shrubs.

Size Height 1 ft (30 cm) min. Single or multi-stemmed. Minimum five short side shoots.

Foliage Evergreen. Mid green, grey-green or white variegated. Premature basal leaf drop.

Roots Pots 5 in (12 cm) min. dia.

Hints Any well-prepared soil. May be scarce. If kept under cover in winter, avoid planting until spring frosts have finished. Hardiness in doubt in cold

areas. Needs winter protection in first few years after planting.

Most widely available *Cornilla emerus*. *C. glauca*. *C. g.* 'Variegata'.

CORTADERIA
Pampas Grass

Time to buy Pot-grown, any time except January. Avoid adverse weather conditions.

Where to find Outside in Shrubs or Perennials.

Size Winter, height 6 in–1½ ft (15–50 cm) min. Summer, height 1½–2½ ft (50–80 cm) min.

Foliage Evergreen. Mid green. Premature basal leaf drop.

Roots Pots 5 in (12 cm) min. dia.

Hints Any well-prepared soil. Named forms may be scarce. Care needed when transporting, as leaf edges are razor-sharp.

Most widely available *Cortaderia selloana*. *C. s.* 'Gold Band'. *C. s.* 'Pumila'. *C. s.* 'Rendatieri'. *C. s.* 'Silver Cornet'. *C. s.* 'Sunningdale Silver'.

CORYLOPSIS
Cowslip Bush, Winter Hazel, Spike Winter Hazel

Time to buy Pot-grown, any time except January. Balled, October–May. Avoid adverse weather conditions.

Where to find Outside in Shrubs or Acid-loving Plants.

Size Height 1½ ft (50 cm) min. Single or multi-stemmed. Minimum five side shoots. *Corylopsis pauciflora*, height 9 in (23 cm) min. Multi-stemmed. Minimum three shoots.

Foliage Deciduous. Spring/summer, green. Premature autumn colour and leaf drop.

Roots Pots 5 in (12 cm) min dia. Balled, good fibrous root system.

Hints Well-prepared acid soil, plus extra organic material. May be scarce. Balled European stock slow to establish.

Most widely available *Corylopsis glabre-*

*scens. C. pauciflora. C. spicata. C. veit-
chiana. C. willmottiae. C. w.* 'Spring
Purple'.

CORYLUS ORNAMENTAL FORMS
Ornamental Hazel, Ornamental Filbert,
Ornamental Cobnut
Time to buy Pot-grown, any time except
January. Balled, October–May. Avoid ad-
verse weather conditions.
Where to find Outside in Shrubs.
Size Height 1½ ft (50 cm) min. Single or
multi-stemmed. Limited side shoots.
Foliage Deciduous. Spring/summer, gold,
purple or mid green. Premature autumn
colour and leaf drop.
Roots Pots 6 in (15 cm) min. dia. Balled,
good fibrous root system.
Hints Any well-prepared soil, plus extra
organic material. Fragile when being
transported. *Corylus avellana* 'Contorta'
grafted, ensure there are no suckers.
Most widely available *Corylus avellana.
C. a.* 'Aurea' (Golden-leaved Hazel). *C. a.*
'Contorta' (Corkscrew Hazel, Harry
Lauder's Walking Stick, Contorted
Hazel). *C. maxima* 'Purpurea' (*C. m.* 'At-
ropurpurea') (Purple-leaved Filbert,
Purple Giant Filbert).

CORYNABUTILON syn. *Abutilon vitifolium*
Flowering Maple, Vine-leaved Abutilon
Time to buy Pot-grown, April–July. Avoid
adverse weather conditions.
Where to find Outside in Shrubs.
Size Height 1½ ft (50 cm) min. Single-
stemmed. Limited short side shoots.
Foliage Deciduous. Spring/summer, mid
to grey-green. Premature autumn colour
and leaf drop.
Roots Pots 5 in (12 cm) min. dia.
Hints Any well-prepared soil, plus extra
organic material. Scarce. If kept under
cover in winter, avoid planting until
spring frosts have finished. Hardiness in
doubt. Research overall ultimate size.

Most widely available *Corynabutilon
sutense. C. vitifolium. C. v. album. C. v.*
'Veronica Tennant'.

COTINUS
Smoke Tree, Smoke Bush, Burning Bush
Time to buy Pot-grown, any time except
January. Balled, October–May. Avoid ad-
verse weather conditions.
Where to find Outside in Shrubs.
Size Height 1 ft (30 cm) min. Single or
multi-stemmed. Balled from Europe may be
taller, and of value if in excess of 1½ ft
(50 cm) in height and multi-stemmed.
Foliage Deciduous, Spring/summer, mid
green or purple. Premature autumn colour
and leaf drop.
Roots Pots 5 in (12 cm) min. dia. Balled,
good fibrous root system.
Hints Any well-prepared soil, plus extra
organic material. Slow to establish.
Balled European stock resents different
UK garden soil.
Most widely available *Cotinus coggygria. C. c.* 'Flame'. *C. c.* 'Foliis Purpureis'. *C. c.* 'Notcutt's Variety'. *C. c.*
'Royal Purple'. *C. c.* 'Rubrifolius'. *C. ob-
ovatus* (*C. o. americanus*) (Chitam
Wood).

COTONEASTER
Time to buy Pot-grown, any time except
January. Balled, October–May. Avoid adverse weather conditions.
Where to find Outside in Shrubs.
Size LOW-GROWING Height 9 in (23 cm)
min. MEDIUM AND TALL-GROWING Height
15 in (40 cm) min. All single or multi-
stemmed.
Foliage DECIDUOUS Spring/summer, light
to mid green. Premature autumn colour
and leaf drop. EVERGREEN Mid to dark
green. Premature basal leaf drop.
Roots Pots 5 in (12 cm) min. dia. Balled,
good fibrous root system.
Hints Any well-prepared soil. Wide range
of forms.

Most widely available

LOW-GROWING *Cotoneaster adpressus var. praecox* (E). *C. buxifolia* (E). *C. congestus* (E). *C. c. var. procumbens* (E). *C.* 'Coral Beauty' (D). *C. dammeri* (E). *C. d. var. radicans* (E). *C.* 'Donard's Gem' (E). *C. horizontalis* 'Major' (D). *C. h.* 'Robusta' (D). *C. h.* 'Variegatus' (D). *C. microphyllus* (E). *C. m. var. cochleatus* (E). *C. m. var. thymifolius* (E). *C. salicifolius* 'Gnone' (E). *C. s.* 'Parkteppich' (Park Carpet) (E). *C. s.* 'Repens' (E). *C.* 'Skogholme' (E).

MEDIUM-GROWING *Cotoneaster conspicuus* (E). *C. c.* 'Decorus' (E). *C.* 'Coral Beauty' (D). *C. horizontalis* (Fishbone or Herringbone Cotoneaster) (D). *C. h.* 'Major' (D). *C. h.* 'Robusta' (D). *C. h.* 'Variegatus' (D). *C.* 'Hybridus Pendulus' (E). *C. salicifolius* 'Autumn Fire' (E).

TALL-GROWING *Cotoneaster bullatus* (D). *C.* 'Cornubia' (E). *C. distichus* (*C. rotundifolius*) (D). *C. divaricatus* (D). *C.* 'Exburiensis' (E). *C.* 'Firebird' (D). *C. franchetii* (E). *C. f. var. sternianus* (*C. wardii*) (E). *C. frigidus* (E). *C. henryanus* (E). *C.* 'Inchmery' (E). *C. lacteus* (E). *C. pannosus* (E). *C.* 'Rothschildianus' (E). *C. salicifolius var. floccosus* (E). *C. simonsii* (D). *C.* 'St Monica' (E). *C.* × *watereri* (E).

CRINODENDRON HOOKERANUM
syn. *Tricuspidaria lanceolata*
Lantern Tree
Time to buy Pot-grown, April–July. Balled, October–May. Avoid adverse weather conditions.
Where to find Outside in Shrubs.
Size Height 1 ft (30 cm) min. Single or multi-stemmed.
Foliage Evergreen. Mid to dark green. Premature basal leaf drop.
Roots Pots 5 in (12 cm) min. dia. Balled, good fibrous root system.
Hints Well-prepared acid soil, plus extra organic material. May be scarce. Research overall size.

CYTISUS BATTANDIERI
Moroccan Broom, Pineapple Broom
Time to buy Pot-grown, any time except January. Avoid adverse weather conditions.
Where to find Outside in Shrubs.
Size Height 1½ ft (50 cm) min. Single or multi-stemmed.
Foliage Deciduous. Spring/summer, greygreen. Premature autumn colour and leaf drop.
Roots Pots 5 in (12 cm) min. dia.
Hints Any well-prepared soil except alkaline. May be scarce. Grafted plants have larger flowers and more attractive foliage. For wall use plant 15–18 in (40–50 cm) away from wall.

CYTISUS
Broom
Time to buy Pot-grown, any time except January. Avoid adverse weather conditions.
Where to find Outside in Shrubs.
Size LOW-GROWING Height 9 in (23 cm) min. TALL-GROWING Height 1½ ft (50 cm) min. *Cytisus praecox* forms 9 in (23 cm) min. All single or multi-stemmed.
Foliage Deciduous. Spring/summer, greygreen. Premature autumn colour and leaf drop.
Roots LOW-GROWING Pots 4 in (10 cm) min. dia. TALL-GROWING Pots 5 in (12 cm) min. dia.
Hints Any well-prepared soil, plus extra organic material. Wide range. Uninteresting outside flowering period.
Most widely available
LOW-GROWING *Cytisus* × *beanii*. *C. decumbens*. *C.* × *kewensis*. *C. procumbens*. *C. purpureus* (Purple Broom).
TALL-GROWING *Cytisus multiflorus* **forms**: *C. multiflorus* (*C. albus*). *Cytisus* × *praecox* **forms**: *C.* × *praecox*. *C.* × *p.* 'Albus'. *C.* × *p.* 'Allgold'. *C.* × *p.* 'Buttercup'. *C.* 'Hollandia'. *C.* 'Zeelandia'. *Cytisus scoparius* **forms**: *C. nigricans*. *C. scoparius*. *C. s.* 'Andreanus'. *C. s.* 'Cor-

nish Cream'. *C. s.* 'Fulgens'. *C. s.* 'Red
Favourite'. ***Cytisus* hybrids**: *C.* 'Burk-
woodii'. *C.* 'C. E. Pearson'. *C.* 'Criterion'.
C. 'Daisy Hill'. *C.* 'Donard Seedling'. *C.*
'Dorothy Walpole'. *C.* 'Eastern Queen'. *C.*
'Golden Cascade'. *C.* 'Goldfinch' *C.* 'Kil-
liney Salmon'. *C.* 'Lord Lambourne'. *C.*
'Minstead'. *C.* 'Moonlight'. *C.* 'Windles-
ham Ruby'.

DABOECIA
Connemara Heath, St Daboec's Heath,
Irish Heath
Time to buy Pot-grown, any time except
January. Avoid adverse weather condi-
tions.
Where to find Outside in Shrubs, Heath-
ers or Acid-loving Plants.
Size Height 2 in (5 cm) min. Single or
multi-stemmed.
Foliage Evergreen. Dark green to purple-
green. Premature basal leaf drop.
Roots Pots 3 in (8 cm) min. dia.
Hints Well-prepared acid soil, plus extra
organic material. Scarce. Often looks
small and uninteresting.
Most widely available *Daboecia canta-
brica (Menziesia polifolia)*. *D. c.* 'Alba'.
D. c. 'Atropurpurea'. *D. c.* 'Bicolor'. *D. c.*
'Praegerae'.

DANAE RACEMOSA syn. *Ruscus racemosus*
Alexandrian Laurel
Time to buy Pot-grown, any time except
January. Balled, root-wrapped and bare-
rooted, October–May. Avoid adverse wea-
ther conditions.
Where to find Outside in Shrubs.
Size Height 9 in (23 cm) min. Single or
multi-stemmed.
Foliage Evergreen. Mid green. Premature
basal leaf drop.
Roots Pots 5 in (12 cm) min. dia. Balled,
root-wrapped and bare-rooted, good
fibrous root system.
Hints Any well-prepared soil, plus extra
organic material. Very scarce.

DAPHNE
Garland Flower, Rose Daphne, Sourge
Laurel, February Daphne, Mezereon
Time to buy Pot-grown, March–August.
Balled, October–May. Avoid adverse weather conditions.
Where to find Outside in Shrubs.
Size Height 6 in (15 cm) min. *Daphne
cneorum*, *D. collina*, *D. retusa* and *D. tangutica*, height 3 in (8 cm) min. All single
or multi-stemmed.
Foliage DECIDUOUS Spring/summer mid
to light green. Premature autumn colour
and leaf drop. EVERGREEN Mid green. Premature basal leaf drop.
Roots Pots 5 in (12 cm) min. dia. *Daphne
cneorum*, *D. collina*, *D. retusa* and *D. tangutica*, pots 4 in (10 cm) min. dia. Balled,
good fibrous root system.
Hints Well-prepared neutral to acid
soils, plus extra organic material. Wide
range. If kept under cover in winter,
avoid planting until spring frosts have
finished.
Most widely available *Daphna bholua*
(D). *D. blagayana* (D). *D. × burkwoodii*
(Burkwood's Daphne) (D). *D. × b.* 'Somer-
set' (D). *D. × b.* 'Somerset Gold Edge' (D).
D. cneorum (Garland Flower, Rose
Daphne) (E). *D. c.* 'Alba' (E). *D. c.* 'Eximia'
(E). *D. c.* 'Pygmaea' (E). *D. c.* 'Variegata' (E).
D. collina (E). *D. c. var. neapolitana* (E). *D.
genkwa* (D). *D. laureola* (Spurge Laurel)
(E). *D. l. var. philippi* (E). *D. mezereum*
(February Daphne, Mezereon) (D). *D. m.*
'Rubrum' (D). *D. odora* (Fragrant Daphne,
Winter Daphne) (E). *D. o.* 'Alba' (E). *D. o.*
'Aureomarginata' (E). *D. pontica* (E). *D.
retusa* (E). *D. tangutica* (E).

DECAISNEA FARGESII
Time to buy Pot-grown, any time except
January. Balled, October–May. Avoid ad-
verse weather conditions.
Where to find Outside in Shrubs.
Size Height 1½ ft (50 cm) min. Single or
multi-stemmed.
Foliage Deciduous. Spring/summer, mid

green. Early autumn colour and leaf drop.
Roots Pots 6 in (15 cm) min. dia. Balled,
good fibrous root system.
Hints Any well-prepared soil, plus extra
organic material. Scarce. Research overall
ultimate size.

DESFONTAINEA SPINOSA
Time to buy Pot-grown, any time except
January. Balled, October–May. Avoid ad-
verse weather conditions.
Where to find Outside in Shrubs or
Acid-loving Plants.
Size Height 6 in (15 cm) min. Single or
multi-stemmed.
Foliage Evergreen. Mid green. Premature
basal leaf drop.
Roots Pots 5 in (12 cm) min. dia. Balled,
good fibrous root system.
Hints Well-prepared acid soil, plus extra
organic material. Scarce. Winter protec-
tion in cold areas.

DEUTZIA
Time to buy Pot-grown, any time except
January. Root-wrapped, bare-rooted and
prepacked, October–May. Avoid adverse
weather conditions.
Where to find Outside in Shrubs. Pre-
packs under limited cover.
Size Height 2 ft (60 cm) min. *Deutzia kal-
miflora* and *D. × elegantissima* 'Rosalind'
height 1 ft (30 cm) min. All, minimum two
main shoots. Limited side shoots.
Foliage Deciduous. Spring/summer, mid
green. Premature autumn colour and leaf
drop.
Roots Pots 5 in (12 cm) min. dia. Root-
wrapped and bare-rooted, good fibrous
root system.
Hints Any well-prepared soil. May be
scarce. Hardiness in doubt, particularly
in first year following planting. Suffers
from drying out, attention should be
given to watering. Offered as pre-packs
in supermarkets: not always a good buy.
Most widely available *Deutzia chunii.*
D. 'Contraste'. *D. corymbosa. D. × ele-*

gantissima. D. × e. 'Rosealind'. *D. gracilis. D. × kalmiiflora. D. longifolia* 'Veitchii'. *D.* 'Magician'. *D. × magnifica. D.
monbeigii. D.* 'Mont Rose'. *D. pulchra.
D. × rosea* 'Carminea'. *D. scabra* (Fuzzy
Deutzia). *D. s.* 'Candidissima'. *D. s.*
'Plena'. *D. s.* 'Pride of Rochester'. *D. set-
chuensis.*

DIERVILLA
Bush-Honeysuckle
Time to buy Pot-grown, any time except
January. Root-wrapped and bare-rooted,
October–May. Avoid adverse weather conditions.
Where to find Outside in Shrubs.
Size *Diervilla rivularis* and *D. sessilifolia*,
height 1 ft (30 cm) min. *D. × splendens*,
height 2 ft (60 cm) min. Minimum two
main shoots. Limited side shoots.
Foliage Deciduous. Spring/summer, mid
green. Premature autumn colour and leaf
drop.
Roots Pots 5 in (12 cm) min. dia. Root-
wrapped and bare-rooted, good fibrous
root system.
Hints Any well-prepared soil. *Diervilla
sessilifolia* and *D. × splendens* are confused in production as ultimate height
is only major difference. Some outlets
may say *Diervilla* not available and is
now named *Weigela*.
Most widely available *Diervilla rivularis*
(Georgia Bush Honeysuckle). *D. sessilifolia* (Southern Bush Honeysuckle).
D. × splendens.

DIPELTA FLORIBUNDA
Time to buy Pot-grown, any time except
January. Avoid adverse weather condi-
tions.
Where to find Outside in Shrubs.
Size Height 1½ ft (50 cm) min. Single or
multi-stemmed.
Foliage Deciduous. Spring/summer, mid
green. Premature autumn colour and leaf
drop.
Roots Pots 5 in (12 cm) min. dia.

1. *Acer griseum* (Paper-bark Maple). Showing off its winter stems.

2. *Betula jacquemontii*. One of the finest silver-stemmed Birchs.

3. *Fagus sylvatica* 'Purpurea' (Purple Beech). Contrasting with a carpet of Myosotis (Forget-me-not) and Buttercups for spring effect.

4. *Elaeagnus pungens* 'Maculata', one of the boldest of golden-variegated leaved shrubs.

5. *Dorycnium hirsutumn*. A low shrub with attractive foliage, flowers and fruit for all summer effect.

6. *Cotinus coggygria.* Few other large shrubs offer such spectacular autumn colours.

7. *Rhodochiton atrosanguineum.*
A summer-flowering perennial climber for sheltered sunny aspects.

8. Apple 'Cox's Orange Pippin'. Still one of the finest of English apples.

9. *Clematis* 'Niobe'. One of the darkest coloured large-flowering clematis.

11. *Rosa rugosa* 'Alba'. Showing off its tomato-shaped fruits in autumn.

10. Rambling Rose 'Alberic Barbier', with creamy-white flowers shown-off against its semi-evergreen foliage.

12. Floribunda Rose (Cluster Rose) 'Iceberg'. Displaying its pure-white flowers throughout summer.

13. *Rosa gallica* 'Complicata'. So simple yet attractive flowers.

14. *Liquidambar styraciflua* showing off its autumn colours.

15. *Cedrus atlantica* 'Glauca' (The Blue Atlas Cedar) showing its colour, size and stature.

16. *Rosa moschata* 'Penelope' as a hedge and at its base *Lavandula angustifolia* 'Hidcote'.

17. (*above*) Cabbage and Cos Lettuce ready for a summer salad.

18. (*right*) Curled-Leaved Parsley (*Petroselinum crispum*) a spring and early summer sown annual herb.

19. *Allium aflatunense* 'Purple Sensation'. One of the giants of the onion family, often reaching up to 3 ft (1 m) in height.

20. (*above*) Crocus 'Pickwick' with its spring flowers looking like striped pyjamas.

21. (*right*) Snake's Head Fritillary (*Fritillaria meleagris*). One of the most elegant of all small bulbous plants.

22. Winter Aconite (*Eranthis hyemalis*). Flowering in the spring then disappearing for the rest of the year.

23. Houseplant Cyclamen (*Cyclamen persicum*). One of the finest of all flowering houseplants.

24. *Dipladenia splendens*. An attractive climber for conservatories and large greenhouses.

25. *Hibiscus rosa-sinensis*. A magnificent, tender shrub for use as a houseplant.

Hints Any well-prepared soil, except alkaline, plus organic material. Scarce.

DISANTHUS CERCIDIFOLIUS
Time to buy Pot-grown, April–August. Balled, October–May. Avoid adverse weather conditions.
Where to find Outside in Shrubs or Acid-loving Plants.
Size Height 15 in (40 cm) min. Single or multi-stemmed.
Foliage Deciduous. Spring/summer, dark green. Premature autumn colour and leaf drop.
Roots Pots 5 in (12 cm) min. dia. Balled, good fibrous root system.
Hints Well-prepared acid soil, plus extra organic material. Scarce.

DISTYLIUM RACEMOSUM
Time to buy Pot-grown, April–August. Balled, October–May. Avoid adverse weather conditions.
Where to find Outside in Shrubs or Acid-loving Plants.
Size Height 9 in (23 cm) min. Single or multi-stemmed.
Foliage Evergreen. Dark green. Premature basal leaf-drop.
Roots Pots 5 in (12 cm) min. dia. Balled, good fibrous root system.
Hints Well-prepared acid soil, plus extra organic material. Very scarce.

DORYCNIUM HIRSUTUM
Time to buy Pot-grown, April–August. Avoid adverse weather conditions.
Where to find Outside in Shrubs or grey-leaf plants.
Size Height 4 in (10 cm) min. Single or multi-stemmed.
Foliage Deciduous to semi-evergreen. Spring/summer, grey-green. Some premature autumn colour and leaf drop.
Roots Pots 3 in (8 cm) min. dia.
Hints Any well-prepared soil. May be scarce. Cut back all previous season's growth by three-quarters in April. Repeat

annually. Looks 'floppy' from July. Correct pruning will rectify this.

DRIMYS WINTERI
Winter's Bark
Time to buy Pot-grown, March–August. Balled, October–May. Avoid adverse weather conditions.
Where to find Outside in Shrubs or Acid-loving Plants.
Size Height 1½ ft (50 cm). Single or multi-stemmed.
Foliage Evergreen. Grey-green. Premature basal leaf drop.
Roots Pots 5 in (12 cm) min. dia. Balled, good fibrous root system.
Hints Well-prepared acid soil, plus extra organic material. Scarce.

ELAEAGNUS
Time to buy Pot-grown, any time except January. Avoid adverse weather conditions.
Where to find Outside in Shrubs.
Size Height 9 in (23 cm) min. Single or multi-stemmed.
Foliage DECIDUOUS Spring/summer, grey-green to silver. Premature autumn colour and leaf drop. EVERGREEN Grey-green, dark green, golden or golden variegated. New growth on variegated forms brownish/grey. Premature basal leaf drop.
Roots Pots 5 in (12 cm) min. dia.
Hints Any well-prepared soil, plus extra organic material. May be scarce. *Elaeagnus pungens* forms may appear loosely rooted in pots. If grafted, avoid those with suckers.
Most widely available *Elaeagnus angustifolia* (Oleaster. Russian Olive) (D). *E.* × *ebbingei* (E). *E.* × *e.* 'Gilt Edge' (E). *E.* × *e.* 'Limelight' (E). *E. commutata* (*E. argentea*) (Silver Berry) (D). *E. macrophylla* (E). *E. multiflora* (Cherry Elaeagnus) (D). *E. pungens* (E). *E. p.* 'Dicksonii' (E). *E. p.* 'Fredericia' (E). *E. p.* 'Gold Rim' (E). *E. p.* 'Maculata' (E). *E. p.* 'Variegata' (E). *E. umbellata* (Autumn Olive) (D).

ELSHOLTZIA STAUNTONII
Time to buy Pot-grown, March–August. Balled, October–May. Avoid adverse weather conditions.
Where to find Outside in Shrubs.
Size Height 15 in (40 cm) min. Single or multi-stemmed.
Foliage Deciduous. Spring/summer, light to grey-green. Premature autumn colour and leaf drop.
Roots Pots 5 in (12 cm) min. dia. Balled, good fibrous root system.
Hints Any well-prepared soil, plus extra organic material. Scarce. Hardiness in doubt.

EMBOTHRIUM
Chilean Fire Bush
Time to buy Pot-grown, March–July. Balled, October–May. Avoid adverse weather conditions.
Where to find Outside in Shrubs or Acid-loving Plants.
Size Height 1½ ft (50 cm) min. Single or multi-stemmed.
Foliage Semi-evergreen. Grey-green. Some premature autumn colour and leaf drop.
Roots Pots 5 in (12 cm) min. dia. Balled, good fibrous root system.
Hints Well-prepared acid soil, plus extra organic material. Scarce. Hardiness in doubt.

ERICA
Heather
Time to buy Pot-grown, any time except January. Avoid adverse weather conditions.
Where to find Outside in Heathers, Ground-cover or Acid-loving Plants.
Size Year-old, height and spread 2 in (5 cm) min. Three-year-old, height and spread 3 in (8 cm) min. Short multiple branches.
Foliage Evergreen. Mid green, silver-grey, gold or purple. Premature basal leaf drop.

Roots One-year-old, pots 3 in (8 cm) min. dia. Two-year-old, pots 4 in (10 cm) min. dia.
Hints Well-prepared soil according to needs. Wide range. Winter or summer-flowering, and acid or alkaline forms not always clearly divided in outlets.
Most widely available
ACID-LOVING SUMMER-FLOWERING *Erica arborea* (Tree Heath. Briar). *E. a.* 'Alpina'. *E. australis. E. a.* 'Mr Robert'. *E. a.* 'Riverslea'. *E. ciliaris* (Dorset Heath). *E. c.* 'Corfe Castle'. *E. c.* 'David Maclintock'. *E. c.* 'Globosa'. *E. c.* 'Maweana'. *E. c.* 'Mrs C. H. Gill'. *E. c.* 'Multiflora'. *E. c.* 'Stoborough'. *E. cinerea* (Bell Heather. Bell Flower Heather). *E. c.* 'Alba Minor'. *E. c.* 'Atropurpurea'. *E. c.* 'C. D. Eason'. *E. c.* 'Cindy'. *E. c.* 'Contrast'. *E. c.* 'Elan Valley'. *E. c.* 'Foxhollow'. *E. c.* 'Golden Drop'. *E. c.* 'Knaphill Pink'. *E. c.* 'Lavender Lady'. *E. c.* 'Pentreath'. *E. c.* 'Pink Ice'. *E. c.* 'P. S. Patrick'. *E. c.* 'Purple Beauty'. *E. c.* 'Pygmea'. *E. c.* 'Rosabelle'. *E. c.* 'Rozanne Waterer'. *E. c.* 'Stephen Davis'. *E. c.* 'Vivienne Patricia'. *E. erigena* (*E. mediterranea*) (Mediterranean Heath). *E. e.* 'Alba'. *E. e.* 'Brightness'. *E. e.* 'Inch Salmon'. *E. e.* 'Superba'. *E. e.* 'W. T. Rackliff'. *E. terminalis* (*E. stricta*) (Corsican Heath). *E. t.* 'Thelma Woolner'. *E. tetralix* (Cross-Leaved Heath. Bog Heather). *E. t.* 'Alba Mollis'. *E. t.* 'Alba Praecox'. *E. t.* 'Con Underwood'. *E. t.* 'Moonstone Pink'. *E. t.* 'Melbury White'. *E. t.* 'Pink Glow'. *E. t.* 'Pink Star'. *E. t.* 'Rosea'. *E. × watsonii* 'Dawn'. *E. × williamsii. E. vagans* (Cornish Heath). *E. v.* 'Alba'. *E. v.* 'Brick Glow'. *E. v.* 'Dianna Hookstone'. *E. v.* 'Mrs D. F. Maxwell'. *E. v.* 'Pyrenees Pink'. *E. v.* 'St Keverne'. *E. v.* 'Valerie Proudley'. LIME-TOLERANT WINTER-FLOWERING *Erica × darleyensis. E. × d.* 'Arthur Johnson'. *E. × d.* 'Darley Dale'. *E. × d.* 'Furzey'. *E. × d.* 'Ghost Hills'. *E. × d.* 'George Rendell'. *E. × d.* 'Jack H. Brummage'. *E. × d.* 'Silberschmelze' (*E. × d.* 'Alba') (Molten Silver. Silver Beads). *E.*

herbacea (*E. carnea*). *E. h.* 'Aurea'. *E. h.* 'Ann Sparks'. *E. h.* 'December Red'. *E. h.* 'James Backhouse'. *E. h.* 'Myretown Ruby'. *E. h.* 'Pink Spangles'. *E. h.* 'Queen Mary'. *E. h.* 'Roby Glow'. *E. h.* 'Spring-wood Pink'. *E. g.* 'Springwood White'. *E. h.* 'Startler'. *E. h.* 'Vivellii'. *E. h.* 'West-wood Yellow'. *E. h.* 'Winter Beauty'. Many other forms.

ERYTHRINA CRISTA-GALLI
Coral Tree, Coxcomb

Time to buy Pot-grown, April–July. Avoid adverse weather conditions.

Where to find Outside in Shrubs or Perennials.

Size Height 1 ft (30 cm) min. Single or multi-stemmed.

Foliage Deciduous. Spring/summer, mid green. Premature autumn colour and leaf drop.

Roots Pots 4 in (10 cm) min. dia.

Hints Any well-prepared soil, plus extra organic material. Scarce. Hardiness in doubt. Take care in selecting suitable planting site. For wall use, plant 15–18 in (40–50 cm) away from wall.

ESCALLONIA

Time to buy Pot-grown, any time except January. Root-wrapped, bare-rooted and pre-packed, October–May. Avoid adverse weather conditions.

Where to find Outside in Shrubs. Pre-packs under limited cover.

Size Height 2 ft (60 cm) min. Minimum two main shoots. Limited side shoots. *Escallonia* 'Gwendolyn Anley' and *E. rubra* 'Woodside' height 9 in (23 cm) min. Minimum two main shoots. Numerous side shoots.

Foliage Evergreen. Mid to dark green. Premature basal leaf drop.

Roots Pots 5 in (12 cm) min. dia. Root-wrapped and bare-rooted, good fibrous root system.

Hints Any well-prepared soil. Wide range. May need protection first winter

after planting. Offered as pre-packs in supermarkets, but not always a good purchase. Suffers from drying out; attention should be given to watering.

Most widely available *Escallonia* 'Apple Blossom'. *E.* 'C. F. Ball'. *E.* 'Crimson Spires'. *E.* 'Donard Beauty'. *E.* 'Donard Brilliance'. *E.* 'Donard Gem'. *E.* 'Donard Radiance'. *E.* 'Donard Seedling'. *E.* 'Donard Star'. *E.* 'Edinensis'. *E. fortunei* 'Golden Pillar'. *E. f.* 'Sheridan Gold'. *E.* 'Gwendolyn Anley'. *E.* 'Ingramii'. *E.* 'Iveyi'. *E.* 'Langleyensis'. *E. macrantha*. *E.* 'Peach Blossom'. *E. rubra* 'Woodside' ('Pygmaea'). *E.* 'Slieve Donard'. Many other forms.

EUCRYPHIA
Brush Bush

Time to buy Pot-grown, any time except January. Balled, October–May. Avoid adverse weather conditions.

Where to find Outside in Shrubs.

Size Height 1½ ft (50 cm) min. Single stemmed. Limited side shoots.

Foliage Evergreen. Grey-green. Premature basal leaf drop. *Eucryphia glutinosa* deciduous. Premature autumn colour and leaf drop.

Roots Pots 5 in (12 cm) min. dia. Balled, good fibrous root system.

Hints Well-prepared neutral to acid soil, plus extra organic material. Except for *Eucryphia* × *nymansensis* 'Nymansay' scarce. Requires winter protection, first few years after planting.

Most widely available *Eucryphia cordifolia* (*E. ulmo*). *E. glutinosa*. *E.* × *intermedia* 'Rostrevor'. *E. lucida*. *E. milliganii*. *E.* × *nymansensis* 'Nymansay'.

EUONYMUS

Time to buy Pot-grown, any time except January. Balled, October–May. Avoid adverse weather conditions.

Where to find Outside in Shrubs.

Size Height 2 ft (60 cm) min. Single or multi-stemmed. Height and spread 6 in

(15 cm) min. for the following varieties: *Euonymus fortunei*, *E. f.* 'Coloratus', *E. f.* 'Emerald Gaiety', *E. f.* 'Emerald 'n' Gold', *E. f.* 'Gold Spot', *E. f.* 'Kewensis', *E. f. var radicans*, *E. f.* 'Silver Queen', *E. f.* 'Sunshine', *E. f.* 'Variegatus', *E. f.* 'Vegetus'.
Foliage DECIDUOUS Spring/summer, mid green. Premature autumn colour and leaf drop. EVERGREEN Dark green, silver or golden variegated. Premature basal leaf drop. Golden and silver variegated may have orange-red band on outer edges in winter.
Roots Pots 5 in (12 cm) min. dia. Balled, good fibrous root system.
Hints Any well-prepared soil. Wide range.
Most widely available
DECIDUOUS *Euonymous alatus* (Winged Euonymus). *E. a.* 'Compacta'. *E. europaeus* (Spindle. Common Spindle. European Euonymus). *E. e.* 'Albus'. *E. e.* 'Red Cascade'. *E. fortunei*. *E. japonicus* 'Microphyllus Variegatus'. *E. phellomanus*. *E. sachalinensis* (*E. planipes*).
EVERGREEN *Euonymus radicans* (Wintercreeper Euonymus). *E. fortunei* 'Coloratus'. *E. f.* 'Emerald Gaiety'. *E. f.* 'Emerald 'n' Gold'. *E. f.* 'Gold Spot'. *E. f.* 'Kewensis'. *E. f. var radicans*. *E. f.* 'Silver Queen'. *E. f.* 'Sunshine'. *E. f.* 'Variegatus'. *E. f.* 'Vegetus'. *E. japonicus* (Japanese Euonymus). *E. j.* 'Albomarginatus'. *E. j.* 'Macrophyllus'. *E. j.* 'Macrophyllus Albus'. *E. j.* 'Microphyllus Pulchellus' (*E.* 'Microphyllus Aureus'). *E. j.* 'Ovatus Aureus' (*E.* 'Aureovariegatus'). *E. j. robusta*. *E. kiautschovicus* (*E. patens*) (Spreading Euonymus). *E. k.* 'Manhattan'.

EXOCHORDA
Time to buy Pot-grown, any time except January. Balled, root-wrapped and bare-rooted, October–May. Avoid adverse weather conditions.
Where to find Outside in Shrubs.
Size Height 1½ ft (50 cm) min. Single or multi-stemmed.
Foliage Deciduous. Spring/summer, mid

green. Premature autumn colour and leaf drop.
Roots Pots 5 in (12 cm) min. dia. Balled, root-wrapped and bare-rooted, good fibrous root system.
Hints Any well-prepared soil. May be scarce. Ungainly when young. Needs time to establish.
Most widely available *Exochorda giraldii*. *E.* × *macrantha*. *E.* × *m.* 'The Bride'. *E. racemosa*.

FABIANA
Time to buy Pot-grown, any time except January. Balled, October–May. Avoid adverse weather conditions.
Where to find Outside in Shrubs or Acid-loving Plants.
Size Height 9 in (23 cm) min. Single or multi-stemmed.
Foliage Evergreen. Bright green. Premature basal leaf drop.
Roots Pots 5 in (12 cm) min. dia. Balled, good fibrous root system.
Hints Well-prepared acid soil, plus extra organic material. Scarce.
Most widely available *Fabiana imbricata*. *F. i.* 'Prostrata'. *F. i. var. violacea*.

× FATSHEDERA
Aralia Ivy
Time to buy Pot-grown, any time except January. Avoid adverse weather conditions.
Where to find Outside in Shrubs or Climbers.
Size Height 1 ft (30 cm) min. Normally single stemmed, multi-stemmed for preference.
Roots Pots 5 in (12 cm) min. dia.
Foliage Evergreen. Dark to mid green. Premature basal leaf drop.
Hints Any well prepared soil, plus extra organic material. May show leaf scorch. Hardiness in doubt. Needs shade. Either offered as shrub or climber.
Most widely available × *Fatshedera lizei*. × *F. l.* 'Variegata'.

FATSIA

Castor Oil Plant, Japanese Fatsia

Time to buy Pot-grown, any time except January. Avoid adverse weather conditions.

Where to find Outside in Shrubs. Indoors as House Plants.

Size Height 1 ft (30 cm) min. Normally single-stemmed.

Foliage Evergreen. Dark green or variegated. Premature basal leaf drop.

Roots Pots 5 in (12 cm) min. dia.

Hints Any well-prepared soil, plus extra organic material. Avoid using plants grown as house plants for outside use. Variegated forms hardiness in doubt.

Most widely available *Fatsia japonica. F. j.* 'Variegata'.

FEIJOA

Guava, Pineapple Guava

Time to buy Pot-grown, April–August. Avoid adverse weather conditions.

Where to find Outside in Shrubs or Fruit. Indoors in Conservatory.

Size Height 1 ft (30 cm) min. Single or multi-stemmed.

Foliage Evergreen. Grey-green or white variegated. Premature basal leaf drop.

Roots Pots 5 in (12 cm) min. dia.

Hints Any well-prepared soil, except alkaline, plus extra organic material. Scarce. Not possible to grow for its edible fruit in the U.K., but flowers are attractive.

Most widely available *Feijoa sellowiana. F. s.* 'David'. *F. s.* 'Variegata'.

FORSYTHIA

Golden Ball

Time to buy Pot-grown, any time except January. Root-wrapped, bare-rooted and pre-packed, October–May. Avoid adverse weather conditions.

Where to find Outside in Shrubs. Pre-packs under limited cover.

Size Height 2 ft (60 cm) min. Minimum two main shoots and limited side shoots.

Forsythia 'Arnold Dwarf', *F. ovata*, *F. o.* 'Tetragold', *F. viridissima* and *F. v.* 'Bronxensis', height 5 in (12 cm) min.

Foliage Deciduous. Spring/summer, green. Premature autumn colour and leaf drop.

Roots Pots 5 in (12 cm) min. dia. Root-wrapped and bare-rooted, good fibrous root system. *Forsythia* 'Arnold Dwarf', *F. ovata*, *F. o.* 'Tetragold', *F. viridissima* and *F. v.* 'Bronxensis', pots 4 in (10 cm) min. dia. Pot-grown for preference.

Hints Any well-prepared soil. Wide range. Offered as pre-packs in supermarkets: not always a good purchase. *Forsythia suspensa* due to climbing habit, looks open and straggly. Forms not always named.

Most widely available *Forsythia* 'Arnold Dwarf'. *F.* 'Arnold Giant'. *F.* 'Beatrix Farrand'. *F. giraldiana. F.* 'Golden Nugget'. *F.* × *intermedia* (Border Forsythia). *F.* × *i.* 'Spectabilis'. *F.* 'Karl Sax'. *F.* 'Lynwood'. *F. ovata* (Korean Lilac). *F.* 'Robusta'. *F.* 'Spring Glory'. *F. suspensa* (Climbing Forsythia. Weeping Forsythia). *F. s. var. atrocaulis. F. s.* 'Nymans'. *F.* 'Tremonia'. *F. viridissima* (Green stem Forsythia). *F. v.* 'Bronxensis'.

FOTHERGILLA

Time to buy Pot-grown, any time except January. Balled, October–May. Avoid adverse weather conditions.

Where to find Outside in Shrubs or Acid-loving Plants.

Size Height 15 in (40 cm) min. Single or multi-stemmed.

Foliage Deciduous. Spring/summer, green. Premature autumn colour and leaf drop.

Roots Pots 5 in (12 cm) min. dia. Balled, good fibrous root system.

Hints Well-prepared acid soil, plus extra organic material. Scarce.

Most widely available *Fothergilla gardenii* (Dwarf Fothergilla). *F. major* (Large Fothergilla). *F. monticolar* (Alabama Fothergilla).

FREMONTODENDRON
Fremontia

Time to buy Pot-grown, any time except January. Avoid adverse weather conditions.

Where to find Outside in Shrubs.

Size Height 1½ ft (50 cm) min. Normally single-stemmed. Limited side shoots.

Foliage Evergreen. Grey-green. Premature basal leaf drop.

Roots Pots 5 in (12 cm) min. dia.

Hints Any well-prepared soil, plus extra organic material. Scarce. If kept under cover in winter, avoid planting until spring frosts have finished. Dust on flowers, stems and foliage can be an irritant. Research overall size.

Most widely available *Fremontodendron californicum*. *F. c.* 'California Glory'. *F. c. mexicanum*.

FUCHSIA
Hardy Fuchsia, Shrubby Fuchsia

Time to buy Pot-grown, any time except January. Avoid adverse weather conditions.

Where to find Outside in Shrubs.

Size Spring, height 4 in (10 cm) min. Summer, 12 in (30 cm) min. *Fuchsia* 'Lady Thumb' and *Fuchsia* 'Tom Thumb', 3 in (8 cm) and 6 in (15 cm). Single or multi-stemmed.

Foliage Deciduous. Spring/summer, mid to dark green or variegated. Premature autumn colour and leaf drop.

Roots Pots 4 in (10 cm) min. dia. Smaller may be available in spring.

Hints Any well-prepared soil, plus extra organic material. Wide range. If kept under cover in winter, avoid planting until spring frosts have finished. It is best to attempt to purchase named forms. Those listed below are the most hardy.

Most widely available *Fuchsia* 'Alice Hoffman'. *F.* 'Chillerton Beauty'. *F.* 'Eva Boerg'. *F.* 'Golden Treasure'. *F.* 'Lady Thumb'. *F.* 'Madame Cornelissen'. *F.*

magellanica 'Alba'. *F. m* 'Pumila'. *F. m.* 'Riccartonii'. *F. m.* 'Variegata' (*F. gracilia* 'Variegata'). *F. m.* 'Versicolor' (*F. m.* 'Tricolor'). *F.* 'Margaret'. *F.* 'Mrs Popple'. *F. procumbens*. *F.* 'Tom Thumb'.

GARRYA
Tassel Bush, Silk Tassel Tree

Time to buy Pot-grown, any time except January. Avoid adverse weather conditions.

Where to find Outside in Shrubs or Climbers.

Size Height 9 in (23 cm) min. Single or multi-stemmed.

Foliage Evergreen. Grey-green, dark green. Premature basal leaf drop.

Roots Pots 5 in (12 cm) min. dia.

Hints Any well-prepared soil, plus extra organic material. May be scarce. For wall use, plant 15–18 in (40–50 cm) away from wall.

Most widely available *Garrya elliptica*. *G. e.* 'James Roof'. *G. fremontii*.

GENISTA
Mount Etna Broom

Time to buy Pot-grown, any time except January. Avoid adverse weather conditions.

Where to find Outside in Shrubs.

Size LOW-GROWING Height 6 in (15 cm) min. TALL-GROWING Height 1 ft (30 cm) min. Single or multi-stemmed.

Foliage Deciduous. Spring/summer, grey-green. Premature autumn colour and leaf drop.

Roots Pots 4 in (10 cm) min. dia.

Hints Any well-prepared soil, plus extra organic material. Short stake and ties. May be scarce. Research overall size.

Most widely available

LOW-GROWING *Genista hispanica* (Spanish Gorse). *C. lydia*. *G. pilosa*. *G. p.* 'Lemon Spreader'. *G. p.* 'Vancouver Gold'. *G. tinctoria* 'Royal Gold'. (Dyer's Greenwood, Common Woadwaxen).

TALL-GROWING *Genista aetnensis*. *G.*

tenera 'Golden Showers' (*G. cinerea* 'Golden Showers').

GRISELINIA
Time to buy Pot-grown, any time except January. Avoid adverse weather conditions.
Where to find Outside in Shrubs.
Size Height 9 in (23 cm) min. Single or multi-stemmed. Limited side shoots.
Foliage Evergreen. Bright green, dark green or golden. Premature basal leaf drop.
Roots Pots 5 in (12 cm) min. dia.
Hints Any well-prepared soil, plus extra organic material. Hardiness in doubt.
Most widely available *Griselinia littoralis*. *G. l.* 'Dixon's Gold. *G. l.* 'Variegata'.

HALESIA
Mountain Silverbell, Mountain Snowball Tree, Carolina Silverbell
Time to buy Pot-grown, any time except January. Avoid adverse weather conditions.
Where to find Outside in Shrubs or Acid-loving Plants.
Size Height 1 ft (30 cm) min. Single or multi-stemmed. Limited side shoots.
Foliage Deciduous. Spring/summer, grey-green. Premature autumn colour and leaf drop.
Roots Pots 5 in (12 cm) min. dia.
Hints Well prepared acid to neutral soil, plus extra organic material. Scarce.
Most widely available *Halesia carolina* (*H. tetraptera*) (Carolina Silverbell). *H. monticola* (Mountain Silverbell). *H. m. vestita*.

× HALIMIOCISTUS
Time to buy Pot-grown, any time except January. Avoid adverse weather conditions.
Where to find Outside in Shrubs.
Size Height and spread 9 in (23 cm) min. Single or multi-stemmed.

Foliage Evergreen. Dark green to grey-green. Premature basal leaf drop.
Roots Pots 5 in (12 cm) min. dia.
Hints Any well-prepared soil. May be scarce. If kept under cover in winter, avoid planting until spring frosts have finished.
Most widely available × *Halimiocistus ingwersenii*. × *H. sahucii*. × *H. wintonensis*.

HALIMIUM
Time to buy Pot-grown, any time except January. Avoid adverse weather conditions.
Where to find Outside in Shrubs.
Size Height 9 in (23 cm) min. Single or multi-stemmed.
Foliage Evergreen. Grey-green. Premature basal leaf drop.
Roots Pots 5 in (12 cm) min. dia.
Hints Any well-prepared soil. May be scarce. If kept under cover in winter, avoid planting until spring frosts have finished. May need protection first winter after planting.
Most widely available *Halimium lasianthum* (*Cistus formosus*). *H. ocymoides* (*Helianthemum algarvense*). *H. umbellatum*.

HAMAMELIS
Witch Hazel
Time to buy Pot-grown, any time except January. Balled, October–May. Avoid adverse weather conditions.
Where to find Outside in Shrubs or Acid-loving Plants.
Size Height 15 in (40 cm) min. Single or multi-stemmed.
Foliage Deciduous. Spring/summer, grey-green. Premature autumn colour and leaf drop.
Roots Pots 8 in (20 cm) min. dia. Balled, good fibrous root system.
Hints Well-prepared acid soil, plus extra organic material. May be scarce.
Most widely available *Hamamelis* ×

intermedia 'Diane'. *H.* × 'Jelena'. *H.* ×
'Ruby Glow'. *H.* × 'Westersteide'. *H. ja-
ponica* 'Zuccariniana' (Japanese Witch
Hazel). *H. mollis* (Chinese Witch Hazel).
H. m. 'Brevipetala'. *H. m.* 'Pallida'.

HEBE
Veronica
Time to buy Pot-grown, March–August,
or April–July in northerly areas. Avoid
adverse weather conditions.
Where to find Outside in Shrubs.
Size LOW-GROWING Height or diameter
6 in (15 cm) min. TALL-GROWING Height
or diameter 15 in (40 cm) min. Single or
multi-stemmed.
Foliage Evergreen. Light, mid to grey-
green or variegated. Premature basal leaf
drop.
Roots LOW-GROWING Pots 4 in (10 cm)
min. dia. TALL-GROWING Pots 5 in (12 cm)
min. dia.
Hints Any well-prepared soil, plus extra
organic material. May be scarce. If under
cover in winter, avoid planting until
spring frosts have finished. Hardiness in
doubt. May need protection first winter
after planting. Purchase young fleshy-
looking plants.
Most widely available
LOW-GROWING *Hebe albicans. H. a.*
'Pewter Dome'. *H. a.* 'Red Edge'. *H.*
'Autumn Glory'. *H.* 'Carl Teschner'. *H.
glaucophylla* 'Variegata' (*H. darwiniana
variegata*). *H. macrantha. H. pinguifolia*
'Pagei'. *H. p.* 'Quick Silver'. *H. rakaiensis*
(*H. subalpina*).
TALL-GROWING *Hebe* 'Alicia Amherst'.
H. × *andersonii. H.* × 'Variegata'. *H. ano-
mala. H.* 'Bowles Hybrid'. *H. brachy-
siphon* (*H. traversii*). *H.* × *franciscana*
'Blue Gem' (*H.* 'Blue Gem'). *H.* × *f.* 'Vari-
egata' (*elliptaca*). *H.* 'Great Orme'. *H. Hul-
keana. H.* 'La Seduisante'. *H.* 'Marjorie'.
H. 'Mauvena'. *H.* 'Midsummer Beauty'. *H.*
'Mrs E. Tennant'. *H.* 'Mrs Winder'. *H.*
'Purple Queen'. *H. salicifolia. H. s.* 'Vari-
egata'. *H.* 'Simon Delaux'. *H.* 'Waikiki'.

HEDERA
Ivy
Time to buy Pot-grown, any time except
January. Avoid adverse weather conditions.
Where to find Outside in Shrubs or
Ground Cover.
Size Height or spread, 9 in (23 cm) min.
Foliage Evergreen. Mid, dark or light
green, or golden variegated. Premature
basal leaf drop.
Roots SHRUB FORM Pots 5 in (12 cm)
min. dia. GROUND-COVER Pots 4 in
(10 cm) min. dia.
Hints Any well-prepared soil. Wide
range. Plants of small sizes can be used
for *en masse* planting. For ground-cover,
plant three plants per sq. yard (sq.
metre), but many not specifically grown
for this purpose.
Most widely available
GROUND-COVER *Hedera canariensis*
'Gloire de Marengo'. *H. colchica* (Persian
Ivy). *H. c.* 'Dentata Variegata'. *H. c.* 'Sulphur Heart' (Paddy's Pride). *H. helix* 'Buttercup'. *H. h.* 'Cristata'. *H. h.* 'Glacier'.
H. h. 'Gold Heart' (*H. h.* 'Jubilee'). *H. h.*
'Hibernica' (Irish Ivy).
SHRUB FORM *Hedera colchica* 'Arbore-
scens' (Shrubby Persian Ivy). *H. helix*
'Arborescens'. *H. h.* 'Conglomerata'
(Shrubby Common Ivy). *H. h.* 'Erecta'.

HELIANTHEMUM
Rock Rose, Sun Rose
Time to buy Pot-grown, any time except
January. Avoid adverse weather condi-
tions.
Where to find Outside in Shrubs or
Alpines.
Size Height 2 in (5 cm) min. Single or
multi-stemmed.
Foliage Evergreen. Glossy or grey-green.
Premature basal leaf drop.
Roots Pots 4 in (10 cm) min. dia.
Hints Any well-prepared soil. Wide
range.
Most widely available *Helianthemum al-*

pestre (*H. serpyllifolium*). *H. lunulatum.*
H. nummularium 'Afflick'. *H. n.* 'Amy
Baring'. *H. n.* 'Ben Hope'. *H. n.* 'Ben Ledi'.
H. n. 'Ben More'. *H. n.* 'Ben Nevis'. *H. n.*
'Cerise Queen'. *H. n.* 'Cherry Pink'. *H. n.*
'Fireball' (*H. n.* 'Mrs Earl'). *H. m.* 'Fire
Dragon' (*H. n.* 'Mrs Clay'). *H. m.* 'Henfield
Brilliant'. *H. n.* 'Jubilee'. *H. n.* 'Lemon
Queen'. *H. n.* 'Old Gold'. *H. n.* 'Raspberry
Ripple'. *H. n.* 'Rhodanthe Carneum' (*H. n.*
'Wisley Pink'). *H. n.* 'Rose Perfection'.
H. n. 'Salmon Bee'. *H. n.* 'St John's Col-
lege'. *H. n.* 'Sudbury Gem'. *H. n.* 'The
Bride'. *H. n.* 'Wisley Primrose'. *H. n.*
'Wisley Yellow'. *H. n.* 'Wisley White'.
H. n. 'Yellow Queen'.

HELICHRYSUM

Time to buy Pot-grown, any time except
January. Avoid adverse weather conditions.
Where to find Outside in Shrubs, Perennials or Herbs.
Size Spring, height 3 in (8 cm) min.
Summer 6 in (15 cm) min. Single or
multi-stemmed.
Foliage Evergreen. Grey-green. Premature
basal leaf drop.
Roots Pots 4 in (10 cm) min. dia.
Hints Any well-prepared soil. Wide
range. If kept under cover in winter,
avoid planting until spring frosts have
finished. Research overall size. Cut back
previous season's growth within 2 in
(5 cm) of its origin in April. Repeat
annually.
Most widely available *Helichrysum
petiolatum. H. plicatum. H. serotinum* (*H.
angustifolia*) (Curry Plant). *H. splen-
didum* (Everlasting Immortelles).

HIBISCUS

Tree Hollyhock, Flower of an Hour, Rose
of Sharon, Shrub Alethea
Time to buy Pot-grown, any time except
January. Balled, October–May. Avoid ad-
verse weather conditions.
Where to find Outside in Shrubs.

Size Height 15 in (40 cm) min. May be
single-stemmed. Multi-stemmed for preference.
Foliage Deciduous. Spring/summer, mid
green. Premature autumn colour and leaf
drop.
Roots Pots 5 in (12 cm) min. dia. Balled,
good fibrous root system.
Hints Any well-prepared soil, plus extra
organic material. Late to produce foliage.
Most widely available *Hibiscus syriacus*
'Admiral Dewey'. *H. s.* 'Ardens' (*H.* 'Caer-
uleus Plenus'). *H. s.* 'Blue Bird'. *H. s.* 'Duc
de Brabant'. *H. s.* 'Hamabo'. *H. s.* 'Jeanne
d'Arc'. *H. s.* 'Lady Stanley' (*H. s.* 'Ele-
gantissimus'). *H. s.* 'Leopoldi'. *H. s.*
'Mauve Queen'. *H. s.* 'Rubus'. *H. s.* 'Russian Violet'. *H. s.* 'Speciosus'. *H. s.* 'Violet
Clair Double' (*H. s.* 'Puniceus Plenus').
H. s. 'Roseus Plenus'. *H. s.* 'William E.
Smith'. *H. s.* 'Woodbridge'.

HIPPOPHAE RHAMNOIDES
Sea Buckthorn
Time to buy Pot-grown, any time except
January. Balled, root-wrapped and bare-
rooted, October–May. Avoid adverse wea-
ther conditions.
Where to find Outside in Shrubs.
Size Height 1½ ft (50 cm) min. Single or
multi-stemmed.
Foliage Deciduous. Spring/summer,
silver-grey to grey-green. Premature
autumn colour and leaf drop.
Roots Pots 5 in (12 cm) min. dia. Balled,
root-wrapped and bare-rooted, good
fibrous root system.
Hints Any well-prepared sandy soil.
Weak and straggly. Can become invasive,
particularly in the Channel Islands.
Female plants berry, but are rarely
offered sexed. This leads to the problem
of planting males for pollination.

HOHERIA
Time to buy Pot-grown, any time except
January. Avoid adverse weather condi-
tions.

Where to find Outside in Shrubs.
Size Height 15 in (40 cm) min. Single or multi-stemmed.
Foliage Deciduous. Spring/summer, mid green. Premature autumn colour and leaf drop.
Roots Pots 5 in (12 cm) min. dia.
Hints Any well-prepared soil, except alkaline, plus extra organic material. Scarce. Stunted and irregular in habit. Almost impossible to obtain correctly named forms.
Most widely available *Hoheria glabrata* (*Gaya lyallii*) (*Plagianthus lyallii*). *H. lyalli* (*Gaya lyallii*) (*Gaya lyalli ribifolia*) (*Plagianthus lyalli*). *H. populnea*.

HOLODISCUS DISCOLOR
Ocean Spray
Time to buy Pot-grown, any time except January. Balled, root-wrapped and bare-rooted, October–May. Avoid adverse weather conditions.
Where to find Outside in Shrubs.
Size Height 1½ ft (50 cm) min. Single or multi-stemmed.
Foliage Deciduous. Spring/summer, mid green. Premature autumn colour and leaf drop.
Roots Pots 5 in (12 cm) min. dia. Balled, root-wrapped and bare-rooted, good fibrous root system.
Hints Any well-prepared soil, plus extra organic material. May be scarce. Young plants look weak and insipid. Can become invasive. European stock often fails.

HYDRANGEA ARBORESCENS
Smooth Hydrangea, Tree Hydrangea
Time to buy Pot-grown, any time except January. Balled, October–May. Avoid adverse weather conditions.
Where to find Outside in Shrubs.
Size Height 15 in (40 cm) min. Minimum three main stems.
Foliage Deciduous. Spring/summer, light green. Premature autumn colour and leaf drop.

Roots Pots 6 in (15 cm) min. dia. Balled, good fibrous root system.
Hints Any well-prepared soil, plus extra organic material. Scarce. If kept under cover in winter, avoid planting until spring frosts have finished. Looks dishevelled and some die-back in winter. Cut back all previous season's growth to within 2 in (5 cm) of origin in April. Repeat annually.
Most widely available *Hydrangea arborescens* 'Annabelle'. *H. a.* 'Grandiflora'.

HYDRANGEA ASPERA
Rough-leaved Hydrangea
HYDRANGEA SARGENTIANA
Sargent's Hydrangea
Time to buy Pot-grown, any time except January. Balled, October–May. Avoid adverse weather conditions.
Where to find Outside in Shrubs.
Size Height 6 in (15 cm) min. Single-stemmed or multi-stemmed.
Foliage Deciduous. Spring/summer, felty-red to red-green. Premature autumn colour and leaf drop.
Roots Pots 6 in (15 cm) min. dia. Balled, good fibrous root system.
Hints Any well-prepared soil, plus extra organic material. Scarce. If kept under cover in winter, avoid planting until spring frosts have finished. Needs protection in first and second winter after planting. Looks short and stunted.

HYDRANGEA MACROPHYLLA
(hortensia forms)
Bigleaf Hydrangea and Mop-headed Hydrangea
HYDRANGEA MACROPHYLLA
(lace-cap forms)
Lace-cap Hydrangea
Time to buy Pot-grown, any time except January. Balled, October–May. Avoid adverse weather conditions.

Where to find Outside in Shrubs.
Size Height 6 in (15 cm) min. Minimum two main stems.
Foliage Deciduous. Spring/summer, mid green. Premature autumn colour and leaf drop.
Roots Pots 5 in (12 cm) min. dia. Balled, good fibrous root system.
Hints Any well-prepared soil, except alkaline, plus extra organic material. If kept under cover in winter, avoid planting until spring frosts have finished. Wide range. Avoid purchasing any showing signs of growth prior to late April. Plants used as house plants can be planted out once flowering is over. Needs protection during first two years after planting.
Most widely available
MOP-HEADED *Hydrangea macrophylla* 'Altona'. *H. m.* 'Ami Pasquier'. *H. m.* 'Amethyst'. *H. m.* 'Ayesha'. *H. m.* 'Blue Prince'. *H. m.* 'Deutschland'. *H. m.* 'Europa'. *H. m.* 'Generale Vicomtesse de Vibraye'. *H. m.* 'Hamburg'. *H. m.* 'Harry's Red'. *H. m.* 'Holstein'. *H. m.* 'King George'. *H. m.* 'Klus Supreme'. *H. m.* 'Madame Emile Mouilliere'. *H. m.* 'Maréchal Foch'. *H. m.* 'Miss Belgium'. *H. m.* 'Niedersachsen'. *H. m.* 'President Doumer'. *H. m.* 'Sister Teresa'.
LACE-CAP *Hydrangea macrophylla* 'Blue Wave'. *H. m.* 'Lanarth White'. *H. m.* 'Lilacina'. *H. m.* 'Mariesii'. *H. m.* 'Sea Foam'. *H. m.* 'Tricolor'. *H. m.* 'White Wave'.

HYDRANGEA PANICULATA
Panick Hydrangea
Time to buy Pot-grown, any time except January. Balled, October–May. Avoid adverse weather conditions.
Where to find Outside in Shrubs.
Size Height 1 ft (30 cm) min. Single or multi-stemmed.
Foliage Deciduous. Spring/summer, mid green. Premature autumn colour and leaf drop.

Roots Pots 5 in (12 cm) min. dia. Balled, good fibrous root system.
Hints Any well-prepared soil, except alkaline, plus extra organic material. May be scarce. If kept under cover in winter, avoid planting until spring frosts have finished. Late to show foliage. Damages easily in transit. Cut back all previous season's growth to within 2 in (5 cm) of origin in April. Repeat annually.
Most widely available *Hydrangea paniculata* 'Grandiflora' (Pee Gee Hydrangea). *H. p.* 'Kyushu'. *H. p.* 'Praecox'. *H. p.* 'Tardiva'.

HYDRANGEA PETIOLARIS
Climbing Hydrangea
Time to buy Pot-grown, any time except January. Balled, October–May. Avoid adverse weather conditions.
Where to find Outside in Shrubs.
Size Height 9 in (23 cm) min. Single stemmed. Multi-stemmed as it gains height.
Foliage Deciduous. Spring/summer, mid green. Premature autumn colour and leaf drop.
Roots Pots 5 in (12 cm) min. dia. Balled, good fibrous root system.
Hints Any well-prepared soil, except alkaline, plus extra organic material. If kept under cover in winter, avoid planting until spring frosts have finished. One-sided and irregular in growth. Dying brown leaves from July. For wall use, plant 15–18 in (40–50 cm) away from wall.

HYDRANGEA QUERCIFOLIA
Oak Leaf Hydrangea
Time to buy Pot-grown, any time except January. Balled, October–May. Avoid adverse weather conditions.
Where to find Outside in Shrubs.
Size Height 8 in (20 cm) min. Single or multi-stemmed.
Foliage Deciduous. Spring/summer, mid green. Premature autumn colour and leaf drop.

Roots Pots 5 in (12 cm) min. dia. Balled, good fibrous root system.

Hints Any well-prepared soil, except alkaline, plus extra organic material. May be scarce. If kept under cover in winter, avoid planting until spring frosts have finished. Always straggly, never upright. For wall use, plant 15–18 in (40–50 cm) away from wall.

HYDRANGEA SERRATA
Time to buy Pot-grown, any time except January. Balled, October–May. Avoid adverse weather conditions.

Where to find Outside in Shrubs.

Size Height 6 in (15 cm) min. Minimum two main stems. *Hydrangea pia*, height 2 in (5 cm) min., with normally no side shoots.

Foliage Deciduous. Spring/summer, mid green. Premature autumn colour and leaf drop.

Roots Pots 5 in (12 cm) min. dia. *Hydrangea pia*, pots 3 in (8 cm) min. dia. Balled, good fibrous root system.

Hints Any well-prepared soil, except alkaline, plus extra organic material. Wide range. If kept under cover in winter, avoid planting until spring frosts have finished. Needs protection in first and second years after planting. Avoid plants with signs of leaf prior to April. Needs light shade.

Most widely available *Hydrangea serrata* 'Bluebird' (*H. s.* var. *acuminata*). *H. s.* 'Grayswood'. *H. s.* 'Preziosa'. *H. s.* 'Rosalba'. *H. acuminata* 'Bluebird'. *H. pia*.

HYDRANGEA VILLOSA syn.
Hydrangea rosthornii
Time to buy Pot-grown, any time except January. Balled, October–May. Avoid adverse weather conditions.

Where to find Outside in Shrubs.

Size Height 6 in (15 cm) min. Minimum two upright stems.

Foliage Deciduous. Spring/summer, grey-green with velvet texture. Premature autumn colour and leaf drop.

Roots Pots 5 in (12 cm) min. dia. Balled, good fibrous root system.

Hints Any well-prepared soil, except alkaline, plus extra organic material. Normally available. If kept under cover in winter, avoid planting until spring frosts have finished. Needs protection from spring frosts first year after planting.

HYPERICUM CALYCINUM
St John's Wort, Aaronsbeard
Time to buy Pot-grown, any time except January. Balled, root-wrapped and bare-rooted, October–May. Avoid adverse weather conditions.

Where to find Outside in Shrubs or Ground-Cover.

Size Height 2 in (5 cm) min. Minimum three upright shoots. All signs of growth may disappear in winter.

Foliage Evergreen. Mid green. Premature basal leaf drop.

Roots Pots 3 in (8 cm) min. dia. Balled, root-wrapped and bare-rooted, good fibrous root system.

Hints Any well-prepared soil. Avoid plants showing orange/red rust on leaves. Dislikes being grown in containers and may look unattractive at time of purchase. For ground-cover, use three plants per sq. yard. Need for weed control until established.

HYPERICUM (grown as shrub)
Rose of Sharon, St John's Wort
Time to buy Pot-grown, any time except January. Balled, root-wrapped and bare-rooted, October–May. Avoid adverse weather conditions.

Where to find Outside in Shrubs.

Size Height 1 ft (30 cm) min. Minimum two upright shoots. *Hypericum coris*, *H.* × *moseranum*, *H.* × *m.* 'Tricolor' and *H.* 'Ysella', height 6 in (15 cm) min.

Foliage Deciduous. Spring/summer, mid green, gold or variegated. Premature autumn colour and leaf drop.

Roots Pots 5 in (12 cm) min. dia. Balled, root-wrapped and bare-rooted, good fibrous root system.

Hints Any well-prepared soil. Wide range. Cut back all previous season's growth to within 2 in (5 cm) of ground level in April. Repeat annually.

Most widely available *Hypericum androsaemum* (Tutsan Hypericum) *H. a.* 'Variegatum' *H. a.* 'Mrs Gladys Brabazon'). *H. beanii* 'Gold Cup'. *H. coris. H. forrestii* (*H. patulus forrestii*). *H. p. henryi. H.* 'Hidcote' (*H. patulum* 'Hidcote'). *H. p.* 'Hidcote Gold'. *H. × inodrum* (*H. androsaemum × hircinum*). *H. elatum. H. kouytchense* (*H. penduliflorus*). *H. patulum grandiflorum. H. p.* 'Sungold'. *H. p.* 'Variegata'. *H. × moseranum. H. × m.* 'Tricolor'. *H. persistens* 'Elstead' (*H. elatum* 'Elstead'). *H. prolificum. H.* 'Rowallane'. *H.* 'Summer Gold'. *H.* 'Ysella'.

ILEX

Altaclar Holly, Highclere Holly, Common Holly, English Holly

Time to buy Pot-grown, any time except January. Balled, October–May. Avoid adverse weather conditions.

Where to find Outside in Shrubs.

Size Height 1½ ft (50 cm) min. *Ilex × altaclarensis* 'Ferox' forms, height 8 in (20 cm) min. All normally single-stemmed.

Foliage Evergreen. Dark green, golden or silver variegated. Premature basal leaf drop.

Roots Pots 5 in (12 cm) min. dia. Balled, good fibrous root system.

Hints Any well-prepared soil, plus extra organic material. Wide range. If kept under cover in winter, avoid planting until spring frosts have finished. Needs protection from cold winds for two years after planting. Research overall size. Can be trimmed, but if started must be repeated annually.

Most widely available *I. × altaclarensis* (M). *I. × a.* 'Atkinsonii' (M). *I. × a.* 'Camelliifolia' (F). *I. × a.* 'Golden King' (F). *I. × a.* 'Hodginsii' (M). *I. × a.* 'Lawsoniana'(F). *I. × a.* 'Silver Sentinel' (F). *I. aquifolium. I. a.* 'Argentea Marginata' (Broad-leaved Silver Holly) (F). *I. a.* 'Argentea Pendula' (Perry's Silver Weeping Holly) (F). *I. a.* 'Bacciflava' (*I.a.* 'Fructuluteo') (Yellow-fruited Holly), (F). *I.a.* 'Golden Milkboy' (*I. a.* 'Aurea Mediopicta Latifolia') (M). *I. a.* 'Ferox' (Hedgehog Holly) (M). *I. a.* 'Ferox Argentea' (Silver Hedgehog Holly). *I. a.* 'Ferox Aurea' (M). *I. a.* 'Golden Queen' (*I. a.* 'Aurea Regina') (M). *I. a.* 'Golden van Tol' (F). *I. a.* 'Handsworth New Silver' (F). *I. a.* 'J. C. van Tol' (F). *I. a.* 'Madame Briot' (F). *I. a.* 'Myrtifolia Aureomaculata' (M). *I. a.* 'Pendula' (F). *I. a.* 'Pyramidalis' (F). *I. a.* 'Silver Milkboy' (M). *I. a.* 'Silver Queen (M)'. *I. × meserveae. I. × m.* 'Blue Angel' (F)'. *I. × m.* 'Blue Prince' (M). *I. × m.* 'Blue Princess' (F). *I. pernyi* (F). *I. p.* var. *veitchii* (F) (*I. bioritsensis*).

ILEX CRENATA

Box-leaved Holly, Japanese Holly

Time to buy Pot-grown, any time except January. Balled, October–May. Avoid adverse weather conditions.

Where to find Outside in Shrubs.

Size Height 4 in (10 cm) min. Spread 6 in (15 cm) min. Normally single-stemmed, with side shoots giving a cushion or bun effect.

Foliage Evergreen. Dark green or golden variegated. Premature basal leaf drop.

Roots Pots 5 in (12 cm) min. dia. Balled, good fibrous root system.

Hints Any well-prepared soil, plus extra organic material. Golden readily available. Green scarce. *Ilex crenata* 'Golden Gem' scorches in full sun. If kept under cover in winter, avoid planting until spring frosts have finished.

Most widely available *Ilex crenata* 'Aureovariegata' (*I. c.* 'Variegata'). *I. c.* 'Convexa'. *I. c.* 'Golden Gem'. *I. c.* 'Helleri'. *I. c.* 'Mariesii'. *I. c.* 'Stokes Variety'.

ILEX VERTICILLATA
Winterberry
Time to buy Pot-grown, any time except January. Balled, October–May. Avoid adverse weather conditions.
Where to find Outside in Shrubs.
Size Height 15 in (40 cm) min. Normally single-stemmed.
Foliage Deciduous. Spring/summer, mid green. Premature autumn colour and leaf drop.
Roots Pots 5 in (12 cm) min. dia. Balled, good fibrous root system.
Hints Any well-prepared soil, plus extra organic material. May be scarce. If kept under cover in winter, avoid planting until spring frosts have finished.

INDIGOFERA HETERANTHA syn.
Indigofera gerardiana
Indigo Bush
Time to buy Pot-grown, any time except January. Avoid adverse weather conditions.
Where to find Outside in Shrubs.
Size Spring, height 6 in (12 cm) min. Summer, 1 ft (30 cm) min. Normally single-stemmed, but possibly multi-stemmed.
Foliage Deciduous. Spring/summer, grey-green. Premature autumn colour and leaf drop.
Roots Pots 5 in (12 cm) min. dia.
Hints Any well-prepared soil, plus extra organic material. Scarce. If kept under cover in winter, avoid planting until spring frosts have finished. Wispy and insipid in growth.
Most widely available Indigofera heterantha. I. potaninii.

ITEA ILICIFOLIA
Holly-Leaf, Sweetspire
Time to buy Pot-grown, any time except January. Avoid adverse weather conditions.
Where to find Outside in Shrubs.
Size Height 9 in (23 cm) min. Single-stemmed. Minimum three side shoots.

Foliage Evergreen. Dark green. Premature basal leaf drop.
Roots Pots 5 in (12 cm) min. dia.
Hints Any well-prepared soil, plus extra organic material. May be scarce. If kept under cover in winter, avoid planting until spring frosts have finished. Often loosely rooted in pot. Slow to establish. Hardiness in doubt. Needs sheltered position. For wall use, plant 15–18 in (40–50 cm) away from wall.

ITEA VIRGINICA
Virginia Sweetspire
Time to buy Pot-grown, any time except January. Balled, October–May. Avoid adverse weather conditions.
Where to find Outside in Shrubs.
Size Height 1½ ft (50 cm) min. Single or multi-stemmed.
Foliage Deciduous. Spring/summer, mid green. Premature autumn colour and leaf drop.
Roots Pots 5 in (12 cm) min. dia. Balled, good fibrous root system.
Hints Any well-prepared soil. Scarce. Uninteresting in pots. Slow to establish.

JASMINUM (grown as shrub)
Shrubby Jasmine, Jessamine
Time to buy Pot-grown, any time except January. Avoid adverse weather conditions.
Where to find *Jasminum fruticosa, J. humile revolutum* and *J. nudiflorum* outside in Shrubs or Climbers. *Jasminum parkeri* outside in Shrubs or Alpines.
Size Jasminum fruticosa, J. nudiflorum, height 1 ft (30 cm) min. Jasminum humile revolutum, height 1½ ft (50 cm) min., multi-stemmed. All, minimum two main stems. Jasminum parkeri, height 3 in, (8 cm) min. Several wispy side shoots.
Foliage DECIDUOUS Spring/summer, mid green. Premature autumn colour and leaf drop. EVERGREEN Glossy light to mid green. Premature basal leaf drop.

Roots Pots 5 in (12 cm) min. dia. *Jasminum parkeri*, pots 3 in (8 cm) min. dia.
Hints Any well-prepared soil. Scarce, except *Jasminum nudiflorum*. If kept under cover in winter, avoid planting until spring frosts have finished. Poor and unsightly in growth habit. *Jasminum parkeri* dwarf and small. Needs time to develop. For wall use, plant 15–18 in (40–50 cm) away from wall.
Most widely available DECIDUOUS *Jasminum fruticosa*. *J. nudiflorum* (Winter Jasmine). *J. parkeri*. EVERGREEN *Jasminum humile revolutum*.

KALMIA

Time to buy Pot-grown, any time except January. Balled, October–May. Avoid adverse weather conditions.
Where to find Outside in Shrubs or Acid-loving Plants.
Size LOW-GROWING Height 6 in (15 cm) min. Single or multi-stemmed. TALL GROWING Height 1 ft (30 cm) min. Multi-stemmed.
Foliage Evergreen. Mid green to grey-green. Premature basal leaf drop.
Roots LOW-GROWING Pots 5 in (12 cm) min. dia. TALL-GROWING Pots 6 in (15 cm) min. dia. Balled, good fibrous root system.
Hints Well-prepared acid soil, plus extra organic material. Scarce. Normally available when in flower. If kept under cover in winter, avoid planting until spring frosts have finished. May need winter protection in cold areas.
Most widely available
LOW-GROWING Sheep Laurel, Bog Myrtle *Kalmia angustifolia*. *K. a.* 'Rubra'. *K. polifolia*.
TALL-GROWING Calico Bush, Spoon Wood, Mountain Laurel *Kalmia latifolia*. *K. l.* 'Clementine Churchill'. *K. l.* 'Myrtifolia'. *K. l.* 'Ostbo Red'.

KERRIA

Japanese Kerria, Jew's Mallow, Bachelor's Button, Sailor's Button

Time to buy Pot-grown, any time except January. Balled, root-wrapped, and bare-rooted, October–May. Avoid adverse weather conditions.
Where to find Outside in Shrubs.
Size Height 1½ ft (50 cm) min. Multi-stemmed. *Kerria japonica* 'Variegata' height 6 in (15 cm) min.
Foliage Deciduous. Spring/summer, light green. Premature autumn colour and leaf drop.
Roots Pots 5 in (12 cm) min. dia. Balled, root-wrapped and bare-rooted, good fibrous root system.
Hints Any well-prepared soil. Usually readily available. *Kerria japonica* 'Variegata' may show all-green leaves, avoid. *Kerria japonica* 'Pleniflora' for wall use, plant 15–18 in (40–50 cm) away from wall. Requires wires or other forms of training support.
Most Widely available *Kerria japonica*. *K. j.* 'Golden Guinea'. *K. j.* 'Pleniflora' (*K. j.* 'Flore Pleno'). *K. j.* 'Splendens'. *K. j.* 'Variegata' (*K. j.* 'Picta').

KOLKWITZIA AMABILIS
Beauty Bush
Time to buy Pot-grown, any time except January. Balled, root-wrapped and bare-rooted, October–May. Avoid adverse weather conditions.
Where to find Outside in Shrubs.
Size Height 1½ ft (50 cm) min. Single or multi-stemmed.
Foliage Deciduous. Spring/summer, mid green. Premature autumn colour and leaf drop.
Roots Pots 5 in (12 cm) min. dia. Balled, root-wrapped and bare-rooted, good fibrous root system.
Hints Any well-prepared soil. Wide range. Can look tired August onwards.

LAURUS
Bay, Sweet Bay, Bay Laurel, Poet's Laurel
Time to buy Pot-grown, any time except

January. Avoid adverse weather conditions.
Where to find Outside in Shrubs or Herbs.
Size SHRUB Height 15 in (40 cm) min. Single or multi-stemmed. PYRAMID Height 1½ ft (50 cm) min. Good preformed pyramid shape. MOP-HEADED STANDARD clear stem 3 ft (1 m), min, but not more than 6 ft (2 m). Head of branches, 1 ft (30 cm) min. dia. Standard with twisted or plaited stems may be available. Other shapes available.
Foliage Evergreen. Dark green or gold. Premature basal leaf drop.
Roots Pots 5 in (12 cm) min. dia. Trained pyramid and standard, pots 1 ft (30 cm) min. dia.
Hints Any well-prepared soil. Bushes of *Laurus nobilis* and *L. n.* 'Aurea' readily available. Pyramid and standard of *Laurus nobilis* may be scarce. Hardiness suspect. Trained trees should be kept under protection in winter. If grown in permanent containers use good quality potting compost, with regular feeding and watering. For wall use, plant 15–18 in (40–50 cm) away.
Most widely available *Laurus nobilis*. *L. n.* 'Aurea'.

LAVANDULA
Lavender, French Lavender, Spanish Lavender
Time to buy Pot-grown, any time except January. Avoid adverse weather conditions.
Where to find Outside in Shrubs, Herbs or Hedging.
Size *Lavandula angustifolia* 'Hidcote', *L. a.* 'Munstead', *L. stoechas* and *L. s.* 'Pendunculata', height 3 in (8 cm) min. Large for preference. Other forms, height 9 in (23 cm) min. All multi-stemmed. Minimum eight upright shoots.
Foliage Evergreen. Grey-green. Premature basal leaf drop.

Roots Pots 3 in (8 cm) min. dia. Pots 5 in (12 cm) min., if used for hedging.
Hints Any well-prepared soil. May be scarce July onwards. Avoid tired and dejected looking plants.
Most widely available *Lavandula angustifolia* (*L. officinalis*. *L. spica*) (Old English Lavender). *L. a.* 'Alba'. *L. a.* 'Folgate'. *L. a.* 'Grappenhall'. *L. a.* 'Hidcote'. *L. a.* 'Loddon Pink'. *L. a.* 'Munstead'. *L. a.* 'Nana Alba'. *L. a.* 'Twickel Purple'. *L. a.* 'Vera' (Dutch Lavender). *L. stoechas. L. s.* 'Pendunculata'.

LAVATERA THURINGIACA syn.
Lavatera olbia
Tree Mallow, Tree Lavatera
Time to buy Pot-grown, any time except January. Avoid adverse weather conditions.
Where to find Outside in Shrubs.
Size Height 1 ft (30 cm) min. Single or multi-stemmed.
Foliage Deciduous. Spring/summer, grey-green. Premature autumn colour and leaf drop.
Roots Pots 5 in (12 cm) min. dia. Cuttings, pots 3 in (8 cm) min. dia.
Hints Any well-prepared soil. Hardiness suspect in northern areas. If kept under cover in winter, avoid planting until spring frosts have finished. Flowers produced daily throughout summer, and plant will always have dead flowers on it. May need support of a cane in windy positions. Cut back all previous season's growth to 3 in (8 cm) or its origin in April. Repeat annually.
Most widely available *Lavatera thuringiaca* 'Barnsley'. *L. t.* 'Rosea'. *L. t.* 'Burgundy Red'.

LEPTOSPERMUM
Manuka, Tea Tree, New Zealand Tea Tree
Time to buy Pot-grown, any time except January. Occasionally balled, October–April. Avoid adverse weather conditions.
Where to find Outside in Shrubs or

Acid-loving Plants.
Size Height 1½ ft (50 cm) min. Single or multi-stemmed.
Foliage Evergreen. Purple-green. Premature basal leaf drop.
Roots Pots 5 in (12 cm) min. dia. Balled, good fibrous root system.
Hints Well-prepared acid soil, plus extra organic material. May be scarce. Hardiness suspect in northern areas. If kept under cover in winter, avoid planting until spring frosts have finished. Research overall size. For wall use, plant 15–18 in (40–50 cm) away.
Most widely available *Leptospermum cunninghamii. L. scoparium* 'Chapmanii'. *L. s.* 'Decumbens'. *L. s.* 'Jubilee'. *L. s.* 'Nichollsii'. *L. s.* 'Red Damask'. *L. s.* 'Snow Flurry'. *L. s.* 'Spectro Color'.

LESPEDEZA
Thunberg Lespedeza, Bush Clover
Time to buy Pot-grown, any time except January. Avoid adverse weather conditions.
Where to find Outside in Shrubs.
Size Height 1 ft (30 cm) min. Single or multi-stemmed.
Foliage Deciduous. Spring/summer, grey-green. Premature autumn colour and leaf drop.
Roots Pots 5 in (12 cm) min. dia.
Hints Any well-prepared soil, plus extra organic material. If kept under cover in winter, avoid planting until spring frosts have finished. Always floppy. Late to produce leaf. End of shoot die-back may occur in spring. Requires short stake for life.
Most widely available *Lespedeza thunbergii (L. sieboldii).*

LEUCOTHOE FONTANESIANA syn. *Leucothoe catesbaei*
Drooping Leucothoe, Fetterbush
Time to buy Pot-grown, any time except January. Balled, October–May. Avoid adverse weather conditions.

Where to find Outside in Shrubs or Acid-loving Plants.
Size Height 15 in (40 cm) min. Minimum three main stems. Limited side shoots.
Foliage Evergreen. Mid green. Premature basal leaf drop.
Roots Pots 5 in (12 cm) min. dia. Balled, good fibrous root system.
Hints Well-prepared acid soil, plus extra organic material. Scarce. If kept under cover in winter, avoid planting until spring frosts have finished. Can look straggly and open in habit.
Most widely available *Leucothoe fontanesiana. L. f.* 'Rainbow' (*L. f.* 'Multicolor'). *L. f.* 'Rollissonii'.

LEYCESTERIA FORMOSA
Himalayan Honeysuckle, Pheasant Berry
Time to buy Pot-grown, any time except January. Balled and bare-rooted, October–May. Avoid adverse weather conditions.
Where to find Outside in Shrubs.
Size Height 1½ ft (50 cm) min. Minimum three main upright stems. Normally no side shoots.
Foliage Deciduous. Spring/summer, mid green. Premature autumn colour and leaf drop.
Roots Pots 5 in (12 cm) min. dia. Balled and bare-rooted, good fibrous root system.
Hints Any well-prepared soil. Dislike being grown in containers. Can look uninteresting in autumn and winter. May show signs of die-back to tips of shoots. Stems are hollow.

LIGUSTRUM
Privet. Ornamental Privet, Variegated Privet
Time to buy Pot-grown, any time except January. Balled, October–May. *Ligustrum ovalifolium* and *L. vulgare* root-wrapped and bare-rooted, October through winter. Avoid adverse weather conditions.
Where to find Outside in Shrubs.

Ligustrum ovalifolium and *L. vulgare* may be found in multiples of five or ten in Hedging.
Size Height 15 in (40 cm) min. Multi-stemmed. Minimum two main stems. *Ligustrum japonicum* 'Rotundifolium', height 6 in (15 cm), single or multi-stemmed.
Foliage *Ligustrum japonicum* 'Rotundifolium' and all forms of *Ligustrum lucidum*, evergreen, dark green or variegated.
All forms of *Ligustrum quihoui*, *L. sinense* and *L. vulgare* deciduous, mid green, gold or variegated.
Ligustrum ovalifolium and *L.* 'Vicaryi' semi-evergreen or deciduous, depending on severity of winter, mid green, silver or golden variegated.
Roots Pots 5 in (12 cm) min. dia.
Ligustrum japonicum 'Rotundifolium' pots 4 in (10 cm) min. dia. Balled, root-wrapped and bare-rooted, good fibrous root system.
Hints Any well-prepared soil. *Ligustrum japonicum* 'Rotundifolium' and *L. lucidum* and its forms benefit from extra organic material. Wide range. Ornamental Privet should not be overlooked. *Ligustrum japonicum* 'Rotundifolium' slow-growing.
Most widely available *Ligustrum japonicum* 'Rotundifolium' (*L. j.* 'Coriaceum') (Japanese Privet). *L. lucidum* (Glossy Privet), Chinese Privet. Waxleaf Privet). *L. l.* 'Aureum'. *L. l.* 'Excellsum Superbum'. *L. l.* 'Tricolor'. *L. ovalifolium* (Oval-leaved Privet. Hedging Privet. California Privet) *L. o.* 'Argenteum'. *L. o.* 'Aureum' (Golden Privet). *L. quihoui*. *L. sinense* (Chinese Privet). *L. s.* 'Variegatum'. *L.* 'Vicaryi' (Golden Vicary Privet. Golden Privet). *L. vulgare* (Common Privet. European Privet).

LIPPIA CITRIODORA syn. *Aloysia triphylla*
Lemon Verbena, Shrubby Verbena, Lemon Plant
Time to buy Pot-grown, April–July. Avoid adverse weather conditions.
Where to find Outside in Shrubs, Herbs or under protection.
Size Height 15 in (40 cm) min. Single or multi-stemmed.
Foliage Deciduous. Spring/summer, grey-green, aromatic. Premature autumn colour and leaf drop.
Roots Pots 4 in (10 cm) min. dia.
Hints Any well-prepared soil, plus extra organic material. May be scarce. Hardiness suspect. If kept under cover in winter, avoid planting until spring frosts have finished. Late to show foliage in spring.

LOMATIA FERRUGINEA
Time to buy Pot-grown, April–July. Avoid adverse weather conditions.
Where to find Outside in Shrubs or Acid-loving Plants.
Size Height 1 ft (30 cm) min. Single or multi-stemmed.
Foliage Deciduous. Spring/summer, grey-green. Premature autumn colour and leaf drop.
Roots Pots 5 in (12 cm) min. dia.
Hints Well-prepared acid soil, plus extra organic material. Scarce. If kept under cover in winter, avoid planting until spring frosts have finished. Slow to show its full potential.

LONICERA
Shrubby Honeysuckle
Time to buy Pot-grown, any time except January. *Lonicera nitida* and *L. n.* 'Yunnan' balled, root-wrapped and bare-rooted, October–April. Avoid adverse weather conditions.
Where to find Outside in Shrubs. Hedging or Climbers. *Lonicera nitida* in Hedging. *Lonicera pileata* in Ground Cover.
Size Height 15 in (40 cm) min. Single or multi-stemmed. *Lonicera pileata*, minimum spread 15 in (40 cm).
Foliage *Lonicera nitida*, evergreen. *Lonicera pileata*, semi-evergreen. Mid to dark

green or gold. Premature basal leaf drop.
Roots Pots 5 in (12 cm) min. dia. Balled, root-wrapped and bare-rooted, good fibrous root system.
Hints Any well-prepared soil. If lifted in cold winters, bare-rooted may defoliate.

Most widely available

SHRUBBY EVERGREEN (Boxleaf Honeysuckle, Poor Man's Box, Privet Honeysuckle) *Lonicera nitida. L. n.* 'Baggesen's Gold'. *L. n.* 'Yunnan' (*L. yunnanensis*). *L. pileata.*

WINTER-FLOWERING SHRUBBY FORMS *Lonicera fragrantissima. L. purpusii. L. standishii.*

SUMMER-FLOWERING SHRUBBY FORMS (Twin Berry, Lilac-Scented Shrubby Honeysuckle, Tatarian Honeysuckle) *Lonicera involucrata. L. maackii* (Amur Honeysuckle). *L. syringantha. L. tatarica. L. t.* 'Alba'. *L. t.* 'Hack's Red'.

LUPINUS ARBOREUS
Tree Lupin
Time to buy Pot-grown, April–July. Avoid adverse weather conditions.
Where to find Outside in Shrubs or Perennials.
Size Height 4 in (10 cm) min. reaching 15 in (40 cm). Single or multi-stemmed.
Foliage Deciduous. Spring/summer, grey-green. Premature autumn colour and leaf drop.
Roots Pots 4 in (10 cm) min. dia.
Hints Any well-prepared soil, plus extra organic material. Scarce. White and blue forms very scarce. If kept under cover in winter, avoid planting until spring frosts have finished. Relatively short-lived.

LYCIUM BARBARUM
Duke of Argyll's Tea Tree
Time to buy Pot-grown, any time except January. Avoid adverse weather conditions.
Where to find Outside in Shrubs.

Size Height 15 in (40 cm) min. Single or multi-stemmed.
Foliage Deciduous. Spring/summer, mid green. Premature autumn colour and leaf drop.
Roots Pots 5 in (12 cm) min. dia.
Hints Any well-prepared soil. Hardiness suspect in cold areas.

MAHOBERBERIS AQUISARGENTII
Time to buy Pot-grown, any time except January. Balled, October–May. Avoid adverse weather conditions.
Where to find Outside in Shrubs.
Size Height 1 ft (30 cm) min. Single or multi-stemmed.
Foliage Evergreen. Mid to dark green. Premature basal leaf drop.
Roots Pots 6 in (15 cm) min. dia. Balled, good fibrous root system.
Hints Any well-prepared soil, plus extra organic material. Scarce. If kept under cover in winter, avoid planting until spring frosts have finished. Thorny nature of leaves makes handling difficult. Carries a mildew which is almost impossible to eradicate, but not detrimental to the plant's overall well-being.

MAHONIA
Time to buy Pot-grown, any time except January. Balled, October–May. *Mahonia aquifolium*, bare-rooted. Avoid adverse weather conditions.
Where to find Outside in Shrubs.
Size Height 1 ft (30 cm) min. Single or multi-stemmed.
Foliage Evergreen. Dark glossy green. Premature basal leaf drop.
Roots Pots 6 in (15 cm) min. dia. *Mahonia aquifolium* and forms 4 in (10 cm) min. dia. Balled, good fibrous root system.
Hints Any well-prepared soil, plus extra organic material. Wide range. If kept under cover in winter, avoid planting until spring frosts have finished. Plants vary in size, check. All but *Mahonia aquifolium* forms should have a leading

rosette of foliage and bud removed in spring. All forms need protection first winter after planting.
Most widely available Mahonia aquifolium (Oregon Grape). M. a. 'Apollo'. M. a. 'Atropurpurea'. M. a. 'Moseri'. M. a. 'Orange Flame'. M. bealei. M. 'Buckland'. M. 'Charity'. M. japonica. M. 'Lionel Fortescue'. M. lomarifolia. M. 'Undulata' (M. aquifolium undulata). M. 'Winter Sun'.

MELIANTHUS MAJOR
Honey Bush
Time to buy Pot-grown, any time except January. Avoid adverse weather conditions.
Where to find Outside in Shrubs or indoors in House Plants.
Size Height 10 in (25 cm). Normally single-stemmed, but multi-stemmed for preference if available.
Foliage Evergreen. Grey-green. Premature basal leaf drop.
Roots Pots 6 in (15 cm) min. dia.
Hints Any well-prepared soil, plus extra organic material. May be scarce. If kept under cover in winter, avoid planting until spring frosts have finished. Hardiness suspect, and may need protection.

MYRICA
Bayberry, Californian Bayberry, Sweet Gale, Bog Myrtle, Wax Myrtle
Time to buy Pot-grown, any time except January. Balled, October–May. Avoid adverse weather conditions.
Where to find Outside in Shrubs or Acid-loving Plants.
Size Height 15 in (40 cm) min. Multi-stemmed,
Foliage DECIDUOUS Spring/summer, mid green with grey or reddish hue. Premature autumn colour and leaf drop. EVERGREEN Mid green. Premature basal leaf drop.
Roots Pots 5 in (12 cm) min. dia. Balled, good fibrous root system.
Hints Well-prepared moist and boggy

acid soil, plus extra organic material. Scarce.
Most widely available Myrica californica (Californian Bayberry) (E). M. cerifera (Wax Myrtle) (E). M. gale (Sweet Gale. Bog Myrtle). M. pennsylvanica (Bayberry).

MYRTUS
Myrtle
Time to buy Pot-grown, April–July. Avoid adverse weather conditions.
Where to find Outside in Shrubs and Herbs or under protection.
Size Height 15 in (40 cm) min. Single or multi-stemmed.
Foliage Evergreen. Mid to dark green. Premature basal leaf drop.
Roots Pots 4 in (10 cm) min. dia.
Hints Any well-prepared soil, plus extra organic material. Scarce. If kept under cover in winter, avoid planting until spring frosts have finished. Hardiness suspect in cold areas.
Most widely available Myrtus apiculata (M. luma). M. communis (Common Myrtle). M. c. tarentina. M. c. 'Variegata'.

NANDINA
Sacred Bamboo, Heavenly Bamboo. Chinese Sacred Bamboo.
Time to buy Pot-grown, any time except January. Balled, October–May. Avoid adverse weather conditions.
Where to find Outside in Shrubs or, wrongly, Perennials.
Size Height 9 in (23 cm) min. Single or multi-stemmed. Nandina domestica and N. d. 'Nana Purpurea' open bamboo-type habit. Nandina domestica 'Fire Power' bushy.
Foliage Evergreen. Yellowish-green spring and summer. Orange, red and purple autumn. Premature basal leaf drop.
Roots Pots 5 in (12 cm) min. dia. Balled, good fibrous root system.
Hints Any well-prepared soil, except al-

kaline, plus extra organic material. May be scarce, but becoming more widely available. If kept under cover in winter, avoid planting until spring frosts over.

Most widely available *Nandina domestica. N. d.* 'Fire Power'. *N. d.* 'Nana Purpurea'.

NEILLIA THIBETICA syn. *Neillia longiracemosa*

Time to buy Pot-grown, any time except January. Balled root-wrapped and bare-rooted, October–May. Avoid adverse weather conditions.

Where to find Outside in Shrubs.

Size Height 15 in (40 cm) min. Single or multi-stemmed.

Foliage Deciduous. Spring/summer, light to mid green. Premature autumn colour and leaf drop.

Roots Pots 5 in (12 cm) min. dia. Balled, root-wrapped and bare-rooted, good fibrous root system.

Hints Any well-prepared soil. Looks uninteresting until established.

NERIUM OLEANDER
Oleander

Time to buy Pot-grown, any time for use under protection.

Where to find Indoors in House Plants. Can only be used outside in summer.

Size Height 2 ft (60 cm) min. Minimum three upright stems. Limited side shoots.

Foliage Evergreen. Light green with reddish hue. Premature basal leaf drop.

Roots Pots 5 in (12 cm) min. dia.

Hints If pot-grown, use good quality lime-free potting compost in large pot. If planted in conservatory or greenhouse beds, any well-prepared soil, plus extra organic material. Scarce. Not hardy in U.K. Can be used in containers outside in summer.

Most widely available Offered in a range of colours – pink, red, purple, white and pale yellow.

OLEARIA
Daisy Bush, Tree Daisy, Tree Aster Australian Daisy Bush.

Time to buy Pot-grown, April–July. Avoid adverse weather conditions.

Where to find Outside in Shrubs.

Size Height 1 ft (30 cm) min. Single or multi-stemmed.

Foliage Evergreen. Grey-green. Premature basal leaf drop.

Roots Pots 4 in (10 cm) min. dia.

Hints Any well-prepared soil, plus extra organic material. If kept under cover in winter, avoid planting until spring frosts have finished. Wide range. May need winter protection.

Most widely available *Olearia × haastii. O. macrodonta* (New Zealand Holly). *O. mollis. O. nummularifolia. O. phlogopappa* (*O. gunniana*) (Tasmanian Daisy Bush). *O. p. subrepanda* (*O. subrepanda*). *O. × scilloniensis. O. stellulata* 'Splendens'.

OSMANTHUS

Time to buy Pot-grown, any time except January. Avoid adverse weather conditions.

Where to find Outside in Shrubs.

Size Height 9 in (23 cm) min. Single or multi-stemmed.

Foliage Evergreen. Mid to dark green. Premature basal leaf drop.

Roots Pots 5 in (12 cm) min. dia.

Hints Any well-prepared soil. May be scarce. If kept under cover in winter, avoid planting until spring frosts have finished. In severe winters, foliage may be damaged by frost.

Most widely available *Osmanthus armatus. O.* 'Burkwoodii' (*Osmarea* 'Burkwoodii'). *O. delavayi. O. heterophyllus* (*O. aquifolium*). *O. ilicifolius* (Holly Osmanthus. False Holly). *O. h.* 'Aureomarginatus'. *O. h.* 'Gulftide'. *O. h.* 'Purpureus'. *O. h.* 'Rotundifolia'. *O. h.* 'Variegatus'.

OSMARONIA CERASIFORMIS syn.
Nuttallia cerasiiformis
Oso Berry
Time to buy Pot-grown, any time. Avoid adverse weather conditions.
Where to find Outside in Shrubs.
Size Height 15 in (40 cm) min. Single or multi-stemmed.
Foliage Deciduous. Spring/summer, light to mid green. Premature autumn colour and leaf drop.
Roots Pots 5 in (12 cm) min. dia.
Hints Any well-prepared soil. Scarce. Looks uninteresting until established.

**OZOTHAMNUS
ROSMARINIFOLIUS**
Time to buy Pot-grown, from April–July. Avoid adverse weather conditions.
Where to find Outside in Shrubs.
Size Height 9 in (23 cm) min. Single or multi-stemmed.
Foliage Evergreen. Dark grey-green.
Roots Pots 5 in (12 cm) min. dia.
Hints Any well-prepared soil, plus extra organic material. Scarce. If kept under cover in winter, avoid planting until spring frosts have finished. Takes some years to show full potential.

PACHYSANDRA
Japanese Pachysandra, Japanese Spurge, Mountain Spurge
Time to buy Pot-grown, any time. Avoid adverse weather conditions.
Where to find Outside in Shrubs.
Size Height 3 in (8 cm) min. Minimum three short shoots from soil level.
Foliage Evergreen. Mid green or variegated. Premature basal leaf drop.
Roots Pots 3 in (8 cm) min. dia.
Hints Well-prepared neutral to acid soil. If kept under cover in winter, avoid planting until spring frosts have finished. Yellowing from July onwards. Dislikes being grown in container.
Most widely available Pachysandra terminalis. P. t. 'Variegata'.

PAEONIA (grown as tree)
Tree Peony
Time to buy Pot-grown, April–July, except *Paeonia lutea* var. 'Ludlowii' planted any time. Avoid adverse weather conditions.
Where to find Outside in Shrubs or Perennials.
Size Height 6 in (15 cm) min. Normally single-stemmed. Multi-stemmed acceptable.
Foliage Deciduous. Spring/summer, green. Premature autumn colour and leaf drop.
Roots Pots 4 in (10 cm) min. dia.
Hints Any well-prepared soil, plus extra organic material. Scarce, apart from *Paeonia lutea* var. 'Ludlowii'. Named forms *Paeonia suffruticosa* extremely scarce. If kept under protection in winter, avoid planting until spring frosts have finished. Hardiness in doubt, except *Paeonia lutea* var. 'Ludlowii'.
Most widely available *Paeonia lutea* var. 'Ludlowii'. *P. delavayi*. *P. suffruticosa* (Japanese Tree Peony. Mountain Peony). Colours: white, flesh pink, rose pink, red, dark red, pale yellow or yellow.

PALIURUS SPINA-CHRISTI
Christ's Thorn, Jerusalem Thorn
Time to buy Pot-grown, any time except January. Avoid adverse weather conditions.
Where to find Outside in Shrubs.
Size Height 15 in (40 cm) min. Single or multi-stemmed.
Foliage Deciduous. Spring/summer, light to mid green. Premature autumn colour and leaf drop.
Roots Pots 5 in (12 cm) min. dia.
Hints Any well-prepared soil. Looks uninteresting in garden centres and needs planting to achieve full potential.

PARAHEBE CATARRACTAE syn.
Veronica catarractae
Time to buy Pot-grown, April–July. Avoid

adverse weather conditions. Can be planted in flower.

Where to find Outside in Shrubs, Alpines or Perennials.

Size Height 3 in (8 cm) min. Single or multi-stemmed.

Foliage Evergreen. Mid green, with purplish hue. Premature basal leaf drop.

Roots Pots 3 in (8 cm) min. dia. Larger for preference.

Hints Any well-prepared soil. Normally only available in spring. Hardiness suspect. If kept under cover in winter, avoid planting until spring frosts have finished. Truly a shrub, but thought of as an alpine.

PERNETTYA

Time to buy Pot-grown, any time except January. Balled, October–May. Avoid adverse weather conditions. Can be planted in flower or fruit.

Where to find Outside in Shrubs or Acid-loving Plants.

Size Height 9 in (23 cm) min. Multistemmed. Minimum three upright shoots.

Foliage Evergreen. Dark green. Premature basal leaf drop.

Roots Pots 5 in (12 cm) min. dia. Balled, good fibrous root system.

Hints Well-prepared neutral to acid soil, plus extra organic material. If kept under cover in winter, avoid planting until spring frosts have finished. Male and female plants needed for fruiting, at a ratio of one male to any number of females, planted not more than twenty yards apart.

Most widely available *Pernettya mucronata* (F). *P. m.* 'Alba' (F). *P. m.* 'Bell's Seedling' (M/F). *P. m.* 'Crimsoniana' (F). *P. m.* 'Davis's Hybrids' (F). *P. m.* 'Lilacine' (F). *P. m.* 'Lillian' (F). *P. m.* 'Mascula' (M). *P. m.* 'Mother of Pearl' (F). *P. m.* 'Mulberry Wine' (F). *P. m.* 'Pink Pearl' (F). *P. m.* 'Sea Shell' (F). *P. m.* 'Signal' (F). *P. m.* 'White Pearl' (F). *P. m.* Wintertime' (F).

PEROVSKIA
Russian Sage

Time to buy Pot-grown, April–July. Avoid adverse weather conditions.

Where to find Outside in Shrubs.

Size Spring, height 4 in (10 cm) min., reaching 1½ ft (50 cm) min. including flower spikes August.

Foliage Deciduous. Spring/summer, grey. Premature autumn colour and leaf drop.

Roots Pots 4 in (10 cm) min. dia. Large for preference.

Hints Any well-prepared soil. Best spring-planted but may be scarce. Usually sold when in flower in August–September. If kept under cover in winter, avoid planting until spring frosts have finished. Cut back all previous season's growth to within 2 in (5 cm) of origin in April. Repeat annually.

Most widely available *Perovskia atriplicifolia. P. s.* 'Blue Spire'.

PHILADELPHUS
Mock Orange

Time to buy Pot-grown, any time except January. Root-wrapped and bare-rooted, October–May. Avoid adverse weather conditions.

Where to find Outside in Shrubs.

Size Height 1½ ft (50 cm) min. Low growing, height 6 in (15 cm). Multi-stemmed.

Foliage Deciduous. Spring/summer, mid green, gold or white variegated. Premature autumn colour and leaf drop.

Roots Pots 5 in (12 cm) min. dia. Rootwrapped and bare-rooted, good fibrous root system.

Hints Any well-prepared soil. Wide range. *Philadelphus coronarius* 'Aureus' and *P. c.* 'Variegatum' require protection from summer sun, if this is not given will show signs of scorching. If kept under cover in winter, avoid planting until spring frosts have finished.

Most widely available

LOW-GROWING *Philadelphus* 'Boule d' Argent'. *P. coronarius* 'Variegata'. *P.*

'Manteau d'Hermine'. *P. microphyllus. P.*
'Silver Showers'.
MEDIUM HEIGHT *Philadelphus* 'Ava-
lanche'. *P.* 'Belle Etoile'. *P.* 'Erectus'. *P.*
'Galahad'. *P.* 'Innocence'. *P.* 'Sybille'.
TALL-GROWING *Philadelphus* 'Beauclerk'.
P. 'Buckley's Quill'. *P.* 'Burfordensis'. *P.*
'Burkwoodii'.   *P.   coronarius.   P. c.*
'Aureus'. *P.* 'Minnesota Snowflake'. *P.*
'Norma'. *P.* 'Virginal'. *P.* 'Voie Lactée'.

PHILLYREA
Jasmine Box
Time to buy Pot-grown, any time except
January. Balled, October–May. Avoid adverse weather conditions.
Where to find Outside in Shrubs.
Size Height 1 ft (30 cm) min. Single or
multi-stemmed.
Foliage Evergreen. Mid to dark green. Premature basal leaf drop.
Roots Pots 5 in (12 cm) min. dia. Balled,
good fibrous root system.
Hints Any well-prepared soil. May be
scarce. If kept under cover in winter,
avoid planting until spring frosts have
finished.
Most widely available *Phillyrea angustifolia. P. decora (P. medwediewii). P.
latifolia.*

PHLOMIS
Time to buy Pot-grown, any time except
January. Avoid adverse weather condi-
tions.
Where to find Outside in Shrubs.
Size Height 9 in (23 cm) min. Single or
multi-stemmed.
Foliage Evergreen. Grey to grey-green.
Premature basal leaf drop.
Roots Pots 5 in (12 cm) min. dia.
Hints Any well-prepared soil, plus extra
organic material. May be scarce. If kept
under cover in winter, avoid planting
until spring frosts have finished.
Most widely available *Phlomis chryso-
phylla. P. fruticosa* (Jerusalem sage). *P.
italica.*

PHORMIUM
New Zealand Flax
Time to buy Pot-grown, April–July. Avoid
adverse weather conditions.
Where to find Outside in Shrubs or
Perennials.
Size Height 9 in (23 cm) min. Minimum
three upright leaf spears.
Foliage Evergreen. Dark green, purple or
red or yellow variegated. Premature basal
leaf drop. Leaf spears bent July onwards.
Roots Pots 5 in (12 cm) min. dia.
Hints Any well-prepared soil, plus extra
organic material. May be scarce. If kept
under cover in winter, avoid planting
until spring frosts have finished. Wide
range, many not entirely hardy. Avoid
newly potted plants in spring.
Most widely available *Phormium cook-
ianum* 'Cream Delight'. *P. colensoi* 'Cream
Delight'. *P. tenax* (New Zealand Flax).
P. t. 'Bronze Baby'. *P. t.* 'Dazzler'. *P. t.*
'Maori Sunrise'. *P. t.* 'Purpureum'. *P. t.*
'Sundowner'. *P. t.* 'Tricolor'. *P. t.* 'Variegatum'. *P. t.* 'Yellow Wave'.

PHOTINIA
Photinia also contains Stranvaesia and
names are listed accordingly.
Time to buy Pot-grown, any time except
January. Avoid adverse weather conditions.
Where to find Outside in Shrubs.
Size Height 1½ ft (50 cm) min. Single or
multi-stemmed.
Foliage Evergreen. Dark green. Premature
basal leaf drop.
Roots Pots 5 in (12 cm) min. dia.
Hints Any well-prepared soil, plus extra
organic material. If kept under cover in
winter, avoid planting until spring frosts
have finished. *Photiniastranvaesia* section
may still be labelled as *Stranvaesia*: this
will take many years to change completely in the industry.
Most widely available
PHOTINIA GROUP *Photinia* × *fraseri* 'Birmingham'. *P.* × *f.* 'Red Robin', *P. glabra*

'Red Robin'. *P. glabra* 'Rubens'. *P. serrulata* (Chinese Hawthorn).
STRANVAESIA GROUP *Photinia davidiana*. *P. d.* 'Fructuluteo'. *P. d.* 'Prostrata'. *P. d. var undulata. P. d. undulata* 'Palett'.

PHYGELIUS
Cape Figwort
Time to buy Pot-grown, April–August, although can be planted any time. Avoid adverse weather conditions.
Where to find Outside in Shrubs and Perennials.
Size April–May, height 6 in (15 cm) min. July, 15 in (40 cm) min. Single or multi-stemmed.
Foliage Deciduous. Spring/summer, light or dark green. Premature autumn colour and leaf drop.
Roots Pots 4 in (10 cm) min. dia. Larger for preference.
Hints Any well-prepared soil. Wide range. *Phygelius aequalis*, hardiness suspect and of perennial nature. All look straggly and misshapen.
Most widely available *Phygelius aequalis* 'Yellow Trumpet'. *P. capensis* 'Coccineus'.

PIERIS syn. *Andromeda*
Pieris, Lily of the Valley Shrub
Time to buy Pot-grown, any time except January. Balled, October–May. Avoid adverse weather conditions.
Where to find Outside in Shrubs or Acid-loving Plants.
Size Height 6 in (15 cm) min. Single or multi-stemmed.
Foliage Evergreen. Dark green or variegated. New growth red to orange-red in spring. Premature basal leaf drop.
Roots Pots 5 in (12 cm) min. dia. Balled, good fibrous root system.
Hints Well-prepared acid to neutral soil, plus extra organic material. If kept under cover in winter, avoid planting until spring frosts have finished. Wide range. Need for acid soil not always stated.

Most widely available *Pieris floribunda*. *P. formosa*. *P. f. forrestii*. *P. f.* 'Wakehurst'. *P. f.* 'Forest Flame'. *P. japonica P. j.* 'Bert Chandler'. *P. j.* 'Christmas Cheer'. *P. j.* 'Fire Crest'. *P. j.* 'Flamingo'. *P. j.* 'Flaming Silver'. *P. j.* 'Little Heath Green'. *P. j.* 'Mountain Fire'. *P. j.* 'Pink Delight'. *P. j.* 'Red Mill'. *P. j.* 'Scarlet O'Hara'. *P. j.* 'Variegata'. *P. j.* 'White Pearl'. *P. taiwanensis*.

PIPTANTHUS
Evergreen Laburnum
Time to buy Pot-grown, any time except January. Avoid adverse weather conditions.
Where to find Outside in Shrubs or Climbers.
Size Height 2 ft (60 cm) min. Multi-stemmed.
Foliage Evergreen. Mid to dark green. Premature basal leaf drop.
Roots Pots 5 in (12 cm) min. dia.
Hints Any well-prepared soil, plus extra organic material. Scarce. If kept under cover in winter, avoid planting until spring frosts have finished. Looks gaunt and straggly. For wall use, plant 15–18 in (40–50 cm) away from wall. Will need wires or other training support.
Most widely available *Piptanthus laburnifolius*.

PITTOSPORUM
Kohuha
Time to buy Pot-grown, April–July. Avoid adverse weather conditions.
Where to find Outside in Shrubs. Indoors in House Plants.
Size Height 9 in (23 cm) min. Normally single-stemmed. Numerous side shoots.
Foliage Evergreen. Grey-green, purple, white or golden variegated. Premature basal leaf drop.
Roots Pots 5 in (12 cm) min. dia.
Hints Any well-prepared soil, plus extra organic material. Wide range. If kept under cover in winter, avoid planting until spring frosts have finished.

Hardiness suspect. Container-grown, use good quality potting compost. For wall use, plant 15–18 in (40–50 cm) away from wall. Will require wires or other training support.

Most widely available *Pittosporum tenuifolium*. *P. t.* 'Garnetti'. *P. t.* 'Irene Paterson'. *P. t.* 'James Stirling'. *P. t.* 'Purpureum'. *P. t.* 'Silver Queen'. *P. t.* 'Tresederi'. *P. t.* 'Warnham Gold'. *P. tobira* (Japanese Pittosporum. Tobiri Pittosporum). *P. t.* 'Variegatum'.

PONCIRUS TRIFOLIATA syn. *Citrus trifoliata*
Hardy Orange, Japanese Bitter Orange, Trifoliate Orange

Time to buy Pot-grown, any time except January. Avoid adverse weather conditions.

Where to find Outside in Shrubs.

Size Height 5 in (12 cm) min. Irregular stiff shoots.

Foliage Deciduous. Spring/summer, mid green. Premature autumn colour and leaf drop.

Roots Pots 4 in (10 cm) min. dia.

Hints Any well-prepared soil, plus extra organic material. Scarce. If kept under cover in winter, avoid planting until spring frosts have finished.

POTENTILLA
Shrubby Cinquefoil, Buttercup Shrub, Five Finger

Time to buy Pot-grown, any time except January. Balled, root-wrapped and bare-rooted, October–May. Avoid adverse weather conditions.

Where to find Outside in Shrubs.

Size Height 6 in (15 cm) min. Single or multi-stemmed. *Potentilla arbusula* 'Beesii' and *P. dahurica* 'Manchu', height 4 in (10 cm) min., spread 6 in (15 cm) min.

Foliage Deciduous. Spring/summer, green to grey-green. Premature autumn colour and leaf drop.

Roots Pots 4 in (10 cm) min. dia. Balled, root-wrapped and bare-rooted, good fibrous root system.

Hints Any well-prepared soil. Wide range. Looks lifeless and dead early spring, quickly grows away.

Most widely available *Potentilla arbuscula*. *P. a.* 'Beesii' (*P. fruticosa* 'Beesii'). *P. a.* 'Nana Argentea'. *P. dahurica* 'Abbotswood'. *P. d.* 'Abbotswood Silver'. *P. d.* 'Manchu' (*P. mandshurica fruticosa*). *P. d.* 'Mount Everest' (*P. fruticosa* 'Mount Everest'). *P. d.* var. *veitchii* (*P. fruticosa veitchii*). *P.* 'Dart's Golddigger', *P.* 'Daydawn'. *P.* 'Elizabeth' (*P. fruticosa* 'Elizabeth'). *P. fruticosa*. *P.* 'Goldfinger'. *P.* 'Goldstar'. *P.* 'Hopley's Orange'. *P.* Kobold'. *P.* 'Pink Pearl'. *P.* 'Jackman's Variety'. *P.* 'Katherine Dykes'. *P.* 'Longacre'. *P.* 'Maanelys (*P.* 'Moonlight'). *P. parvifolia*. *P. p.* 'Buttercup'. *P. p.* 'Klondike' (*P. fruticosa* 'Klondike'). *P. p.* 'Pretty Polly'. *P.* 'Primrose Beauty' (*P. fruticosa* 'Primrose Beauty'). *P.* 'Princess'. *P.* 'Red Ace'. *P.* 'Royal Flush'. *P.* 'Sanved' (*P. sandudana*). *P.* 'Sunset'. *P.* 'Tangerine'. *P.* 'Tilford Cream'. *P.* 'Vilmoriniana'.

PRUNUS (shrub forms)
Laurel, Cherry Laurel, Portuguese Laurel, Purple Plum

Time to buy Pot-grown, any time except January. *Prunus laurocerasus*, *P. l.* 'Rotundifolia', *P. × cistena*, *P. c.* 'Nigra', *P. mume* 'Green Glow' and *P. c. cistena* 'Purple Flash', bare-rooted, October–May. Avoid adverse weather conditions.

Where to find Outside in Shrubs. *Prunus laurocerasus*, *P. l.* 'Rotundifolia', *P. lusitanica*, *P. cerasifera* 'Nigra'. *P. c.* 'Blaze', *P. c.* 'Purple Flash', *P. c.* 'Green Glow' outside in Hedging.

Size Height 1 ft (30 cm) min. Single or multi-stemmed. *P. laurocerasus* and *P. lusitanica* may be found as pre-trained mop-headed standards, clear stem 3–6 ft (1–2 m), height 4 ft (1.2 m) min.

Foliage DECIDUOUS Spring/summer, green or purple. Premature autumn colour and leaf drop. EVERGREEN Mid green, purple-green or variegated. Premature basal leaf drop.

Roots DECIDUOUS Pots 5 in (12 m) min. dia. EVERGREEN Pots 6 in (15 cm) min. dia. Bare-rooted, good fibrous root system.

Hints Any well-prepared soil. Evergreens may show round holes in leaves caused by leaf-cutting bees. Deciduous forms suffer from bacterial leaf and stem canker. *Prunus triloba* is grafted and may produce suckers. European stock of *Prunus tenella* and *P. triloba* need the addition of extra organic material when planting.

Most widely available
DECIDUOUS *Prunus cerasifera* 'Nigra' (Purple Plum). *P. c.* 'Blaze'. *P. c.* 'Purple flash'. *P.* × *cistena* 'Crimson Dwarf'. (Purple-leaf Sand Cherry. Dwarf Crimson Cherry). *P. glandulosa* (Chinese Bush Cherry. Dwarf Flowering Almond). *P. g.* 'Albiplena'. *P. incisa* 'Beniome'. *P. mume* (Japanese Apricot). *P. myrobalum* 'Greenglow'. *P. tenella* (Dwarf Russian Almond). *P. t.* 'Fire Hill'. *P. triloba* (*P. t. multiplex*). *P. t.* 'White Fruits'.
EVERGREEN *Prunus laurocerasus* (English Laurel. Cherry Laurel). *P. l.* 'Camelliifolia'. *P. l.* 'Magnoliifolia'. *P. l.* 'Otto Luyken'. *P. l.* 'Rotundifolia'. *P. l.* 'Schipkaensis'. *P. l.* 'Variegata'. *P. l.* 'Zabeliana'. *P. lusitanica.* (Portuguese Laurel). *P. l. var. azorica. P. l.* 'Variegata'.

PSEUDOSASA syn. *Arundinaria*
Bamboo, Japanese Bamboo, Sassa
Time to buy Pot-grown, any time except January. Balled, October–May. Avoid adverse weather conditions.
Where to find Outside in Shrubs or sometimes Perennials.
Size Height 1½ ft (50 cm) min. Minimum three upright shoots. *Pseudosasa pumila*, *P. pygmaea*, *P. variegata*, *P. viridistriata* and *Sassa palmatum*, height 9 in (23 cm) min.

Foliage Evergreen. Dark green, silver or golden variegated. Premature basal leaf drop. *Sassa palmatum*, off-white band around each leaf edge.
Roots Pots 5 in (12 cm) min. dia. Balled, good fibrous root system.
Hints Any well-prepared soil, plus extra organic material. Avoid tall plants with limited upright shoots.
Most widely available *Pseudosasa japonica. P. humilis. P. murieliae. P. nitida. P. pumila. P. pygmaea. P. variegata. P. viridistriata (P. auricoma). Sassa palmatum.*

PYRACANTHA
Firethorn
Time to buy Pot-grown, any time except January. Avoid adverse weather conditions.
Where to find Outside in Shrubs, Climbers or Hedging.
Size Height 1½ ft (50 cm) min. Normally single-stemmed. Numerous thorny side shoots. Also offered as large shrubs, height 3–5 ft (1–1.5 m) or pre-trained, mop-headed standards, clear stem 3 ft (1 m) min., height 4 ft (1.2 m) min.
Foliage Evergreen. Dark green or white variegated. Premature basal leaf drop.
Roots Pots 5 in (12 cm) min. dia.
Hints Any well-prepared soil. Wide range. If kept under cover in winter, avoid planting until spring frosts have finished. Avoid plants with signs of dieback; this could be a sign of Fire blight. Stake should be provided. For wall use, plant 15–18 in (40–50 cm) away from wall.
Most widely available *Pyracantha* 'Alexander Pendula'. *P. angustifolia. P. atalantiodes (P. gibbsii)* (Gibbs Firethorn). *P. a.* 'Aurea' (*P.* 'Flava') *P. coccinea* 'Lalandei'. *P. c.* 'Sparklers'. *P.* 'Golden Charmer'. *P.* 'Harlequin'. *P.* 'Mojave'. *P.* 'Orange Charmer'. *P.* 'Orange Glow'. *P.* 'Red Cushion'. *P. rogersiana. P. r.* 'Flava'. *P.* 'Shawnee'. *P.* 'Soleil d'Or'. *P.* 'Teton'.

RHAMNUS
Buckthorn

Time to buy Pot-grown, any time except January. Avoid adverse weather conditions.

Where to find Outside in Shrubs. Indoors in House Plants.

Size Height 9 in (23 cm) min. Single-stemmed.

Foliage DECIDUOUS Spring/summer, grey-green. Premature autumn colour and leaf drop. EVERGREEN Grey-green, white variegated. Premature basal leaf drop.

Roots Pots 5 in (12 cm) min. dia.

Hints Any well-prepared soil, plus extra organic material. May be scarce. If kept under cover in winter, avoid planting until spring frosts have finished. *Rhamnus alaterna* 'Argenteovariegata', hardiness suspect. Other forms hardy. *Rhamnus alaterna* 'Argenteovariegata' container-grown, use good quality potting compost. For wall use, plant 15–18 in (40–50 cm) away from wall. Requires wires for training.

RHODODENDRONS

Time to buy Pot-grown, any time except January. Balled, October–May. Avoid adverse weather conditions.

Where to find Outside in Shrubs, Acid-loving Plants or Rhododendron area.

Size DWARF-GROWING Height 5 in (12 cm) min. Numerous side shoots. TALL-GROWING Height 1½ ft (50 cm) min. Minimum three main stems.

Foliage Evergreen. Dark green, golden or white variegated. Premature basal leaf drop.

Roots DWARF Pots 5 in (12 cm) min. dia. TALL Pots 10 in (25 cm) min. dia. Balled, good fibrous root system.

Hints Well-prepared acid soil, plus extra organic material. Wide range normally offered in flower. Outside of this time, may be scarce.

Most widely available
DWARF-GROWING *Rhododendron* 'Blue-

bird'. R. 'Blue Diamond'. R. 'Blue Tit'. R. 'Bow Bells.' R. 'Bric-a-Brac'. R. 'Carmen'. R. 'Elisabeth Hobbie'. R. 'Elizabeth'. R. *ferrugineum* (Alpen Rose of Switzerland). R. *hirsutum*. R. 'Humming Bird'. R. 'Moonstone'. R. *impeditum*. R. *moupinense*. R. *obtusum* 'Amoenum Coccineum'. R. *pemakoense*. R. 'Pink Drift'. R. 'Praecox'. R. *racemosum*. R. *saluenense*. R. 'Scarlet Wonder'. R. *williamsianum*. R. *yakushimanum*. R. 'Yellow Hammer'.

TALL-GROWING, LARGE FLOWERING *Rhododendron* 'Bagshot Ruby'. R. 'Betty Wormald'. R. 'Blue Peter'. R. 'Britannia'. R. 'Coutess of Athlone'. R. 'Countess of Derby'. R. 'Cynthia'. R. 'Earl of Donoughmore'. R. 'Fastuosum Flore Pleno'. R. 'General Eisenhower'. R. 'Goldsworth Orange'. R. 'Gomer Waterer'. R. 'Kluis Sensation'. R. 'Kluis Triumph'. R. 'Lord Roberts'. R. 'Madame de Bruin'. R. 'Moser's Maroon'. R. 'Mrs G. W. Leak'. R. 'Old Port'. R. 'Pink Pearl'. R. *ponticum*. R. *p.* 'Variegatum'. R. 'Purple Splendour'. R. 'Sappho'. R. 'Susan'. R. 'Unique'.
Many other forms.

RHODOTYPOS SCANDENS
White Jew's Mallow, Black Jetbead

Time to buy Pot-grown, any time except January. Avoid adverse weather conditions.

Where to find Outside in Shrubs.

Size Height 1½ ft (50 cm) min. Single or multi-stemmed.

Foliage Deciduous. Spring/summer, mid green. Premature autumn colour and leaf drop.

Roots Pots 5 in (12 cm) min. dia.

Hints Any well-prepared soil. May be scarce. Often look gaunt and spindly when young.

RIBES
Flowering Currant

Time to buy Pot-grown, any time except January. Balled, root-wrapped and bare-

rooted, October–May. Avoid adverse weather conditions.
Where to find Outside in Shrubs. *Ribes
henryi* in Climbers.
Size Height 15 in (40 cm) min. Single or
multi-stemmed. *Ribes sanguineum* 'Broc-
klebankii' 1 ft (30 cm) min.
Foliage Deciduous. Spring/summer, light
to mid green or golden. Premature
autumn colour and leaf drop. *Ribes laurifolium*, grey/green, evergreen foliage.
Roots Pots 5 in (12 cm) min. dia. Balled,
root-wrapped and bare-rooted, good
fibrous root system.
Hints Any well-prepared soil. European
stock potted in winter may not be established by spring. Do not purchase unless
they have good foliage.
Most widely available *Ribes alpinum*
(Alpine Currant). *R. americanum* (American Blackcurrant). *R. × gordonianum. R.
henryi. R laurifolium* (E). *R. odoratum*
(Buffalo Currant. Clove Currant). *R. sanguineum* (Flowering Currant). *R. s.*
'Album'. *R. s.* 'Atrorubens'. *R. s.* 'Brockle-
bankii'. *R. s.* 'King Edward VII'. *R. s.* 'Pulborough Scarlet'. *R. s.* 'Splendens'. *R. s.*
'Tydeman's White'. *R. speciosum. R. vib-
urnifolium.*

ROMNEYA
Tree Poppy, California Tree Poppy
Time to buy Pot-grown, April–July. Avoid
adverse weather conditions.
Where to find Outside in Shrubs or
Perennials.
Size April–May: height 6 in (15 cm) min.
May–August: 1½ ft (50 cm) min.
Foliage Deciduous. Spring/summer, grey-
green. Premature autumn colour and leaf
drop.
Roots Pots 5 in (12 cm) min.
Hints Any well-prepared soil, plus extra
organic material. Scarce. Can become in-
vasive.
Most widely available *Romneya coulteri.
R. × hybrida* 'White Cloud'.

ROSMARINUS
Rosemary
Time to buy Pot-grown, April–August.
Avoid adverse weather conditions.
Where to find Outside in Shrubs or
Herbs.
Size Height 3 in (8 cm) min. Normally
single-stemmed. Limited side shoots.
Foliage Evergreen, grey-green. Premature
basal leaf drop.
Roots Pots 3 in (8 cm) min. dia. with 5 in
(12 cm) min. for preference.
Hints Any well-prepared soil. Wide
range. Hardiness suspect. If kept under
cover in winter, avoid planting until
spring frosts have finished. May need pro-
tection first winter after planting.
Most widely available *Rosmarinus an-
gustifolia* (Narrow-leaved Rosemary).
R. a. 'Corsican Blue'. *R. lavandulaceus* (*R.
officinalis prostratus*). *R. officinalis*
(Common Rosemary). *R. o.* 'Albus'. *R. o.*
'Aurea Variegata'. *R. o* 'Benenden Blue'.
R. o. 'Fastigiatus (*R. o.* 'Pyramidalis').
R. o. 'Roseus'. *R. o.* 'Severn Sea.' *R. o.*
'Tuscan Blue'.

RUBUS
Bramble, Blackberry, Ground-covering
Bramble
Time to buy Pot-grown, any time except
January. Balled October–May. Avoid ad-
verse weather conditions.
Where to find Outside in Shrubs or
Ground-Cover.
Size SHRUBS Height 1½ ft (50 cm) min.
Minimum two upright stems. GROUND-
COVER Spread 1 ft (30 cm) min. Minimum
two main shoots. *Rubus calycinoides*,
spread 4 in (10 cm) min.
Foliage SHRUBS Deciduous. Spring/
summer mid green. Premature autumn
colour and leaf drop. GROUND-COVER
Evergreen. Mid green or variegated. Pre-
mature basal leaf drop.
Roots SHRUBS Pots 5 in (12 cm) min. dia.
GROUND-COVER Pots 4 in (10 cm) min.
dia. Balled, good fibrous root system.

Hints Any well-prepared soil, plus extra organic material. Wide range. Some forms may be scarce. Looks straggly until planted out.
Most widely available
SHRUBS R. *deliciosus* (D). R. *odoratus* (D). R. *spectabilis* (Salmon Berry) (D). R. *tridel* (D). R. t. 'Benenden' (D). R. *ulmifolius* 'Bellidiflorus.
WHITE-STEMMED R. *biflorus*. R. *cockburnianus* (R. *giraldianus*). R. *thibetanus*..
GROUND COVER R. *calycinoides* (R. *fockeanus*) (E). R. *microphyllus* 'Variegatus' (E). R. *tricolor* (E).

RUSCUS
Butcher's Broom, Box Holly
Time to buy Pot-grown, any time except January. Avoid adverse weather conditions.
Where to find Outside in Shrubs.
Size Height 6 in (15 cm). Minimum three upright shoots.
Foliage Evergreen. Dark green. Premature basal leaf drop.
Roots Pots 5 in (12 cm) min. dia.
Hints Any well-prepared soil. Scarce.
Most widely available Ruscus *aculeatus*. R. *hypoglossum*.

RUTA
Rue, Herb of Grace
Time to buy Pot-grown, April–August.
Where to find Outside in Shrubs or Herbs.
Size Height 3 in (8 cm) min. Single-stemmed.
Foliage Evergreen. Grey-green, blue or variegated. Premature basal leaf drop.
Roots Pots 3 in (8 cm) min. dia., 5 in (12 cm) for preference.
Hints Any well-prepared soil. Wide range. If kept under cover in winter, avoid planting until spring frosts have finished. Hardiness in doubt. SKIN CONTACT CAN CAUSE BLISTERS.
Most widely available Ruta *graveolens*. R. g. 'Jackman's Blue'. R. g. 'Variegata'.

SALIX
Willow
Time to buy Pot-grown any time except January. Balled, root-wrapped and bare-rooted, October–May. Avoid adverse weather conditions.
Where to find Outside in Shrubs. Occasionally in Alpines (Low-growing).
Size LOW-GROWING Height 6 in (15 cm) min. Single or multi-shooted. TALL-GROWING Height 1½ ft (50 cm) min. Single or multi-stemmed. Minimum two upright stems. Also hardwood cuttings for growing *in situ*.
Foliage Deciduous. Spring/summer, grey-green, purple-grey or variegated. Premature autumn colour and leaf drop.
Roots Pots 5 in (12 cm) min. dia. Balled, root-wrapped and bare-rooted, good fibrous root system.
Hints Any well-prepared soil. May be scarce. Low-growing, slow-growing, small and irregular.
Most widely available
LOW-GROWING Salix *alba integra maculata* (S. 'Hakuro Nishikii'). S. 'Fuiri-Koriyangi'. S. *bockii*. S. × *boydii*. S. *hastata* 'Wehrhahnii' S. *helvetica*. S. *lanata* (Woolly Willow). S. l. 'Stuartii'. S. *lapponum* (Lapland Willow. Downy Willow). S. *melanostachys* (S. 'Kurome') (Black Catkin Willow). S. *moupinensis*. S. *purpurea* ('Gracilis') (S. p. 'Nana'). S. *repena argentea*.
TALL-GROWING Salix *acutifolia* 'Blue Streak'. S. a. 'Pendulifolia'. S. *adenophylla*. S. *aegyptiaca* (S. *medemii*) (Egyptian Musk Willow) S. *alba* (White Willow). S. a. 'Chermesina (S. a. 'Britzensis') (Scarlet Willow). S. a. 'Sericea' (S. a. 'Argentea') (Silver Willow). S. a. 'Vitellina' (Golden Willow). S. *caprea* (Goat Willow. Great Sallow. Palm Willow. Pussy Willow). S. *cinerea* (Grey Sallow). S. *daphnoides* (Violet Willow). S. d. 'Aglaia'. S. *elaeagnos* (S. *incana*). S. *rosmarinifolia* (Hoary Willow). S. *exigua* (Coyote Willow). S. *fargesii*. S. *graci-*

listyla (Rosegold Pussy Willow). *S.* 'Hakuro'. *S.* 'Harlequin'. *S. humilis* (Prairie Willow). *S. irrorata*. *S. magnifica* (Magnolia-leaved Willow). *S. phylicifolia* (Tea-leaf Willow). *S. purpurea* (Purple Osier Willow). *S. p.* 'Eugenei'. *S. sachalinensis* 'Sekka' (*S.* 'Setsuka). *S.* × *smithiana*. *S.* 'The Hague'. *S.* × *tsugaluensis* 'Ginme'.

SALVIA (grown as shrub)
Sage
Time to buy Pot-grown, April–July. Avoid adverse weather conditions.
Where to find Outside in Shrubs. Can be planted in flower.
Size Spring, height 4 in (10 cm) min. Midsummer, height 6 in (15 cm) min. Multishooted, bushy.
Foliage Evergreen. Green, grey-green, purple, silver or golden variegated. Premature basal leaf drop.
Roots Pots 4 in (10 cm) min. dia.
Hints Any well-prepared soil. If kept under cover in winter, avoid planting until spring frosts have finished. Available all year, best purchased April–July. Except for *Salvia microphylla* (*S. grahamii*), cut back all previous season's growth to within 2 in (5 cm) of ground in April. Repeat annually.
Most widely available *Salvia microphylla* (*S. grahamii*). *S. officinalis*. *S. o.* 'Icterina'(*S. o.aureovariegatus*).*S. o.*'Purpurascens' (Purple-leaf Sage). *S. o.* 'Tricolor' (Tricoloured Sage).

SAMBUCUS
Elder
Time to buy Pot-grown, any time except January. Balled, October–May. Avoid adverse weather conditions.
Where to find Outside in Shrubs.
Size Height 1 ft (30 cm) min. Single or multi-stemmed.
Foliage Deciduous. Spring/summer, green, purple, gold or variegated. Premature autumn colour, leaf drop and brown leaf scorch.

Roots Pots 6 in (15 cm) min. dia. Balled, good fibrous root system.
Hints Any well-prepared soil, plus extra organic material. European stock needs special attention when planting. Resents being grown in containers. Hard pruning advised after planting.
Most widely available *Sambucus canadensis* (American Elderberry). *S. c.* 'Maxima'. *S. nigra* (Common Elder. Bour Tree). *S. n.* 'Albovariegata'. *S. n.* 'Aurea' (Golden Elder). *S. n.* 'Aurea Variegata' (*S. n.* 'Laciniata') (Fern-leaved Elder. Parsley-leaved Elder). *S. n.* 'Pulverulenta'. *S. n.* 'Purpurea'. *S. racemosa* 'Plumosa Aurea' (Red-berried Elder). *S. r.* 'Sutherland.'

SANTOLINA
Cotton Lavender, Lavender Cotton
Time to buy Pot-grown, April–July. Avoid adverse weather conditions.
Where to find Outside in Shrubs or Herbs.
Size April, height 4 in (10 cm) min. July, height 6 in (15 cm) min. Multi-shooted, bushy.
Foliage Evergreen. Grey-green or silver. Premature basal leaf drop.
Roots Pots 4 in (10 cm) min. dia.
Hints Any well-prepared soil. If kept under cover in winter, avoid planting until spring frosts have finished. Offered all year round, best purchased April–July. Cut back all previous season's growth to within 2 in (5 cm) of ground in April. Repeat annually.
Most widely available *Santolina chamaecyparissus* (*S. incana*). *S. c. corsica* (*S. c.* 'Nana'). *S. neapolitana*. *S. n.* 'Sulphurea'. *S. virens* (*S. viridis*).

SAROCOCOCCA
Christmas Box, Sweet Box
Time to buy Pot-grown, any time except January. Balled, October–May. Avoid adverse weather conditions.
Where to find Outside in Shrubs.

Size Height 6 in (15 cm) min. Multistemmed.
Foliage Evergreen. Mid to dark green. Premature basal leaf drop.
Roots Pots 5 in (12 cm) min. dia. Balled, good fibrous root system.
Hints Any well-prepared soil, plus extra organic material. Offered in winter when in flower, scarce at other times. *Sarococacca confusa*, *S. humilis* and *S. ruscifolia* are mixed, and named forms are difficult to find. Balled European stock slow to establish.
Most widely available *Sarococacca confusa. S. hookerana var. digyna. S. h. d.* 'Purple Stem'. *S. humilis. S. ruscifolia. S. r. chinensis.*

SENECIO
Shrubby Ragwort
Time to buy Pot-grown, April–August. Avoid adverse weather conditions. Can be planted in flower.
Where to find Outside in Shrubs, Summer Bedding or Herbs.
Size April, height 4 in (10 cm) min. June, height 9 in (23 cm) min. Single or multistemmed.
Foliage Evergreen. Silver-grey. Premature basal leaf drop.
Roots Pots 5 in (12 cm) min. dia.
Hints Any well-prepared soil. Wide range. Avoid old woody plants. If kept under cover in winter, avoid planting until spring frosts have finished.
Most widely available *Senecio cineraria* (Dusty Miller). *S. compactus. S.* 'Dunedin Sunshine' (*S. laxifolius*). *S. greyi. S. hectori. S. leucostachys. S. monroi. S. reinoldii* (*S. rotundifolia*).

SKIMMIA
Time to buy Pot-grown, any time except January. Balled, October–May. Avoid adverse weather conditions.
Where to find Outside in Shrubs or Acid-loving Plants.
Size Height 6 in (15 cm) min. Multistemmed. Minimum three upright shoots.
Foliage Evergreen. Mid to dark green or purple hue. Premature basal leaf drop.
Roots Pots 6 in (15 cm) min. dia. Balled, good fibrous root system.
Hints Well-prepared neutral to acid soil, plus extra organic material. May be scarce, except when in flower or fruit. If kept under cover in winter, avoid planting until spring frosts have finished. Male and female required for fruiting. Avoid all-yellow foliage, gaunt or woody plants.
Most widely available *Skimmia japonica* (Japanese Skimmia). *S. j.* 'Foremanii' (*S. j.* 'Fisheri') *S. j.* 'Veitchii' (F). *S. j.* 'Fragrans' (M). *S. j.* 'Fructu-alba' (F). *S. j.* 'Nymans' (F). *S. j.* 'Red Princess' (F). *S. j.* 'Rogersii' (F). *S. j.* 'Rubella' (M). *S. laureola.*

SOPHORA (shrub forms)
New Zealand Kowhai
Time to buy Pot-grown, April–August. Avoid adverse weather conditions.
Where to find Outside in Shrubs.
Size Height 6 in (15 cm) min. Single-stemmed. Short side shoots.
Foliage Evergreen. Mid green. Premature basal leaf drop.
Roots Pot-grown, 5 in (12 cm) min. dia.
Hints Any well-prepared soil, plus extra organic material. Scarce. If kept under cover in winter, avoid planting until spring frosts have finished. Sheltered position. Research ultimate overall size.
Most widely available *Sophora tetraptera. S. microphylla.*

SORBARIA
Tree Spiraea
Time to buy Pot-grown, any time except January. Balled, October–May. Avoid adverse weather conditions.
Where to find Outside in Shrubs.
Size Height 2 ft (60 cm) min. Single or multi-stemmed.
Foliage Deciduous. Spring/summer, mid green. Premature autumn colour and leaf drop.

Roots Pots 6 in (15 cm) min. dia.
Hints Any well-prepared soil. May be scarce. Looks gaunt and one-sided. Research ultimate overall size.
Most widely available Sorbaria aitchisonii. S. arborea. S. sorbifolia.

SORBUS REDUCTA
Creeping Mountain Ash
Time to buy Pot-grown, any time except January. Balled, October–May. Avoid adverse weather conditions.
Where to find Outside in Shrubs or Alpines.
Size Height 4 in (10 cm) min. Minimum two shoots from below soil level.
Foliage Deciduous. Spring/summer, green. Bronze to orange-red in autumn. Premature autumn colour and leaf drop.
Roots Pots 4 in (10 cm) min. dia. Balled, good fibrous root system.
Hints Any well-prepared soil, plus extra organic material. Scarce. Always look sparse and unattractive.

SPARTIUM JUNCEUM
Spanish Broom
Time to buy Pot-grown, any time except January. Avoid adverse weather conditions.
Where to find Outside in Shrubs.
Size Height 1½ ft (50 cm) min. Single or multi-stemmed.
Foliage Deciduous. Spring/summer, mid green. Premature autumn colour and leaf drop.
Roots Pots 5 in (12 cm) min. dia.
Hints Any well-prepared soil, plus extra organic material. Sparse, gaunt appearance. Research ultimate overall size.

SPIRAEA
Time to buy Pot-grown, any time except January. Balled, root-wrapped and bare-rooted, October–May. Avoid adverse weather conditions.
Where to find Outside in Shrubs.
Size LOW-GROWING Height 6 in (15 cm)

min. Multi-stemmed. TALL-GROWING Height 1½ ft (50 cm) min. Multi-stemmed. Minimum three upright shoots.
Foliage Deciduous. Spring/summer, mid green or golden. Premature autumn colour and leaf drop.
Roots Pots 5 in (12 cm) min. dia. Balled, root-wrapped and bare-rooted, good fibrous root system.
Hints Any well-prepared soil. Wide range. Refer to pruning techniques required for each form.
Most widely available
LOW-GROWING Spiraea albiflora (S. japonica alba). S. betulifolia aemiliana. S. × bumalda 'Anthony Waterer'. S. × b. 'Gold Flame'. S. japonica 'Alpina'. S. j. 'Bullata' (S. crispifolia. S. bullata). S. j. 'Coccinea'. S. j. var. fortunei (S. j. wulfenii). S. j. 'Golden Princess'. S. j. 'Little Princess'. S. 'Shirobana'.
TALL-GROWING Spiraea arcuata. S. × arguta (Bridal Wreath. Foam of May. Garland Wreath). S. × billardii 'Triumphans' (S. menziesii 'Triumphana') (Billiard Spiraea). S. douglasii. S. menziesii. S. nipponica var. tosaensis (S. 'Snowmound') (Snowmound Nippon Spiraea). S. prunifolia (Bridal Wreath Spiraea). S. thunbergii (Thunberg Spiraea). S. × vanhouttei (Vanhoutte Spiraea).

STACHYURUS
Time to buy Pot-grown, any time except January. Avoid adverse weather conditions. Can be planted in flower.
Where to find Outside in Shrubs.
Size Height 1½ ft (50 cm) min. Single or multi-stemmed.
Foliage Deciduous. Spring/summer mid to dark green, with reddish hue. Premature autumn colour and leaf drop.
Roots Pots 6 in (15 cm) min. dia.
Hints Any well-prepared soil, plus extra organic material. Scarce. Research overall size.
Most widely available Stachyurus praecox. S. chinensis. S. c. 'Magpie'.

STAPHYLEA
Bladdernut, Colchis Bladdernut
Time to buy Pot-grown, any time except
January. Avoid adverse weather conditions.
Where to find Outside in Shrubs.
Size Height 1½ ft (50 cm) min. Single or
multi-stemmed.
Foliage Deciduous. Spring/summer, mid
green. Premature autumn colour and leaf
drop.
Roots Pots 6 in (15 cm) min. dia.
Hints Any well-prepared soil, plus extra
organic material. Scarce. If kept under
cover in winter, avoid planting until
spring frosts have finished. Research
overall size.
Most widely available *Staphylea colchica. S. holocarpa. S. h. 'Rosea'. S. pin-
nata* (Anthony Nut).

STEPHANANDRA
Cutleaf Stephanandra, Tanaka
Stephanandra
Time to buy Pot-grown, any time except
January. Balled, root-wrapped and bare-
rooted, October–May. Avoid adverse wea-
ther conditions.
Where to find Outside in Shrubs.
Size *Stephanandra incisa* forms, height
6 in (15 cm) min. *S. tanakae* height 1½ ft
(50 cm) min. Both multi-stemmed.
Foliage Deciduous. Spring/summer, mid
green. Premature autumn colour and leaf
drop.
Roots Pot-grown, 5 in (12 cm) min. dia.
Balled, root-wrapped and bare-rooted,
good fibrous root system.
Hints Any well-prepared soil. May be
scarce. Foliage may become poor from
July.
Most widely available *Stephanandra
incisa. S. i. 'Crispa'. S. tanakae.*

SYMPHORICARPOS
Snowberry, Coral Berry, Indian Currant
Time to buy Pot-grown, any time except
January. Balled, root-wrapped and bare-

rooted, October–May. Avoid adverse weather conditions. Can be planted in
flower.
Where to find Outside in Shrubs.
Size Height 10 in (25 cm) min. Single or
multi-stemmed. Minimum two upright
stems.
Foliage Deciduous. Spring/summer, grey-
green, greenish-purple, silver or gold
variegated. Premature autumn colour
and leaf drop.
Roots Pots 5 in (12 cm) min. dia. Balled,
root-wrapped and bare-rooted, good
fibrous root system.
Hints Any well-prepared soil. Often look
old and woody, establish once planted
out. Take reference on invasive and non-
invasive forms.
Most widely available *Symphoricarpos
albus* (Snowberry). *S.* × *chenaultii* 'Han-
cock'. *S.* × *doorenbosii. S.* × *d.* 'Erect'.
S. × *d.* 'Magic Berry'. *S.* × *d.* 'Mother of
Pearl'. *S.* × *d.* 'White Hedge'. *S. or-
biculatus (S. vulgaris)* (Indian Currant.
Coral Berry). *S. o.* 'Albovariegatus'. *S. o.*
'Variegatus'. *S. rivularis* (Snowberry).

SYMPLOCOS PANICULATA
Sapphineberry, Asiatic Sweetleaf
Time to buy Pot-grown, any time except
January. Avoid adverse weather condi-
tions.
Where to find Outside in Shrubs.
Size Height 9 in (23 cm) min. Single or
multi-stemmed.
Foliage Deciduous. Spring/summer, mid
green. Premature autumn colour and leaf
drop.
Roots Pots 5 in (12 cm) min. dia.
Hints Well-prepared neutral to acid soil,
plus extra organic material. Scarce. If
kept under cover in winter, avoid plant-
ing until spring frosts have finished.

SYRINGA
Lilac
Time to buy Pot-grown, any time except
January. Balled, root-wrapped and bare-

rooted, October–May. Avoid adverse weather conditions.
Where to find Outside in Shrubs or Rockery.
Size LOW-GROWING Height 1 ft (30 cm) min. *Syringa meyeri palibin*, height 4 in (10 cm) min. TALL-GROWING Height 1½ ft (50 cm) min. Single or multi-stemmed.
Foliage Deciduous. Spring/summer, light to mid green. Premature autumn colour and leaf drop.
Roots LOW-GROWING Pots 5 in (12 cm) min. dia. *Syringa meyeri palibin*, pots 3 in (8 cm) min. dia. TALL-GROWING Pots 6 in (15 cm) min. dia. Balled, root-wrapped and bare-rooted, good fibrous root system.
Hints Any well-prepared soil. Balled European stock, extra organic material. Wide range. Looks gaunt in winter. Care needed when transporting. Many grafted on to *Ligustrum ovalifolium* or *L. vulgaris* (Round-leaf and Common Privets); any suckers must be removed from below ground level by ripping out.
Most widely available
LOW-GROWING *Syringa meyeri var. palibin* (*S. palibiniana*). *S. velutina* (Korean Lilac. Meyer Lilac). *S. microphylla* 'Superba' (Daphne Lilac. Littleleaf Lilac). *S. × persica* (Persian lilac). *S. × p.* 'Alba'. *S. × p.* 'Laciniata (*S. × p. afghanica*).
TALL-GROWING *Syringa amurensis* (Amur Lilac). *S. × chinensis* (Chinese Lilac. Rouen Lilac). *S. × c.* 'Saugeana' (*S. × c.* 'Rubra'). *S. × hyacinthiflora*. *S. × h.* 'Alice Eastwood'. *S. × h.* 'Blue Hyacinth'. *S. × h.* 'Clarke's Giant'. *S. × h.* 'Esther Staley'. *S. × josiflexa* 'Bellicent' (Canadian Lilac). *S. josikaea* (Hungarian Lilac). *S. × prestoniae* (Canadian Lilac). *S. × p.* 'Audrey'. *S. × p.* 'Desdemona'. *S. × p.* 'Elinor'. *S. × p.* 'Isabella'. *S. reflexa*. *S. sweginzowii*. *S. vulgaris* (Common Lilac). *S. × v.* 'Alba'. *S. v.* 'Rubra'.
HYBRID SINGLE-FLOWERING *Syringa* 'Congo'. *S.* 'Etna'. *S.* 'Firmament'. *S.* 'Lavaliensis'. *S.* 'Marechal Foch'. *S.* 'Massena'.

S. 'Maud Nottcutt'. *S.* 'Night'. *S.* 'Primrose'. *S.* 'Reamur'. *S.* 'Sensation'. *S.* 'Souvenir de Louis Spaeth'. *S.* 'Vestale'.
DOUBLE-FLOWERING *Syringa* 'Belle de Nancy'. *S.* 'Charles Joly'. *S.* 'Edward J. Gardener'. *S.* 'Kathleen Havermeyer'. *S.* Madame A. Buchner'. *S.* Madame Lemoine'. *S.* 'Michel Buchner'. *S.* 'Mrs Edward Harding'. *S.* 'Paul Thirlon'. *S.* 'Souvenir d'Alice Harding'.

TAMARIX
Tamarisk
Time to buy Pot-grown, any time except January. Balled, October–May. Avoid adverse weather conditions.
Where to find Outside in Shrubs.
Size Height 1½ ft (50 cm) min. Single or multi-stemmed.
Foliage Deciduous. Spring/summer, mid green. Early autumn colour and leaf drop.
Roots Pots 5 in (12 cm) min. dia. Balled, good fibrous root system.
Hints Any well-prepared soil, plus extra organic material. Looks dejected in containers. Wispy and unattractive when young. Reference to pruning techniques for summer and spring flowering. Allow adequate space.
Most widely available *Tamarix parviflora* (Small-flowered Tamarix). *T. ramosissima* (*T. pentandra*) (Five-stamen Tamarix). *T. r.* 'Rubra'. *T. r.* 'Pink Cascade'. *T. tetandra*.

TEUCRIUM FRUTICANS
Shrubby Germander
Time to buy Pot-grown, April–August. Avoid adverse weather conditions. Can be planted in flower.
Where to find Outside in Shrubs or Herbs.
Size April, height 4 in (10 cm). June, height 18 in (50 cm). Single or multi-stemmed.
Foliage Evergreen. Silver-grey. Premature basal leaf drop.
Roots Pots 5 in (12 cm) min. dia.

Hints Any well-prepared soil. Hardiness suspect. Plant in sheltered position. Avoid old woody plants.

TRACHYCARPUS FORTUNEI
Chusan Palm
Time to buy Pot-grown, any time except January. Avoid adverse weather conditions.
Where to find Outside in Shrubs.
Size Height 1 ft (30 cm) min. Single-stemmed. Large fronded leaves.
Foliage Evergreen. Dark green, fan-shaped.
Roots Pots 5 in (12 cm) min. dia.
Hints Any well-prepared soil, plus extra organic material. Hardiness suspect. If kept under cover in winter, avoid planting until spring frosts have finished. For permanent containers, use good quality potting compost.

ULEX
Furze, Gorse, Whin
Time to buy Pot-grown, any time except January. Avoid adverse weather conditions.
Where to find Outside in Shrubs.
Size Height 6 in (15 cm) min. Single or multi-stemmed.
Foliage Deciduous. Spring/summer, grey-green. Premature autumn colour and leaf drop.
Roots Pots 5 in (12 cm) min. dia.
Hints Any well-prepared soil. May be scarce. Thorns make handling difficult.
Most widely available *Ulex europaeus*. *U. e.* 'Plenus'.

VACCINIUM (grown as ornamental shrub)
Blueberry, Whortleberry
Time to buy Pot-grown, any time except January. Balled, October–May. Avoid adverse weather conditions.
Where to find Outside in Shrubs, Fruit or Acid-loving Plants.

Size Height 9 in (23 cm) min. Single or multi-stemmed.
Foliage EVERGREEN mid green to grey-green. Premature basal leaf drop. DECIDUOUS Spring/summer, green to grey-green. Premature autumn colour and leaf drop.
ROOTS Pots 4 in (10 cm) min. dia. Balled, good fibrous root system.
Hints Well-prepared neutral to acid soil, plus extra organic material. May be scarce.
Most widely available *Vaccinium angustifolium* (Low-bush Blueberry). *V. arboreum* (Farkleberry) (S–E). *V. arctostaphylos* (Caucasian Whortleberry). *V. corymbosum* (Swamp Blueberry. High-bush Blueberry). *V. hirsutum* (Hairy Huckleberry). *V. myrsinites* (Evergreen Blueberry). (E). *V. myrtillus* (Bilberry. Whortleberry. Whinberry. Blueberry). *V. ovatum* (Cranberry) (E). *V. oxycoccos. V. parvifolium* (Red Bilberry). *V. uliginosum* (Bog Whortleberry). *V. virgatum. V. vitisidaea* (Cowberry).

VIBURNUM
Time to buy Pot-grown, any time except January. Balled, October–May. Avoid adverse weather conditions.
Where to find Outside in Shrubs.
Size Height 1½ ft (50 cm) min. Single or multi-stemmed.
Foliage EVERGREEN OR SEMI-EVERGREEN Dark green or white variegated. Some premature basal leaf drop. DECIDUOUS Spring/summer mid-green. Premature autumn colour and leaf drop.
Roots Pots 6 in (15 cm) min. dia. Balled, good fibrous root system.
Hints Any well-prepared soil, plus extra organic material. Wide range. Often looks uninteresting in winter. Research overall size.
Most widely available
EARLY FLOWERING *Viburnum × bodnantense. V. × b.* 'Dawn'. *V. × b.* 'Deben'. *V. fareri (V. fragrans). V. f. candidissimum.*

V. f. 'Nanum' (*V. f.* 'Compactum'). *V. foetens* (*V. koreana*).

SPRING-FLOWERING SCENTED *Viburnum bitchiuense* (Bitchiu Viburnum). *V. × carlcephalum C. carlesii* (Korean Viburnum). *V. c.* 'Aurora'. *V. c.* 'Charis'. *V. c.* 'Diana'. *V. × juddii* (Judd Viburnum).

VIBURNUM PLICATUM LACECAP FLOWERING *Viburnum plicatum. V. p.* 'Cascade'. *V. p.* 'Lanarth'. *V. p.* 'Mariesii'. *V. p.* 'Pink Beauty'. *V. p.* 'Rowallane'. *V. p. var. tomentosum. V. p.* 'Watanabe' (*V. semperflorens*).

SNOWBALL FLOWERING *Viburnum plicatum* 'Grandiflorum' (Japanese Snowball).

VIBURNUM OPULUS *Viburnum opulus* (Guelder Rose. Water Elder. European Cranberrybush Viburnum). *V. o.* 'Aureum'. *V. o.* 'Compactum'. *V. o.* 'Fructuluteo'. *V. o.* 'Nanum'. *V. o.* 'Nottcutt's Variety'. *V. o.* 'Xanthocarpum'. *V. o.* 'Sterile' (*V. o.* 'Roseun') (Snowball Shrub).

INTERESTING FOLIAGE *Viburnum acerifolium* (dock-mackie). *V. alnifolium* (Hobble Bush). *V. furcatum*.

EVERGREEN *Viburnum buddleifolium. V. cinnamomifolium. V. cylindricum. V. henryi. V. japonicum* (Japanese Viburnum). *V.* 'Pragense'. *V. × rhytidophylloides* (*lantanaphyllum viburnum*). *V. rhytidophyllum* (Leatherleaf Viburnum). *V. r.* 'Roseum'. *V. r.* 'Variegatum'. *V. utile* (Service Viburnum). *V. tinus* (Laurustinus). *V. t.* 'Eve Price'. *V. t.* 'French White'. *V. t.* 'Gwenllian'. *V. t. lucidum. V. t.* 'Purpureum'. *V. t.* 'Variegatum'.

SEMI-EVERGREEN *Viburnum × burkwoodii* (Burkwood Viburnum). *V. × b.* 'Anne Russell'. *V. × b.* 'Chenaultii'. *V. × b.* 'Park Farm Hybrid'. *V. × hillieri* (*V. × hillieri* 'Winton'). *V. macrocephalum*.

BEST FRUITING *Viburnum betulifolium. V. huphense. V. lantana* (Wayfaring Tree). *V. l.* 'Variegatum' (*V. l.* 'Auratum'). *V. lentago* (Sheepberry. Nannyberry). *V. l.* 'Pink Beauty'. *V. prunifolium* (Black Haw). *V. sargentii.*

VIBURNUM DAVIDII
David's Viburnum
Time to buy Pot-grown, any time except January. Balled, October–May. Avoid adverse weather conditions.
Where to find Outside in Shrubs.
Size Height 6 in (15 cm) min. Multistemmed.
Foliage Evergreen. Dark, glossy green. Premature basal leaf drop.
Roots Pots 5 in (12 cm) min. dia. Balled, good fibrous root system.
Hints Any well-prepared soil, plus extra organic material. Male and female required to produce turquoise berries, but rarely offered sexed.

VINCA
Periwinkle
Time to buy Pot-grown, any time except January. Avoid adverse weather conditions.
Where to find Outside in Shrubs or Ground Cover.
Size Small-leaved, spread 3 in (8 cm) min. Large-leaved, 9 in (23 cm).
Foliage Evergreen. Mid green, silver or golden variegated. Premature basal leaf drop.
Roots Small-leaved, pots 3 in (8 cm) min. dia. Large-leaved, pots 4 in (10 cm) min. dia.
Hints Any well-prepared soil. Named forms may be scarce. Gaunt and insipid, apart from a short period in spring.
Most widely available

LARGE-LEAVED *Vinca major* (Greater Periwinkle. Large Periwinkle). *V. difformis. V. m.* 'Maculata'. *V. m.* 'Variegata'.

SMALL-LEAVED *Vinca minor* (Common Periwinkle. Lesser Periwinkle). *V. m.* 'Alba'. *V. m.* 'Atropurpurea'. *V. m.* 'Aureovariegata'. *V. m.* 'Aureovariegata Alba'. *V. m.* 'Aureo Flore Pleno'. *V. m.* 'Bowles' Variety'. *V. m.* 'Gertrude Jekyll'. *V. m.* 'Multiplex'. *V. m.* 'Variegata'.

WEIGELA
Time to buy Pot-grown, any time except January. Bare-rooted, October–May. Avoid adverse weather conditions.
Where to find Outside in Shrubs.
Size Height 1½ ft (50 cm) min. Single or multi-stemmed.
Foliage Deciduous. Spring/summer, dark to mid green, gold and silver variegated. Premature autumn colour and leaf drop.
Roots Pots 6 in (15 cm) min. dia. Bare-rooted, good fibrous root system.
Hints Any well-prepared soil. Wide range. Looks uninteresting in winter. Research ultimate overall size.
Most widely available Weigela 'Abel Carrière'. W. 'Avalanche'. W. 'Boskoop Glory'. W. 'Bristol Ruby'. W. 'Bristol Snowflake'. W. 'Candida'. W. 'Dart's Colourdream'. W. 'Eva Rathke'. W. 'Evita'. W. florida 'Albovariegata'. W. f. 'Aureovariegata'. W. f. 'Foliis Purpureis'. W. 'Looymansii Aurea'. V. middendorffiana. W. f. 'Minuet'. W. 'Mont Blanc'. W. 'Newport Red'. W. praecox 'Variegata'. W. 'Rumba'. W. 'Stelzneri'. W. 'Styriaca'. W. 'Victoria'.

XANTHOCERAS SORBIFOLIUM
Yellowhorn
Time to buy Pot-grown, any time except January. Avoid adverse weather conditions.
Where to find Outside in Shrubs.
Size Height 1½ ft (50 cm) min. Single or multi-stemmed.
Foliage Deciduous. Spring/summer, mid to dark green. Premature autumn colour and leaf drop.
Roots Pots 6 in (15 cm) min. dia.
Hints Any well-prepared soil, plus extra organic material. Scarce. If kept under cover in winter, avoid planting until spring frosts have finished. Research overall size. For wall use plant 15–18 in (40–50 cm) away from wall.

YUCCA
Time to buy Pot-grown any time except January. Avoid adverse weather conditions.
Where to find Outside in Shrubs.
Size Height 6 in (15 cm) min.
Foliage Evergreen. Grey-green white variegated. Minimum five upright, sword-like leaves.
Roots Pots 5 in (12 cm) min. dia.
Hints Any well-prepared soil, plus extra organic material. Allow space for architectural shape.
Most widely available Yucca brevifolia (Joshua Tree). Y. filamentosa (Adam's Needle Yucca). Y. f. 'Variegata'. Y. flaccida. Y. f. 'Bright Edge'. Y. f. 'Ivory'. Y. f. 'Variegata'. Y. gloriosa (Spanish Dagger. Moundlily Yucca). Y. recurvifolia. Y. r. 'Variegata'. Y. whipplei.

ZENOBIA PULVERULENTA
Dusty Zenobia
Time to buy Pot-grown, any time except January. Balled, October–May. Avoid adverse weather conditions. Can be planted in flower.
Where to find Outside in Shrubs or Acid-loving Plants.
Size Height 9 in (23 cm) min. Single or multi-stemmed.
Foliage Deciduous. Spring/summer, mid green. Premature autumn colour and leaf drop.
Roots Pots 4 in (10 cm) dia. Balled, good fibrous root system.
Hints Well-prepared neutral to acid soil, plus extra organic material. May be scarce. Hardiness suspect.

Climbers

Even the smallest garden can accommodate one or more climbers and so add a third dimension of growing area. Walls and fences can be turned into green hedges of foliage, flower and fruit. Archways, trellis, trees and pergolas can provide homes for one of the most interesting of all plant groups.

It must be remembered that for the height or spread required, an adequate root-run must be allowed for.

Walls and fences have a 12 in (30 cm) wide dry area at their bases, so it is important to plant the climber at least 15–18 in (40–50 cm) away, laying it back towards the wall and preparing at least a square yard (metre) of soil to a depth of 18 in (50 cm). Organic material should be added to hold the food and moisture the climber will need.

Some form of training support such as wires, trellis or individual anchorage points will be required.

Often climbing plants present themselves as small, sometimes insipid looking plants but overall growth in height and spread can be phenomenal, and reference must be taken to ensure that they will not become over-crowded. The forward-protruding growth must always be accounted for, as this can cause problems in later years.

As well as climbing plants, there are wall shrubs, climbing roses and fruit trees that can be used to cover walls and fences.

Correct pruning techniques are important and research should be done to ensure that these are carried out.

Occasionally, there is the opportunity to buy larger sizes than those recommended, but they may not always establish quickly or well.

When climbers are required for growing in containers, they will normally reach only one-third of their open ground potential; if grown in this way, always use a good-quality potting compost and give adequate spring and summer feeding.

ACTINIDIA KOLOMIKTA
Time to buy Pot-grown, any time. Avoid adverse weather conditions.
Where to find Outside in Climbers.
Size 1–3 ft (30 cm–1 m). One or more shoots tied to cane.
Foliage Deciduous. Spring/summer, mid green. May not show white or pink markings. Brown scorching may be seen by July.
Roots Pots 5 in (12 cm) min. dia.
Hints Any well-prepared soil, except alkaline. May be scarce. If kept under cover in winter, avoid planting until spring

frosts have finished. Plant on sunny wall 15–18 in (40–50 cm) away from wall.

AKEBIA QUINATA
Time to buy Pot-grown, any time. Avoid adverse weather conditions.
Where to find Outside in Climbers.
Size 9 in–4 ft (23 cm–1.2 m). Minimum one shoot tied to cane. Single-stemmed acceptable.
Foliage Deciduous. Light green. Brown scorching and leaf drop by August.
Roots Pots 5 in (12 cm) min. dia.
Hints Any well-prepared soil. May be scarce. If kept under cover in winter avoid planting until spring frosts have finished. Plant 15–18 in (40–50 cm) away from support.

AMPELOPSIS
Time to buy Pot-grown, any time. Avoid adverse weather conditions.
Where to find Outside in Climbers. *Ampelopsis brevipedunculata* 'Elegans' also indoors as House Plants.
Size 1–3 ft (30 cm–1 m). One shoot tied to cane.
Foliage Deciduous. Mid green. Signs of scorching early autumn. Variegated may have all-green shoots – remove.
Roots Pots 5 in (12 cm) min. dia.
Hints Any well-prepared soil. Offered newly potted, avoid until established. May be scarce. Plant 15–18 in (40–50 cm) away from support.
Most widely available *Ampelopsis brevipedunculata*. *A. b.* 'Elegans'.

ARISTOLOCHIA MACROPHYLLA
syn. *Aristolochia sipho*
Dutchman's Pipe
Time to buy Pot-grown, any time. Avoid adverse weather conditions.
Where to Find Outside in Climbers or inside in House Plants.
Size 1½–4 ft (50 cm–1.2 m). Minimum two shoots tied to cane.
Foliage Deciduous. Spring/summer, light to mid green. Brown scorching from August.
Roots Pots 5 in (12 cm) min. dia.
Hints Any well-prepared soil, plus extra organic material. If kept under cover in winter, avoid planting until spring frosts have finished. European stock may require additional organic material. Plant 15–18 in (40–50 cm) away from support.

BILLARDIER'A LONGIFLORA
Time to buy Pot-grown, any time. Avoid adverse weather conditions.
Where to find Outside in Climbers or inside in House Plants.
Size 1–3 ft (30 cm–1 m). One or more shoots tied to cane. Single-shooted acceptable.
Foliage Evergreen. Dark green.
Roots Pots 4 in (10 cm) min. dia.
Hints Any well-prepared soil. Scarce. If kept under cover in winter, avoid planting until spring frosts have finished. Plant 15–18 in (40–50 cm) away from support.

CAMPSIS
Trumpet Climber
Time to buy Pot-grown, any time. Avoid adverse weather conditions.
Where to find Outside in Climbers.
Size 1½–4 ft (50 cm–1 m). One or more shoots tied to cane. Single-stemmed acceptable.
Foliage Deciduous. Spring/summer, mid green. Premature autumn colour and leaf drop.
Roots Pots 5 in (12 cm) min. dia.
Hints Any well-prepared soil. May be scarce. If kept under cover in winter, avoid planting until spring frosts have finished. Plant 15–18 in (40–50 cm) away from support. Requires sunny wall.
Most widely available *Campsis grandiflora*. *C. radicans*. *C. r.* 'Flava' *C. r.* 'Flamingo'. *C. r.* 'Yellow Trumpet'. *C. tagliabuana* 'Madame Galen'.

CELASTRUS ORBICULATUS
Time to buy Pot-grown, any time. Avoid adverse weather conditions.
Where to find Outside in Climbers.
Size 1½–4 ft (50 cm–1.2 m). Minimum two shoots tied to cane.
Foliage Deciduous. Spring/summer, light green. Premature autumn colour.
Roots Pots 5 in (12 cm) min. dia.
Hints Any well-prepared soil. If kept under cover in winter, avoid planting until spring frosts have finished. Plant 15–18 in (40–50 cm) away from support.

CLEMATIS
Time to buy Pot-grown, August–December mature plants, April–July young plants. Avoid adverse weather conditions.
Where to find Outside in Climbers or Clematis.
Size 1–3 ft (30 cm–1 m). One or more shoots tied to cane.
Foliage Deciduous. Spring/summer, mid green. May show leaf scorch late summer.
Roots Pots, young plants min. 2¾ in (7 cm) square, mature plants min. 5 in (12 cm).
Hints Any well-prepared soil, except very dry. 2¾ in (7 cm) pot sizes require extra organic material. Cover roots with stones, tiles or other shading material. Wide range. If purchased prior to March, keep under limited protection until frosts have finished. Plant 15–18 in (40–50 cm) away from support.
Most widely available
SPRING FLOWERING Clematus alpina and forms. C. macropetala and forms. C. montana and forms.
LARGE FLOWERING SUMMER FLOWERING HYBRIDS Clematis 'Comtesse de Bouchard'. C. 'Dr Ruppel'. C. 'Ernest Markham'. C. 'Hagley Hybrid'. C. 'H. F. Young'. C. 'Jackmanii'. C. 'Lasurstern'. C. 'Marie Boisselot'. C. 'Mrs Cholmondley'. C. 'Nelly Moser'. C. 'Rouge Cardinale'. C. 'The President'. C. 'Ville de Lyon'. C. 'Vyvyan Pennell'. C. 'William Kennet'.
AUTUMN FLOWERING Clematis flammula. C. × jouiniana praecox. C. orientalis and forms. C. tangutica. Many other forms.

DECUMARIA
Time to buy Pot-grown April–August. Avoid adverse weather conditions.
Where to find Outside in Shrubs or Climbers. May be under protection in winter.
Size Height 9 in (23 cm) min. Single stemmed, becoming multi-stemmed.
Foliage Deciduous. Spring/summer, mid green. Premature autumn colour and leaf drop.
Roots Pots 5 in (12 cm) min. dia.
Hints Any well-prepared soil, except alkaline, plus extra organic material. If kept under cover in winter, avoid planting until spring frosts have finished. May need protection for 2–3 years after planting. One-sided and irregular. Plant 15–18 in (40–50 cm) away from support.
Most widely available Decumaria barbara. D. sinensis.

ECCREMOCARPUS
Time to buy Pot-grown, April–June. Avoid adverse weather conditions. Can be purchased as seed.
Where to find Outside in Climbers or Annual Bedding Plants.
Size 3 in–2 ft (6–60 cm). One or more shoots tied to cane.
Foliage Although evergreen, foliage does not normally survive through winter. Light green.
Roots Pots 4 in (10 cm) min. dia.
Hints Any well-prepared soil, except waterlogged. May be scarce. Hardiness in doubt. If kept under cover in winter, avoid planting until spring frosts have finished. Plant 15–18 in (40–50 cm) away from support.
Most widely available Eccremocarpus scaber. E. s. 'Lutea'. E. s. 'Rubra'.

PARTHENOCISSUS
Virginia Creeper (*Parthenocissus Quinquefolia*)
Boston Ivy (*Parthenocissus Veitchii*)
Time to buy Pot-grown, any time. Avoid adverse weather conditions.
Where to find Outside in Climbers.
Size 1–3 ft (30 cm–1 m). Single shoot or more tied to cane.
Foliage Deciduous. Light green spring, turning darker. Brown scorching September onwards.
Roots Pots 5 in (12 cm) min. dia.
Hints Any well-prepared soil. Looks fragile. Confusion regarding common names and care must be taken. Plant 15–18 in (40–50 cm) away from support.
Most widely available *Parthenocissus henryana. P.quinquefolia. P. tricuspidata* 'Beverley Brook'. *P. t.* 'Veitchii'.

PASSIFLORA CAERULA
Passion Flower
Time to buy Pot-grown April–July. Avoid adverse weather conditions.
Where to find Outside in Climbers.
Size 1½–3 ft (50 cm–1 m). One or more shoots tied to cane.
Foliage Semi-evergreen to deciduous. Dark green with no grey/brown blotches.
Roots Pots 5 in (12 cm) min. dia.
Hints Any well-prepared soil, except waterlogged. If kept under cover in winter, avoid planting until spring frosts have finished. Cut back top growth by 40% in spring. Plant 15–18 in (40–50 cm) away from support.
Most widely available *Passiflora caerulea. P. c.* 'Constance Elliot'.

PILEOSTEGIA VIBURNOIDES
Evergreen Viburnum
Time to buy Pot-grown, any time. Avoid adverse weather conditions.
Where to find Outside in Climbers or Rare Plants.
Size 6 in–3 ft (15 cm–1 m). One or more shoots tied to cane.

Foliage Evergreen. Dark green. Occasional die-back, February–March.
Roots Pots 5 in (12 cm) min. dia.
Hints Any well-prepared soil, except alkaline. May be scarce. If kept under cover in winter, avoid planting until spring frosts over. Slow-growing. Plant 15–18 in (40–50 cm) away from support.

POLYGONUM BALDSCHUANICUM
syn. *Polygonum aubertii*
Russian Vine, Mile-a-minute
Time to buy Pot-grown, any time. Avoid adverse weather conditions.
Where to find Outside in Climbers.
Size 1½–3½ ft (50 cm–1 m). One or more shoots tied to cane.
Foliage Deciduous. Spring/summer, light green. Autumn, russet-red. Premature leaf drop.
Roots Pots 4 in (10 cm) min. dia.
Hints Any well-prepared soil. May entwine itself with other climbers. Large, wide, spreading climber. Plant 15–18 in (40–50 cm) away from support.

SCHISANDRA RUBRIFOLIA
Time to buy Pot-grown, any time. Avoid adverse weather conditions.
Where to find Outside in Climbers or Rare Plants.
Size 1–4 ft (30 cm–1.2 m). Size will vary in season. Single shoot acceptable.
Foliage Deciduous. Spring/summer, light to mid green. Premature leaf drop and scorching.
Roots Pots 5 in (12 cm) min. dia.
Hints Any well-prepared soil. Scarce. Less vigorous. Plant 15–18 in (40–50 cm) away from support.

SCHIZOPHRAGMA
Time to buy Pot-grown, any time. Avoid adverse weather conditions.
Where to find Outside in Climbers or Rare Plants.
Size 1–3 ft (30 cm–1 m). One or more shoots tied to cane.

Foliage Deciduous. Spring/summer, light to mid green. Brown scorching from July.
Roots Pots 5 in (12 cm) min. dia.
Hints Any well-prepared soil. Scarce. Looks straggly and wilted. Plant 15–18 in (40–50 cm) away from support.
Most widely available *Schizophragma hydrangeoides*. *S. h.* 'Roseum'. *S. intergrifolium*.

SOLANUM JASMINOIDES
Jasmine-scented Solanum
Time to buy Pot-grown, any time. Avoid adverse weather conditions.
Where to find Outside in Climbers or Rare Plants.
Size 1–4 ft (30 cm–1.2 m). One or more shoots tied to cane.
Foliage Deciduous. Spring/summer, light green. Premature autumn colour.
Roots Pots 5 in (12 cm) min. dia.
Hints Any well-prepared soil. May need winter protection first two years after planting. Straggly with foliage and flowers only at top; quickly grows away. Fruits are poisonous. Plant 15–18 in (40–50 cm) away from support.
Most widely available *Solanum jasminoides*. *S. j.* 'Album'.

SOLLYA FUSIFORMIS
Australian Bluebell Creeper
Time to buy Pot-grown, any time. Avoid adverse weather conditions.
Where to find Outside in Climbers or Rare Plants. Indoors in House Plants.
Size 1–3 ft (30 cm–1 m). One or more shoots tied to cane.
Foliage Evergreen. Dark green. May show signs of leaf drop April.
Roots Pots 6 in (15 cm) min. dia.
Hints Any well-prepared soil. Scarce. If kept under cover in winter, avoid planting until spring frosts have finished. Hardiness in doubt. In cold areas, use as conservatory plant. Plant 15–18 in (40–50 cm) away from support.

STAUTONIA HEXAPHYLLA
Time to buy Pot-grown, any time. Avoid adverse weather conditions.
Where to find Outside in Climbers or Rare Plants.
Size 2–4 ft (60 cm–1.2 m). One or more shoots tied to cane.
Foliage Evergreen. Dark green. May show signs of older leaves dying in autumn.
Roots Pots 5 in (12 cm) min. dia.
Hints Any well-prepared soil. Scarce. If kept under cover in winter, avoid planting until spring frosts have finished. May need winter protection. Plant 15–18 in (40–50 cm) away from support.

TRACHELOSPERMUM
Time to buy Pot-grown, any time. Avoid adverse weather conditions.
Where to find Outside in Climbing or Rare Plants.
Size 6 in–3 ft (15 cm–1 m). One or more shoots tied to cane. Single-stemmed acceptable.
Foliage Evergreen. Dark green or white variegated. Some leaf drop in winter.
Roots Pots 5 in (12 cm) min. dia.
Hints Any well-prepared soil, plus extra organic material. Scarce. If kept under cover in winter, avoid planting until spring frosts have finished. May need winter protection. Plants often small. Needs time to establish. Plant 15–18 in (40–50 cm) away from support.
Most widely available *Trachelospermum asiaticum*. *T. a.* 'Variegata'. *T. jasminoides*. *T. j.* 'Variegatum'.

VITIS (ornamental)
Vines, Ornamental Vines
Time to buy Pot-grown, any time. Avoid adverse weather conditions.
Where to find Outside in Climbers. *Vitis* 'Brant' may be in Fruit.
Size 1½–4 ft (50 cm–1.2 m). One or more shoots tied to cane. Single shoot is acceptable.

Foliage Deciduous. Spring/summer, mid to dark green or purple. Premature leaf drop.

Roots Pots 4 in (10 cm) min. dia.

Hints Any well prepared soil. May look ragged from mid summer. Plant 15–18 in (40–50 cm) away from support. Train into vine formation on support.

Most widely available *Vitis* 'Brant'. *V. coignetiae*. *V. vinifera* 'Incana'. *V. v.* 'Purpurea'.

WISTERIA

Time to buy Pot-grown, any time. Balled, root-wrapped and bare-rooted, October–March. Avoid adverse weather conditions.

Where to find Outside in Climbers.

Size 1–6 ft (30 cm–2 m). One or more shoots tied to cane.

Foliage Deciduous. Spring/summer, light green. Premature autumn colour and leaf drop.

Roots Pots 6 in (15 cm) min. dia. Balled, root-wrapped and bare-rooted, good fibrous root system.

Hints Any well prepared soil, except alkaline. Named forms may be scarce. Avoid seed-raised plants. Plant 15–18 in (40–50 cm) away from support, with adequate space and root run of 10 ft (3 m) minimum. Train into vine formation, main vines $1\frac{1}{2}$ ft (50 cm) apart over support. Best on sunny south or west wall.

Most widely available *W. formosa* 'Issai'. *W. f.* 'Macrobotrys'. *W. f.* 'Pink Ice'. *W. f.* 'Rosea'. *W. sinensis*. *W. s.* 'Alba'. *W. s.* 'Domino'. *W. s.* 'Black Dragon'. *W. s.* 'Prematura'. *W. s.* 'Prematura Alba'. *W. s.* 'Peaches and Cream'. *W. s.* 'Purple Patches'. *W. s.* 'Snow Showers'.

Conifers

When buying conifers, the most common mistake is to underestimate the ultimate overall size. Conifers can be split into two groups, specimen and dwarf. Some straightforward research will give an understanding of a specimen's overall size. It does pay to check. 'Dwarf', however, is a very misleading description. 'Slow-growing' is far better, as there is really no such thing as a 'dwarf' conifer. In time all so-called 'dwarfs' become giants, and this can mean a heartbreaking decision on whether to remove the conifer, and so lose years of development.

With all conifers, hardiness is not normally a problem, but good soil preparation is important. A hole at least 3 ft (1 m) in diameter should be dug to a depth of 18 in (50 cm), keeping the top-soil at the top throughout the operation. Adequate organic material must be added to aid root development.

Larger specimens may be planted, but those over 4 ft (1.2 m) can often be in some danger. For all conifers planted in exposed areas, some form of protection from wind may be necessary. Spraying from overhead with water, once a day during April and May will be beneficial.

Conifers can be found in spreading, upright, globe, round and obelisk shapes, and so they are widely used as architectural features in the garden.

Often ground-covering forms, in particular *Juniperus* 'Pfitzerana' and *J. media* give ground-cover but also reach a height of 6–8 ft (2–2.5 m). Low-growing forms such as *Juniperus sabina tamariscifolia*, *J. communis* 'Repanda' and *J. c.* 'Depressa Aurea' make true low-growing carpets.

Heathers, when used in association with conifers, are often planted too close to them, causing damage. Small bulbs, such as Crocus, Narcissus and Iris, are shown off to their best advantage when used to brighten the planting in the spring.

Dogs can cause damage to conifers by water fouling, particularly in open-planned areas.

There are some deciduous conifers, and these offer autumn colours. Metasequoia, Larix (Larch) and *Ginkgo biloba* are good examples. Often rightly offered by nurseries and garden centres as Trees, but technically they are conifers.

Tall evergreen conifers are at risk when planted, but tall deciduous conifers are not.

Conifers are offered in a wide range of sizes, but it would be impractical for any garden centre or nursery to stock every size. In the author's opinion, choosing a smaller size is always better.

Conifers look best in good sunlight where their golds, blues and greys are shown off to advantage.

Not all conifers are suitable for hedging, and reference should be sought on the best forms to use. See under Hedging (p. 145).

ABIES (slow-growing/dwarf)
Fir
Time to buy Pot-grown, any time except December–February. Balled, October–November or March–April. Avoid adverse weather conditions.
Where to find Outside in Slow-Growing/ Dwarf or Specimen Conifers.
Size
10–20 cm (4–8 in)
20–30 cm (8–12 in)
30–40 cm (12–15 in)
40–60 cm (15 in–2 ft)
Balled, more than 60 cm (2 ft) difficult to establish.
Abies nordmanniana 'Golden Spreader' and *A. procera* 'Glauca Prostrata', heights should be translated into spread, however, may not have neat spreading habit.
Foliage Evergreen short needles. Mid, dark or grey-green, gold or blue. Limited needle drop spring.
Roots Height purchased:
10 cm (4 in), pots 4 in (10 cm) min. dia.
10–20 cm (4–8 in), pots 5 in (12 cm) (1 litre) min. dia.
20–30 cm (8–12 in), pots 7 in (17 cm) (2 litre) min. dia.
30–40 cm (12–15 in), pots 7 in (17 cm) (2 litre) min. dia.
40–60 cm (15 in–2 ft), pots 8 in (20 cm) (3 litre) min. dia.
Balled up to 60 cm (2 ft), good fibrous root system.
Hints Well-prepared soil, except alkaline. Over 60 cm (2 ft) in height, extra organic material. May be scarce. Avoid drying out of pots or root-balls. Research overall ultimate size.

Most widely available: *Abies balsamea* 'Nana' (*A. b.* 'Hudsonia'). *A. cephalonica* 'Nana'. *A. concolor* 'Compacta' (Dwarf Colorado White Fir). *A. c.* 'Violacea'. *A. delavayi* 'Nana'. *A. koreana* (Korean Fir). *A. k.* 'Aurea'. *A. k.* 'Horstmann's Silberlocke' (*A. k.* 'Horstmann's Silver Lock'). *A. lasiocarpa* 'Compacta' (Dwarf Arizona Cork Bark Fir). *A. normanniana* 'Golden Spreader' (Spreading Golden Caucasian Fir). *A. pinsapo* 'Glauca' (Blue Creeping Spanish Fir). *A. pinsapo* 'Horstmann's Nana' (Horstmann's Dwarf Spanish Fir). *A. procera* 'Glauca Prostrata' (*A. nobilis* 'Glauca Prostrata') (Spreading Blue Noble Fir).

ABIES (tall-growing)
Fir
Time to buy Pot-grown, any time except December–February. Balled, October–November or March–April. Avoid adverse weather conditions.
Where to find Outside in Conifers, Forestry or Screening Trees.
Size
30–40 cm (12–15 in)
40–80 cm (15 in–2 ft)
60–80 cm (2–2½ ft)
80 cm–1 m (2½–3 ft)
Balled, more than 60–80 cm (2–2½ ft) difficult to establish.
Foliage Evergreen short needles. Mid, dark or grey-green, gold or blue. Limited needle drop spring.
Roots Height purchased:
30–40 cm (12–15 in), pots 7 in (17 cm) (2 litre) min. dia.
40–60 cm (15 in–2 ft), pots 8 in (20 cm) (3 litre) min. dia.

60–80 cm (2–2½ ft), pots 9 in (23 cm) (3 litre) min. dia.

80 cm–1 m (2½–3 ft), pots 10 in (25 cm) (4 litre+) min. dia.

Balled, up to 80 cm (2½ ft), good fibrous root system.

Hints Well-prepared soil, except alkaline. Over 80 cm (2½ ft) in height, extra organic material. May be scarce. Avoid drying out of pots or root balls. Research overall size.

Most widely available Abies alba (European Silver Fir). A. amabilis (Red-Silver Fir). A. cephalonica (Grecian Fir). A. concolor (Colorado White Fir). A. delavayi. A. firma (Japanese Fir). A. grandis (Giant Fir). A. holophylla (Manchurian Fir). A. homolepsis (Nikko Fir). A. magnifica Californian Red Fir). A. nordmanniana (Caucasian Fir). A. pindrow (West Himalayan Fir). A. pinsapo (Spanish Fir). A. procera (Noble Fir). A. spectabilis (Himalayan Fir).

ARAUCARIA ARAUCANA
Monkey Puzzle Tree, Chile Pine

Time to buy Pot-grown, any time except December–February. Balled, October–November or March–April. Avoid adverse weather conditions.

Where to find Outside in Specimen Conifers.

Size

40–60 cm (15 in–2 ft)

60–80 cm (2–2½ ft)

80 cm–1 m (2½–3 ft)

60 cm–1 m (2–3 ft) scarce.

Balled, more than 80 cm (2½ ft) difficult to establish.

Foliage Evergreen sharp flat needles. Mid green. Limited needle drop spring.

Roots Height purchased:

30–40 cm (12–15 in), pots 7 in (17 cm) (2 litre) min. dia.

40–60 cm (15 in–2 ft), pots 8 in (20 cm) (3 litre) min. dia.

Balled up to 60 cm (2 ft), good fibrous root system.

Hints Any well-prepared soil. Over 60 cm (2 ft) in height, extra organic material. May be scarce. Avoid drying out of pots or root-balls.

CALOCEDRUS forms
Incense Cedar

Time to buy Pot-grown, any time except December–January. Balled, October–November or March–April. Avoid adverse weather conditions.

Where to find Outside in Specimen Conifers.

Size

30–40 cm (12–15 in)

40–60 cm (15 in–2 ft)

60–80 cm (2–2½ ft)

80 cm–1 m (2½–3 ft)

Balled, more than 1 m (3 ft) difficult to establish.

Foliage Evergreen flat fronds. Mid to dark green, or golden-splashed variegated. Limited needle drop spring.

Roots Height purchased:

Up to 10 cm (4 in), pots 4 in (10 cm) min. dia.

30–40 cm (12–15 in), pots 7 in (17 cm) (2 litre) min. dia.

40–60 cm (15 in–2 ft), pots 8 in (20 cm) (3 litre) min. dia.

Balled, up to 1 m (3 ft), good fibrous root system.

Hints Any well-prepared soil. Over 1 m (3 ft) in height, extra organic material. May be scarce. Avoid drying out of pots or root-balls.

Most widely available: Calocedrus decurrens (libocedrus decurrens). C. d. 'Aureovariegata' (Golden Variegated Incense Cedar).

CEDRUS (slow-growing/dwarf)
Cedar

Time to buy Pot-grown, any time except December–February. Balled, October–November or March–April. Avoid adverse weather conditions.

Where to find Outside in Slow-growing (Dwarf), Spreading or Specimen Conifers.

Size
10–20 cm (4–8 in)
20–30 cm (8–12 in)
30–40 cm (12–15 in)
40–60 cm (15 in–2 ft)
60–80 cm (2–2½ ft)
Balled, more than 60 cm (2 ft) difficult to establish.

Foliage Horizontal branches carrying needles, grey-green, blue-green or golden. Limited needle drop spring.

Roots Height purchased:
Up to 10 cm (4 in), pots 4 in (10 cm) min. dia.
10–20 cm (4–8 in), pots 5 in (12 cm) (1 litre) min. dia.
20–30 cm (8–12 in), pots 7 in (17 cm) (2 litre) min. dia.
30–40 cm (12–15 in), pots 7 in (17 cm) (2 litre) min. dia.
40–60 cm (15 in–2 ft), pots 8 in (20 cm) (3 litre) min. dia.
Balled, up to 3 ft (1 m), good fibrous root system.

Hints Any well-prepared soil, except alkaline. Over 60 cm (2 ft) in height, extra organic material. Sold for use on rockeries, but quickly exceed space allowed. Avoid drying out of pots or root-balls.

Most widely available Cedrus deodora 'Cream Puff'. C. d. 'Golden Horizon'. C. d. 'Karl Fuchs'. C. d. 'Nana Aurea'. C. libani 'Sargentii'.

CEDRUS (tall-growing)
Cedar
Time to buy Pot-grown, any time except December–February. Balled, October–May or March–April. Avoid adverse weather conditions.
Where to find Outside in Specimen Conifers.
Size
30–40 cm (12–15 in)
40–60 cm (15 in–2 ft)
60–80 cm (2–2½ ft)
80 cm–1 m (2½–3 ft)
1–1.20 m (3–4 ft)
Balled, more than 1.2 m (4 ft) difficult to establish.

Foliage Evergreen short needles in clusters. Light to dark grey, blue to blue-green or golden. Limited needle drop spring.

Roots Height purchased:
Up to 60 cm (2 ft), pots 6 in (15 cm) min. dia.
80 cm–1 m (2½–3 ft), pots 10 in (25 cm) (3 litre) min. dia.
1 m (3 ft) and above, pots 15 in (40 cm) min. dia.
Balled, up to 1 m (3 ft), good fibrous root system.

Hints Any well-prepared soil. Over 1 m (3 ft) in height, extra organic material. May be scarce, particularly taller plants. Avoid drying out of pots or root-balls. Research ultimate overall size.

Most widely available Cedrus atlantica (Atlas Cedar). C. a. 'Aurea' (Golden Atlas Cedar). C. a. 'Fastigiate' (Upright Atlas Cedar). C. a. (Blue Atlas Cedar). C. a. 'Glauca Pendula' (Weeping Blue Atlas Cedar). C. deodora (The Deodar, Indian Cedar). C. d. 'Aurea' (Golden Deodar, Golden Indian Cedar). C. libani (Cedar of Lebanon).

CEPHALOTAXUS forms
Chinese Plum Yew
Time to buy Pot-grown, any time except December–February. Balled, October–November or March–April. Avoid adverse weather conditions.
Where to find Outside in Slow-growing (Dwarf) or Specimen Conifers.
Size
20–30 cm (8–12 in)
30–40 cm (12–15 in)
40–60 cm (15 in–2 ft)
60–80 cm (2–2½ ft)
Balled, more than 60 cm (2 ft) difficult to establish.

Foliage Evergreen short soft needles.
Dark green with silver reverse. Limited
needle drop spring.
Roots Height purchased:
30–40 cm (12–15 in), pots 7 in (17 cm) (2
litre) min. dia.
40–60 cm (15 in–2 ft), pots 8 in (20 cm) (3
litre) min. dia.
Balled, up to 1 m (3 ft), good fibrous root
system.
Hints Any well-prepared soil, except alkaline. Scarce. Avoid drying out of pots
or root-balls. Research overall size.
Most widely available Cephalotaxus fortunei. C. harringtonia drupacea (Cow's
Tail Pine). C. h. 'Fastigiata' (Upright
Cow's Tail Pine, Upright Japanese Plum
Yew).

CHAMAECYPARIS (slow-growing/
dwarf)
Time to buy Pot-grown, any time except
December–February. Balled, October–
November or March–April. Avoid adverse
weather conditions.
Where to find Outside in Slow-growing
(Dwarf) or Specimen Conifers.
Size
Up to 10 cm (4 in)
10–20 cm (4–8 in)
20–30 cm (8–12 in)
30–40 cm (12–15 in)
Balled, more than 60 cm (2 ft) difficult to
establish.
Foliage Evergreen soft fronds. Mid, dark
or grey-green, gold, blue or white variegated. Limited needle drop spring.
Roots Height purchased:
Up to 10 cm (4 in), pots 4 in (10 cm) min.
dia.
10–20 cm (4–8 in), pots 5 in (12 cm) (1
litre) min. dia.
20–30 cm (8–12 in), pots 7 in (17 cm) (2
litre) min. dia.
30–40 cm (12–15 in), pots 7 in (17 cm) (2
litre) min. dia.
Balled, up to 1 m (3 ft), good fibrous root
system.

Hints Any well-prepared soil. Wide
range. Avoid drying out of pots or root-
balls. Although considered dwarf, allow
adequate space for development.
Most widely available
Chamaecyparis lawsoniana (Slow-grow-
ing) Chamaecyparis lawsoniana. C. l.
'Albospica'. C. l. 'Aurea Densa'. C. l.
'Elwoodii'. C. l. 'Ellwood's Gold'. C. l.
'Ellwood's Pillar'. C. l. 'Ellwood's White'
(C. l. 'Ellwood's Variegata'). C. l. 'Gimbor-
nii'. C. l. 'Gnome'. C. l. 'Golden Pot'. C. l.
'Green Globe'. C. l. 'Little Spire'. C. l.
'Lutea Compacta'. C. l. 'Lutea Nana'. C. l.
'Minima'. C. l. 'Minima Aurea'. C. l. 'Nidi-
formis'. C. l. 'Nymph'. C. l. 'Pygmaea Arg-
entea'. C. l. 'Rijnhof'. C. l. 'Silver Threads'.
C. l. 'Summer Snow'.
Chamaecyparis obtusa (Slow-growing)
Chamaecyparis obtusa 'Fernspray Gold'.
C. o. 'Intermedia'. C. o. 'Juniperoides'.
C. o. 'Kosteri'. C. o. 'Nana'. C. o. 'Nana
Aurea'. C. o. 'Nana Gracilis'. C. o. 'Nana
Lutea'. C. o. 'Tetragona Aurea'.
Chamaecyparis pisifera (Slow-growing)
Chamaecyparis pisifera 'Boulevard'. C. p.
'Filifera Aurea'. C. p. 'Filifera Aureovar-
iegata'. C. p. 'Gold Spangle'. C. p. 'Nana'.
C. p. 'Nana Aureovariegata'. C. p. 'Plum-
osa Aurea Nana'. C. p. 'Plumosa Com-
pressa'. C. p. 'Plumosa Purple Dome'.
C. p. 'Silver and Gold'. C. p. 'Snow'. C. p.
'Squarrosa Lombarts'. C. p. 'Squarrosa
Sulphurea'. C. p. 'White Pygmy'.
Chamaecyparis thyoides (Slow-growing)
Chamaecyparis thyoides 'Ericoides'. C. t.
'Rubicon'.

CHAMAECYPARIS (specimen and
screening)
False Cypress
Time to buy Pot-grown, any time except
December–February. Balled, October–
November or March–April. Avoid ad-
verse weather conditions.
Where to find Outside in Specimen or
Screening Conifers.

Size

30–40 cm (12–15 in)

40–60 cm (15 in–2 ft)

60–80 cm (2–2½ ft)

80 cm–1 m (2½–3 ft)

1–1.2 m (3–4 ft)

Foliage Evergreen flat, feathery fronds. Mid, dark or grey-green, gold or blue, splashed white. Upright or pendulous. Limited yellowing of fronds.

Roots Height purchased:

Up to 60 cm (2 ft), pots 6 in (15 cm) min. dia.

80 cm–1 m (2½–3 ft), pots 10 in (25 cm) (3 litre) min. dia.

1 m (3 ft) and above, pots 15 in (40 cm) (5 litre) min. dia.

Balled, up to 1 m (3 ft), good fibrous root system.

Hints Any well-prepared soil. Over 60 cm (2 ft) in height, extra organic material. Wide range. May be scarce. Avoid drying out of pots or root-balls. Avoid planting larger material which is difficult to establish. *Chamaecyparis lawsoniana* often offered mail order. Care should be taken when purchasing this way. Research overall size.

Most widely available:

Chamaecyparis lawsoniana. C. l. 'Alumii'. C. l. 'Broomhill Gold'. C. l. 'Chilworth Silver'. C. l. 'Columnaris'. C. l. 'Erecta'. C. l. 'Fletcheri'. C. l. 'Fraseri'. C. l. 'Golden Wonder'. C. l. 'Green Hedger'. C. l. 'Green Pillar'. C. l. 'Kilmacurragh'. C. l. 'Lane'. C. l. 'Lutea'. C. l. 'Pembury Blue'. C. l. 'Pottenti'. C. l. 'Pyramidalis'. C. l. 'Somerset'. C. l. 'Stardust'. C. l. 'Stewartii'. C. l. 'Triomf van Boskoop'. C. l. 'Westermannii'. C. l. 'Winston Churchill'. C. l. 'Wisselii'.

Chamaecyparis nootkatensis Chamaecyparis nootkatensis (Nootka Cypress). C. n. 'Glauca;. C. n. 'Lutea'. C. n. 'Pendula'.

Chamaecyparis obtusa forms Chamaecyparis obtusa 'Crippsii'.

Chamaecyparis pisifera forms Chamaecyparis pisifera 'Plumosa'. C. p. 'Plumosa Aurea'.

CRYPTOMERIA (slow-growing/dwarf)

Dwarf Cypress

Time to buy Pot-grown, any time except December–February. Balled, October–November or March–April. Avoid adverse weather conditions.

Where to find Outside in Slow-growing (Dwarf) or Specimen Conifers.

Size

Up to 10 cm (4 in)

10–20 cm (4–8 in)

20–30 cm (8–12 in)

30–40 cm (12–15 in)

Balled, more than 60 cm (2 ft) difficult to establish.

Foliage Evergreen cord-like stems, covered in flat close-clinging needles. Mid to dark green, tinged purple.

Roots Height purchased:

Up to 10 cm (4 in), pots 4 in (10 cm) min. dia.

10–20 cm (4–8 in), pots 5 in (12 cm) (1 litre) min. dia.

20–30 cm (8–12 in), pots 7 in (17 cm) (2 litre) min. dia.

30–40 cm (12–15 in), pots 7 in (17 cm) (2 litre) min. dia.

Balled, up to 60 cm (2 ft), good fibrous root system.

Hints Any well-prepared soil. May be scarce. Avoid drying out of pots or root-balls. Relatively small when purchased, allow adequate space for development.

Most widely available Cryptomeria japonica 'Compressa'. C. j. 'Elegans Compacta'. C. j. 'Sakken Sugi'. C. j. 'Vilmoriniana'.

CRYPTOMERIA (specimen forms)

Japanese Cedar

Time to buy Pot-grown, any time except December–February. Balled, October–November or March–April. Avoid adverse weather conditions.

Where to find Outside in Specimen Conifers. *Cryptomeria japonica* 'Elegans' may be found under slow-growing dwarf forms, which it is not.

Size

40–60 cm (15 in–2 ft)

60–80 cm (2–2½ ft)

80 cm–1 m (2½–3 ft)

60 cm–1 m (2–3 ft) scarce.

Foliage Evergreen long cord-like branches closely covered in flat overlapping needles. Light to mid green. *Cryptomeria japonica* reddish hue in autumn. *Cryptomeria japonica* 'Elegans' plum to brown from autumn through winter, with soft-yellow foliage in spring.

Roots Height purchased:

Up to 60 cm (2 ft), pots 6 in (15 cm) min. dia.

80 cm–1 m (2½–3 ft), pots 10 in (25 cm) (3 litre) min. dia.

1 m (3 ft) and above, pots 15 in (40 cm) (5 litre) min. dia.

Balled, up to 1 m (3 ft), good fibrous root system.

Hints Any well-prepared soil. Over 60 cm (2 ft) in height, extra organic material. Some forms scarce. Avoid drying out of pots or root-balls. Research overall size. Rarely show-off full potential when young.

Most widely available *Cryptomeria japonica*. *C. j.* 'Cristata'. *C. j.* 'Elegans'. *C.* 'Dacrydioides'.

× CUPRESSOCYPARIS LEYLANDII

Lawson Cupressus

Time to buy Pot-grown, any time except December–February. Avoid adverse weather conditions.

Where to find Outside in Specimen Conifers, Hedging or Screening.

Size

20–30 cm (8–12 in)

30–40 cm (12–15 in)

40–60 cm (15 in–2 ft)

60–80 cm (2–2½ ft)

80 cm–1 m (2½–3 ft)

1–1.2 m (3–4 ft)

1.2–1.5 m (4–5 ft)

1.5–2 m (5–6 ft)

In the author's opinion, the preferred planting height is 60–80 cm (2–2½ ft). 1.2–2 m (4–6 ft) may be scarce.

Foliage Evergreen flat, soft fronds. Mid green, golden or white variegated.

Roots Should always be purchased pot-grown. Height purchased:

Up to 60 cm (2 ft), pots 6 in (15 cm) min. dia.

80 cm–1 m (2½–3 ft), pots 10 in (25 cm) (3 litre) min. dia.

1 m (3 ft), pots 15 in (40 cm) (5 litre) min. dia.

Above 1 m pots 15–24 in (40–60 cm) (5–10 litre) min. dia.

Hints Any well-prepared soil. Over 1.2 m (4 ft) in height, extra organic material. Avoid drying out of pots or root-balls. Research overall size, very fast growing.

Most widely available × *Cupressocyparis leylandii*. *C. l.* 'Castlewellan Gold'. *C. l.* 'Golconda'. *C. l.* 'Howarth's Gold'. *C. l.* 'Robinson's Gold'. *C. l.* Variegata.

CUPRESSUS

Cypress

Time to buy Pot-grown, any time except December–February. Golden foliage forms April–July. Avoid adverse weather conditions.

Where to find Outside in Specimen Conifers.

Size

40–60 cm (15 in–2 ft)

60–80 cm (2–2½ ft)

80 cm–1 m (2½–3 ft)

Foliage Evergreen soft upright fronds. Dark green, grey-green, blue or gold.

Roots Height purchased:

30–40 cm (12–15 in), pots 7 in (17 cm) (2 litre) min. dia.

40–60 cm (15 in–2 ft), pots 8 in (20 cm) (3 litre) min. dia.

Hints Any well-prepared soil. Over 60 cm (2 ft) in height, extra organic material. May be scarce. Avoid drying out of pots or root-balls. *Cupressus macrocarpa* hardiness in doubt.

Most widely available: Cupressus glabra
'Pyramidalis' (C. 'Arizonica Conica'). C.
macrocarpa. C. m. 'Donard Gold'. C. m.
'Goldcrest'. C. m. 'Golden Pillar'. C. m.
'Lutea'. C. sempervirens (Italian Cypress).
C. s. 'Aurea'.

GINKGO
Maidenhair Tree
Time to buy Pot-grown, any time except
December–February. Balled, October–
November or March–April. Avoid adverse weather conditions.
Where to Find Outside in Specimen Conifers or Trees.
Size
20–30 cm (8–12 in)
30–40 cm (12–15 in)
40–60 cm (15 in–2 ft)
60–80 cm (2–2½ ft)
80 cm–1 m (2½–3 ft)
Preferred planting height 40 cm–1 m
(15 in–3 ft).
Above 1 m (3 ft) scarce.
Balled, more than 1 m (3 ft) difficult to
establish.
Foliage Deciduous. Spring/summer, flat,
heart-shaped, mid green. Premature
autumn colour and leaf drop.
Roots Height purchased:
Up to (60 cm) (2 ft), pots 10 in (25 cm)
min. dia.
80 cm–1 m (2½–3 ft), pots 10 in (25 cm) (3
litre) min. dia.
1 m (3 ft), pots 15 in (40 cm) (5 litre), min.
dia.
Balled, up to 1 m (3 ft), good fibrous root
system.
Hints Any well-prepared soil, except alkaline. Over 80 cm (2½ ft) in height, extra
organic material. Ginkgo biloba 'Fastigiata' and Ginkgo biloba 'Variegata' scarce.
Avoid drying out of pots or root-balls. Leading shoot often missing, once planted will
produce new leader. Straight stems impossible to obtain. Research overall size.
Most widely available: Ginkgo biloba.
G. b. 'Variegata'. G. 'Fastigiata'.

JUNIPERUS (slow-growing/dwarf)
Juniper
Time to buy Pot-grown, any time except
December–February. Balled, October–
November or March–April. Avoid ad-
verse weather conditions.
Where to find Outside in Slow-growing
(Dwarf) or Specimen Conifers.
Size
Up to 10 cm (4 in)
10–20 cm (4–8 in)
20–30 cm (8–12 in)
30–40 cm (12–15 in)
Balled more than 60 cm (2 ft) difficult to
establish.
Foliage Evergreen sharp pointed needles.
Green, blue or gold. Limited needle drop
spring.
Roots Height purchased:
Up to 10 cm (4 in), pots 4 in (10 cm) min.
dia.
10–20 cm (4–8 in), pots 5 in (12 cm) (1
litre) min. dia.
20–30 cm (8–12 in), pots 7 in (17 cm) (2
litre) min. dia.
30–40 cm (12–15 in), pots 7 in (17 cm) (2
litre) min. dia.
Balled, up to 60 cm (2 ft), good fibrous
root system.
Hints Any well-prepared soil. May be
scarce. Avoid drying out of pots or root-
ball. Although considered dwarf, allow
adequate space for development
Most widely available Juniperus chinensis 'Aurea'. J. c. 'Kuriwao Gold'. J. c.
'Pyramidalis'. J. c. 'Blue Pygmy'. J. c.
'Compressa'. J. c. 'Gold Cone'. J. c.
'Golden Showers'. J. c. 'Sentinel'. J. hori-
zontalis 'Blue Chip'. J. h. 'Grey Pearl'.
J. h. 'Plumosa Aurea'. J. h. 'Plumosa
Youngstown'. J. h. 'Prince of Wales'. J.
procumbens 'Nana'. J. squamata 'Blue
Alps'. J. s. 'Blue Star'. J. s. 'Blue Swede'.
J. s. 'Chinese Silver'. J. virginiana. J. v.
'Skyrocket'.

JUNIPERUS (spreading)
Spreading Juniper

Time to buy Pot-grown, any time except
December–February. Balled, October–
November or March–April. Avoid ad-
verse weather conditions.

Where to find Outside in Slow-growing
(Dwarf), Specimen, Ground-cover, or
Spreading Conifers.

Size
30–40 cm (12–15 in)
40–60 cm (15 in–2 ft)
60–80 cm (2–2½ ft)
80 cm–1 m (2½–3 ft)
1–1.2 m (3–4 ft)
Balled, more than 60 cm (2 ft) difficult to
establish.

Foliage Evergreen sharp pointed needles.
Green, blue or gold. Branches ground-
hugging or arching. Limited needle drop
spring.

Roots Height purchased:
Up to 10 cm (4 in), pots 4 in (10 cm) min.
dia.
10–20 cm (4–8 in), pots 5 in (12 cm) (1
litre) min. dia.
20–30 cm (8–12 in), pots 7 in (17 cm) (2
litre) min. dia.
30–40 cm (12–15 in), pots 7 in (17 cm) (2
litre) min. dia.
Balled, up to 60 cm (2 ft), good fibrous
root system.

Hints Any well-prepared soil. May be
scarce. Avoid drying out of pots or root-
balls. Although considered dwarf, allow
adequate space for development.

Most widely available *Juniperus com-
munis* 'Depressa Aurea'. *J. c.* 'Green
Carpet'. *J. c.* 'Hornibrookii'. *J. c.* 'Re-
panda'. *J. conferta. J. c.* 'Blue Pacific'. *J.
horizontalis* 'Banff'. *J. h.* 'Bar Habror'. *J. h.*
'Douglassii'. *J. h.* 'Glauca'. *J. h.* 'Hetzii'.
J. h. 'Hughes' *J. × m.* 'Blue and Gold'.
J. × m. 'Gold Coast'. *J. × m.* 'Gold Sove-
reign'. *J. × m.* 'Mint Julep'. *J. × m.* 'Old
Gold'. *J. × m.* 'Pfitzerana Glauca'. *J. ×
m.* 'Sulphur Spray'. *J. sabina* 'Blue
Danube'. *J. s. tamariscifolia. J. scopulo-
rum* 'Tabletop Blue'. *J. squamata* 'Blue
Carpet'.

JUNIPERUS (upright growing)
Juniper
Time to buy Pot-grown, any time except
December–February. Balled, October–
December or March–April. Avoid adverse
weather conditions.

Where to find Outside in Slow-growing
(Dwarf) or Specimen Conifers.

Size
20–30 cm (8–12 in)
30–40 cm (12–15 in)
40–60 cm (15 in–2 ft)
60–80 cm (2–2½ ft)
80 cm–1 m (2½–3 ft)
1–1.2 m (3–4 ft)
Balled, more than 60 cm (2 ft) difficult to
establish.

Foliage Evergreen sharp pointed needles.
Green, blue or gold. Neat, tight, upright
habit. Limited needle drop spring.

Roots Height purchased:
Up to 10 cm (4 in), pots 4 in (10 cm) min.
dia.
10–20 cm (4–8 in), pots 5 in (12 cm) (1
litre) min. dia.
20–30 cm (8–12 in), pots 7 in (17 cm) (2
litre) min. dia.
30–40 cm (12–15 in), pots 7 in (17 cm) (2
litre) min. dia.
40–60 cm (15 in–2 ft), pots 8 in (20 cm) (3
litre) min. dia.
Balled, up to 1 m (3 ft), good fibrous root
system.

Hints Any well-prepared soil. Over
60 cm (2 ft) in height, extra organic
material. May be scarce. Avoid drying
out of pots or root-balls. Smaller heights
establish better.

Most widely available *Juniperus communis* 'Hibernica' (Irish Juniper). *J. recurva coxii. J. scopulorum* 'Blue Heaven'.
J. s. 'Moonglow'. *J. s.* 'Skyrocket'. *J. s.*
'Springbank'. *J. s.* 'Witchita Blue'. *J. squamata* 'Meyeri'.

LARIX (slow-growing/dwarf)
Dwarf Larch
Time to buy Pot-grown, any time except

December–February. Avoid adverse weather conditions.
Where to find Outside in Slow-growing (Dwarf) or Specimen Conifers.
Size
Up to 10 cm (4 in)
10–20 cm (4–8 in)
20–30 cm (8–12 in)
30–40 cm (12–15 in)
40–60 cm (15 in–2 ft)
Foliage Deciduous. Spring/summer blue, grey-green to light green. Premature autumn colour and leaf drop.
Roots Height purchased:
Up to 10 cm (4 in), pots 4 in (10 cm) min. dia.
10–20 cm (4–8 in), pots 5 in (12 cm) (1 litre) min. dia.
20–30 cm (8–12 in), pots 7 in (17 cm) (2 litre) min. dia.
30–40 cm (12–15 in), pots 7 in (17 cm) (2 litre) min. dia.
40–60 cm (15 in–2 ft), pots 8 in (20 cm) (3 litre) min. dia.
Hints Any well-prepared soil. Over 60 cm (2 ft) in height, extra organic material. Scarce. Avoid drying out of pots or root-balls. Although dwarf, research overall size.
Most widely available Larix kaempferi 'Blue Dwarf'. L. k. 'Nana'.

LARIX (specimen forms)
Larch
Time to buy Pot-grown, any time except December–February. Balled, October–November or March–April. Larix decidua, bare-rooted from November–March. Avoid adverse weather conditions.
Where to find Outside in Specimen or Screening Conifers.
Size
30–40 cm (12–15 in)
40–60 cm (15 in–2 ft)
60–80 cm (2–2½ ft)
80 cm–1 m (2½–3 ft)
1–1.2 m (3–4 ft)
Larix kaempferi 'Pendula', feathered,

1.2 m (4 ft) min. Minimum five side branches, minimum 30 cm (1 ft) long. Top-worked, stems 1.5 m (5 ft) min. Minimum three main branches originating from graft or budded union, 50 cm (1½ ft) min. long. Balled, more than 1 m (3 ft) difficult to establish.
Foliage Deciduous. Spring/summer, light green. Premature autumn colour and leaf drop.
Roots Height purchased:
Up to 10 cm (4 in), pots 4 in (10 cm) min. dia.
Up to 60 cm (2 ft), pots 6 in (15 cm) (1 litre) min. dia.
80 cm–1 m (2½–3 ft), pots 10 in (25 cm) (3 litre) min. dia.
1 m (3 ft), pots 15 in (40 cm) (5 litre) min. dia.
Larix kaempferi 'Pendula', pots 12 in. (30 cm) min. dia.
Balled, up to 1 m (3 ft) good fibrous root system.
Hints Any well-prepared soil. Over 60 cm (2 ft) in height, extra organic material. Larix kaempferi 'Pendula' scarce. Larix decidua from forestry outlets. Avoid drying out of pots or root-balls.
Most widely available Larix decidua (European Larch). L. kaempferi (Japanese Larch). L. k. 'Pendula' (Weeping Larch).

MICROBIOTA DECUSSATA
Time to buy Pot-grown, any time except December–February. Avoid adverse weather conditions.
Where to find Outside in Conifers.
Size
Up to 10 cm (4 in)
10–20 cm (4–8 in)
20–30 cm (8–12 in)
30–40 cm (12–15 in)
40–60 cm (15 in–2 ft)
Foliage Evergreen or mid green in summer. Dark green with bronze hue in autumn and winter.
Roots Height purchased:

Up to 10 cm (4 in), pots 4 in (10 cm) min. dia.

10–20 cm (4–8 in), pots 5 in (12 cm) (1 litre) min. dia.

20–30 cm (8–12 in), pots 7 in (17 cm) (2 litre) min. dia.

30–40 cm (12–15 in), pots 7 in (17 cm) (2 litre) min. dia.

40–60 cm (15 in–2 ft), pots 8 in (20 cm) (3 litre) min. dia.

Hints Any well-prepared soil. Over 60 cm (2 ft) in height, extra organic material. Scarce. Avoid drying out of pots or rootballs. Research overall size.

METASEQUOIA GLYPTOSTROBOIDES
Dawn Redwood

Time to buy Pot-grown, any time except December–February. Balled October–November or March–April. Avoid adverse weather conditions.

Where to Find Outside in Specimen Conifers or Trees.

Size

20–30 cm (8–12 in)

30–40 cm (12–15 in)

40–60 cm (15 in–2 ft)

60–80 cm (2–2½ ft)

80 cm–1 m (2½–3 ft)

1–1.2 m (3–4 ft)

1.2–1.5 m (4–5 ft)

1.5–2 m (5–6 ft)

Balled, more than 60 cm (2 ft) difficult to establish.

Foliage Deciduous. Spring/summer, soft green. Flat, fern-like. Yellow to bronze-brown late summer. Premature autumn colour and leaf drop.

Roots Height purchased:

Up to 60 cm (2 ft), pots 6 in (15 cm) min. dia.

80 cm–1 m (2½–3 ft), pots 10 in (25 cm) min. dia.

1 m (3 ft), pots 15 in (40 cm) (5 litre) min. dia.

Balled, up to 1 m (3 ft), good fibrous root system.

Hints Any well-prepared soil. Over 1.2 m (4 ft) in height, extra organic material. May be scarce. Often stored amongst trees, but is truly a conifer.

PICEA (slow-growing/dwarf)
Dwarf Spruce

Time to buy Pot-grown, any time except December–February. Balled, October–November or March–April. Avoid adverse weather conditions.

Where to find Outside in Slow-growing (Dwarf) or Specimen Conifers.

Size

Up to 10 cm (4 in)

10–20 cm (4–8 in)

20–30 cm (8–12 in)

30–40 cm (12–15 in)

Balled, more than 60 cm (2 ft) difficult to establish.

Foliage Evergreen short stiff spines. Green, grey-green or gold. Limited needle drop spring.

Roots Height purchased:

Up to 10 cm (4 in), pots 4 in (10 cm) min. dia.

10–20 cm (4–8 in), pots 5 in (12 cm) (1 litre) min. dia.

20–30 cm (8–12 in), pots 7 in (17 cm) (2 litre) min. dia.

30–40 cm (12–15 in), pots 7 in (17 cm) (2 litre) min. dia.

Balled, up to 60 cm (2 ft) good fibrous root system.

Hints Any well-prepared soil. May be scarce. Avoid drying out of pots or rootball. Research overall size.

Most widely available *Picea abies* 'Argenteo-spica'. *P. a.* 'Nidiformis'. *P. a.* 'Formanek'. *P. a.* 'Little Gem'. *P. a.* 'Will's Zwerg' (Will's Dwarf). *P. glauca* 'Alberta Globe'. *P. g.* 'Laurin'. *P. mariana* 'Aureo-variegata'. *P. m.* 'Nana'. *P. obovata* 'Glauca'. *P. omorika* 'Minimax'. *P. o.* 'Nana'. *P. orientalis* 'Wittbold'. *P. pungens* 'Globosa'. *P. p.* 'Prostrata'. *P. sitchensis* 'Papoose'. *P. s.* 'Tenas'.

PICEA (specimen forms)
Spruce
Time to buy Pot-grown, any time except December–February. Balled, October–November or March–April. Avoid adverse weather conditions.
Where to find Outside in Specimen Conifers.
Size
40–60 cm (15 in–2 ft)
60–80 cm (2–2½ ft)
80 cm–1 m (2½–3 ft)
60 cm–1 m (2–3 ft) scarce.
Balled, more than 80 cm (2½ ft) difficult to establish.
Foliage Evergreen. Close, short, sharp needles along branches. Mid green, grey-green to bright blue. Limited needle drop spring.
Roots Height purchased:
30–40 cm (12–15 in), pots 7 in (17 cm) (2 litre) min. dia.
40–60 cm (15 in–2 ft), pots 8 in (20 cm) (3 litre) min. dia.
Balled, up to 80 cm (2½ ft), good fibrous root system.
Hints Any well-prepared soil. Over 60 cm (2 ft), extra organic material. Wide range. Avoid drying out of pots or root-ball. Research overall size.
Most widely available Picea abies. P. a. 'Columnaris'. P. a. 'Frohburg'. P. a. 'Inversa Major'. P. a. 'Magnifica Aurea' (Norway Spruce). P. bicolor. P. brewerana (Brewer's Weeping Spruce). P. engelmannii 'Glauca'. P. omorika (Serbian Spruce). P. o. 'Pendula'. P. orientalis 'Aurea' (P. o. 'Albospica'). P. pungens (Blue Spruce). P. p. 'Endtz'. P. p. 'Hoopsii'. P. p. 'Hoto'. P. p. 'Koster'. P. p. 'Moerheimii'. P. p. 'Pendula'. P. p. 'Thomsen'.

PINUS (slow-growing/dwarf)
Dwarf Pine
Time to buy Pot-grown, any time except December–February. Balled, October–November or March–April. Avoid adverse weather conditions.

Where to find Outside in Slow-growing (Dwarf) or Specimen Conifers.
Size
Up to 10 cm (4 in)
10–20 cm (4–8 in)
20–30 cm (8–12 in)
30–40 cm (12–15 in)
Balled more than 60 cm (2 ft) difficult to establish.
Foliage Evergreen needles in clumps. Green, blue, gold or variegated. Limited needle drop spring.
Roots Height purchased:
Up to 10 cm (4 in), pots 4 in (10 cm) min. dia.
10–20 cm (4–8 in), pots 5 in (12 cm) (1 litre) min. dia.
20–30 cm (8–12 in), pots 7 in (17 cm) (2 litre) min. dia.
30–40 cm (12–15 in), pots 7 in (17 cm) (2 litre) min. dia.
Balled, up to 60 cm (2 ft), good fibrous root system.
Hints Any well-prepared soil. Wide range. Avoid drying out of pots or root-ball. Although considered dwarf, allow adequate space of development.
Most widely available Pinus aristata 'Sherwood Compact'. P. cembra 'Glauca'. P. contorta 'Frisian Gold'. P. c. 'Spaan's Dwarf'. P. leucodermis 'Compact Gem'. P. l. 'Schmidtii'. P. l. 'Stellit'. P. mugo 'Corley's Mat'. P. m. 'Humpy'. P. m. 'Mops'. P. m. 'Ophir'. P. m. 'Wintergold'. P. parviflora 'Glauca'. P. p. 'Negishii'. P. p. 'Dwarf Blue'. P. p. 'Globe'. P. radiata 'Aurea'. P. strobus 'Nana'. P. s. 'Pyramidalis'. P. s. 'Reinhaus'. P. sylvestris 'Inverleith'. P. thunbergii 'Sayonara'.

PINUS (specimen and screening)
Pine
Time to buy Pot-grown, any time except December–February. Balled, October–November or March–April. Pinus sylvestris, bare-rooted November–March. Avoid adverse weather conditions.

Where to find Outside in Specimen or Screening Conifers.
Size
20–30 cm (8–12 in)
30–40 cm (12–15 in)
40–60 cm (15 in–2 ft)
60–80 cm (2–2½ ft)
80 cm–1 m (2½–3 ft)
1–1.2 m (3–4 ft)
1.2–1.5 m (4–5 ft)
1.5–2 m (5–6 ft)
Best planting height 60–80 cm (2–2½ ft).
1.2 m–2 m (4–6 ft) may be scarce.
Balled, more than 60 cm (2 ft) difficult to establish.
Foliage Evergreen long sharp needles in clusters. Dark or grey-green, gold or blue. Limited needle drop spring.
Roots
Height purchased:
Up to 10 cm (4 in), pots 4 in (10 cm) min. dia.
10–20 cm (4–8 in), pots 5 in (12 cm) (1 litre) min. dia.
20–30 cm (8–12 in), pots 7 in. (17 cm) (2 litre) min. dia.
30–40 cm (12–15 in), pots 7 in (17 cm) (2 litre) min. dia.
40–60 cm (15 in–2 ft), pots 8 in (20 cm) (3 litre) min. dia.
Balled, up to 60 cm (2 ft), good fibrous root system.
Hints Any well-prepared soil. Over 60 cm (2 ft) in height, extra organic material. Wide range, many from forestry outlets, particularly *Pinus sylvestris*. Avoid drying out of pots or root-ball. Research ultimate overall size.
Most widely available *Pinus jeffreyi. P. leucodermis* (Bosnian Pine). *P. nigra* (Austrian Pine). *P. parviflora* 'Brevifolia'. *P. pinea* (Stone Pine). *P. ponderosa* (Western Yellow Pine). *P. radiata* (Monterey Pine). *P. strobus* (Weymouth Pine). *P. s.* 'Nana'. *P. sylvestris* (Scots Pine). *P. s.* 'Aurea'. *P. s.* 'Beuvronensis'. *P. s.* 'Fastigiata'. *P. s.* 'Watereri'. *P. wallichiana* (Bhutan Pine).

PODOCARPUS
Time to buy Pot-grown, April–October. Avoid adverse weather conditions.
Where to find Outside in Slow-growing (Dwarf) or Specimen Conifers.
Size
10–20 cm (4–8 in)
20–30 cm (8–12 in)
30–40 cm (12–15 in)
Foliage Evergreen flat fronds. Grey-green to blue-green.
Roots Height purchased:
Up to 10 cm (4 in), pots 4 in (10 cm) min. dia.
10–20 cm (4–8 in), pots 5 in (12 cm) (1 litre) min. dia.
20–30 cm (8–12 in), pots 7 in (17 cm) (2 litre) min. dia.
30–40 cm (12–15 in), pots 7 in (17 cm) (2 litre) min. dia.
Hints Any well-prepared soil. Over 60 cm (2 ft) extra organic material. Scarce. Hardiness suspect. Research ultimate overall size.
Most widely available *Podocarpus alpinus* 'Blue Gem'. *P. nivalis* 'Alpine Totara'.

PSEUDOTSUGA (slow-growing/dwarf)
Douglas Fir
Time to buy Pot-grown, any time except December–February. Avoid adverse weather conditions.
Where to find Outside in Slow-growing or Specimen Conifers.
Size
10–20 cm (4–8 in)
20–30 cm (8–12 in)
30–40 cm (12–15 in)
Foliage Evergreen soft fronds. Dark green or silver blue.
Roots Height purchased:
Up to 10 cm (4 in), pots 4 in (10 cm) min. dia.
10–20 cm (4–8 in), pots 5 in (12 cm) (1 litre) min. dia.
20–30 cm (8–12 in), pots 7 in (17 cm) (2 litre) min. dia.

30–40 cm (12–15 in), pots 7 in (17 cm) (2 litre) min. dia.

Hints Any well-prepared soil. Over 60 cm (2 ft) in height, extra organic material. Scarce. Avoid drying out of pots. Research overall size.

Most widely available *Pseudotsuga menziesii* 'Blue Wonder'. *P. m.* 'Hillside Pride'.

PSEUDOTSUGA MENZIESII
Oregon Douglas Fir

Time to buy Pot-grown, any time except December–February. Balled, October–November or March–April. Avoid adverse weather conditions.

Where to find Outside in Specimen Conifers.

Size
40–60 cm (15 in–2 ft)
60–80 cm (2–2½ ft)
80 cm–1 m (2½–3 ft)
Balled, more than 60 cm (2 ft) difficult to establish.

Foliage Evergreen soft fronds. Summer, grey to mid green. Autumn, darker with bronze tinge.

Roots
Height purchased:
30–40 cm (12–15 in), pots 7 in (17 cm) (2 litre) min. dia.
40–60 cm (15 in–2 ft), pots 8 in (20 cm) (3 litre) min. dia.
Balled, up to 60 cm (2 ft) good fibrous root system.

Hints Well-prepared neutral to acid soil. Over 60 cm (2 ft) in height, extra organic material. May be scarce. Avoid drying out of pots or root-ball.

Most widely available *Pseudotsuga menziesii*.

SCIADOPITYS VERTICILLATA
Umbrella Pine

Time to buy Pot-grown, any time except December–February. Balled, October–November to March–April. Avoid adverse weather conditions.

Where to find Outside in Specimen Conifers.

Size
40–60 cm (15 in–2 ft)
60–80 cm (2–2½ ft)
80 cm–1 m (2½–3 ft)
60 cm–1 m (2–3 ft) scarce.
Balled, more than 80 cm (2½ ft) difficult to establish.

Foliage Evergreen long thin needles in clusters. Dark green, bronze-green tinge in autumn and winter.

Roots Height purchased:
30–40 cm (12–15 in), pots 7 in (17 cm) (2 litre) min. dia.
40–60 cm (15 in–2 ft), pots 8 in (20 cm) (3 litre) min. dia.
Balled, up to 80 cm (2½ ft) good fibrous root system.

Hints Any well-prepared soil. Over 60 cm (2 ft) in height, extra organic material. Scarce. Avoid drying out of pots or rootball. Slow to establish. Wind screen advised in exposed positions in first and second winters.

SEQUOIA
Redwood

Time to buy Pot-grown, any time except December–February. Avoid adverse weather conditions.

Where to find Outside in Specimen Conifers.

Size
40–60 cm (15 in–2 ft)
60–80 cm (2–2½ ft)
80 cm–1 m (2½–3 ft)
60 cm–1 m (2–3 ft) scarce.
Sequoia sempervirens 'Depressa' heights should be interpreted as spreads. Height up to 60–80cm (2–2½ ft).

Foliage Evergreen soft fronds. Silver-green in spring, dark green in summer, Maroon or brown hue in autumn and winter.

Roots Height purchased:
30–40 cm (12–15 in), pots 7 in (17 cm) (2 litre) min. dia.

40–60 cm (15 in–2 ft), pots 8 in (20 cm) (3 litre) min. dia.

Hints Any well-prepared soil. Over 60 cm (2 ft) in height, extra organic material. Scarce. *Sequoia sempervirens* 'Adpressa' and *S. s.* 'Depressa' offered as dwarf conifers, although slower, reach considerable heights and have spreading habit. Avoid drying out of pots or rootball.

Most widely available *Sequoia sempervirens* (Californian Redwood). *S. s.* 'Adpressa'. *S. s.* 'Depressa'.

SEQUOIADENDRON GIGANTEUM
Wellingtonia

Time to buy Pot-grown, any time except December–February. Balled, October–November or March–April. Avoid adverse weather conditions.

Where to find Outside in Specimen Conifers.

Size
40–60 cm (15 in–2 ft)
60–80 cm (2–2½ ft)
80 cm–1 m (2½–3 ft)
60 cm–1 m (2–3 ft) scarce.
Balled, more than 80 cm (2½ ft) difficult to establish.

Foliage Evergreen long cord-like needles in bunches. Dark green.

Roots Height purchased:
30–40 cm (12–15 in), pots 7 in (17 cm) (2 litre) min. dia.
40–60 cm (15 in–2 ft), pots 8 in (20 cm) (3 litre) min. dia.
Balled, up to 80 cm (2½ ft) good fibrous root system.

Hints Any well-prepared soil. Over 60 cm (2 ft) in height, extra organic material. Scarce. Avoid drying out of pots or rootball. Research overall size.

TAXODIUM
Swamp Cypress

Time to buy Pot-grown, any time except December–February. Balled, October–

November or March–April. Avoid adverse weather conditions.

Where to find Outside in Specimen Conifers or Trees.

Size
20–30 cm (8–12 in)
30–40 cm (12–15 in)
40–60 cm (15 in–2 ft)
60–80 cm (2–2½ ft)
80 cm–1 m (2½–3 ft)
Balled, more than 60 cm (2 ft) difficult to establish.

Foliage Deciduous. Spring/summer, soft green. Yellow to bronze-brown, August/September. Flat fern-like. Premature autumn colour and leaf drop.

Roots Height purchased:
Up to 60 cm (2 ft), pots 6 in (15 cm) min. dia.
80 cm–1 m (2½–3 ft), pots 10 in (25 cm) (3 litre) min. dia.
1 m (3 ft) and above, pots 15 in (40 cm) (5 litre) min. dia.
Balled, up to 1 m (3 ft), good fibrous root system.

Hints Any well-prepared soil. Over 1.2 m (4 ft) height, extra organic material. Often stocked in garden centres in Trees, but truly a Conifer.

Most widely available *Taxodium ascendens* 'Nutans'. *T. distichum* (Swamp Cypress). *T. d.* 'Pendens' (Weeping Swamp Cypress).

TAXUS BACCATA
Yew, Common Yew, English Yew

Time to buy Pot-grown, any time except December–February. Balled, October–November or March–April. Avoid adverse weather conditions.

Where to find Outside in Specimen Conifers or Hedging.

Size
20–30 cm (8–12 in)
30–40 cm (12–15 in)
40–60 cm (15 in–2 ft)
60–80 cm (2–2½ ft)
80 cm–1 m (2½–3 ft)

60 cm–1 m (2–3 ft) scarce.

Balled, more than 80 cm (2½ ft) difficult to establish.

Foliage Evergreen flat fronds. Dark green. Limited needle drop spring.

Roots Height purchased:

Up to 10 cm (4 in), pots 4 in (10 cm) min. dia.

10–20 cm (4–8 in), pots 5 in (12 cm) (1 litre) min. dia.

20–30 cm (8–12 in), pots 7 in (17 cm) (2 litre) min. dia.

30–40 cm (12–15 in), pots 7 in (17 cm) (2 litre) min. dia.

40–60 cm (15 in–2 ft), pots 8 in (20 cm) (3 litre) min. dia.

Balled, up to 80 cm (2½ ft) good fibrous root system.

Hints Any well-prepared soil. Over 60 cm (2 ft) in height, extra organic material. Large sizes scarce. Avoid drying out of pots or root-ball. Wind screen advised in exposed positions in first and second winters.

FOLIAGE AND FRUIT CAN BE POISONOUS TO ANIMALS.

Most widely available Taxus baccata. T. b. 'Hicksii'. T. b. 'Overeynderi'.

TAXUS BACCATA

(ornamental forms)

Yew

Time to buy Pot-grown, any time except December–February. Balled, October–November or March–April. Avoid adverse weather conditions.

Where to find Outside in Slow-growing (Dwarf) or Specimen Conifers.

Size

Up to 10 cm (4 in)

10–20 cm (4–8 in)

20–30 cm (8–12 in)

30–40 cm (12–15 in)

40–60 cm (15 in–2 ft)

60 cm–1 m (2–3 ft) scarce.

Balled, more than 80 cm (2½ ft) difficult to establish.

Foliage Evergreen flat fronds. Mid to

dark green or golden and golden variegated. Limited needle drop spring.

Roots Height purchased:

Up to 10 cm (4 in), pots 4 in (10 cm) min. dia.

10–20 cm (4–8 in), pots 5 in (12 cm) (1 litre) min. dia.

20–30 cm (8–12 in), pots 7 in (17 cm) (2 litre) min. dia.

30–40 cm (12–15 in), pots 7 in (17 cm) (2 litre) min. dia.

40–60 cm (15 in–2 ft), pots 8 in (20 cm) (3 litre) min. dia.

Balled, up to 80 cm (2½ ft) good fibrous root system.

Hints Any well-prepared soil. Over 60 cm (2 ft) in height, extra organic material. May be scarce. Often small when purchased, but research overall size. Avoid drying out of pots and root-ball. FOLIAGE AND FRUIT CAN BE POISONOUS TO ANIMALS.

Most widely available Taxus baccata 'Adpressa Aurea'. T. b. 'Dovastonii'. T. b. 'Dovastonii Aurea'. T. b. 'Dwarf White'. T. b. 'Fastigiata'. T. b. 'Fastigiata Aureomarginata'. T. b. 'Fastigiata Robusta'. T. b. 'Repandens'. T. b. 'Repens Aurea'. T. b. 'Semperaurea'. T. b. 'Standishii'. T. b. 'Summergold'.

THUJA (slow-growing)

Western Red Cedar

Time to buy Pot-grown, any time except December–February. Balled, October–November or March–April. Avoid adverse weather conditions.

Where to find Outside in Slow-growing (Dwarf) or Specimen Conifers.

Size

Up to 10 cm (4 in)

10–20 cm (4–8 in)

20–30 cm (8–12 in)

30–40 cm (12–15 in)

Balled, more than 60 cm (2 ft) difficult to establish.

Foliage Evergreen soft fronds. Mid, dark or grey-green, gold or blue.

Roots Height purchased:
Up to 10 cm (4 in), pots 4 in (10 cm) min.
dia.
10–20 cm (4–8 in), pots 5 in (12 cm) (1
litre) min. dia.
20–30 cm (8–12 in), pots 7 in (17 cm) (2
litre) min. dia.
30–40 cm (12–15 in), pots 7 in (17 cm) (2
litre) min. dia.
Balled, up to 60 cm (2 ft), good fibrous
root system.
Hints Any well-prepared soil. Over 60 cm
(2 ft) in height, extra organic material.
Wide range. Avoid drying out of pots
and root-ball. Research overall size.
Most widely available Thuja occi-
dentalis 'Danica'. T. o. 'Europe Gold'. T. o.
'Holmstrup'. T. o. 'Rheingold'. T. o. 'Smar-
agd'. T. o. 'Sunkist'. T. o. 'Yellow Ribbon'.
T. o. 'Aurea Nana'. T. o. 'Conspicua'. T. o.
'Golden Rail'. T. o. 'Golden Sceptre'. T.
orientalis 'Rosedalis'.

THUJA (specimen and screening)
Western Red Cedar
Time to buy Pot-grown, any time except
December–February. Balled, October–
November or March–April. Avoid ad-
verse weather conditions.
Where to find Outside in Specimen or
Screening Conifers.
Size
40–60 cm (15 in–2 ft)
60–80 cm (2–2½ ft)
80 cm–1 m (2½–3 ft)
1–1.2 m (3–4 ft)
80 cm–1.2 m (2½–4 ft) scarce.
Balled, more than 1.2 m (4 ft) difficult to
establish.
Foliage Evergreen soft fronds. Mid, dark
green or gold.
Roots Height purchased:
40–60 cm (15 in–2 ft), pots 8 in (20 cm) (3
litre) min. dia.
Balled, up to 80 cm (2½ ft), good fibrous
root system.
Hints Any well-prepared soil. Over 1 m
(3 ft) in height, extra organic material. Lar-

ger sizes scarce. Avoid drying out of pots or
root-ball. Wind screen advised in exposed
positions in first and second winters.
Most widely available Thuja plicata
(Western Red Cedar). T. p. 'Coles Variety'. T. p. 'Semperaurescens'. T. p. 'Zebrina'.

TSUGA (slow-growing/dwarf)
Hemlock
Time to buy Pot-grown, any time except
December–February. Balled, October–
November or March–April. Avoid adverse weather conditions.
Where to find Outside in Slow-growing
(Dwarf) or Specimen Conifers.
Size
Up to 10 cm (4 in)
10–20 cm (4–8 in)
20–30 cm (8–12 in)
30–40 cm (12–15 in)
Balled, more than 60 cm (2 ft) difficult to
establish.
Foliage Evergreen soft fronds. Light to
grey-green.
Roots Height purchased:
Up to 10 cm (4 in), pots 4 in (10 cm) min.
dia.
10–20 cm (4–8 in), pots 5 in (12 cm) (1
litre) min. dia.
20–30 cm (8–12 in), pots 7 in (17 cm) (2
litre) min. dia.
30–40 cm (12–15 in), pots 7 in (17 cm) (2
litre) min. dia.
Balled, up to 60 cm (2 ft), good fibrous
root system.
Hints Any well-prepared soil. Over 60 cm
(2 ft) in height, extra organic material.
Scarce. Avoid drying out of pots or root-
ball. Tsuga canadensis 'Nana' and T. c.
'Pendula' research overall size.
Most widely available Tsuga canadensis
'Nana'. T. c. 'Pendula'.

TSUGA (specimen and screening)
Hemlock
Time to buy Pot-grown, any time except
December–February. Balled, October–

November or March–April. Avoid adverse weather conditions.

Where to find Outside in Specimen or Screening Conifers.

Size

40–60 cm (15 in–2 ft)

60–80 cm (2–2½ ft)

80 cm–1 m (2½–3 ft)

60 cm–1 m (2–3 ft) scarce.

Balled, more than 80 cm (2½ ft) difficult to establish.

Foliage Evergreen soft fronds. Mid to grey-green.

Roots Height purchased:

30–40 cm (12–15 in), pots 7 in (17 cm) (2 litre) min. dia.

40–60 cm (15 in–2 ft), pots 8 in (20 cm) (3 litre) min. dia.

Balled, up to 80 cm (2½ft) good fibrous root system.

Hints Any well-prepared soil. May be scarce. Avoid drying out of pots and root-ball.

Most widely available *Tsuga canadensuis* (Eastern Hemlock). *T. heterophylla* (Western Hemlock).

Roses

The rose must surely be the queen of all flowering garden plants, and quite rightly it finds its way into almost every garden, offering colour, scent and a wide range of usages.

Roses are offered in two seasons, bare-rooted or root-wrapped plants in the autumn and early spring, and pot-grown plants throughout the rest of the year. From a financial point of view, bare-rooted and root-wrapped will be the least expensive; but they have to be planted from autumn to early spring.

Before purchasing, the quality of roses should be checked, as there is a fringe supply market offering second-grade material, often at first-grade prices. This will not normally happen in reputable nurseries or garden centres, but in markets and other non-horticultural outlets.

Some varieties of Hybrid Tea (H.T.), Floribunda (Fl.) and Climbing (Clg.) will be seen to be under 'Plant Breeder's Rights'. These will command a higher price, as they are new or relatively new varieties.

New varieties are being introduced all the time. Some of these may not be universally suitable for all aspects in all areas, and care must be taken to ensure that new varieties are hardy enough to take the rigours of all aspects.

With shrub roses, the principal mistake that gardeners make is not taking note of the ultimate size. These plants can very rapidly reach quite substantial proportions, outgrowing the allocated area. As they are often used in mixed plantings with perennials and other shrubs, they can become totally overpowering.

Attack by black spot and mildew is always a problem, although one should not be paranoid about it. It is almost impossible to eradicate completely, but good cultivation methods will keep it under control. It has always been the author's opinion that blackspot and mildew in gardens is a good sign for human beings, because it indicates pollution-free air.

A principal form of supply is by mail-order from reputable rose growers. Orders are normally placed through late spring and summer for delivery in the autumn and winter. Delivery will be made when the roses are 'ripe' and ready for lifting. Weather conditions at the time may bring supply forward or delay it, often to as late as Christmas. Purchasers should not be worried by late delivery, assuming the order has been acknowledged: the grower is simply sending out the material at the correct time. Supply and planting can continue by this method through to early spring.

In addition to the cost of the roses themselves, there will be a charge for packing and carriage.

Preparation of the soil is important; and the planting area should be double-dug to a depth of 18 in (50 cm) and good quantities of organic material added. Cultivation practices such as mulching, feeding and pruning are all-important and research should be done into the correct method for each individual group.

Prices may vary, and it is a good idea to shop around. Some specific varieties may have to be sought from one or more outlets.

Note: In this chapter, the following abbreviations are used for rose habits: Clg. – Climbing; Fl. – Floribunda; H.T. – Hybrid Tea; Min. – Miniature; Min. Std. – Miniature Standard; W/S – Weeping Standard.
   The following abbreviations are used for rose colours: (A) – Apricot; (C) – Crimson; (L) – Lavender; (M) – Mauve; (O) – Orange; (P) – Pink; (R) – Red; (S) – Salmon; (W) – White; (Y) – Yellow.

CLIMBING, RAMBLER and CLIMBING SPECIES ROSES

Time to buy Pot-grown, any time. Root-wrapped, bare-rooted or pre-packed, October–April. Avoid adverse weather conditions. Mail order is acceptable.

Where to find Outside in Roses. Pre-packed under limited protection.

Size 6 in (15 cm) min. Minimum two strong branches. May be hard pruned.

Foliage Deciduous. Spring/summer, mid to dark green. Premature autumn colour and leaf drop.

Roots Pots 5 in (12 cm) min. dia. Root-wrapped, bare-rooted and pre-packed, good fibrous root system.

Hints Any well-prepared soil. Wide range. Mildew and black spot may be seen in summer. If not excessive, not a long-term problem. Avoid pre-packed if signs of growth are seen. Climbing, Rambler and Climbing Species Roses, if grown-up trees, must be planted weather side and if grown against support, planted 15–18 in (40–50 cm) away. *Rosa banksiae* 'Lutea' and *Rosa bracteata* 'Mermaid' should always be purchased pot-grown.

Most widely available
CLIMBING ROSES 'Allen Chandler' (R). Clg. 'Allgold' (Y). 'Aloha' (P). 'Altissimo' (R). 'Bantry Bay' (P). Clg. 'Bettina' (O). 'Casino' (Y). Clg. 'Cécile Brunner' (P). Clg. 'Com-passion' (P). 'Copenhagen' (R). Clg. 'Crimson Glory' (C). 'Danse du Feu' (O/R). 'Dreaming Spires' (Y). 'Dublin Bay' (R). 'Dortmund' (Y). 'Elegance' (Y). 'Elizabeth Heather Grierson' (Mattnot) (P). 'Étoile de Hollande' (R). 'Galway Bay' (P). 'Gloire de Dijon' (Y). 'Golden Showers' (Y). 'Grand Hotel' (R). 'Guinée' (R). 'Hamburger Phoenix' (C). 'Handel' (P). Clg. 'Iceberg' (W). Clg. 'Josephine Bruce' (C). Clg. 'Korona' (P). Clg. 'Lady Hillingdon' (Y). Clg. 'Lady Sylvia' (P). 'Lady Waterlow' (P). 'Leverkusen' (Y). 'Maigold' (Y). 'Malaga' (P). Clg. 'Masquerade' (Y/R). 'Meg' (P). 'Mme Alfred Carrière' (W/P). 'Mme Grégoire Staechelin' (P). 'Morning Jewel' (P). 'Mrs Sam McGredy' (O). Clg. 'Ophelia' (P). 'Parade' (R). 'Parkdirektor Riggers' (C). 'Paul's Lemon Pillar' (W/Y). 'Paul's Scarlet' (R). 'Pink Perpetue' (P). 'Rosy Mantle' (P). 'Royal Gold' (Y). 'Senateur Amic' (P). 'Schoolgirl' (O). Clg. 'Shot Silk' (P). 'Sparkling Scarlet' (R). 'Summer Wine' (P). Clg. 'Super Star' (R). 'Swan Lake' (W/P). 'Sympathie' (R). 'The New Dawn' (P). Clg. 'Wendy Cussons' (P). 'White Cockade' (W). 'Zéphirine Drouhin' (P).

RAMBLER ROSES 'Albéric Barbier' (Y/W). 'Albertine' (P). 'American Pillar' (R). 'Crimson Shower' (C). 'Dorothy Perkins' (P). 'Dr Van Fleet' (P). Easlea's Golden Rambler' (Y). 'Emily Gray' (Y). 'Excelsa' (C). 'Félicité et Perpétue' (W/R) 'François Juran-ville' (P). 'Rambling Rector' (W). 'Sander's White' (W).

CLIMBING SPECIES ROSES *Rosa banksiae* 'Lutea' (Y). *Rosa bracteata* 'Mermaid' (Y). *Rosa filipes* 'Kiftsgate' (W). *Rosa longi-cuspis* (W). *Rosa noisettiana* 'Bobbie James' (W). *Rosa sino-wilsonii* 'Wedding Day' (W). 'Paul's Himalayan Musk' (W). 'Rambling Rector' (W). 'Seagull' (W). 'The Garland' (W/P).

GROUND COVER ROSES

Time to buy Pot-grown, any time. Root-wrapped, bare-rooted or pre-packed October–April. Avoid adverse weather conditions. Mail order is acceptable.

Where to find Outside in Roses or Ground Cover. Pre-packs under limited protection.

Size 5 in (12 cm) min. Minimum two shoots.

Foliage Deciduous. Spring/summer, mid green. Premature autumn colour and leaf drop.

Roots Pots 4 in (10 cm) min. dia. Root-wrapped, bare-rooted and pre-packed, good fibrous root system.

Hints Any well-prepared soil. Wide range. Mildew and black spot may be seen in summer. If not excessive, not a long term problem. Cut back all previous season's shoots to 2–3 in (5–8 cm) of origin in spring. Repeat annually. Research overall size.

Most widely available 'Bonica' (*Meidomanac**) (P). 'Essex' (P). 'Ferdy' (*Keitoli**) (P). 'Fiona' (*Meibeluxen**) (R). 'Frau Dagmar Hartop' ('Frau Dagmar Has-trup') (P). 'Grouse' (*Korimo**) (P). 'Hamp-shire' (*Korhamp**) (R). 'Hansa' (R). 'Kent' (*Poulcov**) (W). 'Moje Hammarberg' (R). R. r. 'Max Graff' (P). 'Nozomi' (P). 'Par-tridge' (*Korweirim*) (W). 'Pheasant' (*Kor-dapt*) (P). 'Pink Bells' (*Poulbells**) (P). 'Pink Drift' (*Poulcat**) (P). 'Pink Wave' (*Mattgro**) (P). 'Raubritter' (P). 'Red Bells' (*Poulred**) (C). 'Red Blanket' (*Intercell**) (R).

'Red Max Graf' (*Kormax**) (R). *Rosa nitida* (P). *Rosa pauli* (W). 'Rosy Cushion' (*Interall**) (P). 'Rutland' (*Poulshine**) (P). 'Scarlet Mediland' (O). 'Smarty' (P). 'Surrey' (*Korlanum**) (P). 'Swany' (*Meiburenac**) (W). 'White Bells' (*Poulwhite**) (W) R. rugosa. 'White Max Graf' (*Korgram**) (W).

*Varieties that may be offered in their Euro-pean language of origin and have not been translated.

HYBRID TEA and FLORIBUNDA ROSES

Time to buy Pot-grown, any time. Root-wrapped, bare-rooted or pre-packed, October–March. Avoid adverse weather conditions. Mail order acceptable.

Where to find Outside in Roses. Pre-packed under limited protection.

Size 5 in (12 cm) min. Minimum two strong shoots. May or may not be hard pruned.

Foliage Deciduous. Spring/summer, mid to dark green. Premature autumn colour and leaf drop.

Root Pots 5 in (12 cm) min. dia. Root-wrapped, bare-rooted and pre-packed, good fibrous root system.

Hints Any well-prepared soil. Wide range. Black spot and mildew may be seen in summer. If not excessive, not a long term problem. Cut back all previous season's growth within $1\frac{1}{2}$ in (4 cm) of origin in Hybrid Tea and 3–4 in (8–10 cm) in Floribunda in spring. Repeat annually.

Most widely available

HYBRID TEA 'Alec's Red' (C). 'Alexander' (R). 'Alpine Sunset ' (Y). 'Anne Watkins' (cream/A). 'Apricot Silk' (A). 'Beauté (A). 'Bettina' (O/P) 'Blessings' (P). 'Blue Moon' (L). 'Cheshire Life' (R/O). 'Chicago Peace' (P/Y). 'City of Gloucester' (Y). 'Double De-light' (W/R). 'Duke of Windsor' (O). 'Ernest S. Morse' (R). 'Fragrant Cloud' (R). 'Gail Borden' (P/Y). 'Gay Gordons' (O/Y). 'Gold Crown' (Y). 'Grandpa Dickson' (Y). 'Jose-phine Bruce' (C). 'Just Joey' (O). 'King's

Ransom' (Y). 'Mischief' (S). 'Miss Harp' (Y). 'Miss Ireland' (O). 'Mr Lincoln' (C). 'My Choice' (P). 'National Trust' (R). 'Pascali' (W). 'Peace' (Y/P). 'Peer Gynt' (Y/P). 'Piccadilly' (R/Y). 'Pink Favourite' (P). 'Prince William' (R). 'Red Devil' (R). 'Rose Gaujard' (R). 'Silver Jubilee' (A). 'Silver Lining' (P). 'Silver Wedding' (W). 'Summer Holiday' (R). 'Summer Sunshine' (Y). 'Sunblest' (Y). 'Super Star' (O/R). 'Super Sun' (Y). 'Susan Hampshire' (P). 'Sutter's Gold' (R/Y). 'Uncle Walter' (C). 'Virgo' (W). 'Wendy Cussons' (P). 'Whisky Mac' (A).
FLORIBUNDA 'Allgold' (Y). 'Apricot Nectar' (A). 'Arthur Bell' (Y). 'Baby Bio' (Y). 'Burma Star' (A/Y) 'Carolle' ('Pink Garnette') (P). 'Chanelle' (A). 'Chinatown' (Y). 'Circus' (Y). 'City of Belfast' (R). 'City of Leeds' (S). 'City of Portsmouth' (P). 'Copper Pot' (O/Y). 'Dearest' (P). 'Dickson's Flame' (R). 'Elizabeth of Glamis' (P). 'Europeana' (R). 'Evelyn Fison' (R). 'Frensham' (C). 'Garnette' (C). 'Glenfiddich' (Y). 'Goldgleam' (Y). 'Iceberg' (W). 'Joyfulness' (A). 'Korresia' (Y). 'Lily Marlene' (R). 'Masquerade' (Y/P/R). 'Mountbatten' (Y). 'Paddy McGredy' (P). 'Paint Box' (Y/P/R). 'Pineapple Poll' (Y/O). 'Poppy Flash' (O/R). 'Priscilla Burton' (R). 'Queen Elizabeth' (P). Polyantha Rose 'Rosemary Rose' (R). 'Scarlet Queen Elizabeth' (O/R). 'Sea Pearl' (peach). 'Sir Lancelot' (A/Y). 'Southampton' (A/O). 'Tip Top' (P). 'Topsi' (R). 'Trumpeter' (R). 'Violet Carson' (peach). 'Woburn Abbey' (O).

MINIATURE ROSES

Time to buy Pot-grown, any time. Rootwrapped, bare-rooted and pre-packed, October–April. Avoid adverse weather conditions. Mail order is acceptable.
Where to find Outside in Roses or Miniature Roses. Indoors in House Plants, but avoid these for planting out.
Size 2 in (5 cm) min. Minimum two shoots.
Foliage Deciduous. Spring/summer, green. Premature autumn colour and leaf drop.

Roots Pots 3 in (8 cm) min. dia. Rootwrapped, bare-rooted and pre-packed, good fibrous root system.
Hints Any well-prepared soil, plus extra organic material. Wide range. Budded stock preferred for garden use, rather than cuttings. Light trimming in first year.
Most widely available 'Baby Crimson' (C). 'B. Masquerade' (Y/R). 'B. Ophelia' (P). 'B. Sunrise' (O/Y). 'Cinderalla' (W). 'Colibre' (O/R). 'Darling Flame' (O). 'Diane' (P). 'Gold Pin' (Y). 'Lavender Jewel' (L). 'New Pin' (Y). 'Perle D' Alcanada' (C). 'Perle de M. Monserrat' (R). 'Pour Toi' (W). 'Rosina' (Y). 'Scarlet Gem' (O/R). 'Scarlet Pimpernel' (R). 'Snowball' (W). 'Sweet Fairy' (L/P).

MINIATURE STANDARD ROSES

Time to buy Pot-grown, any time. Rootwrapped and bare-rooted, October–April. Avoid adverse weather conditions. Mail order is acceptable.
Where to find Outside in Miniature Roses.
Size Stem 12–18 in (30–50 cm) min. Minimum two bunches of shoots emerging 2–3 in (5–8 cm) apart, minimum 2 in (5 cm) long.
Foliage Deciduous. Spring/summer, mid green. Premature autumn colour and leaf drop.
Roots Pots 4 in (10 cm) min. dia. Rootwrapped and bare-rooted, good fibrous root system.
Hints Any well-prepared soil. Wide range. Light trimming only in early years. Stake and ties for life.
For varieties see MINIATURE ROSES.

PATIO ROSES

Time to buy Pot-grown, any time. Rootwrapped, bare-rooted or pre-packed October–April. Avoid adverse weather conditions. Mail order is acceptable.
Where to find Outside in Roses or Patio Roses. Pre-packed under limited protection.

Size 4 in (10 cm) min. Minimum two shoots.

Foliage Deciduous. Spring/summer, mid green. Premature autumn colour and leaf drop.

Roots Pots 4 in (10 cm) min. dia. Root-wrapped, bare-rooted and pre-packed, good fibrous root system.

Hints Any well-prepared soil. Wide range. Mildew and black spot may be seen in summer. If not excessive, not a long term problem. Cut back all previous season's growth to 2–3 in (5–8 cm) of origin in spring. Repeat annually.

Most widely available 'Angela Rippon' (*Ocaru-ocarina**). 'Benson and Hedges Special' (*Macshana**) (Y). 'Bright Smile' (*Dicdance*) (Y). 'Chelsea Pensioner' (*Mattche**) (R). 'Gentle Touch' (*Diclulu**) (P). 'Longleat' (*Macinc**) (R). 'Peek-A-Boo' (*Dicgrow**) (P). 'Penelope Keith' (*Macfreego**) (Y). 'Regensberg' (*Macyour**) (P). 'Royal Salute' (P). 'St Boniface' (*Kormatt**) (R). 'Sweet Dream' (*Fryminicot**) (A). 'Sweet Magic' (*Dicmagic**) (O).

*Varieties that may be offered in their European language of origin and have not been translated.

SHRUB ROSES

Time to buy Pot-grown, any time. Root-wrapped, bare-rooted or pre-packed, October–April. Avoid adverse weather conditions. Mail order is acceptable.

Where to find Outside in Shrub Roses. Pre-packed under limited protection.

Size 5 in (12 cm) min. Minimum two shoots 9 in (23 cm) min. long.

Foliage Deciduous. Spring/summer, mid green. Premature autumn colour and leaf drop.

Roots Pots 5 in (12 cm) min. dia. Root-wrapped, bare-rooted and pre-packed, good fibrous root system.

Hints Any well-prepared soil. Wide range. Mildew and black spot may be seen in summer. If not excessive, not a long term problem. Avoid pre-packs if signs of growth are seen. Research overall size.

Most widely available

SPECIES ROSES *R. californica* 'Plena' (P). *R. × cantabrigiensis* (Y). *R. foetida* 'Austrian Yellow' (Y). *R. f.* 'Bicolor' (R). *R. glauca* syn. *rubrifolia* (P). *R. hugonis* (Y). *R. nitida* (P). *R. omeiensis pteracantha* (W). *R. × paulii* (W). *R. × p.* 'Rosea' (P). *R. pomifera duplex* (P). *R. virginiana* (P). *R. webbiana* (P). *R. willmottiae* (P). *R. woodsii fendleri* (P). *R. xanthia* 'Canary Bird' (Y).

OLD FASHIONED ROSES *R. alba* 'Celestial' (P). *R. a.* 'Félicité Parmentier' (P). *R. a.* 'Maiden's Blush' (P). *R. a. maxima* (W). *R. a.* 'Queen of Denmark' (P). *R. bourboniana* 'Adam Messerich' (R). *R. b.* 'Boule de Neige' (W) *R. b.* 'Kathleen Harrop' (P). *R. b.* 'La Reine Victoria' (P). *R. b.* 'Louise Odier' (P). *R. b.* 'Mme Ernst Calvat' (P). *R. b.* 'Mme Isaac Pereire' (R). *R. b.* 'Mme Pierre Oger' (P). *R. b.* 'Prince Charles' (R). *R. b.* 'Variegata di Bologna' (L/R). *R. b.* 'Zéphirine Drouhin' (P). *R. b.* 'Ziguener Knabe'. *R.* 'Canary Bird' (Y). *R. centifolia* 'Chapeau de Napoleon' (P). *R. c.* 'Fantin Latour' (P). *R. c.* 'La Noblesse' (P). *R. c.* 'Petite de Hollande' (P). *R. chinensis* 'Bloomfield Abundance' (P). *R. c.* 'Cécile Brunner' (P). *R. c.* 'Mutabilis' (P). *R. c.* 'Old Blush' (P). *R. c.* 'Perle d'Or' (Y). *R. damascena* 'Belle Amour' (P). *R. d.* 'Blush Damask' (P). *R. d.* 'Mme Hardy' (W). *R. ecea* (Y). *R. e.* 'Helen Knight' (Y). *R. gallica* 'Belle de Crécy' (M). *R. g.* 'Camaieux' (P). *R. g.* 'Cardinal Richelieu' (L). *R. g.* 'Charles de Mills' (C). *R. g.* 'Complicata' (P). *R. g.* 'Officinalis' (C). *R. g.* Tuscany (C). *R. g.* 'Tuscany Superb' (C). *R. g.* 'Versicolor' syn. *R. g.* 'Mundi' (C/P/W). *R. moschata* 'Buff Beauty' (Y). *R. m.* 'Cornelia' (P). *R. m.* 'Felicia' (P). *R. m.* 'Moonlight' (W). *R. m.* 'Pax' (W). *R. m.* 'Penelope' (W/P). *R. m.* 'Pink Prosperity' (P). *R. m.* 'Prosperity' (W). *R. m.* 'Wilhelm' (C). *R. m.* 'Will Scarlet' (R). *R. moyesii* (R). *R. m.* 'Eddie's Jewel' (R). *R. m.* 'Geranium' (R). *R. m.* 'Sealing Wax' (P). *R. muscosa* 'Blanche Moreau' (W). *R. m.* 'James Mit-

chell' (P). *R. m.* 'William Lobb' (C). *R. nois-*
ettiana 'Mme Plantier' (W). *R. rubiginosa*
'Anne of Geierstein' (R). *R. r.* 'Flora
McIvor' (P). *R. r.*'Greenmantle' (R). *R. r.*
'Lady Penzance' (R). *R. r.* 'Lord Penzance'
(P). *R. rugosa* 'Agnes' (Y). *R. r.* 'Blanc
double de Coubert' (W). *R. r.* 'Conrad F.
Meyer' (P). *R. r.* 'Frau Dagmar Hartop' (P)
(*R. r.* 'Frau Dagmar Hastrup'). *R. r.* 'Groot-
endorst supreme' (C). *R. r.* 'Mrs Anthony
Waterer' (C). R. r. 'Parfum de L'Hay (R).
R. r. 'Pink Grootendorst' (P). *R. r.* 'Roser-
aie de L'Hay' (C). *R. r.* 'Rubra' (R). *R. r.*
'Sarah van Fleet' (P). *R. r.* 'Scabrosa' (C).
R. r. 'Schneezwerg' (W). *R. sempervirens*
'Little White Pet' (W). *R. spinosissima*
'Frühlingsgold' (Y). *R. s.* 'Frühlings-
morgen' (P). *R. s.* 'Frühlingszauber' (P).
R. s. 'Stanwell Perpetual' (P).

MODERN SHRUB ROSES *R. hybrida* 'Aloha'
(P). *R. h.* 'Ballerina' (P). *R. h.* 'Bonn' (R).
R. h. 'Cerise Bouquet' (P). *R. h.* 'Constance
Spry' (P). *R. h.* 'Elmshorn' (C). *R. h.* 'Erfurt'
(P). *R. h.* 'Fred Loads' (O). *R. h.* 'Fritz
Nobis' (P). *R. h.* 'Golden Wings' (Y). *R. h.*
'Joseph's Coat' (Y/R). *R. h.* 'Kassel' (R).
R. h. 'Lavender Lassie' (L). *R. h.* 'Maigold'
(Y). *R. h.* 'Marguerite Hilling' (P). *R. h.*
'Nevada' (W). *R. h.* 'Raubritter' (P). *R. h.*
'Scarlet Fire' (R). *R. h.* 'White Wings' (W).
R. h. 'Yesterday' (P). *R. h. perpetual* 'Frau
Karl Druschki' (W). *R. h. p.* 'Mrs John
Laing' (P). *R. h. p.* 'Vick's Caprice' (P/W).

MODERN ENGLISH ROSES 'English Garden'
(*Ausbuff**)   (Y).   'Gertrude   Jekyll'
(*Ausbord**)   (P).   'Graham   Thomas'
(*Ausmas**) (Y). 'Heritage' (*Ausblush**) (P).
'*Mary Rose*' (*Ausmary**) (P). 'William
Shakespeare' (*Ausroyal**) (C).

*Varieties that may be offered in their European
language of origin and have not been translated.

STANDARD ROSES

Time to buy Pot-grown, any time. Root-
wrapped, bare-rooted or pre-packed,
October–April. Avoid adverse weather
conditions. Mail order is acceptable.
Where to find Outside in Standard Roses.

Size Stem 3½ ft (1.1 m) min. Minimum two
sets of shoots emerging 2–3 in (5–8 cm)
apart on main stem. Each shoot minimum
6 in (15 cm) long. Industry term to describe this is double or treble budded.
Foliage Deciduous. Spring/summer, mid
to dark green. Premature autumn colour
and leaf drop.
Roots Pots 8 in (20 cm) min. dia. Root-
wrapped and bare-rooted, good fibrous
root system.
Hints Any well-prepared soil. Wide
range. Mildew and black spot may be
seen in summer. If not excessive, not a
long-term problem. Cut back all previous
season's growth to within 1½ in (4 cm) of
origin in Hybrid Tea and 3–4 in (8–10 cm)
in Floribunda in spring. Repeat annually.
Stake and ties for life.
Most widely available

HYBRID TEA 'Alec's Red' (C). 'Apricot Silk'
(A). 'Bettina' (O). 'Blessings' (P). 'Blue
Moon' (). 'Duke of Windsor' (R/O),
'Ernest H. Morse' (R). 'Fragrant Cloud' (R).
'Gay Gordons' (O/Y). 'Grandpa Dickson' (Y).
'Just Joey' (O). 'King's Ransom' (Y). 'Mr
Lincoln' (C). 'Mischief' (R). 'My Choice'
(P/Y). 'Pascali' (W). 'Pink Favourite' (P).
'Prima Ballerina' (P). 'Silver Jubilee' (A).
'Super Star' (O/R).

FLORIBUNDA 'Allgold' (Y). 'Anne Cocker'
(O/S). 'Arthur Bell' (Y). 'Chinatown' (Y).
'Dearest' (P) 'Elizabeth of Glamis' (S).
'Evelyn Fison' (R). 'Glenfiddich' (Y). 'Ice-
berg' (W). 'Joyfulness' (A). 'Masquerade'
(R/Y/P). 'Paddy McGredy' (P). 'The Queen
Elizabeth' (P). 'Trumpeter' (R). 'Woburn
Abbey' (O).

STANDARD SHRUB ROSES

Time to buy Pot-grown, any time. Root-
wrapped, bare-rooted or pre-packed,
October–April. Avoid adverse weather
conditions. Mail order acceptable.
Where to find Outside in Standard
Roses or Roses.
Size Stem height 2–4 ft (60 cm–1.2 m)
min. Minimum two bunches of shoots 3–

4 in (8–10 cm) apart originating from main stem, each bunch minimum three shoots 6 in (15 cm) min. long.

Foliage Deciduous. Spring/summer, mid to dark green. Premature autumn colour and leaf drop.

Roots Pots 8 in (20 cm) min. dia. Root-wrapped and bare-rooted, good fibrous root system.

Hints Any well-prepared soil. Wide range. Mildew and black spot may be seen in summer. If not excessive, not a long-term problem. Stake and ties for life.

Most widely available

R. *hybrida* 'Ballerina' (P). R. *xanthia* 'Canary Bird' (Y). 'Essex' (P). 'Nozomi' (P). *Rosa hugonis* (Y). 'Snow Carpet' (W). 'Suffolk' (R). 'Surrey' (P). 'Floribunda (Polyanthus) Rose The Fairy' (P).

WEEPING STANDARD ROSES

Time to buy Pot-grown, any time. Root-wrapped, bare-rooted or pre-packed, October–April. Avoid adverse weather conditions. Mail order acceptable.

Where to find Outside in Standard Roses.

Size Stem 5 ft (1.5 m) min. One to three bunches of shoots emerging from main stem, minimum 12 in (30 cm) long.

Foliage Deciduous. Spring/summer, mid to dark green. Premature autumn colour and leaf drop.

Roots Pots 8 in (20 cm) min. dia. Root-wrapped and bare-rooted, good fibrous root system.

Hints Any well-prepared soil. Wide range. Mildew and black spot may be seen in summer. If not excessive, not a long-term problem. No pruning first year. Stake and ties for life. Requires wire umbrella frame in order to train into a weeping formation.

Most widely available 'Albéric Barbier' (Y). 'Albertine' (P). 'Canary Bird' (Y). 'Crimson Shower' (C). 'Dorothy Perkins' (P). 'Emily Gray' (Y). 'Excelsa' (C). 'François Juranville' (P). 'Golden Showers' (Y). 'Paul's Scarlet' (R). 'Pink Perpetue' (P). 'Sander's White' (W). 'Sparkling Scarlet' (R).

Fruit

Fruit covers two groups: top-fruit, including apples, pears, cherries or plums; and soft-fruit, which are the shrubby blackcurrants, gooseberries, and the canes of raspberries and loganberries. In addition, fruit covers perennial plants such as strawberries.

Once the variety is chosen, consideration must be given to pollination, particularly with top-fruit. In these cases a pollination guide is included. With the proliferation of small gardens, the pollination becomes a little easier and a little less critical, but should still be considered.

Aspect is always important, and it may well be that in certain aspects a fruit-tree can be grown, flower and bear fruit but possibly the fruit may not always ripen to its full potential. Therefore care must be taken to ensure that the planting position is adequate.

With top-fruit, the rules of staking and tying are important. As always, soil preparation should be a paramount concern, with holes at least 3 ft (1 m) in diameter and dug to a depth of 18 in (50 cm) keeping the top-soil at the top throughout the operation. The planting area for soft-fruit should be double-dug. Adequate organic material should be added to aid root development to all.

Many fruit-trees will need the protection of a fruit-cage, and there are a number of models on the market which are adequate for the purpose. One word of warning, always remember never to leave the top net on overwinter, as heavy snow will lie on it, even though it is perforated, and will quickly break the support holes.

With top-fruit there is the choice of a number of root-stocks that will influence and instil into the variety its ultimate height and spread. Apples are the main area where research has been done and root stocks are available, although garden centres and nurseries are often shy to state exactly what the root-stocks are. New root-stocks are being evolved all the time, and pears and plums have now got a limited number of stocks which are becoming more widely available.

Fruit is often isolated and thought of as a subject on its own, as in the orchard or the fruit-cage, but all top-fruit make attractive garden trees and when researching the choice of a tree these may well be included for their ornamental attraction as well as their fruiting ability.

If fruit is the prime objective, then care needs to be taken to ensure that there are adequate wind-breaks, not to protect them from winter cold but to protect the pollinating insects that have to fly between the individual blossoms. If they encounter high winds then they will be unable to do their jobs properly.

ACTINIDIA CHINENSIS
Kiwi Fruit, Chinese Gooseberry
Time to buy Pot-grown, any time. Avoid adverse weather conditions.
Where to find Outside in Fruit or Climbers.
Size 1–4 ft (30 cm–1.2 m). Minimum one shoot tied to cane.
Foliage Deciduous. Spring/summer, large, 2 in (5 cm) min. dia. Mid green, fleshy.
Root Pots 5 in (12 cm) min. dia.
Hints Any well-prepared soil. For wall use, plant 15–18 in (40–50 cm) away from wall. Supply training wires. Open ground, posts and wires for support.
Most widely available FEMALE FLOWERING 'Abbott'. 'Bruno'. 'Gracie'. 'Hayward'. MALE FLOWERING 'Matua'. 'Tomuri'.
Pollination To achieve fruiting purchase male and female. Open sunny position or under protection.

CITRUS (various)
Orange, Lemon, Tangerine, Grapefruit, Lime
Time to buy Always require protection within the U.K., therefore can be purchased all year round.
Where to find Indoors in Conservatory or House Plants.
Size 1–4 ft (30 cm–1.2 m). Minimum three branches.
Foliage Evergreen. Very light green, possibly slightly yellow, sickly looking. Avoid any with no foliage.
Roots Pots 4 in (10 cm) min. dia.
Hints Always pot-grown. Re-pot as required, using good quality soil-based potting compost. Keep under protection in winter. Minimum temperature 41°F (5°C). Do not overwater. Can stand outside in summer in sheltered areas. May

be scarce. *Citrus* 'Clerya Meyer' only decorative. Fruiting of all varieties limited in U.K.

CORYLUS AVELLANA and CORYLUS MAXIMA
Hazel Nuts, Filberts, Cob Nuts
Time to buy Pot-grown, any time. Balled, root-wrapped and bare-rooted, October–March. Avoid adverse weather conditions.
Where to find Outside in Fruit or Shrubs.
Size Pot-grown, 1–2½ ft (30–70 cm). Minimum one main shoot. Balled, root-wrapped and bare-rooted, height 1½–3 ft (50 cm–1 m). Minimum two main shoots.
Foliage Deciduous. Spring/summer, light green.
Roots Pots 5 in (12 cm) min. dia. Balled, root-wrapped and bare-rooted, good fibrous root system.
Hints Any well-prepared soil. Although widely used, not always stocked. May have to be sought. Not always named. Stake and ties for five years.
Most widely available *Corylus avellana*. *C. a.* 'Nottingham'. *C. maxima* 'Kent Cobb'.

CYDONIA OBLONGA and varieties
Quince
Time to buy Pot-grown, any time. Root-wrapped and bare-rooted, October–March. Avoid adverse weather conditions.
Where to find Outside in Fruit or Trees.
Size MAIDEN One-year-old. Height 3–4 ft (1–1.2 m). Limited side branches. FEATHERED Two-year-old. Height 1½–4 ft (50 cm–1.2 m). Minimum four 1½ ft

(50 cm) long side branches. BUSH Height
3–5 ft (1–1.5 m). Minimum three 1½ ft
(50 cm) long branches. HALF-STANDARD
stem 4 ft (1.2 m) min. Height 6 ft (2 m)
min. Minimum three 2 ft (60 cm) long
branches. STANDARD Four to six-year-old.
Stem 6–8 ft (2–2.5 m). Height 9 ft (2.7 m).
Minimum three 2 ft (60 cm) long
branches.
Foliage Deciduous. Spring/summer, mid
green. Premature autumn colour and leaf
drop.
Roots Maiden, pots 8 in (20 cm) min. dia.
Feathered, bush, half-standard and standard, pots 10 in (25 cm) min. dia. Root-
wrapped and bare-rooted, good fibrous
root system.
Hints Any well-prepared soil. Varieties
may not be named. *Chaenomeles* (Ornamental Quince) is a substitute for *Cydonia*. Thin bent stems, except *Cydonia*
'Vranja'. Half-standard, stake and ties for
five years. Maiden and feathered, further
training.
Most widely available 'Champion'.
'Ludovic'. Pear-shaped 'Serbian'. 'Por-
tugal'. 'Vranja' ('Bereczi').

FICUS CARICA varieties
Fig
Time to buy Pot-grown, any time. Avoid
adverse weather conditions.
Where to find Outside in Fruit, Climbers
or Shrubs.
Size Height 12–36 in (30 cm–1 m).
Minimum one 1 ft (30 cm) long branch,
tied to cane.
Foliage Deciduous. Spring/summer, large,
mid green. Premature autumn colour and
leaf drop.
Roots Pots 6 in (15 cm) min. dia.
Hints Any well-prepared soil. Roots
should be contained in brick-built box
4 ft (1.2 m) min. square, depth 4 ft (1.2 m).
For wall use, plant 15–18 in (40–50 cm)
away from wall. Varieties not always
named. Old plants should not be dis-
regarded. May be scarce.

Most widely available 'Brown Turkey'.
'Brunswick'.

FRAGARIA
Strawberry
Time to buy Pot-grown runners and
bare-rooted, July–September. Pot-grown
plants may be available September–
April.
Where to find Outside in Fruit or Soft
Fruit. Alpine varieties outside in Alpines,
Perennials or Ground Cover.
Size Bare-rooted runners 3–5 in (8–12 cm)
long bundled in fives or tens with good
fibrous root system, or in pots. Alpines,
pot-grown only, with central cluster of
leaves.
Foliage Mid to late summer, dark green.
Bare-rooted may have wilted leaves.
Roots Pots 2–4 in (5–10 cm) min. dia.
Alpine, pots 3 in (8 cm) min. dia. Bare-
rooted, good fibrous root system.
Hints Any well-prepared soil. Plant 15–
18 in (40–50 cm) apart. Protect fruit from
birds at ripening time. Plants renewed
every three–five years. Purchase Ministry
of Agriculture certified stock.
Most widely available 'Cambridge
Favourite'. 'Cambridge Gauntlet'. 'Cambridge Royal'. 'Cambridge Vigour'. 'Gran-
dee'. 'Gorella'. 'Hapil'. 'Hampshire Maid'.
'Ostara'. 'Red Gauntlet'. 'Royal Sovereign'. 'Sequoia'. 'Talisman'. 'Tamella'.
Fragaria vesca semperflorens Alpine
Strawberry. 'Alexandria'. 'Baron Solem-
acher'. 'Delicious'.

MALUS PUMILA
Apple
Time to buy Pot-grown, any time. Root-
wrapped and bare-rooted, October–
March. Avoid adverse weather condi-
tions.
Where to find Outside in Fruit Trees.
Size WHIP 1½–2½ ft (50–80 cm). Limited
side branches. MAIDEN One-year-old.
Height 1–4 ft (30 cm–1.2 m). Limited side

branches. FEATHERED Two-years-old. Height 4 ft (1.2 m) min. Minimum four 1½ ft (30 cm) long side branches. BUSH Three- to five-years-old. Stem 2–3 ft (60 cm–1 m). Height 5 ft (1.5 m) min. Minimum three 1½ ft (30 cm) long branches. Trees on root-stock M.9 and M.27 may be smaller. HALF-STANDARD Four- to six-years-old. Stem 4–5 ft (1.2–1.5 m) Height 7 ft (2.2 m) min. Minimum three 2 ft (60 cm) long branches. STANDARD Four- to six-years-old. Stem 6–8 ft (2–2.5 m). Height 9 ft (2.7 m) min. Minimum three 2 ft (60 cm) branches. CORDON Height 2–6 ft (60 cm–2 m). Minimum four short side-fruiting spurs. HORIZONTAL TRAINED (espalier) Two tier, four- to five-years-old. Height 3–6 ft (1–2 m). Minimum two tiers of pre-trained 1½ ft (50 cm) horizontal opposite branches. HORIZONTAL TRAINED (espalier) Three tier, five- to seven-years-old. Height 3–6 ft (1–2 m). Minimum three tiers of pre-trained 2 ft (60 cm) horizontal opposite branches. FAMILY TREES Three varieties grown on same tree, normally bush or half-standard. Range of collections normally available:

'Red Ellison', 'Cox's Orange Pippin',
    'Laxton's Superb'.
'Discovery', 'Fortune', 'Sunset'.
'Grenadier', 'Worcester Pearmain',
    'Charles Ross'.
'James Grieve', 'Cox's Orange Pippin',
    'Spartan'.
'Merton Knave', 'Egremont Russet',
    'Golden Delicious'.
'Howgate Wonder', 'Bramley's Seedling',
    'Idared'.

Foliage Deciduous. Spring/summer, mid green. Grey mildew or brown spots indicate 'apple scab'. Brown scorching may be seen August–September.

Roots Whip, maiden, cordon and feathered, pots 8 in (20 cm) min. dia. Bush, half-standard, standard and fan-trained, pots 12 in (30 cm) min. dia. Root-wrapped and bare-rooted, good fibrous root system. Should be grafted on to a named or numbered rootstock to induce specific height, spread and fruiting capacity.

Root stocks and use
MM106 Bush and trained.
MM111 Half-standard.
M9 Dwarf bush or trained.
M27 Very dwarf bush or trained for growing in tubs.
M26 Dwarf bush or trained.
Crab stocks for half-standard and standard – avoid as size can be variable.

Hints Any well-prepared soil. Wide range. Research to obtain specific requirements. Avoid trees retained more than two years after reaching saleable size. Purchase named varieties. Check rootstock number and name. Check graft point for good union. Whip, maiden and feathered, further training. Bush, half-standard and standard, stakes and ties for five years. Cordon, horizontal-trained (espalier) and fan-trained for walls, plant 15–18 in (40–50 cm) away with training wires. Open ground, posts and training wires. Allow adequate space.

Most widely available Numbers in brackets indicate pollination group. Varieties of each number will pollinate each other. Numbers can also be moved up or down one with good results.

LATE SUMMER DESSERT RIPENING 'Discovery' (2). 'Epicure' (2). 'Merton Knave' (2). 'Red George Cave' (2). EARLY AUTUMN DESSERT RIPENING 'Dr Harvey' (3). 'Ellison's Orange' (4). 'James Grieve' (3). 'Jester' (3). 'Tydeman's Early Worcester' (3). 'Red Ellison' (3). 'Worcester Pearmain' (3).

LATE AUTUMN DESSERT RIPENING 'American Mother' (5). 'Charles Ross' (3). 'Dr Harvey' (3). 'Egremont Russet' (2). 'Fortune' (3). 'Greensleeves' (3). 'Jonagold' (3). 'Katy' (3). 'Kidd's Orange Red' (3). 'Lord Lambourne' (2). 'Norfolk Royal Russet' (3). 'Sunset' (3).

MID WINTER DESSERT RIPENING 'Blenheim Orange' (3). 'Cox's Orange Pippin' (3).

'Crispin' (2). 'Fiesta' (3). 'Fulstaff' (3). 'Gala' (3). 'Golden Delicious' (3). 'Queen Cox' (3). 'Red Delicious' (3). 'Ribston Pippin' (3). 'Rosemary Russet' (3). 'Spartan' (3). 'Tydeman's Late' (3). 'Welspur' (3).

NEW YEAR DESSERT RIPENING 'Ashmead's Kernel' (3). 'Idared' (4). 'Jupiter' (4). 'Laxton's Superb' (4). 'Malling Kent' (4). 'Orleans Reinette' (4). 'Smoothie' (4). 'Suntan' (4). 'Winston' (5).

SUMMER AND AUTUMN COOKING RIPENING 'Grenadier' (3). 'Howgate Wonder' (3). 'Lord Derby' (5). 'Rev. W. Wilks' (2).

LATE KEEPING COOKING RIPENING 'Bramley Seedling' (3). 'Edward VII' (6). 'Lane's Prince Albert' (4). 'Newton Wonder' (5). Many other varieties available.

MESPILUS GERMANICA
Medlar

Time to buy Pot-grown, any time. Balled and bare-rooted, October–March. Avoid adverse weather conditions.
Where to find Outside in Fruit or Trees.
Size MAIDEN Height 3–4 ft (1–1.2 m). Single stemmed. Limited side branches. BUSH Stem 2 ft (60 cm) min. Height 5 ft (1.5 m) min. Minimum three 1½ ft (50 cm) long branches. HALF-STANDARD Four- to six-years-old. Stem 4–5 ft (1.2 m–1.5 m). Height 6–8 ft (2–2.5 m) min. Minimum three 2 ft (60 cm) long branches.
Foliage Deciduous. Spring/summer, mid green. Premature autumn colour and leaf drop.
Roots Pots 9 in (23 cm) min. dia. Balled and bare-rooted, good fibrous root system.
Hints Any well-prepared soil, plus extra organic material. Irregular growth pattern. Stems bent. May be scarce. Grafted on to *Crataegus monogyna* understock, which may send up suckers. Bush and half-standard, stake and ties for five years. Maiden, further training.
Most widely available 'Nottingham'.

MORUS NIGRA
Mulberry

Time to buy Pot-grown, any time. Balled, October–March. Avoid adverse weather conditions.
Where to find Outside in Fruit or Trees.
Size MAIDEN Height 2–4 ft (60 cm–1.2 m) Single stem. Limited side branches. HALF-STANDARD Four–six-years-old. Stem 4 ft (1.2 m) min. Height 5 ft (1.5 m) Minimum three 2 ft (60 cm) long branches. STANDARD Four–six-years-old. Stem height, 6–8 ft (2–2.5 m). Height 9 ft (2.7 m) min. Minimum three 2 ft (60 cm) long branches.
Foliage Deciduous. Spring/summer, light to mid green, sparse. Premature autumn colour and leaf drop.
Roots Pots 6 in (15 cm) min. dia. Half-standard, pots 12 in. (30 cm) min. dia. Balled, good fibrous root system.
Hints Any well-prepared soil. May be scarce. Maiden, further training. Half-standard, stake and ties for five years.

PRUNUS ARMENIACA hybrids
Apricot

Time to buy Pot-grown, any time. Root-wrapped and bare-rooted, October–March. Avoid adverse weather conditions.
Where to find Outside in Fruit Trees.
Size MAIDEN One-year-old. Height 3–4 ft (1–1.2 m). Limited side branches. FEATHERED Two-year-old. Height 1½–4 ft (50 cm–1.2 m). Minimum four 1½ ft (50 cm) long side branches. BUSH Three–five-years-old. Stem 2–3 ft (60 cm–1 m). Height 5 ft (1.5 m) min. Minimum three 2 ft (60 cm) long branches. HALF-STANDARD Four–six-years-old. Stem 4–5 ft (1.2–1.5 m). Height 7 ft (2.2 m) min. Minumum three 2 ft (60 cm) long branches. FAN-TRAINED Five–seven-years-old. 3–6 ft (1–2 m). Minimum five 3 ft (1 m) long fan-trained branches.
Foliage Deciduous. Spring/summer, light to mid green. Premature autumn colour and leaf drop.

Roots Maiden, pots 6 in (15 cm) min. dia. Feathered, bush and fan-trained, pots 10 in (25 cm) min. dia. Root-wrapped and bare-rooted, good fibrous root system.

Hints Any well-prepared soil. Sold as fan-trained when in fact they are maiden or feathered. Look for prune marks and new branch systems to ensure fan-trained. Not always named. Dwarf varieties for containers may be scarce and hardiness suspect. May suffer attacks of Silver Leaf. Maiden and fan-trained for wall use, plant 15–18 in (40–50 cm) away from wall. Specific pruning to form fan-shapes. Open ground, stake and ties for five years.

Most widely available 'Farmindale'. 'Moorpark'. DWARF: 'Aprigold'. 'Garden Annie'. 'Golden Glow'. 'Katy Cot'.

PRUNUS AVIUM. P. CERASUS. P. MAHALEB hybrids

Cherry, Sweet Cherry

Time to buy Pot-grown, any time. Root-wrapped and bare-rooted, October–March. Avoid adverse weather conditions.

Where to find Outside in Fruit Trees.

Size MAIDEN Height 3–4 ft (1–1.2 m). Limited side branches. FEATHERED Height 3–6 ft (1–2 m). Minimum five 9 in (23 cm) long side branches. BUSH Stem 3½ ft (1.1 m). Height 5 ft (1.5 m) min. Minimum three 2 ft (60 cm) long branches. HALF-STANDARD Stem 4–5 ft (1.2–1.5 m). Height 8 ft (2.5 m) min. Minimum three 2 ft (60 cm) long branches. STANDARD Stem 6–8 ft (2–2.5 m). Height 9 ft (2.7 m) min. Minimum three 2 ft (60 cm)

Cherry pollinators (see **Pollinators** on p. 124)

		Pollinators	Fruiting time
1.	Amber Heart	5.6.11.12.19.21	Mid
2.	Bradbourne Late	4.16	Very late
3.	Early Rivers	15.18	Early
4.	Florence	2.13.16.17.20	Late
5.	Frogmore	6.14.15.17.21.22	Early to mid
6.	Governor Wood	5.6.11.14.17.19.20.21.22	Early to mid
7.	Inga	20.21.22	Mid
8.	Kent Bigarreau	4.5.11.12.13.16.17.19.20.21	Mid to late
9.	Merchant	3.5.6.10.11.12.15.18.19.21	Early to mid
10.	Mermat	3.6.11.12.14.15.18	Early to mid
11.	Merton Bigarreau	6.14.15.17.19.20.22	Early to late
12.	Merton Bounty	6.8.9.15.17.19.20	Mid
13.	Merton Crane	4.6.16.17.19	Mid
14.	Merton Glory	5.6.11.15.17.19.22	Early to mid
15.	Merton Heart	3.5.11.14.19	Early to mid
16.	Merton Late	2.8.13.17.20	Very late
17.	Napoleon Bigarreau	5.6.11.14.19.20.22	Mid to late
18.	Noir de Guben	3.9.10.14.15	Early to mid
19.	Roundel	5.6.11.14.15.17.20.21.22	Mid
20.	Stella	Self-fertile	Mid to late
21.	Van	Self-fertile	Mid
22.	Morello	Self-fertile	Mid

---

long branches. FAN-TRAINED Half-standard may be scarce.

Foliage Deciduous. Spring/summer, mid to dark green. Premature leaf drop.

Roots Maiden and feathered, pots 9 in (23 cm) min. dia. Bush, half-standard and standard, pots 10 in (25 cm) min. dia. Root-wrapped and bare-rooted, good fibrous root system.

Hints Any well-prepared soil. Except for 'Cherry Stella', 'C. Van' and 'C. Morello', all others must have pollination. Varieties not correctly named. Full range may have to be sought from different outlets. Bush and half-standard, stake and ties for five years. Fan-trained for wall use, plant 15–18 in (40–50 cm) away from wall. Open ground, post and wires.

Most widely available 'Amber Heart' (W). 'Bradbourne Black' (B). 'Early Rivers' (B). 'Florence' (W). 'Frogmore' (W). 'Governor Wood' (W). 'Inga' (W). 'Kent Bigarreau' (W). 'Merchant' (B). 'Merpet' (B). 'Merton Bigarreau' (W). 'Merton Bounty' (B). 'Merton Crane' (B). 'Merton Glory' (W). 'Merton Heart' (B). 'Merton Late' (W). 'Napoleon Bigarreau' (W). 'Noir de Guben' (B). 'Roundel' (B).

SELF-FERTILE VARIETIES 'Stella' (B). 'Van' (B).

SOUR OR COOKING 'Morello' (R/B).

Pollinators (See table, p. 123). Numbers relate to pollination variety. Only certain varieties pollinate certain other varieties. Take the list of numbers given after the variety name to identify the other varieties which can be used to pollinate it.

W – white. B – black. R – red.

PRUNUS CERASIFERA
Cherry Plum

Time to buy Pot-grown, any time. Balled, root-wrapped and bare-rooted, October–March. Avoid adverse weather conditions.

Where to find Outside in Fruit Trees.

Size MAIDEN Height 3–4 ft (1–1.2 m) Limited side branches. FEATHERED

Height 3–6 ft (1–2 m). Minimum five branches. BUSH Stem 3½ ft (1.1 m). Height 5 ft (1.5 m) min. Minimum three 1 ft (30 cm) long branches. HALF-STANDARD Stem 4–5 ft (1.2–1.5 m). Height 8 ft (2.5 m) min. Minimum three 2 ft (60 cm) long branches. STANDARD Stem 6–8 ft (2–2.5 m). Height 10 ft (3 m) min. Minimum three 2 ft (60 cm) long branches.

Foliage Deciduous. Spring/summer, mid green. May show brown scorching from July.

Roots Maiden and feathered, pots 6 in (15 cm) min. dia. Bush and half-standard, pots 10 in (25 cm) min. dia. Balled, root-wrapped and bare-rooted good fibrous root system.

Hints Any well-prepared soil. May be scarce. Half-standard and standard very scarce. Bush and half-standard, stake and ties for five years. Fan-trained for wall use, plant 15–18 in (40–50 cm) away. Open ground, post and wires.

PRUNUS DOMESTICA
Damson, Gage, Greengage, Plum

Time to buy Pot-grown, any time. Root-wrapped and bare-rooted, October–March.

Where to find Outside in Fruit Trees.

Size MAIDEN Height 3–4 ft (1–1.2 m). Limited side branches. FEATHERED Height 3–6 ft (1–2 m). Minimum four 1½ ft (60 cm) long side branches. BUSH Three-five-year-old. Stem 2–3 ft (60 cm–1 m). Height 5 ft (1.5 m). Minimum three 2 ft (60 cm) long branches. DWARF BUSH Stem 2–3 ft (60 cm–1 m). Height 5 ft (1.5 m) min. Minimum three 2 ft (60 cm) long branches. HALF-STANDARD Stem 4–6 ft (1.2–2 m). Height 6–8 ft (2–2.5 m) min. Minimum three 2 ft (60 cm) long branches. STANDARD Stem 6–8 ft (2–2.5 m). Height 9 ft (2.7 m) min. Minimum three 2 ft (60 cm) long branches. FAN-TRAINED Height 3–6 ft (1–2 m). Minimum five 3 ft (1 m) long fan-trained branches.

Foliage Deciduous. Spring/summer, mid

green. May show brown scorching July onwards.

Roots Maiden and feathered, pots 8 in (20 cm) min. dia. Bush, half-standard and standard, pots 12 in (30 cm) min. dia. Root-wrapped and bare-rooted, good fibrous root system.

All plums will be grafted on to one or other of named rootstock. Dwarf bush Plums some fan-trained Pixie, non-dwarf bush, half-standard, standard, some fan-trained on 'St Julien A.'

Hints Any well-prepared soil. May be scarce. Stake and ties for five years. For wall use, plant 15–18 in (40–50 cm) away. Purchase named varieties.

Most widely available Numbers in brackets indicate pollination group and can be moved up or down by one with good results. Damson, Greengage and Plum all work together.

DAMSON 'Damson Merryweather' (3).

GREENGAGE, Mid Summer Ripening: 'Denniston's Superb' (2). 'Early Transparent Gage' (4). Early Autumn Ripening: 'Cambridge Gage' (4). 'Old Greengage' (2). 'Oullin's Gage' (4). Mid Autumn Ripening: 'Jefferson Gage' (1). 'Reine Claude de Bavay' (2).

PLUM, Mid Summer Ripening: 'Czar' (3). Late Summer Ripening: 'Victoria' (3) Also self-pollinating. Early Autumn Ripening: 'Kirk's Blue' (3).

PRUNUS INSITITIA
Bullace

Time to buy Pot-grown, any time. Balled, root-wrapped and bare-rooted, October–March. Avoid adverse weather conditions.

Where to find Outside in Fruit Trees, Forestry or Native Plants.

Size MAIDEN Height 3–4 ft (1–1.2 m). Limited side branches. FEATHERED Overall height 3–6 ft (1–2 m). Minimum five 1½ ft (50 cm) long side branches. BUSH Stem not more than 2–2½ ft (60–80 cm). Height 5 ft (1.5 m) min. Minimum three

2 ft (60 cm) long branches. HALF-STANDARD Stem 3½–4 ft (1.1–1.2 m) min. Height 6–8 ft (2–2.5 m) min. Minimum three 2 ft (60 cm) long branches. Limited availability.

Foliage Deciduous. Spring/summer, mid green. May show brown scorching from July.

Roots Pots 6 in (15 cm) min. dia. Balled, root-wrapped and bare-rooted, good fibrous root system.

Hints Any well-prepared soil. Normally scarce. Possibly only Red Bullace available. Stake and ties for five years.

Most widely available Red, yellow and black fruiting varieties.

PRUNUS PERSICA
Peach and Nectarine

Time to buy Pot-grown, any time. Root-wrapped and bare-rooted, October–March. Avoid adverse weather conditions.

Where to find Outside in Fruit Trees.

Size MAIDEN One-year-old, height 3–4 ft (1–1.2 m). Limited side branches. FEATHERED Two-years-old, height 1½–4 ft (50 cm–1.2 m). Minimum four 1½ ft (50 cm) long side branches. BUSH Three–five-years-old. Stem 2–3 ft (60 m–1 m). Height 5 ft (1.5 m). Minimum three 2 ft (60 cm) long branches. DWARF BUSH Two-years-old. Stem 1½ ft (50 cm) min. Minimum three side branches. FAN-TRAINED Five–seven-years-old. Height 3–6 ft (1–2 m). Minimum five 3 ft (1 m) long fan-trained branches. HALF-STANDARD Two-years-old. Stem 4 ft (1.2 m) min. Height 8 ft (2.5 m) min. Minimum three 2 ft (60 cm) long branches.

Foliage Deciduous. Spring/summer, light to mid green. Premature autumn colour and leaf drop.

Roots Maiden and dwarf bush, pots 6 in (15 cm) min. dia. Feathered, bush, fan-trained and half-standard, pots 10 in (25 cm) min. dia. Root-wrapped and bare-rooted, good fibrous root system.

Hints Any well-prepared soil. Sold as fan-trained when no more than maidens. Some have very coarse root systems. Named varieties rarely offered. For container-growing only, use dwarf varieties but these may not be fully hardy. Nectarines and peaches may suffer from peach leaf curl. For wall or fence use, plant 15–18 in (40–50 cm) away. Half-standard, stake and ties for five years. Maiden and feathered, additional pruning and training.

Most widely available
PEACHES 'Amsden June'. 'Duke of York'. 'Peregrine'. 'Rochester'. Dwarf Varieties 'Bonanza II'. 'Honeybaby'.
NECTARINES 'Early Rivers'. 'Lord Napier'. 'Pineapple'. Dwarf Varieties 'Garden Delight'. 'Nectar Baby'.

PRUNUS SPINOSA
Sloe, Blackthorn
Time to buy Pot-grown, any time. Balled, root-wrapped and bare-rooted, October–March. Avoid adverse weather conditions.
Where to find Outside in Fruit Trees, Forestry or Native Plants.
Size MAIDEN Height 3–4 ft (1–1.2 m). Limited side branches. FEATHERED Height 3–6 ft (1–2 m). Minimum five 1½ ft (50 cm) long branches. BUSH Stem 2–4 ft (60 cm–1.2 m). Height 6 ft (2 m) min. Minimum three 2 ft (60 cm) long branches. HALF-STANDARD Stem 3½–6 ft (1.1–2 m). Height 7–9 ft (2–2.7 m). Minimum three 2 ft (60 cm) long branches.
Foliage Deciduous. Spring/summer, light green. May show brown scorching July onwards.
Roots Pots, Maiden and feathered 6 in (15 cm) min. dia. Bush and half-standard 10 in (23 cm) min. dia.
Hints Any well-prepared soil. May be scarce, particularly Half-standard. Stake and ties for minimum five years.

PYRUS COMMUNIS hybrids
Pear
Time to buy Pot-grown, any time. Root-wrapped or bare-rooted, October–March. Avoid adverse weather conditions.
Where to find Outside in Fruit Trees.
Size MAIDEN One-year-old, height 3–4 ft (1–1.2 m). Limited side branches. FEATHERED Two-years-old, height 1½–4 ft (50 cm–1.2 m). Minimum four 1½ ft (50 cm) long side branches. BUSH Three–five-years-old, stem height 2–3 ft (60 cm–1 m). Height 5 ft (1.5 m) min. Minimum three 2 ft (60 cm) long branches. HALF STANDARD Four–six-years-old, stem height 4–5 ft (1.2–1.5 m) Height 7 ft (2.2 m) min. Minimum three 2 ft (60 cm) long branches. STANDARD Four–six-years-old, stem height 6–8 ft (2–2.5 m). Height 7 ft (2.2 m) min. Minimum three 2 ft (60 cm) long branches. CORDON Height 2–6 ft (60 cm–2 m). Minimum four short side-fruiting spurs. HORIZONTAL TRAINED (espalier) Two-tier. Four–five-years-old, 3–6 ft (1–2 m) over all. Minimum two tiers pre-trained horizontal 1½ ft (50 cm) opposite branches. HORIZONTAL TRAINED (espalier) Three-tier. Five–seven-years-old, 3–6 ft (1–2 m) over all. Minimum three tiers pre-trained horizontal 2 ft (60 cm) long opposite branches. FAN-TRAINED Five–seven-years-old, 3–6 ft (1–2 m) over all. Minimum five 3 ft (1 m) long fan-trained branches. FAMILY TREES Three varieties on same tree, bush or half-standard. Normally comprised of: 'William Bon Chrétien', 'Conference', 'Doyenné du Comice'.
Foliage Deciduous. Spring/summer, mid green. May show brown scorching from July onwards.
Roots Maiden, pots 6 in (15 cm) min. dia. Other sizes, pots 10 in (25 cm) min. dia. Root-wrapped and bare-rooted, good fibrous root system. All pear varieties grafted on to root-stock Quince C. No dwarf stocks exist at present time.
Hints Any well-prepared soil, plus extra organic material. Poor root system. All

varieties may not be available from one outlet. More than one variety needed for pollination. Half-standard, standard and bush, stake and ties for five years. Horizontal (espalier) and fan-trained for wall use, plant 15–18 in (40–50 cm) away from wall. Open ground, needs posts and wires. Allow adequate space.

Most widely available Numbers in brackets indicate pollination group. Varieties of same number will pollinate each other. Numbers can be moved up or down one with good results.

SEPTEMBER AND OCTOBER RIPENING 'Beth' (3). 'Onward' (4). 'Wlliam's Bon Chretien' (3).

LATE OCTOBER AND NOVEMBER RIPENING 'Beurre Hardy' (4). 'Conference' (3). Also self-pollinating. 'Doyenne du Comice' (4). 'Fertility' (3) syn. 'Improved Fertility'. 'Louise Bonne of Jersey' (3).

DECEMBER AND JANUARY RIPENING 'Winter Nelis' (4).

LATE COOKING 'Pitmaston Duchess' (4).

RHEUM RHAPONITICUM
Rhubarb

Time to buy Pot-grown, any time. Rootwrapped or bare-rooted February–March. Avoid adverse weather conditions.

Where to find Outside in Fruit or Vegetables. Pre-packed under limited cover.

Size Root-wrapped or bare-rooted clumps 4 in (10 cm) min. dia. Pre-packed 3 in (8 cm) min. dia.

Foliage Deciduous. Pot-grown, mid green. Can look long and leggy, but root crown is the important part.

Roots Pots 5 in (12 cm) min. dia. Resembles lumps of dead tree-stump. Barerooted clumps kept moist. Exposure to frost is advantage. Pre-packed stored in cool environment.

Hints Any well-prepared soil, plus extra organic material. Pre-packed has a short shelf-life. April, avoid excessive growth. Not always named. Do not force in first spring and summer after planting.

Most widely available 'Cawood Delight'. 'Champagne'. 'Early Albert'. 'Timperley Early'. 'Sutton Victoria'.

RIBES GROSSULARIA
Gooseberry

Time to buy Pot-grown, any time. Rootwrapped and bare-rooted, October–February. Pre-packed available. Avoid adverse weather conditions.

Where to find Outside in Fruit. Prepacks under limited protection.

Size ONE-YEAR-OLD 8 in–1$\frac{1}{2}$ ft (20–50 cm). Limited branches. TWO-YEARS-OLD 1–2 ft (30–60 cm). Minimum two 12 in (30 cm) long branches. THREE-YEARS-OLD 1$\frac{1}{2}$–2$\frac{1}{2}$ ft (50–80 cm). Minimum three 1$\frac{1}{2}$ ft (50 cm) long branches. Should have a 1 ft (30 cm) 'leg' (small trunk) from ground level to first branches. For training cordons, choose one-year-old. Trained forms must be grown and trained *in situ*.

Foliage Deciduous. Spring/summer, light green. August, yellowing.

Roots Pots 10 in (25 cm) min. dia. Rootwrapped, bare-rooted and pre-packed, good fibrous root system.

Hints Any well-prepared soil. For wall use, plant 15–18 in (40–50 cm) away from wall. Supply training wires. Open ground, cordon-trained, needs post and wires. Requires protection from birds at harvest time. Varieties not always named. Avoid plants showing signs of gooseberry mildew.

Most widely available 'Captivator'. 'Careless'. 'Invicta'. 'Jostaberry'. 'Jubilee'. 'Keepsake'. 'Lancer'. 'Leveller'. 'Whinham's Industry'. 'Whitesmith Hybrid'. 'Worcesterberry'.

RIBES hybrid

Boysenberry, Boysenberry Thornless, Dewberry, Japanese Wineberry (*Rubus phoenicolasius*), John Innes Berry, King's Acre Berry, Marionberry, Silvanberry, Sunberry, Tayberry, Worcesterberry.

Time to buy Pot-grown, February–June.

Root-wrapped, bare-rooted or pre-packed, October–February. Avoid adverse weather conditions.

Where to find Outside in Fruit. Pre-packed under limited cover.

Size Pot-grown, root-wrapped or bare-rooted, 6 in–3 ft (15 cm–1 m). Height not important. Stems thicker than pencil.

Foliage Deciduous. Spring/summer, mid to dark green. Premature autumn colour and leaf drop.

Roots Pots 4 in (10 cm) min. dia. Root-wrapped, bare-rooted and pre-packed, good fibrous root system.

Hints Any well-prepared soil, plus extra organic material. Often stored too close together, with drying out. This can be terminal. Avoid plants with signs of early growth. Cut back all growth to within two buds of ground level in March. Repeat annually. Needs protection from birds at harvest time.

RIBES NIGRUM hybrids
Blackcurrant

Time to buy Pot-grown, any time. Root-wrapped, bare-rooted or pre-packed, October–March. Avoid adverse weather conditions.

Where to find Outside in Fruit. Pre-packs under limited cover.

Size ONE-YEAR-OLD 6 in–1½ ft (15–50 cm). Single shoot.

TWO-YEARS-OLD 1–2 ft (30–60 cm). Minimum two 1½-ft (50 cm) long shoots.

THREE-YEARS-OLD 1½–3 ft (50 cm–1 m). Minimum three 2 ft (60 cm) long shoots.

Foliage Deciduous. Spring/summer, mid green. Premature autumn colour and leaf drop.

Roots Pots 6 in (15 cm) min. dia. Root-wrapped, bare-rooted and pre-packed good fibrous root system.

Hints Any well-prepared soil in full sun. If purchasing in winter, inspect terminal buds, which should be narrow and pointed; if round and fat, suspect big bud disease and avoid. Not always named.

Avoid plants with signs of early growth. One and two-years-old, planted and cut back in March to within two buds from the ground. Three-years-old, three main shoots left unpruned, remainder cut back to within two buds of ground level. One and two-years-old, no fruit in first year. Protection from birds at harvest time.

Most widely available 'Amos Black'. 'Baldwins'. 'Ben Lomond'. 'Ben Moore'. 'Ben Sarek'. 'Black Reward'. 'Boskoop Giant'. 'Malling Jet'. 'Mendip Cross'. 'Seabrook's Black'. 'Tsema'. 'Wellington XXX'.

RUBUS hybrids
Blackberry, Loganberry, Boysenberry, John Innes Berry, Tayberry, Worcesterberry, Japanese Wineberry

Time to buy Pot-grown, any time. Root-wrapped and bare-rooted, October–March. Avoid adverse weather conditions.

Where to find Outside in Fruit Trees, occasionally Climbers. Pre-packed under limited cover.

Size Pot-grown up to 2 ft (60 cm) height. Minimum one shoot tied to cane. Height not important.

Foliage Deciduous. Spring/summer, dark green.

Roots Pots 4 in (10 cm) min. dia. Root-wrapped, bare-rooted or pre-packed clumps, good fibrous root system.

Hints Any well-prepared soil, plus extra organic material. Pre-packed, avoid if showing growth. *Rubus fruticans*, (Wild Blackberry) scarce. For wall use, plant 15–18 in (40–50 cm) away, with wires for training. Open ground, posts and wires. Protection required for fruit. Allow adequate space. Cut back all previous season's growth to within 2 in (5 cm) of ground level in April. No fruit first year of planting.

Most widely available
BLACKBERRY Varieties with thorns: 'Ashton Cross'. 'Bedfordshire Giant'.

'Black Satin'. 'Fantasia'. 'Himalayan Giant'. Wild Blackberries (*Rubus fruticans*). Without thorns: 'Loch Ness'. 'Merton Thornless'. 'Oregon Thornless'. LOGANBERRY Thorned variety 'LY59' Thornless variety 'Thornless LY654'.

RUBUS IDAEUS hybrids
Raspberry
Time to buy Root-wrapped, bare-rooted or pre-packed canes September–March. Avoid adverse weather conditions. Normally bundles of fives or tens.
Where to find Outside in Fruit or Soft Fruit. May be plunged in moist material. Pre-packs under limited cover. Avoid canes stored indoors.
Size Canes, 9 in–3 ft (23 cm–1 m). Strong, firm canes, diameter of pencil min. Purchase Ministry of Agriculture certified stock.
Foliage Deciduous. Limited foliage during planting period.
Roots Good fibrous root system. Main root ends may be broken, this is part of propagation process.
Hints Well-prepared soil plus extra organic material. Open sunny position. Allow adequate space. Never plant where raspberries have been before. Post and wire support. Protection from birds at harvest time. Summer fruiting varieties pruned to within 9 in (23 cm) of ground level in April. No fruit first year of planting. Autumn fruiting, no pruning.
Most widely available
SUMMER RED FRUITING 'Glen Cova'. 'Glen Moy'. 'Glen Prosen'. 'Malling Admiral'. 'Malling Delight'. 'Malling Exploit'. 'Malling Jewel'. 'Malling Joy'. 'Malling Leo'. 'Malling Orion'. 'Malling Promise'. 'Norfolk Giant'.
SUMMER YELLOW FRUITING 'Fall Gold'. 'Golden Everest'.
SUMMER BLACK FRUITING 'Munger'.
AUTUMN FRUITING 'Autumn Bliss'. 'Heritage'. 'September'. 'Zeva'.

VACCINIUM hybrids
Blueberry
Time to buy Pot-grown, any time. Avoid adverse weather conditions.
Where to find Outside in Fruit or Shrubs.
Size 1–3 ft (30 cm–1 m). Minimum two 12 in (30 cm) long shoots.
Foliage Deciduous. Spring/summer, grey-green, narrow, sparse.
Roots Pots 5 in (12 cm) min. dia.
Hints Well-prepared acid soil, which is not always made clear at time of purchase.
Most widely available 'Berkeley'. 'Bluetta'. 'Bluecrop'. 'Colville'. 'Patriot'. 'Spartan'.

VITIS VINIFERA hybrids
Grape
Time to buy Balled, root-wrapped, and bare-rooted October–March. Avoid adverse weather conditions.
Where to find Outside for outdoor varieties. Inside for indoor. In Fruit or Climbers.
Size POT-GROWN 1½–4 ft (50 cm–1.2 m). Single or multi-stemmed tied to cane. BARE-ROOTED 4 in–3 ft (10 cm–1 m).
Foliage Deciduous. Spring/summer light green. Yellowing of foliage in autumn.
Roots Pots 5 in (12 cm) min. dia. Balled, root-wrapped and bare-rooted, good fibrous root system.
Hints Any well-prepared soil. Water before planting. Plant 15–18 in (40–50 cm) away from support. Wire or individual anchorage points to secure on walls and fences. Open ground, posts and wires or some other structure. Be sure to select either wine or desert varieties as per requirements. Vines particularly grown for foliage effect see under Climbers.
Most widely available 'Ali cante' (D/B/I). 'Baco' 1 (W). 'Black Hamburg' (D/W/B/O). 'Brant' (W/B). 'Buckland Sweetwater' (D/WH/I). 'Chardonnay' (W/WH). 'Chasselas

D'Or' (D/WH/I). 'Leon Millot' (W/B). 'Madeleine Angevine' 7972 (W/WH). 'Madeleine Sylvaner' 2851 (D/W/WH/O). 'Marshall Joffre' (W/B). 'Millers Burgundy' (Pinot Meunier) (W/B). 'Mueller-Thurgau' (W/WH). 'Muscat de Saumur' (W/WH). 'Muscat of Alexandria' (D/WH/I). Nimrod (W/WH). Pint Blanc (W/WH). 'Pirovano' 14 (D/W/B/O). 'Precoce de Malingre' (D/WH/O). 'Schuyler' (W/B). 'Seibel 13053' (W/B). 'Seyval' (W/WH). 'Seyve-Villar' 5–276 (D/W/WH/O). 'Siegerrebe' (D/WH/O). 'Strawberry Grape' (D/B/O). 'Traiminer' (W/WH). 'Triomphe d'Alsace' (W/B).

(D) – Dessert; (W) – Wine; (WH) – White; (B) – Black; (O) – Outdoor; I – Indoor.)

Perennials (Herbaceous Plants)

Perennials, herbaceous plants, hardy plants and garden plants are all names for this group, and also included are ferns and grasses. Some are evergreen and may offer all-year-round attraction but the majority are deciduous, dying to ground level in winter.

They can be used in the traditional herbaceous border but more and more are being used in mixed plantings or for interplanting. Many forms are now being used in containers and hanging baskets, and there simply are no hard and fast rules about how they can be used.

There is a wide range and it is impossible for any one nursery or garden centre to stock the myriad different forms. You will therefore need to shop around, and the use of reputable mail-order companies for supply is recommended. However, care must be taken with substitution, as many forms have different characteristics within their own groupings. If substitutes are offered, care must be taken to ensure they fit the colour scheme, aspect and area in which they are intended to grow.

They are available in two main forms, bare-rooted or pot-grown. Some will also be found pre-packed and as long as these are purchased early in the recommended purchasing period, they can be successful.

Traditionally, perennials were easy-going plants, but now the range is much wider and you will need to check on the individual requirements of any chosen plant. Aspect, soil-type and final performance all need to be researched.

A pattern of supply is emerging as follows: up until early spring, bare-rooted material can be purchased with confidence, they then appear in garden centres in small pots, 7–9 cm ($2\frac{3}{4}$–$3\frac{1}{2}$ in), and by the end of June the plants are supplied in 1 and 2 litre pots. These larger plants command a premium price but are 'instant' in their effect.

Pre-planning of any perennial planting is important, to be sure that all the various characteristics are allowed for and that the final effect will be that which is desired.

Soil-preparation and cultivation procedures should be followed just as exhaustively as with any other plant: they should not be curtailed in any way. The soil should be dug to a depth of, at the very least, 9 in (23 cm), deeper if possible, and good quantities of organic material added.

PERENNIALS (HERBACEOUS)
offered bare-rooted by mail order

Time to buy Light soils, August–December. Heavy soils, March onwards. Other types, February–April.

Where to find If offered for immediate sale, covered with moist material.

Size Size of clump will vary according to species, should consist of minimum one full root system.

Foliage Deciduous and evergreen. Evergreens may look limp.

Roots Root-clumps, good fibrous root system. Packed moist, contained in polythene bags. Consignment watertight, packed to prevent crushing or pilfering. Each labelled, singly or in units. Take care with unpacking.

Hints Most well-prepared soil types, plus extra organic material. Take individual reference. Research overall size. Becoming less common as a method of supply. Good for large numbers. Delivery charge will be made.

Most widely available *Acanthus spinosus.* Achillea. *Aconitum arendsii.* Agapanthus 'Headbourne Hybrids'. Alchemilla. Allium. Althaea (Hollyhock). Anaphalis. Aquilegia. Artemisia. Asphodelus. Aster. Astilbe. Astrantia. Bergenia. Caltha. Campanula. Catanache. Centaurea. Chelone. Chrysanthemum. Cimicifuga. Cirsium. Coreopsis. Crocosmia. Cynoglossum. Delphinium. Dicentra. Doronicum. Echinacea. Echinops. Erigeron. Eryngium. Euphorbia. Filipendula. Gaillardia. Geranium (Hardy). Geum. Glyceria. Gypsophila. Helenium. Helianthus. *Helichrysum* 'Sulphur Light'. Heliopsis. Helleborus. Hemerocallis. Heuchera. Hosta. Incarvillea. Iris. Kniphofia. Liatris. Ligularia. Limonium. Liriope. Lupinus. Lychnis. Lysimachia. Lythrum. Macleava. Martensia. Meum. Oenothera. Paeonia. Papaver. Peltiphyllum. Pennisetum. Phlox. Physalis. Physostegia. Polemonium. Polygonatum. Polygonum. Potentilla. Pulmonaria. Rodgersia. Rudbeckia. Salvia. Scabiosa. Sedum. Sidalcea. Smilacina. Solidago. Stachys. Symphytum. Tellima. Thalictrum. Tradescantia. Tricyrtis. Trollium. Veratrum. Verbascum. Veronica. Zygadenus. Others may be available.

PERENNIALS (HERBACEOUS) best purchased pot-grown

Time to buy Pot-grown $2\frac{3}{4}$ in (7 cm) or $3\frac{1}{2}$ in (9 cm) February–April. After May, offered at reduced price. Pot-grown 4 in (10 cm) (1 litre) May–September. Avoid adverse weather conditions.

Where to find Outside in Perennials. May be under light protection.

Size Heights vary.

Foliage December–March, little or no top growth. April–August, more height. After October will deteriorate and reduce in height.

Roots Pots $2\frac{3}{4}$ in (7 cm), $3\frac{1}{2}$ in (9 cm), and 4 in (10 cm) (1 litre).

Hints Well-prepared soil. Take individual reference. Wide range, some forms from various outlets. Should be well labelled and when transporting ensure these are not lost. If kept under cover in winter, avoid planting until spring frosts have finished. Research ultimate overall size.

Species best purchased in this way Agapanthus. Alstroemeria. Artemisia. Arum. Asphodeline. Bupleurum. Caltha. Cheiranthus. Chelone (Turtles Head). Clematis (Perennial forms). Cynara. Dictamnus. Dierama. Epimedium. Euphorbia (Spurge). Gentiana. Gunnera. Gypsophila (Baby's Breath). Houttuynia. Incarvillea (Garden Gloxinia). *Lobelia cardinalis.* Lysichitum (Skunk Cabbage). Meconopsis. Mimulus. Oenothera (Evening Primrose). Ophiopogon. Orchis. Peltiphyllum (Umbrella Plant). Platycodon (Balloon Flower). Primula (all forms). Some forms are also listed as prepacked; for preference, purchase pot-grown.

PERENNIALS (HERBACEOUS)
offered pot-grown
Time to buy Pot-grown $2\frac{1}{4}$ in (7 cm) or $3\frac{1}{2}$ in (9 cm) February–April. After May offered at reduced price. Pot-grown 4 in (10 cm) (1 litre) or 6 in (15 cm) (2 litre) May–September. Avoid adverse weather conditions. Mail order acceptable.

Where to find Outside in Perennials. May be under protection in winter.

Size Height will vary. December–March, little or no top growth. April–August, more height. October, will deteriorate and reduce.

Foliage Most deciduous. Spring/summer, should be firm, unfaded in colour and not drawn. From September, less attractive.

Roots Pots $2\frac{3}{4}$ in (7 cm), $3\frac{1}{2}$ in (9 cm), 4 in (10 cm) (1 litre) or 6 in (15 cm) (2 litre).

Hints Well-prepared soil. Take individual reference. Quantities and some forms from various outlets. Well established and clearly labelled. When transporting, ensure labels are not lost. Research overall size. If kept under cover in winter, avoid planting until spring frosts have finished.

Most widely available Achillea. Aconitum. Agapanthus. Alchemilla. Allium. Althaea (Hollyhock). Anemone. Anthemis. Aquilegia. Artemisia. Aruncua. Asphodelus. Aster. Astilbe. Astrantia. Bergenia. Calamintha. Caltha. Campanula. Centaurea. Centranthus. Chelone. Chrysanthemum. Coreopsis. Crocosmia. Delphinium. Dianthus (border types). Dicentra. Digitalis. Doronicum. Echinacea. Echinops. Epimedium. Erigeron. Eryngium. Euphorbia. Filipendula. Gaillarida. Geranium (Hardy). Geum. Gypsophila. Helianthus. *Helichrysum* 'Sulphur Light'. Heliopsis. Helleborus. Hemerocallis. Heuchera. Hosta. Houttuynia. Inula. Iris. Kniphofia syn. Tritoma (Red Hot Poker). Lamium. Liatris. Ligularia. Limonium. Liriope. *Lobelia cardinalis*. Lupinus. Lychnis. Lythrum. Meconopsis. Monarda. Oenothera. Omphalodes. Paeonia. Papaver. Phlox. Phygelius. *Physalis franchetii* (Chinese Lantern). Physostegia. Plarycodon. Polygonum. Potentilla. Prunella. Pyrethrum. Rodgersia. Rudbeckia. Salvia. Scabiosa. Schizostylis. Sedum. Sidalcea. Solidago. Stachys. Symphytum. Tellima. Thalictrum. Tradescantia. Tricyrtis. Trollius. Verbascum. Veronica. Zantedeschia. Many others available.

PERENNIALS (HERBACEOUS)
offered as pre-packs
Time to buy March–April. Avoid later, as plants grow artificially after this time.

Where to find Inside, pre-packed on racks, or outside under limited cover.

Size Root-clumps, good fibrous root system, in polythene.

Foliage Deciduous, none visible. If seen, avoid.

Roots Substantial clump, packed moist.

Hints Store in light, cool, frost and rodent-free environment. Plant as soon as possible after purchasing. Read instructions on packaging. Well-prepared soil, plus extra organic material. Often offered over too long a period. Correct botanical name not always used.

Most widely available Agapanthus (Blue or White African Lily). Alstroemeria. Aquilegia. Astilbe. *Bergenia cordifolia*. Commelina. Coelestis. Crocosmia (Montbretia). *Dicentra spectabilis. D. s.* 'Alba' (Bleeding Heart). *Gypsophila* (Baby's Breath). *Heliopsis scabra*. Hemerocallis (Day Lily). *Hosta. Incarvillea delavayi* (Garden Gloxinia). *Iris germanica* (Flag Iris). *Iris sibirica* (Wild Iris). Kniphofia syn. Tritoma (Red Hot Poker). Liatris. Lychnis (Maltese Cross). *Oenothera missouriensis* (Evening Primrose). Paeonia double-flowered. *Phlox paniculata*. Physalis (Chinese Lantern). Schildanthus. *Tricyrtis hirta*. Yucca.

PERENNIALS (HERBACEOUS)
supplied as root-cuttings
Time to buy February–April. Avoid adverse weather conditions.

Where to find Indoors as pre-packs. Mail order acceptable.

Size Sections of root minimum 3 in (8 cm) long. Diameter from pencil to large cigar-thickness. *Rheum*, a lump approximately 4 in (10 cm) length and diameter.

Foliage Deciduous. No foliage.

Roots Firm, moist, with no signs of rot. Top cut square and bottom tapered.

Hints Well-prepared plus extra organic material. Take individual reference. Soil preparation of paramount importance. Plant as soon as possible on arrival, square or thickest end upwards.

Most widely available Aconitum. Anchusa. Crambe. Dicentra. Gypsophila (Baby's Breath). Incarvillea. Macelaya (Plume Poppy). Ranunculus. Rheum. Tricyrtis (Toad Lily). Tropaeolum. Zantedeschia (Arum Lily).

PERENNIALS (HERBACEOUS)
grown from seed
Time to buy December–April. Sown as per instructions on packet.

Where to find Inside on seed racks. Normally alphabetical, both Latin and common names used.

Hints Follow instructions on seed packet. The growing from seed of perennials is not universal. Some do not come true. Perennials take time to grow from seed.

Most widely available *Acanthus mollis* (Bear's Breeches). Achillea. *Alchemilla mollis* (Lady's Mantle). *Alstroemeria* 'Ligtu Hybrids' (Peruvian Lilies). *Amaranthus caudatus. Anaphalis margaritacea* (Pearly Everlasting). *Anemone japonica.* Anthemis 'Kelway's Gold'. *Aquilegia* (Columbine). *Asphodelus luteus* 'Yellow Candle' (King's Spear). *Aster novi-*

belgii (Michaelmas Daisy). Astilbe. *Calceolaria biflora. Campanula persicifolia. Campanula pyramidalis. Catananche coerulea.* (Cupid's Dart). *Centaurea dealbata* (Perennial Cornflower) *Centranthus ruber* (Valerian). *Chrysanthemum maxima* (Shasta Daisy). *Chrysanthemum* 'Korean Hybrids, Glorious Mixed'. *Coreopsis* 'Early Sunrise'. *Corydalis lutea* (Golden Bleeding Heart). *Dictamnus fraxinella* (Flame Flower). Delphinium 'Blue Fountains'. Delphinium 'Pacific Giants Mixed'. Dodecatheon (Shooting Stars). Doronicum 'Yellow Splendour' (Leopard's Bane). Echinops 'Ritro' (Globe Thistle). *Erigeron speciosus. Euphorbia polychroma.* Gaillardia. *Geum chiloense. Gypsophila paniculata. Helleborus niger* (Christmas Rose). *Heuchera sanguinea* (Coral Bells). *Incarvillea delavayi* (Garden Gloxinia). *Inula orientalis. Iris versicolor.* Kniphofia syn. Tritoma (Red Hot Poker). *Liatris spicata. Liatris pycnostachya* (Blazing Star). *Lathyrus latifolius* (Everlasting Sweet Pea). *Linum* 'Dwarf Blue Saphyr' (Flax). *Lobelia fulgens* 'Queen Victoria' (Perennial Lobelia). Lupin. *Lupin* 'Dwarf Minarette'. *Lychnis chalcedonica* (Maltese Cross). *Lysimachia punctata* (Loosestrife). *Lythrum salicaria. Meconopsis betonicifolia* syn. *M. baileyi* (Blue Himalayan Poppy). *Meconopsis* 'Cambrica' (Welsh Poppy). *Monarda* 'Panorama Mixed' (Sweet Bergamot). *Nepeta mussinii* (Catmint). *Oenothera* 'Missouri' (Evening Primrose). *Oenothera pallida* 'Wedding Bells'. *Physalis franchetti* (Chinese Lanterns). *Physotegia virginiana* 'Crown of Snow' (Obedient Plant). *Papaver orientalis. Primula japonica* mixed. *Primula rosea* 'Grandiflora' (Hardy Primula). *Primula littoniana* 'Vialtii'. *Prunella* 'Pagoda'. Pyrethrum. Ranunculus 'Amalia Giants Mixed'. Solidago (Golden Rod). Trollius Choice Mixture (Kingcup). *Veronica teucrium. Viola odorata* 'Queen Charlotte'.

ORNAMENTAL GRASSES
Time to buy Pot-grown any time, except January–February. Avoid adverse weather conditions.

Where to find Outside in Grasses or Perennials.

Size Height 4 in–3 ft (10 cm–1 m). Ten leaves per pot min. *Miscanthus* three shoots min.

Foliage Deciduous. Spring/summer, green, blue, gold or variegated. Premature autumn colour and leaf drop.

Roots Pots 4 in (10 cm) min. dia. *Miscanthus* 5 in (12 cm) min. dia.

Hints Any well-prepared soil. May be scarce. Research overall size.

Most widely available *Alopecurus pratensis* 'Aureo-variegatus' (Golden Foxtail). *Arrhenatherum elatus* 'Bulbosum Variegatum' (Bulbous Oat Grass). *Bouteloua gracilis* (Blue Camma Grass). *Briza media* (Quaking Grass). *Carex morrowii* 'Variegata' (Sedge). *C. omithopoda* 'Variegata' (Variegated Birds-foot Sedge). *C. pendula* (Pendulous Sedge). *Festuca glauca* (Blue Fescue). *Glyceria maxima* 'Variegata' (Reed Sweet Grass). *Helictotrichon sempervirens* (Oak Grass). *Holcus lanatus* 'Albovariegatus' (Yorkshire Fog). *Juncus inflexus* (Hard Rush). *Koelaria g. Luxula n.* (Snowy Wood-Rush). *L. pilosa* (Hairy Wood-Rush). *L. sylvatica* (Great-Wood). *Milium effusum Aureum* (Bowle's Golden Grass). *Miscanthus floridus* (Silver Grass). *M. sinensis* (Chinese Silver Grass). *Molinia caerulea* 'Variegata' (Purple Moor Grass). *Panicum virgatum* (Switch Grass). *P. v.* 'Rubrum'. *Phalaris arundinacea* 'Picta' (Gardeners' Garters). *Sesleria caerulea* (Blue Sesleria). *Spartina pectinata* 'Aureomarginata' (Cord Grass). *Stipa gigantea. S. pennata* (Feather Grass).

HARDY FERNS
Time to buy Pot-grown, any time except December–February. Avoid adverse weather conditions.

Where to find Outside in Ferns or Perennials.

Size Heights will vary according to season. EVERGREEN Four leaf shoots min. all year. DECIDUOUS Four leaf shoots min. May–September.

Foliage Evergreen and deciduous. No browning.

Roots Pots 4 in (10 cm) min. dia.

Hints Well-prepared soil as per requirements. Wide range. Unattractive in containers, except in spring. Research ultimate overall size.

Most widely available *Adiantum pedatum* (Maidenhair Fern). *Asplenium adiantum-nigrum* (The Black Spleenwort). *Asplenium scolopendrium* (The Hartstongue Fern). *Asplenium trichomanes* (Maidenhair Spleenwort). *Athyrium filix-femina* (Lady Fern) *Athyrium filix-femina frizelliae* (The Tatting Fern). *Athyrium filix-femina plumosum. Blechnum spicant* (Hard Fern). *Dryopteris filix-mas* (Male Fern). *Matteuccia struthiopteris* (Shuttlecock Fern). *Onoclea sensibilis* (Sensitive Fern). *Osmunda regalis* (The Royal Fern). *Phegopteris connectilis* (The Beech Fern). *Polystichum acrostichioides* (The Dagger or Christmas Fern). *Polypodium vulgare* (The Common Polypody). *Pteridium aquilinum* (The Brake Fern. The Common Bracken). Others may be available.

Alpines

These gems of the plant world are well-known, and the range available is ever-increasing.

Because they are predominantly spring-flowering, they are stocked in nurseries and garden centres mainly at that time. This can lead to difficulty when later planting is attempted.

As rockeries and alpine areas are planted in the spring, with plants chosen from those in flower at the time, this can mean that in following years they only provide interest in the spring. So it is a good idea to visit nurseries and garden centres through the summer and autumn and even in winter, to see if there are any other forms available that will expand the seasonal interest.

Heights, spreads and cultural requirements must be taken into account: some forms need an acid soil, others need dry, well-drained and sunny positions, others need shade, so some research is needed in order to attempt a mixed planting.

Alpines are normally found in small 7 cm and 9 cm ($2\frac{3}{4}$ in and $3\frac{1}{2}$ in) pots but an increasing number are being grown in 1 litre, 4–5 in (10–12 cm) or 2 litre 5–6 in (12–15 cm) pots.

Dwarf bulbs are often included in pots as rockery specimens. 'Dwarf' conifers are also offered, but with these, a lot of consideration should be given to their ultimate size because in fact there is no such thing as a 'dwarf' conifer, they are only 'slow-growing'. Often a well-planned rockery is thrown right out of perspective by an ill-chosen conifer.

Mail-order from reputable nurseries is still a very good method of purchasing alpines, particularly specific species where a planned planting is required. The number of nurseries providing good mail-order service is decreasing but with customer support, they should survive and the full range of alpines will be available to all.

Raising alpines from seed is a possible method of propagation. It is cheaper, but the range is limited and the time it takes can outweigh the advantages of cost against 'instant' planting.

Soil should be dug to a depth of 9 in (23 cm) and in most cases the incorporation of sharp-sand is beneficial, as is covering the soil surface to a depth of 2 in (5 cm) to stop rain splashing.

Some forms may need a winter covering of glass or clear plastic to stop extreme weather conditions causing damage.

ALPINES (ROCKERY PLANTS)
supplied pot-grown

Time to buy All year round, except November–February. Avoid adverse weather conditions.

Where to find Outside in Alpines or Rockery Plants. Mail order acceptable.

Size Pot-grown, with or without top-growth. Height normally 3–8 cm (1–3 in).

Foliage EVERGREEN Lush, healthy foliage, May–July. DECIDUOUS April–October, healthy foliage in range of colours. Some browning, July–October.

Roots Pots 7 cm (2¾ in) or 9 cm (3½ in) dia. Some in 1 litre (5 in) pots.

Hints Wide range of well-prepared soil types which should be researched, as should overall ultimate size. Sold in flower, and entire species or form may sell out rapidly. Some are not always clearly labelled.

Most widely available Acaena. *Achillea argentea. Acinos alpinus. Aconitum anglicum.* Acorus. *Adenophora bulleyana.* Aethionema. Ajuga. *Alchemilla abyssinica.* Allium. Alopercurus. Alyssoides. Alyssum. Amsonia. Anacyclus. Anagallis. Androsace. Andryala. Anemone. *Angelica archangelica. Antennaria aprica. Anthemis cupaniana. Anthericum ramosum.* Anthyllis. *Antirrhinum molle. Aquilegia alpina.* Arabis. Arenaria. Arisaema. Arisarum. Armeria. *Arnica alpina.* Arrhenatherum. Artemisia. Arthropodium. Asarina. Asperula. Asplenium *Aster alpinus.* Asyneuma. Athalmanta. Aubrieta. Bellium. Bolax. Bulbinella. *Calceolaria arachnoides.* Campanula. Camphorosma. Cassiope. *Celsioverbascum* 'Golden Wings'. *Centaurea simplicicaulis.* Cerastium. Cheiranthus. Chiastophyllum. *Chrysanthemum arcticum.* Codonopsis. Coptis. Cotula. Crassula. Crepsis. Curtonus. Cyclamen. Delosperma. *Dianthus alpinus.* Diascia. *Disporum hookeri.* Dodecatheon. Draba. Drosanthemum. Dryas. Ephedra. Epilobium. Epimedium. *Erigeron auranti-*

acus. Erinus. Eriophyllum. Erodium. Eryngium. Erysimum. Erythronium. Euryops. Fragaria. Francoa. Frankenia. Galium. Gentiana. Geranium. Gillenia. Globularia. Haberlea. Hacquetia (Dondia). Haplopappus. Hepatica. Herniaria. Heuchera. Hieraceum. Horminum. Hugeuninia. Hutchinsia. Hydrocotyle. Hypsella. Iberis. Iris (dwarf). Jasione. Kalmiopsis. Leiophyllum. *Leontopodium alpinum* (Edelweiss). Leucanthemopsis. Leucopogon. Lewisia. Libertia. *Linaria alpina.* Linnaea. *Linum perenne.* Lithodona (Lithospermum). Lithophragma. *Lobelia lindblomii.* Lotus. Luzuriaga. *Lychnis alpina. Lysimachia nummularia.* Margyricarpus. Melittis. Mibora. Mimulus. Minuartia. Mitella. Moltkia. Montia. Morisia. Muehlenbeckia. Myosotis. Neopaxia. Nierembergia. Oakesiella. *Oenothera glaber.* Omphalodes. Osteospermum. Ourisia. *Papaver alpinum.* Parochetus. Patrinia. Petrophytum. *Phlox* 'Camla Nana'. Pimelia. Pinellia. Plantago. Pleione. Polygonatum. *Polygonum affine.* Potentilla (low growing). Pratia. Pterocephalus. Ptilotrichum. Ramonda. Raoulia. Reineckia. Rhodohypoxis. Romanzoffia. Rosularia. Saponaria. Saxifrages (Mossy Saxifrages). Saxifrages (Silver and encrusted Saxifrages). Saxifrages (Kabschia and Engleria Saxifrages). *Saxifrages robertsoniana* (London Pride group). *Scaiosa alpina.* Schivereckia. Scutellaria. Sedum. *Selaginella kraussiana. Semiaquilegia adoxioides.* Sempervivum. Senecio. Serratula. Silene. Sisyrinchium. Soldanella. Solidago. Symphyandra. Talinum. *Tanacetum densum* 'Amani' (*Chrysanthemum haradjanii*). Teucrium. *Thalictrum minus.* Thlaspi. Thymus. Townsendia. Trifolium. *Trollius ledebourii.* Tsusiophyllum. Tuberaria. *Tunica saxifraga.* Vancouveria. Verbena. Veronica. *Viola cornuta.* Waldsteinia. Wulfenia. Zauschneria. Zygadenus.

ALPINES (ROCKERY PLANTS)
supplied pre-packed
Time to buy March–April.
Where to find Inside with autumn or spring-planted bulbs.
Size Root clumps.
Foliage Deciduous. No growth visible.
Roots Good clump of roots, fleshy nature, in moist material in a polythene bag.
Hints Plant as soon as possible after purchasing. Read instructions on packaging. Any well-prepared soil, plus extra organic material. Avoid late purchasing. Full botanical names rarely stated.
Most widely available Leontopodium (Edelweiss). *Primula vialii. Sedum spurium.* Sprekelia.

ALPINES (ROCKERY PLANTS)
grown from seed
Time to buy Seed, December–April.
Where to find Inside on seed racks.
Hints Follow instructions on seed packet. A number of alpines can be grown from seed, but not universal and some forms do not come true. Those listed are most reliable. Takes time. Requires seed raising and plant nurturing conditions which may not be in the average garden.
Most widely available Acaena. *Achillea ageratum* (Sweet Nancy). Aethionema. *Alchemilla alpina. A. erythropoda. Alyssum montanum.* Anacyclus. Androsace. Anemone. Antennaria. *Aquilegia alpina.* Arabis. Arenaria. Armeria. Artemisia (low-growing). Asarina. *Astilbe chinensis pumila. Astrantia minor.* Aubrietia. Campanula (Bell Flower). Dianthus. Draba. Dryas. Erinus. Eryngium. Erysimum. Geranium (low growing). Gnaphalium. *Gypsophila repens.* Hepatica. Herniaria. *Hypericum olympicum.* Leontopodium (Edelweiss) Lewisia. Linaria. Linum. Mimulus. *Papaver alpinum* (Poppy). *Penstemon alpinus.* Phyteuma. Pinguicula. Potentilla. *Pulsatilla alpina.* Ramonda. Sagina. Sanguinaria. Saxifraga. *Scutellaria alpina.* Semiaquilegia. Sempervivum. Silene. Sisyrinchium. Soldanella. Succisa. Thymus. Viola. *Viscaria alpina.*

Herbs

The diversity of herbs is almost as wide as the range of plants themselves, and over the centuries many forms have been used in a herbal context, whether for culinary, medicinal or commercial purposes, or simply for adorning the garden with scent, foliage or flowers.

Their commercial interest is in the production of perfume or dyes or as a constituent part of a catalyst between other ingredients.

The following section contains a selection of those which are principally used and supplied for various herbal purposes.

There are many different forms available, produced by various growing techniques. The entries cover those grown by nurseries or offered in garden centres specifically in a herbal context. As well as being sold singly, they may also be offered as selections of different forms, and as long as the collection covers the needs of the planter, this is a very good way of purchasing.

Some herbs are poisonous and these have been clearly marked within the entries. However, the use of any herb for culinary, medicinal or commercial purposes should only be undertaken when careful reference has been made to a more authoritative source of reference.

Soil preparation is to a depth of 9 in (23 cm), with a good supply of organic material added to ensure good plant growth.

BIENNIAL HERBS

Time to buy Pot-grown, August–September, April–May.

Where to find Outside in Herbs or Winter Bedding.

Size 6–12 in (15–30 cm) of top growth.

Foliage EVERGREEN dark to mid green. DECIDUOUS mid, dark or light green, or variegated. Premature autumn colour and leaf drop.

Roots Pots 3 in (8 cm) min. dia. Foxglove (*Digitalis*) also in trays.

Hints Any well-prepared soil. Wide range available. Sown in one year to flower the following. Research ultimate overall size.

Most widely available

CULINARY Angelica (*Angelica archan-gelica*). Burdock (*Artiumlappa*). Caraway (*Carum carvi*). Clover, Red (*Trifolium pratense*). Celery, Wild (*Apium graveolens*). Evening Primrose (*Oenothera biennis*). Melilot (*Melilotus officinalis*). Musk Mallow (*Malva moschata*). Parsley, Curled (*Petroselinum crispum*). Parsley, French (*P. carum*).

MEDICINAL/COMMERCIAL Herb Robert (*Geranium Robertianum*). Mullein (*Verbascum thapsis*). Clary (*Salvia sclarea*). Vipers Bugloss (*Echium vulgare*). Woad (*Isatis tinctoria*).

DECORATIVE Teazle (*Dipsacus fullonom*).

POISONOUS Caper Spurge (*Euphorbia lathyrus*). Foxglove (*Digitalis purpurea*). Foxglove, Woolly (*D. lanata*). Foxglove, Yellow (*D. lutea*).

HALF-HARDY AND ANNUAL HERBS

Time to buy Seed, January onwards. Pot-grown, April–May when danger of frost has passed.

Where to find Seed, indoors on seed racks. Pots, outside in Herbs.

Size Pot-grown, 2–4 in (5–10 cm) high.

Foliage Mid to dark green.

Roots Pots 3 in (8 cm) min. dia.

Hints Any well-prepared soil. Seed sown as per directions on packet. Grown for one year for foliage and flower. Short planting period, so they tend to sell out quickly. Research ultimate overall size.

Most widely available CULINARY – ANNUAL Ambrosia (*Chenopodium botrys*). Anise (*Pimpinella anisum*). Bergamot, Lemon (*Monarda citriodora*). Borage (*Borago officinalis*). Chervil (*Anthriscus cerefolium*). Chives (*Allium schoenaprasum*). Clary (*Salvia horminum*). Coriander (*Coriandrum sativum*). Dill (*Anethum graveolens*). Garlic (*Allium tuberosum*). Milk Thistle (*Silybum marianum*). Pot Marigold (*Calendula officinalis*). Red Orach (*Atriplex hortensis rubra*). Rocket, Sweet (*Eruca sativa*). Roman Wormwood (*Artemisias absinthium*). Savory, Summer (*Satureia hortensis*).

CULINARY – HALF-HARDY Basil, Bush (*Ocimum minimum*). Basil, Red or Dark Opal (*O. purpurea*).

MEDICINAL/COMMERCIAL – ANNUAL Centuary (*Centaurum erythraea*). Cumin (*Cuminum cyminum*). Holy Thistle (*Cnicus benedictus*). Safflower (*Carthamus tinctoria*).

DECORATIVE – ANNUAL Ambrosia (*Chenopodium botrys*). Woodruff, Annual (*Asperula orientalis*).

POISONOUS – ANNUAL Indian Tobacco (*Lobelia inflata*). Thornapple (*Datura stramonium*).

HARDY HERBS

Time to buy Pot-grown, any time. Avoid adverse weather conditions. Garlic cloves, March–April or pot-grown. Horseradish, pre-packs March–April. Mail order acceptable.

Where to find Outside in Herbs. Horseradish, inside.

Size Pots 3 in (8 cm) min. height. Thymus will be less.

Foliage EVERGREEN Dark to mid green. DECIDUOUS Spring/summer mid, dark or light green, purple or variegated. Premature autumn colour and leaf drop.

Roots Pots 3 in (8 cm) min. dia.

Hints Any well-prepared soil. Wide range. Can look leggy and gaunt. Research overall size.

Most widely available CULINARY Alecost (*Balsimita vulgaris*). Basil Thyme (*Acinos arvensis*). Bay (*Laurus nobilis*). Bergamot (*Monarda didyma*). Chamomile (*Matricaria chamomilla*). Chicory (*Cicorium intybus*). Chives (*Allium schoenaprasum*). Chives, Garlic (*A. tuberosum*). Cowslip (*Primula veris*). Curry Plant (*Helichrysum angustifolium*). Dandelion (*Taraxacum officinale*). Dropwort (*Filipendula vulgaris*). Fennel Green (*Foeniculum vulgare*). Fennel Bronze. Garlic (*Allium sativa*). Good King Henry (*Chenopodium bonushenricus*). Hops (*Humulus lupus*). Horseradish (*Cochlearis armoracia*). Hyssop (*Hyssopus officinalis*). Ladies Mantle (*Alchemilla mollis*). Lemon Balm (*Melissa officinalis*). Lemon Balm, variegated (*M. o. variegata*) Lovage (*Levisticum officinalis*). Lungwort (*Pulmonaria officinalis*). Mace (*Achillea decolorans*). Marjoram (*Origanum*). Oregano (*Oreganum vulgare* 'Wild Marjoram'). Marsh Mallow (*Althaea officinalis*). Meadowsweet (*Spirea ulmaria*). Mint (*Mentha*). Apple Mint (*M. rotundifolia*). Apple White, variegated 'Pineapple'. Basilmint. Lemon Mint (*M. citrata*). Bowles Mint (*M. rotundifolia* 'Bowles'). Corsican Mint (*M. requienii*). Curly Mint

(M. crispa). Eau-de-Cologne Mint (M. citrata). Ginger Mint (M. gentilis). Moroccan Mint. Peppermint Black Mint (M. piperita). Peppermint White Mint. Mint (Rubra raripila syn. raripila rubra). Spearmint Mint (M. spicata). Horsemint (M. longifolia). Myrtle (Myrtus communis). Roman Wormwood (Artemisias absinthium). Rosemary (Rosmarinus officinalis). Sage, Common (Salvia officinalis). Savory, Creeping (Satureia repandra). Savory, Winter (S. montana). Sorrel, French broadleaf (Rumex acetosa). Sweet Cicely (Myrrhis odorata). Tarragon French, (Artemesia dracunculus). Thyme (T. pulegioides). Broadleaf. Thyme, Common Culinary (T. vulgaris) Common, Culinary or French Thyme. Welsh Onion (Allium fistulosum). Woodruff Sweet (Asperula odorata).

MEDICINAL/COMMERCIAL Agrimony (Agrimonia eupatoria). Avens (Geum urbanum). Bear's Breech (Acanthus mollis). Betony (Stachys officinalis). Bistort (Polygonum bistorta). Box (Buxus sempervirens). Broom Dyers (Genista tinctoria). Bugle (Ajuga reptans). Calamint (Calamintha grandiflora). Calamint (Lesser C. nepetiodes). Camphor Plant (Balsamita vulgaris). Catnip (Nepeta cataria). Catsfoot (Antennaria dioica). Celandine, Greater (Chelidonium majus). Chamomile, Dyers (Anthemis tinctoria). Coltsfoot (Tussilago farfara). Comfrey (Symphytum officinalis). Coneflower (Echinacea purpurea). Elecampane (Inula helenium). Feverfew, Green (Chrysanthemum parthenium). Figwort, Knotted (Scrophularia nodosa). Goats Rue (Galega officinalis). Golden Rod (Solidago virgaura). Gravelroot (Eupatorium purpureum). Heartsease (Viola tricolor). Hedge Hyssop (Gratiol officinalis). Horehound, White (Marrubium vulgare). Horehound, Black (Ballota nigra). Houseleek (Sempervivum tectorum). Juniper (Juniperus communis). Lobelia, Great (Lobelia siphilitica). Motherwort (Leonurus cardiaca). Orris, Purple

(Iris florentina). Pasque Flower (Pulsatilla vulgaris). Penny Royal (Mentha pulegium. Upright) Penny Royal (Creeping). Periwinkle, Greater. (Vinca major, variegated). Periwinkle, Lesser (V. minor). Pokeroot (Phytolacca decandra). Primrose (Primula vulgaris). Rue (Ruta graveolens 'Jackman's Blue'). Rosmarinus angustifolius. Rosmarinus officinalis angustissimus 'Corsican Blue'. Corsican Rosemary. Rosmarinus o. 'Albus'. White Rosemary. Rosmarinus o. 'Benenden Blue'. Rosmarinus o. 'Fota Blue'. Rosmarinus o. 'Frimley Blue'. Rosmarinus o. 'Majorca'. Rosmarinus o. 'Miss Jessopp's Upright'. Rosmarinus o. 'Seven Seas'. Rosmarinus o. 'Tuscan Blue'. Rosmarinus lavandulaceus syn. R. officinalis prostrata. Creeping Rosemary. Salvia (Glutinosa). Sea Holly (Eryngium maritimum). Self Heal (Prunella vulgaris). Sneezewort (Achillea ptarmica). Soapwort (Saponaris officinalis). Solomon's Seal (Polygonatum multiflorum). St. John's Wort (Hypericum perforatum). Strawberry, Alpine (Fragaria vesca 'Alexandria'). Sweetbriar, Eglantine. (Rosa rubiginosa). Toadflax (Linaria vulgaris). Tree Lupin (Lupinus arboreus). Valerian (Valeriana officinalis). Vervain (Verbena officinalis). Virginian Scullcap (Scutellaria laterifolia). Wild Wallflower (Cheiranthus cheiri). Yarrow (Achillea millefolium).

DECORATIVE Anise Hyssop (Agastache anethiodora). Anthemis cupaniana. Artemisias (Lanata Pedamonta). Catmint (Nepeta mussinii). Chamomile, Double flowered (Anthemis nobilis). Chamomile, Roman (A. nobilis). Chamomile, Treneague (A. nobilis 'Treneague'). Cotton Lavender (Santolina serratifolia). Cotton Lavender (S. viridis). Creeping Jenny (Lysimachia nummularia). Curry Plant, Dwarf. (Helichrysum angustifolium 'Nana'). Flax (Linum perenne). Geranium (Pratense. Meadow Cranesbill). Geranium (Sanguineum. Bloody Cranesbill). Geranium (Macrorrhizum). Jacob's

Ladder (*Polemonium caeruleum*). Jerusalem Sage (*Phlomis fruticosa*). Ladies Bedstraw (Cheese Rennet. *Galium verum*) Lavender (*Lavandula spica alba*). Lavender (*L. s.* 'Grappenhall'). Lavender (*L. s.* 'Lodden Pink'). Lavender (*L. s.* 'Munstead Dwarf'). Lavender (*L. s.* 'Nana'). Lavender (*L. s.* 'Royal Purple'*). Lavender (*L. s.* 'Seale'). Lavender (*L. stoechas*). Madder (*Rubia tinctorium*). Marjoram, Compact (*Origanum vulgare compactum*). Marjoram, Golden (*O. aureum*) Marjoram, Golden curly. Marjoram, Gold-tipped or splashed Myrtle (*Myrtus communis* 'Tarentina'). Myrtle (*M. c.* 'Tarentina' *variegata*). *Nepeta nervosa*. Pink, Clove (*Dianthus caryophyllus*). Pink, Cheddar. (*D. caesius*). Pink, Maiden. (*D. deltoides*). Rosemary ('Benenden Blue'). Rosemary ('Corsican'*). Rosemary ('Frimley Blue'). Rosemary ('Fota Blue'). Rosemary ('Miss Jessops Upright'). Rosemary ('Majorca') Rosemary (Prostrate. *R. lavendulaceous*). Rosemary ('Severn Sea'). Rosemary ('Tuscan Blue'). Rosemary, White. (*R. albus*). Russian Sage (*Perovskia atriplicifolia*). Salvia hormium 'Clary' (Painted Sage). Salvia officinalis 'Icterina' (Golden-leaved Sage). Salvia officinalis 'Purpurascens' (Red or Purple Sage). Salvia officinalis 'Tricolor' (Tricoloured Sage). Sedum Acre (Yellow Stonecrop or Wall-pepper). Sedum ('Album'). Southernwood (*Artemesia arbrotanum*). Sweet Rocket (*Hesperis matronalis*). Tansy, Curled or Feathered (*Tanacetum vulgare crispum*). Tansy, Plain leaf (*T. vulgare*). *Teucrium fruticans*. Thrift (*Armeria maritima*) Thymus caespititius 'Aureus'. Golden-leaved Lemon Thyme. Thymus × citriodorus. Lemon Thyme. Thymus × c. 'Aureus'. Golden-leaved Lemon Thyme. Thymus × c. 'Nyewoods'. Thymus × c. 'Silver Queen'. Thymus × c. 'Golden King'. Thymus × c. 'Lemon Curd'. Thymus doerfleri 'Doone Valley'. Thymus erectus. Upright-growing Thyme.

Thymus nitida. Small-leaved Thyme. Thymus serpyllum coccineus. Crimson Thyme. Thymus serpyllum 'Annie Hall'. Thymus serpyllum 'Snowdrift'. Thymus serpyllum 'Pink Chintz'. Thymus fragrantissimus. Scented Thyme. Thymus vulgaris 'Archer's Gold'. Archer's Golden-leaved Thyme. Thymus vulgaris aureus. Golden-leaved Thyme. Thymus vulgaris 'Silver Posie'. Violet, Sweet (*Viola odorata*). Violet, Tufted (*V. cornuta*). Winter Heliotrope (*Petasites fragrans*). Wolly Yarrow (*Achillea tomentosum* 'Aurea').

POISONOUS Arnica (*Arnica montana*). Celandine, Lesser. (*Ranunculus ficaria*). Lily of the Valley (*Convallaria majalis*)

TENDER or SEMI-TENDER HERBS
Time to buy Pot-grown, April–June. Mail order acceptable.
Where to find Outside in Herbs or Shrubs.
Size Root clumps, with or without foliage, not more than 12 in (30 cm) in full growth.
Foliage EVERGREEN Grey or dark to mid green. DECIDUOUS Spring/summer mid, light or dark green, or variegated. Premature autumn colour and leaf drop.
Roots Pots 3 in (8 cm) min. dia.
Hints Any well-prepared soil. Wide range. Avoid planting until spring frosts have finished.
Most widely available
CULINARY Alexanders (*Smyrnium olusatrum*). Lemon Verbens (*Lippia citriodora*). Marjoram Sweet Knotted (*Origanum majoram*). Sage, Pineapple (*Salvia rutilans*). Skirret (*Sium sisarum*).
MEDICINAL/COMMERCIAL Pellitory-of-the-Wall (*Patrietaria officinalis*). Pilewort, Lesser Celandine (*Ranunculus ficaria*). Wood Sage (*Teucrium scordonia*).
DECORATIVE 'Balm of Gilead' (*Cedronella triphylla*). Eucalyptus (*E. citriodorus*) Lavender (*Lavandula canariensis*). (*L. dendata*). (*L. stoechas pendunculata*). Sage (*Salvia officinalis*). Salvia 'Grahamii'. S. 'Patens'. S. uliginosa.

Hedging

Hedging is like building a wall, allowing a yearly build-up, layer by layer, shortening back the annual growth by one third ever year will do this and help to create a thick dense hedge.

Planting distances are important. Each selection will have its own requirements. It may be planted in a single or double staggered row. The distance between the plants is important; remember that the last in each row, where it meets a path or gateway, needs to be planted at half the recommended planting distance from the end.

Often planting preparation is neglected when hedging is planted. There is a misconception that hedging is tough and so does not need the same preparation as other plants. A 3 ft (1 m) wide, 18 in (50 cm) deep trench with good amounts of organic compost added is a minimum. Hedging plants are expected to produce a thick, dense screen and to produce new growth on a regular basis and to do this they need a good root-run.

Feeding is often also overlooked and a general fertilizer, or in the case of conifers, dried blood, in mid to late spring will encourage strong growth.

The required height is often specified but rarely is the spread considered, so an attempt has been made to show minimum and maximum heights and spread that hedges should achieve over five to ten years.

The shape of a hedge is important. It is good practice to make the top narrower than the bottom so rain and snow can fall off freely. Conifers suffer badly from heavy snow, so following a fall, shake off as much snow as possible.

Grass allowed to grow up to the base will restrict growth. A 15–18 in (40–50 cm) clear band should be maintained so the root-system can feed and obtain necessary moisture.

The temptation is to plant tall plants in excess of 3 ft (1 m) to achieve a quick screen. However experience shows that a hedge needs to develop over a period of two to three years to form a good dense screen.

ACER CAMPESTRE
Hedge Maple, Field Maple
Height and spread Minimum 4 × 3 ft (1.2 m- × 1 m); maximum 18 × 18 ft (5.5 × 5.5 m).
Time to buy Pot-grown any time, except mid-winter. Bare-rooted November. Avoid adverse weather conditions.

Where to find Outside in Hedging, Shrubs or Trees.
Size 1–1½ ft (30–50 cm). 1½–2 ft (50–60 cm). 2–2½ ft (60–80 cm) 2½–3 ft (80 cm–1 m).
Foliage Deciduous. Pot-grown, mid green. Premature autumn colour and leaf drop.

Roots Pots 5 in (12 cm) min. dia. Bare-rooted, good fibrous root system.

Hints Any well-prepared soil. Scarce. Trench 3 ft (1 m) wide, 18 in (50 cm) deep, well prepared. Planted in single line 2½ ft (80 cm) apart. Reduce 25% of leading shoots in spring after planting. Repeat annually. Best for country locations.

BERBERIS (evergreen and deciduous)
Barberry
Height and spread TALL GROWING Minimum 4 × 3 ft (1.2 × 1 m); maximum 8 × 6 ft (2.5 × 2 m). SLOW GROWING Minimum 1 ft × 9 in (30 × 23 cm); maximum 3 × 3 ft (1 × 1 m).
Time to buy Pot-grown, any time except December–February. Balled, October–November. Avoid adverse weather conditions.
Where to find Outside in Shrubs or Hedging.
Size Pots: Evergreen, tall growing 9–24 in (23–60 cm), deciduous, tall growing 12–30 in (30–80 cm): minimum two main shoots, numerous short side branches. Evergreen, low growing 6–12 in (15–30 cm), deciduous, low growing 6–12 in (15–30 cm): multi-stemmed.
Foliage Evergreen, dark green, glossy. Deciduous. Spring/summer green, purple or purple and pink. Premature autumn colour and leaf drop.
Roots Pots, 5 in (12 cm) min. dia. tall growing. 4 in (10 cm) min. dia. low growing. Balled, good fibrous root system.
Hints Any well-prepared soil. Trench 3 ft (1 m) wide, 18 in (50 cm) deep, well-prepared. Tall growing, plant in single line 2½ ft (80 cm) apart and low growing 15 in (40 cm) apart. Flowering curtailed by 50% minimum. Thorns make cultivation difficult.
Most widely available
TALL-GROWING EVERGREEN *Berberis darwinii. B. julianae. B. × stenophylla. B. s.* 'Autumnalis'.

LOW-GROWING EVERGREEN *Berberis-panlanensis. B. × stenophylla* 'Irwinii'. *B. verruculosa.*
TALL-GROWING DECIDUOUS *Berberis × ottawensis* 'Purpurea'. *B. thunbergii. B. t.* 'Atropurpurea'. *B. t.* 'Gold Ring'. *B. t.* 'Harlequin'. *B. t.* 'Red Chief'. *B. t.* 'Rose Glow'.
LOW-GROWING DECIDUOUS *Berberis thunbergii* 'Atropurpurea Nana'. *B. t.* 'Bagatelle'. *B. t.* 'Kobold'.

BUXUS SEMPERVIRENS
Common Box
Height and spread Minimum 2 × 1 ft (60 × 30 cm); maximum 15 × 6 ft (4.5 × 2 m).
Time to buy Pot-grown, any time except December–February. Balled, October–November, March–April. Avoid adverse weather conditions
Where to find Outside in Shrubs or Hedging.
Size 6–24 in (15–60 cm). Single-stemmed. Numerous side shoots.
Foliage Evergreen. Dark green, golden or silver variegated. Premature basal yellowing.
Roots Pots 4 in (10 cm) min. dia. Balled, good fibrous root system.
Hints Any well-prepared soil. Apart from *Buxus sempervirens* may be scarce. Trench, 3 ft (1 m) wide, 18 in (50 cm) deep, well-prepared. Plant in single line 2 ft (60 cm) apart.
Most widely available *Buxus sempervirens. B. s.* 'Aureovariegata'. *B. s.* 'Elegantissima'. *B. s.* 'Handsworthensis'. *B. s.* 'Rotundifolia'.

BUXUS SEMPERVIRENS 'SUFFRUTICOSA'
Edging Box
Height and spread Minimum 4 × 3 in (10 × 8 cm); maximum 3 × 2 ft (1 m × 60 cm).
Time to buy Pot-grown, any time except

December–February. Balled or bare-rooted, October–November. Avoid adverse weather conditions.
Where to find Outside in Hedging, Shrubs or Herbs.
Size 2–6 in (5–15 cm). Single shooted. Numerous short side branches, creating ball effect.
Foliage Evergreen. Mid green. Bronze, autumn through winter.
Roots Pots 2 in (5 cm) min. dia. Balled and bare-rooted, good fibrous root system.
Hints Any well-prepared soil. May be scarce. Trench 2 ft (60 cm) wide, 1 ft (30 cm) deep, well-prepared. Plant in single line 12 in (30 cm) apart. Plants small at time of purchase.

CARPINUS BETULUS
Hornbeam
Height and spread Minimum $3 \times 2\frac{1}{2}$ ft (1 m × 80 cm); maximum 15×6 ft (4.5 × 2 m).
Time to buy Pot-grown, at any time except December–February. Bare-rooted, November–April. Avoid adverse weather conditions.
Where to find Outside in Hedging or Shrubs
Size 1–1½ ft (30–50 cm). 1½–2 ft (50–60 cm). 2–2½ ft (60–80 cm). 2½–3 ft (80 cm–1 m). 3½–4 ft (1.1 m–1.2 m). Bare rooted bundles of five or ten. From forestry outlets, units of twenty-five or thirty.
Foliage Deciduous. Spring/summer, mid green. Premature autumn colour and leaf drop.
Roots Pots 5 in (12 cm) min. dia. Bare-rooted, good fibrous root system.
Hints Any well-prepared soil. Scarce. Trench 3 ft (1 m) wide, 18 in (50 cm) deep, well-prepared. Planted in single line 18 in (50 cm) apart. Reduce 25% of leading shoots in spring after planting. Repeat annually.

CONIFERS
Height and spread Maximum 4×3 ft (1.2 × 1 m); maximum 20×10 ft (6 × 3 m)
Time to buy Pot-grown, any time except December–February. Balled, October–November, March–April. Avoid adverse weather conditions.
Where to find Outside in Conifers or Hedging.
Size 1–1½ ft (30–50 cm). 1½–2 ft (50–60 cm). 2–2½ ft (60–80 cm). 2½–3 ft (80 cm–1 m).
Foliage Evergreen. Light to dark green, grey-blue or golden fronds.
Roots Pots 5 in (12 cm) min. dia. Balled, good fibrous root system. *Cupressocyparis leylandii* and forms must always be pot-grown.
Hints Any well-prepared soil. Trench 3 ft (1 m) wide, 18 in (50 cm) deep, well-prepared. Plant in single row 3 ft (1 m) apart, except *Taxus baccata* 'Semperaurea' and *T. b.* 'Summergold' planted 2½ ft (80 cm) apart. Chosen forms must allow for hard clipping or be grown informally without clipping.
Most widely available *Chamaecyparis lawsoniana* (Lawson Cypress). *C. l.* 'Allumii'. *C. l.* 'Erecta'. *C. l.* 'Fletcheri'*. *C. l.* 'Green Hedger'. *C. l.* 'Lanei'. *C. l.* 'Pembury Blue'. *C. l.* 'Somerset'*. *C. nootkatensis* (Nootka Cypress). *C. pisifera* 'Plumosa'*. *C. p.* 'Plumosa Aurea'*. *Cupressus glabra* 'Pyramidalis'. *C. macrocarpa. C. m.* 'Lutea'. × *Cupressocyparis leylandii* (Leyland Cypress). *C. l.* 'Castwellan Gold'. *C. l.* 'Robinson's Gold'. *C. l. variegata. Taxus baccata* (Common Yew). *T. b.* 'Semperaurea'. *T. b.* 'Summergold'. *Thuya plicata* (Western Red Cedar). *T. p.* 'Semperaurescens'. *T. p.* 'Zebrina'.

*Informal screening, not for clipping.

CORNUS SANGUINEA
Common Dogwood
Height and spread Minimum 3×2 ft (1 m × 60 cm); maximum 8×4 ft (2.5 × 1.2 m).

Time to buy Pot-grown any time except December–February. Bare-rooted, November or March–April. Avoid adverse weather conditions.

Where to find Outside in Hedging or Shrubs.

Size 2 ft (60 cm) min. Single or multi-stemmed.

Foliage Deciduous. Spring/summer, mid green. Premature autumn colour and leaf drop.

Roots Pots 5 in (12 cm) min. dia. Bare-rooted, good fibrous root system.

Hints Any well-prepared soil. Trench 3 ft (1 m) wide, 18 in (50 cm) deep, well-prepared. Planted in single line $2\frac{1}{2}$ ft (80 cm) apart. Reduce 25% of leading shoots in spring after planting. Repeat annually.

COTONEASTER (evergreen and deciduous)

Height and spread Minimum 6 × 4 ft (2 × 1.2 m); maximum 15 × 8 ft (4.5 × 2.5 m). *Cotoneaster simonsii*: Minimum 4 × 3 ft (1.2 × 1 m); maximum 7 × 4 ft (2.2 × 1.2 m).

Time to buy Pot-grown any time, except December–February. Balled, October–November, March–April. Avoid adverse weather conditions.

Where to find Outside in Shrubs or Hedging.

Size 18 in (50 cm) min. Single or multi-stemmed.

Foliage DECIDUOUS Spring/summer, mid green. Premature autumn colour and leaf drop. EVERGREEN Dark green. Yellowing to basal leaves from July. SEMI-EVER-GREEN Dark green. In severe weather may loose leaf cover.

Roots Pots 4 in (10 cm) min. dia. Balled, good fibrous root system.

Hints Any well-prepared soil. Trench 3 ft (1 m) wide, 18 in (50 cm) deep, well-prepared. Planted in single line 3 ft (1 m) apart. *Cotoneaster simonsii*, planted in single line $2\frac{1}{2}$ ft (80 cm) apart.

Most widely available *Cotoneaster franchettii* (S-E). *C. f. sternianus* (S-E). *C. lacteus* (E). *C. salicifolius floccossus* (S-E). *C. simonsii* (S-E) *C. wardii* (E).

COUNTRY OR MIXED HEDGE*

Hints Any well-prepared soil. Trench 3 ft (1 m) wide, 18 in (50 cm) deep, well-prepared. Plant at distance recommended within individual entries.

Important not to overcrowd, i.e. a particular hedge might be constructed as follows: twenty-four *Fagus sylvatica* (Beech) in a block planted at 18 in (50 cm) apart in a double row; four *Ilex aquifolium* (Holly) planted 3 ft (1 m) apart in a single row and 3 ft (1 m) from *Fagus sylvatica*; twenty-four *Crataegus monogyna* (Thorn) planted at 18 in (50 cm) apart in two rows and staggered.

Most widely available *Carpinus betulus* (Hornbeam). *Crataegus monogyna* (Thorn. Quickthorn. May). *Fagus sylvatica* (Green Beech). *Ilex aquifolium* (Common Holly). *Ligustrum ovalifolium* (Green Privet). *L. vulgare* (Wild Privet).

*For information on **Time to buy**, **Where to find**, **Size**, **Foliage**, **Roots** see under appropriate entry in this chapter.

CRATAEGUS MONOGYNA
Thorn, Quickthorn, May

Height and spread Minimum 3 × $2\frac{1}{2}$ ft (1 m × 80 cm); maximum 15 × 6 ft (4.5 × 2 m)

Time to buy Pot-grown, any time except December–February. Bare-rooted October–November, March–April. Avoid adverse weather conditions.

Size 1–$1\frac{1}{2}$ ft (30–50 cm): one-year seedlings. $1\frac{1}{2}$–2 ft (50–60 cm): one-year transplants. 2–$2\frac{1}{2}$ ft (60–80 cm): two-year transplants. $2\frac{1}{2}$–3 ft (80 cm–1 m): two-year transplants.

Where to find Outside in Hedging or Shrubs.

Foliage Deciduous. Spring/summer, mid

green. Premature autumn colour and leaf drop.

Roots Pots 5 in (12 cm) min. dia. Bare-rooted, good fibrous root system.

Hints Any well-prepared soil. Trench 3 ft (1 m) wide, 18 in (50 cm) deep, well-prepared. Planted in double row, 18 in (50 cm) between plants and 15–18 in (40–50 cm) between rows. Rows staggered. Reduce 25% of leading shoots in spring after planting. Repeat annually. Thorns can make cultivation difficult. Possibly not suitable for suburban areas.

DEUTZIA

Height and spread Minimum 3 × 2 ft (1 m × 60 cm); maximum 8 × 4 ft (2.5 × 1.2 m).

Time to buy Pot-grown any time. Avoid adverse weather conditions.

Where to find Outside in Shrubs or Hedging.

Size 12–30 in (30–80 cm). Minimum two upright stems.

Foliage Deciduous. Spring/summer, mid green. Premature autumn colour and leaf drop.

Roots Pots 5 in (12 cm) min. dia.

Hints Any well-prepared soil. Trench 3 ft (1 m) wide, 18 in (50 cm) deep well-prepared. Planted in single line 2½ ft (80 cm) apart. Reduce 25% of leading shoots in spring following planting. Repeat annually.

Most widely available *Deutzia* 'Contraste'. *D.* 'Mont Rose'. *D. scarba. D. s.* 'Candidissima'. *D. s.* 'Plena'.

ELAEAGNUS

Height and spread Minimum 3 × 2 ft (1 m × 60 cm); maximum 8 × 4 ft (2.5 × 1.4 m).

Time to buy Pot-grown, any time. Avoid adverse weather conditions.

Where to find Outside in Shrubs or Hedging.

Size 12 in (30 cm). Single or multi-stemmed.

Foliage Evergreen. Glossy, grey-green or golden variegated. Yellowing to basal leaves from August.

Roots Pots 5 in (12 cm) min. dia.

Hints Any well-prepared soil. Trench 3 ft (1 m) wide, 18 in (50 cm) deep, well-prepared. Planted in single line 2½ ft (80 cm) apart. Do not intermix forms. Reduce 25% of leading shoots in spring after planting. Repeat annually.

Most widely available *Elaeagnus* × *ebbingei. E.* × *e.* 'Gilt Edge'. *E.* 'Limelight'. *E. pungens* 'Gold Rim'. *E. p.* 'Maculata'. *E. p.* 'Variegata'.

ESCALLONIA

Height and spread Minimum 3 × 2 ft (1 m × 60 cm); maximum 8 × 4 ft (2.5 × 1.2 m)

Time to buy Pot-grown, any time except December–February. Avoid adverse weather conditions.

Where to find Outside in Shrubs or Hedging.

Size 12 in (30 cm). Single or multi-stemmed.

Foliage Evergreen. Glossy, grey-green. Yellowing to basal leaves from August.

Roots Pots 5 in (12 cm) min.

Hints Any well-prepared soil. Trench 3 ft (1 m) wide, 18 in (50 cm) deep. Planted in single line 2½ ft (80 cm) apart. Reduce 25% of leading shoots in spring after planting. Repeat annually. Do not intermix forms. Hardiness suspect in cold areas.

Most widely available *Escallonia* 'Apple Blossom'. *E.* 'Crimson Spire'. *E.* 'Donard Brilliance'. *E.* 'Donard Seedling'. *E.* 'Iveyi'. *E. langleyensis. E.* 'Peach Blossom'.

EUONYMUS

Height and spread TALL GROWING Minimum 3 × 2 ft (1 m × 60 cm); maximum 8 × 4 ft (2.5 × 1.2 m). LOW GROWING Minimum 2 × 1 ft (60 × 30 cm); maximum 3 × 2 ft (1 m × 60 cm)

Time to buy Pot-grown April–July. Avoid adverse weather conditions.

Where to find Outside in Shrubs or Hedging.

Size Tall growing 12 in (30 cm), low growing 5 in (12 cm) min. Single or multistemmed.

Foliage Evergreen. Glossy, grey-green, golden or silver variegated. Premature basal leaf drop.

Roots Pots 4 in (10 cm) min. dia.

Hints Any well-prepared soil. Trench 2 ft (60 cm) wide for low growing, 3 ft (1 m) wide for tall growing, 18 in (50 cm) deep, well-prepared. Tall growing, plant in single line, 2½ ft (80 cm) apart, low growing, 15 in (40 cm) apart. *Euonymus japonicus* good in maritime areas. Hardiness suspect.

Most widely available

TALL GROWING *Euonymus japonicus*. *E. j.* 'Albomarginatus'. *E. j.* 'Aureopictus'. *E. j.* 'Macrophyllus'. *E. j.* 'Macrophyllus Albus'. *E. j.* 'Ovatus Aureus' (*E.* 'Aureovariegatus').

LOW GROWING *Euonymus fortunei* 'Emerald Gaiety'. *E. .f.* 'Emerald and Gold'. *E. f.* 'Silver Queen'. *E. f.* 'Sunshine'.

FAGUS SYLVATICA
Beech

Height and spread Minimum 3 × 3 ft (1 × 1 m); maximum 15 × 6 ft (4.5 × 2 m).

Time to buy Pot-grown, any time except December–February. Bare-rooted, November or March–April. Avoid adverse weather conditions.

Where to find Outside in Hedging or Shrubs.

Size 1–1½ ft (30–50 cm). 1½–2 ft (50–60 cm). 2–2½ ft (60–80 cm). Bare-rooted, bundles of five or ten. From forestry outlets, units of twenty-five or fifty.

Foliage Deciduous. Spring/summer, purple to purple-red. Premature autumn colour and leaf drop.

Roots Pots 5 in (12 cm) min. dia. Bare-rooted, good fibrous root system.

Hints Any well-prepared soil. Trench 3 ft (1 m) wide, 18 in (50 cm) deep well-prepared. Planted in double staggered row 18 in (50 cm) apart, 15–18 in, (40–50 cm) between rows. Reduce 25% of leading shoots in spring after planting. Repeat annually. Bare-rooted difficult to establish.

Most widely available *Fagus sylvatica* (Green Beech). *F. s. purpurea* (Purple Beech).

FORSYTHIA 'Lynwood'
Lynwood's Gold Forsythia

Height and spread Minimum 3 × 2 ft (1 m × 60 cm); maximum 8 × 4 ft (2.5 × 1.2 m).

Time to buy Pot-grown, any time except December–February. Bare-rooted, November or March–April. Avoid adverse weather conditions.

Where to find Outside in Hedging or Shrubs.

Size 2 ft (60 cm) min. Single or multistemmed.

Foliage Deciduous. Spring/summer, mid green. Premature autumn colour and leaf drop.

Roots Pots 5 in (12 cm) min. dia. Bare-rooted, good fibrous root system.

Hints Any well-prepared soil. Trench 3 ft (1 m) wide, 18 in (50 cm) deep, well-prepared. Planted in single line 2½ ft (80 cm) apart. Reduce 25% of leading shoots in spring after planting. Repeat annually.

GRISELINIA

Height and spread Minimum 3 × 2 ft (1 m × 60 cm); maximum 8 × 4 ft (2.5 × 1.2 m).

Time to buy Pot-grown, any time except December–February. Avoid adverse weather conditions.

Where to find Outside in Shrubs or Hedging.

Size 12 in (30 cm) min. Single or multistemmed.

Foliage Evergreen. Glossy, grey-green or golden variegated. Yellowing to basal leaves from August.

Roots Pots 5 in (12 cm) min. dia.

Hints Any well-prepared soil. Trench 3 ft (1 m) wide. 18 in (50 cm) deep, well-prepared. Planted in single line 2½ ft (80 cm) apart. Hardiness suspect, particularly variegated form.

Most widely available Griselinia littoralis. G. l. 'Variegata'.

HEBE
Veronica

Height and spread Minimum 3 × 3 ft (1 × 1 m); maximum 5 × 5 ft (1.5 × 1.5 m).

Time to buy Pot-grown any time except December–February. Avoid adverse weather conditions.

Where to find Outside in Shrubs or Hedging.

Size 12 in (30 cm). Single or multi-stemmed.

Foliage Evergreen. Glossy, grey-green. Yellowing of basal foliage from August to May.

Roots Pots 5 in (12 cm) min. dia.

Hints Any well-prepared soil. Trench 3 ft (1 m) wide, 18 in (50 cm) deep, well-prepared. Planted in single line 2½ ft (80 cm) apart. Do not intermix forms. Informal hedge, not clipped.

Most widely available Hebe brachysiphon. H. 'Great Orme'. H. 'Mauvena'. H. 'Midsummer Beauty'. H. salicifolia.

HIPPOPHAE RHAMNOIDES
Sea Buckthorn

Height and spread Minimum 5 × 3 ft (1.5 × 1 m); maximum 15 × 8 ft (4.5 × 2.5 m).

Time to buy Pot-grown, any time except December–February. Bare-rooted, November or March–April. Avoid adverse weather conditions.

Where to find Outside in Shrubs or Hedging.

Size 2 ft (60 cm) min. Single or multi-stemmed.

Foliage Deciduous. Spring/summer, silver-grey. Premature autumn colour and leaf drop.

Roots Pots 5 in (12 cm) min. dia. Bare-rooted, good fibrous root system.

Hints Any well-prepared soil. Trench 3 ft (1 m) wide, 18 in (50 cm) deep, well-prepared. Planted in single line 2½ ft (80 cm) apart. Reduce 25% of leading shoots in spring after planting. Repeat annually.

HYPERICUM 'HIDCOTE'
St John's Wort

Height and spread Minimum 3 × 3 ft (1 × 1 m): Maximum 3 × 3 ft (1 × 1 m).

Time to buy Pot-grown, any time except December–February. Avoid adverse weather conditions.

Where to find Outside in Shrubs or Hedging.

Size Minimum two main shoots, 15 in (40 cm) min. high. Limited side branches.

Foliage Deciduous. Spring/summer, mid green. Premature autumn colour and leaf drop.

Roots Pots 5 in (12 cm) min. dia.

Hints Any well-prepared soil. Trench 3 ft (1 m) wide, 18 in (50 cm) deep, well-prepared. Planted in single line 2 ft (60 cm) apart. Not trimmed. Forms round-topped hedge.

ILEX
Holly

Height and spread Minimum 5 × 3 ft (1.5 × 1 m); maximum 15 × 8 ft (4.5 × 2.5 m).

Time to buy Pot-grown, any time except December–February. Balled, October–November, March–April. Avoid adverse weather conditions.

Where to find Outside in Shrubs or Hedging.

Size 15 in (40 cm) min. Single or multi-stemmed.

Foliage Evergreen. Glossy, grey-green. Yellowing of basal foliage August–May.

Roots Pots 5 in (12 cm) min. dia. Balled, good fibrous root system.

Hints Any well-prepared soil. Trench 3 ft

(1 m) wide, 18 in (50 cm) deep, well-prepared. Planted in single line 3 ft (1 m) apart. Reduce 25% of leading shoots in spring after planting. Repeat annually. Do not intermix forms. Thorns make cultivation difficult. Berrying will be limited on formal clipped hedges but to improve chances plant a male specimen holly in close proximity. *Ilex Aquifolium* (Common Holly) may not be available sexed at time of purchase.

Most widely available *Ilex* × *altaclarensis* 'Camelliifolia' (F). *I.* × *a.* 'Golden King' (F). *I. aquifolium* (Common Holly) (M/F). *I. a.* 'Argenteomarginata' (Broad-leaved Silver Holly). *I. a.* 'Bacciflava' (F). *I. a.* 'Golden Van Tol' (F). *I. a.* 'Handsworth New Silver' (F). *I. a.* 'Madame Briot' (F).

LAVANDULA
Lavender

Height and spread Minimum 2 × 2 ft (60 × 60 cm); maximum 2½ × 2½ ft (80 × 80 cm). *Lavandula* 'Munstead' and *L.* 'Hidcote': minimum 18 × 18 in (50 × 50 cm): maximum 2 × 2 ft (60 × 60 cm)

Time to buy Pot-grown, April–July. Avoid adverse weather conditions.

Where to find Outside in Shrubs or Hedging.

Size 3 in (8 cm) min. Single or multi-stemmed.

Foliage Evergreen. Grey-green. Yellowing of basal leaves from August.

Roots Pots 2¾ in (6 cm), 3½ in (9 cm), 5 in (1 litre) or 7 in (2 litre).

Hints Any well-prepared soil. Trench 2 ft (60 cm) wide, 18 in (50 cm) deep, well-prepared. Planted in single line 15 in (40 cm) apart. *Lavandula augustifolia* 'Hidcote' and *L. a.* 'Munstead' planted in single line 12 in (30 cm) apart. Cut back to within 1½–2 in (4–5 cm) of ground level, spring after planting. Repeat tri-annually. Not trimmed. Grown into a round topped hedge. May be scarce.

Most widely available *Lavandula augustifolia* (Old English Lavender). *L. a.*

'Hidcote'. *L. a.* 'Munstead'. *L. a.* 'Vera'. *L. stoechas.*

LIGUSTRUM
Green Privet

Height and spread Minimum 3 × 2½ ft (1 m × 80 cm); maximum 12 × 6 ft (3.5 × 2 m).

Time to buy Pot-grown, any time except December–February. Balled, or bare-rooted October–November, March–April. Avoid adverse weather conditions.

Where to find Outside in Hedging or Shrubs.

Size 1–1½ ft (30–50 cm). 1½–2 ft (50–60 cm). 2–2½ ft (60–80 cm). 2½–3 ft (80 cm–1 m). Bare-rooted in bundles of five or ten. Forestry outlets, units of twenty-five or fifty.

Foliage Semi-evergreen. Mid green or golden variegated. Premature leaf drop may occur from August.

Roots Pots 5 in (12 cm) min. dia. Balled or bare-rooted, good fibrous root system.

Hints Any well-prepared soil. Trench 3 ft (1 m) wide, 18 in (50 cm) deep, well-prepared. Planted in double row, 18 in (50 cm) between plants, 15–18 in (40–50 cm) between rows. Rows should be staggered. Reduce 25% of leading shoots in spring after planting. Repeat annually. Should only be planted where gross feeding nature of roots will not affect other garden plantings. Good in maritime areas.

Most widely available *Ligustrum ovalifolium* 'Aureum' (Golden Privet). *L. vulgare* (Wild Privet).

LONICERA NITIDA
Poor Man's Box

Height and spread Minimum 1 ft × 9 in (30 × 23 cm); maximum 4 × 4 ft (1.2 × 1.2 m).

Time to buy Pot-grown, any time except December–February. Balled or bare-rooted, October–November, March–April. Avoid adverse weather conditions.

Where to find Outside in Hedging or Shrubs.

Size 1–1½ ft (30–50 cm). 1½–2 ft (50–60 cm).

Foliage Evergreen. Small, dark to mid green, round or oval. Yellowing of basal leaves from August through winter. Defoliation may occur in spring after planting.

Roots Pots 4 in (10 cm) min. dia. Balled or bare-rooted, good fibrous root system.

Hints Any well-prepared soil. Trench 3 ft (1 m) wide, 18 in (50 cm) deep, well-prepared. Plant in single line 15 in (40 cm) apart. May be scarce.

Most widely available Lonicera nitida 'Bagesson's Gold'. L. yunnanensis.

OSMANTHUS

Height and spread Minimum 3 × 2 ft (1 m × 60 cm); maximum 8 × 4 ft (2.5 × 1.2 m).

Time to buy Pot-grown April–July. Avoid adverse weather conditions.

Where to find Outside in Shrubs or Hedging.

Size 12 in (30 cm). Single or multi-stemmed.

Foliage Evergreen. Glossy, grey-green. Yellowing or basal leaves from August–May.

Roots Pots 5 in (12 cm) min. dia.

Hints Any well-prepared soil. Trench 3 ft (1 m) wide, 18 in (50 cm) deep, well-prepared. Plant in single line 2½ ft (80 cm) apart. Reduce 25% of leading shoots in the spring after planting. Repeat annually. May be scarce. Hardiness suspect. Good in maritime areas.

Most widely available Osmanthus 'Burkwoodii' (× Osmarea 'Burkwoodii'). O. heterophyllus.

PHILLYREA DECORA

Height and spread Minimum 3 × 2 ft (1 m × 60 cm); maximum 8 × 4 ft (2.5 × 1.2 m).

Time to buy Pot-grown, April–July. Avoid adverse weather conditions.

Where to find Outside in Shrubs or Hedging.

Size 12 in (30 cm). Single or multi-stemmed.

Foliage Evergreen. Glossy, grey-green. Yellowing of basal leaves August–May.

Roots Pots 5 in (12 cm) min. dia.

Hints Any well-prepared soil. Trench 3 ft (1 m) wide, 18 in (50 cm) deep, well-prepared. Plant in single row 2½ ft (80 cm) apart. Reduce 25% of leading shoots in spring after planting. Repeat annually. May be scarce. Good in maritime areas.

PITTOSPORUM

Height and spread Minimum 3 × 2 ft (1 m × 60 cm); maximum 8 × 4 ft (2.5 × 1.2 m).

Time to buy Pot-grown, April–July. Avoid adverse weather conditions.

Where to find Outside in Shrubs or Hedging.

Size 12 in (30 cm). Single or multi-stemmed.

Foliage Evergreen. Glossy, grey-green. Yellowing of basal foliage August–May.

Roots Pots 5 in (12 cm) min. dia.

Hints Any well-prepared soil. Trench 3 ft (1 m) wide, 18 in (50 cm) deep, well-prepared. Reduce 25% of leading shoots in spring after planting. Repeat annually. May be scarce. Hardiness suspect. Good in maritime areas.

POTENTILLA

Height and spread Minimum 3 × 3 ft (1 × 1 m); maximum 3 × 3 ft (1 × 1 m).

Time to buy Pot-grown, any time. Avoid adverse weather conditions.

Where to find Outside in Shrubs or Hedging.

Size Minimum two main shoots, 15 in (40 cm) min. height. Limited side branches.

Foliage Deciduous. Spring/summer, mid green. Premature autumn colour and leaf drop.

Roots Pots 5 in (12 cm) min. dia.

Hints Any well-prepared soil. Trench 3 ft (1 m) wide, 18 in (50 cm) deep, well-prepared. Plant in single line 18 in (50 cm) apart. Not trimmed. Will form round topped hedge.

Most widely available Potentilla dahurica 'Abbotswood'. P. 'Elizabeth'. P. 'Jackman's Variety'. P. 'Maanely's ('Moonlight'). P. 'Primrose Beauty'.

PRUNUS
Ornamental Plum

Height and spread Prunus cerasifera Minimum 5 × 3 ft (1.5 × 1 m); maximum 8 × 4 ft (2.5 × 1.2 m). Prunus 'Cistena' Minimum 1 ft × 9 in (30 × 23 cm); maximum 4 × 4 ft (1.2 × 1.2 m).

Time to buy Pot-grown, any time except December–February. Bare-rooted, November–April. Avoid adverse weather conditions.

Where to find Outside in Hedging or Shrubs.

Size Prunus cerasifera, 2 ft (60 cm) min. P. 'Cistena' 15 in (40 cm) min. Single or multi-stemmed.

Foliage Deciduous. Spring/summer, green or purple. Premature autumn colour and leaf drop.

Roots Pots 5 in (12 cm) min. dia. Bare-rooted, good fibrous root system.

Hints Any well-prepared soil. Trench 3 ft (1 m) wide, 18 in (50 cm) deep, well-prepared. Prunus cerasifera, plant 2½ ft (80 cm) apart, P. 'Cistena' 18 in (50 cm) apart in single line. Reduce 25% of leading shoots in spring after planting. Repeat annually.

Most widely available Prunus cerasifera (Myrobalan Plum. Purple Plum). P. c. 'Nigra'. P. c. 'Pissardii'. P. 'Cistena' (Dwarf Purple Plum).

PRUNUS LAUROCERASUS
Cherry Laurel, Common Laurel

Height and spread Minimum 3 × 2½ ft (1 m × 80 cm); maximum 15 × 6 ft (4.5 × 2 m).

Time to buy Pot-grown, any time except December–February. Balled and bare-rooted, October–November, March–April. Avoid adverse weather conditions.

Where to find Outside in Hedging or Shrubs.

Size 1–1½ ft (30–50 cm). 1½–2 ft (50–60 cm). 2–2½ ft (60–80 cm). 2½–3 ft (80 cm–1 m).

Foliage Evergreen, Mid to dark green, shiny upper surface. Yellowing of basal leaves from July onwards. Defoliation may occur in spring after planting.

Roots Pots 5 in (12 cm) min. dia. Balled and bare-rooted, good fibrous root system.

Hints Any well-prepared soil. Trench 3 ft (1 m) wide, 18 in (50 cm) deep, well-prepared. Plant in single line 2½ ft (80 cm) apart. Larger plants may be scarce.

Most widely available Prunus laurocerasus 'Schipkaensis'. P.l. 'Rotundifolia'.

PRUNUS LUSITANICA
Portuguese Laurel

Height and spread Minimum 3 × 2½ ft (1 m × 80 cm); maximum 15 × 6 ft (4.5 × 2 m).

Time to buy Pot-grown, any time except December–February. Balled, October–November, March–April. Avoid adverse weather conditions.

Where to find Outside in Shrubs or Hedging.

Size 15 in (40 cm) min. Single or multi-stemmed.

Foliage Evergreen. Glossy green or silver. Yellowing of basal leaves, August–May.

Roots Pots 5 in (12 cm) min. dia. Balled, good fibrous root system.

Hints Any well-prepared soil. Trench 3 ft (1 m) wide, 18 in (50 cm) deep, well-prepared. Planted in single line 2½ ft (80 cm) apart. Reduce 25% of leading shoots in spring after planting. Repeat annually. Do not intermix forms.

Most widely available Prunus lusitanica azorica. P. l. 'Variegata'.

PYRACANTHA
Firethorn
Height and spread Minimum 5 × 3 ft (1.5 × 1 m); maximum 8 × 4 ft (2.5 × 1.2 m).
Time to buy Pot-grown, any time. Avoid adverse weather conditions.
Where to find Outside in Shrubs or Hedging.
Size 15 in (40 cm) min. Single or multi-stemmed.
Foliage Evergreen. Glossy, grey-green. Yellowing of basal foliage August–May.
Roots Pots 5 in (12 cm) min. dia.
Hints Any well-prepared soil. Trench 3 ft (1 m) wide, 18 in (50 cm) deep, well-prepared. Plant in single line 2½ ft (80 cm) apart. Reduce 25% of leading shoots spring after planting. Repeat annually. Do not intermix forms. Thorns make cultivation difficult. May defoliate in severe winters.
Most widely available *Pyracantha atalantoides* ('Gibbsii'). *P. a.* 'Aurea'. *P.* 'Golden Charmer'. *P.* 'Mojave'. *P.* 'Orange Charmer'. *P.* 'Orange Glow'. *P.* 'Soleil d'Or'. *P.* 'Teton'.

RHODODENDRON
Height and spread Minimum 8 × 4 ft (2.5 × 1.2 m); maximum 20 × 15 ft (6 × 4.5 m).
Time to buy Pot-grown, any time except December–February. Balled, October–November, March–April. Avoid adverse weather conditions.
Where to find Outside in Shrubs, Acid-loving or Hedging.
Size 1½–2 ft (50–60 cm). 2–2½ ft (60–80 cm). 2½–3 ft (80 cm–1 m).
Foliage Evergreen. Glossy, grey-green or golden. Yellowing of basal leaves from August–May.
Roots Pots 6 in (15 cm) min. dia. Balled, good fibrous root system.
Hints Well-prepared acid soil. Trench 3 ft (1 m) wide, 18 in (50 cm) deep, well-prepared. Planted in single row 3 ft (1 m) apart.

Most widely available *Rhododendron ponticum. R. p.* 'Variegatum' and most large flowering forms.

RIBES
Flowering Currant
Height and spread Minimum 3 × 2 ft (1 m × 60 cm); maximum 8 × 4 ft (2.5 × 1.2 m).
Time to buy Pot-grown, any time except December–February. Bare-rooted, November or March–April. Avoid adverse weather conditions.
Where to find Outside in Hedging or Shrubs.
Size 2 ft (60 cm) min. Single or multi-stemmed.
Foliage Deciduous. Spring/summer, mid green. Premature autumn colour and leaf drop.
Roots Pots 5 in (12 cm) min. dia. Bare-rooted, good fibrous root system.
Hints Any well-prepared soil. Trench 3 ft (1 m) wide, 18 in (50 cm) deep, well-prepared. Reduce 25% of leading shoots in spring after planting. Repeat annually.
Most widely available *Ribes odoratum. R. sanguineum* 'King Edward VII'. *R. s.* 'Pulborough Scarlet'. *R. s.* 'Splendens'.

ROSA
Rose
Height and spread HYBRID TEA and FLORIBUNDA Minimum 3 × 2 ft (1 m × 60 cm); maximum 5 × 4 ft (1.5 × 1.2 m). SPECIES AND SHRUB Minimum 5 × 3 ft (1.5 × 1 m); maximum 7 × 5 ft (2.2 × 1.5 m).
Time to buy Pot-grown, any time. One-year-old bare-rooted or pre-packed, October–March. Avoid adverse weather conditions.
Where to find Outside in Roses. Pre-packed under limited protection.
Size Hybrid Tea and Floribunda, minimum two shoots, minimum 12 in (30 cm) long. Species and Shrub, 2 ft (60 cm) min. Single or multi-stemmed.

Foliage Deciduous. Spring/summer, mid green. Premature autumn colour and leaf drop. Mildew and black spot may be seen. If not excessive not a long term problem.

Roots Pots 5 in (12 cm) min. dia. Bare-rooted and pre-packed, good fibrous root system.

Hints Any well-prepared soil. Trench 3 ft (1 m) wide, 18 in (50 cm) deep, well-prepared. Plant in single line 2½ ft (80 cm) apart. Hybrid Tea and Floribunda, prune lighter than for bedding. Shrub and Species, no pruning in first year. Wide range. Research ultimate overall size.

Most widely available

HYBRID TEA ROSES 'Alec's Red'. 'Duke of Windsor'. 'Ernest S. Morse'. 'Fragrant Cloud'. 'Grandmere Jenny'. 'Peace'. 'Red Devil'. 'Super Star'. 'Wendy Cussons'. 'Whisky Mac'.

FLORIBUNDA ROSES 'Allgold'. 'Arthur Bell'. 'Chinatown'. 'Evelyn Fison'. 'Frensham'. 'Iceberg'. 'Joyfulness'. 'Masquerade'. 'Orange Sensation'. 'Queen Elizabeth'. 'Scarlet Queen Elizabeth'. 'Woburn Abbey'.

SPECIES AND SHRUB *R. hybrida* 'Ballerina'. *R. h.* 'Golden Wings'. *R. h.* 'Maigold'. *R. moschata* 'Buff Beauty'. *R. m.* 'Cornelia'. *R. m.* 'Felicia'. *R. m.* 'Penelope'. *R. paulii. R. rugosa* 'Alba'. *R. r.* 'Blanc Double de Coubert'. *R. r.* 'Frau Dagmar Hartop' (*R. r.* 'Frau Dagmar Hastrup'). *R. r.* 'Pink Grootendorst'. *R. r.* 'Roseraie de L'Hay'. *R. r.* 'Rubra'. *R. r.* 'Schneezwerg'.

ROSMARINUS
Rosemary
Height and spread Minimum 2 × 2 ft (60 × 60 cm); maximum 3 × 3 ft (1 × 1 m).
Time to buy Pot-grown, April–July. Avoid adverse weather conditions.
Where to find Outside in Shrubs or Hedging.
Size 3 in (8 cm) min. Single or multi-stemmed.

Foliage Evergreen, grey-green. Yellowing of basal leaves from August.

Roots Pots 2¾ in (7 cm), 3½ in (9 cm), 5 in (1 litre) or 7 in (2 litre).

Hints Any well-prepared soil. Trench 2 ft (60 cm) wide, 18 in (50 cm) deep, well-prepared. Plant in single line, 18 in (50 cm) apart. Cut back to 1½–2 in (4–5 cm) of ground level spring after planting. Repeat tri-annually. Grown into round-topped hedge. May be scarce. Initial pruning important.

Most widely available *Rosmarinus officinalis. R. o.* 'Jessop's Upright'. *R. o.* 'Pyramidalis'.

SANTOLINA
CHAMAECYPARISSUS
Cotton Lavender
Height and spread Minimum 2 × 2 ft (60 × 60 cm); maximum 2½ × 2½ ft (80 × 80 cm).
Time to buy Pot-grown, April–July. Avoid adverse weather conditions.
Where to find Outside in Shrubs or Hedging.
Size 3 in (8 cm) min. Single or multi-stemmed.
Foliage Evergreen. Grey-green. Yellowing of basal leaves from August.
Roots Pots, 2¾ in (7 cm), 3½ in (9 cm), 5 in (1 litre) or 7 in (2 litres).
Hints Any well-prepared soil. Trench 2 ft (60 cm) wide, 18 in (50 cm) deep, well-prepared. Plant in single line 12 in (30 cm) apart. Cut back to within 1½–2 in (4–5 cm) of ground level in spring after planting. Repeat tri-annually. Normally grown into round-topped hedge. May be scarce. Initial pruning important.

SPIRAEA × BUMALDA
Height and spread Minimum 2 × 2 ft (60 × 60 cm); maximum 3 × 3 ft (1 × 1 m).
Time to buy Pot-grown, any time, except December–February. Avoid adverse weather conditions.

Where to find Outside in Shrubs or Hedging.

Size Minimum two main shoots, 15 in (40 cm) min. height. Limited side shoots.

Foliage Deciduous. Spring/summer, mid green. Premature autumn colour and leaf drop.

Roots Pots 5 in (12 cm) min. dia.

Hints Any well-prepared soil. Trench 3 ft (1 m) wide, 18 in (50 cm) deep, well-prepared. Plant in single line 2 ft (60 cm) apart. Not normally trimmed. Will form round-topped hedge.

Most widely available *Spiraea × bumalda* 'Anthony Waterer'. *S. × b.* 'Gold Flame'.

VIBURNUM TINUS
Laurustinus

Height and spread Minimum 3 × 2 ft (1 m × 60 cm); maximum 8 × 4 ft (2.5 × 1.2 m).

Time to buy Pot-grown any time, except December–February. Avoid adverse weather conditions.

Where to find Outside in Shrubs or Hedging.

Size 9 in (23 cm) min. Single or multi-stemmed.

Foliage Evergreen. Glossy, grey-green. Yellowing of basal leaves from August through to May.

Roots Pots 5 in (12 cm) min. dia.

Hints Any well-prepared soil. Trench 3 ft (1 m) wide, 18 in (50 cm) deep, well-prepared. Planted in single line 2½ ft (80 cm) apart. Reduce 25% of leading shoots in spring after planting. Repeat annually. Hardiness suspect in cold areas.

Most widely available *Viburnum tinus* 'Eve Price'. *V. t.* 'Purpureum'. *V.t.* 'Variegatum'.

Autumn-Planted Bulbs,
Corms and Tubers

Few flowering plants that we grow give as much pleasure and excitement as spring-flowering bulbs planted in the autumn period. Bulbs are widely used for mass and spot planting in pots, tubs and containers, but they can also be used outside in hanging baskets, and in conservatories and greenhouses as pot-grown displays.

Some bulbs, such as *Lilium sparaxis*, Anemone and Ranunculus have a double planting season and can also be safely planted in the early spring.

The range, especially of Narcissi and Tulips, is wide. This selection represents the main forms, but many more are worthy of planting and none should be discarded if they attract you.

Bulbs are sold in a range of sizes and prices. Fringe sellers, such as markets, must be watched carefully to make sure you get value for money and that varieties are true to name.

Some bulbs originating in South Africa, such as Nerine, *Amaryllis belladonna* and Sparaxis, require soil conditions to mimic those from their native environment, and these should be researched.

ALLIUM (large-growing forms)
Flowering Onion
Time to buy Bulbs, August–October, February–March. Mail order acceptable. Pot-grown as available.
Where to find Bulbs, indoors on bulbs display, loose or pre-packed. Pot-grown, outside in Perennials or Bulbs.
Size Bulbs, 4 in (10 cm) min. dia., or in pots.
Foliage Deciduous. Pot-grown, mid to dark green.
Bulbs Dry, firm and rot-free. Pots 4 in (10 cm) min. dia. Singly or in three's or five's per pot.
Hints Any well-prepared soil. Wide range not always available from one outlet.
Most widely available *Allium aflatunense* (30 in/80 cm). *A. christophii* 'Al-bopilosum' (24 in/60 cm). A. giganteum (48 in/1.2 m). *A.* 'Purple Sensation' (40 in/1.1 m). *A. sphaerocephalum* (24 in/60 cm).

ALLIUM (short growing forms)
Flowering Onion
Time to buy Bulbs, August–October, February–March. Mail order acceptable. Pot-grown, as available.
Where to find Bulbs, indoors on bulb display, loose or pre-packed. Pot-grown, outside in Alpines or Bulbs.
Size Bulbs, 1–2 in (3–5 cm) dia., or in pots.
Foliage Deciduous. Pot-grown, mid to dark green.
Bulbs Dry, firm and rot free. Pots 3 in (8 cm) min. dia. Three per pot.

Hints Any well-prepared soil. May be scarce.

Most widely available *Allium flavum* (10–12 in/25–30 cm). *A. karataviense* (12 in/30 cm). *A. moly* (12 in/30 cm). *A. nea-politanum* (10 in/25 cm). *A. oreophilum* 'Ostrowskianum' (6 in/15 cm). *A. roseum* (12 in/30 cm) Many other varieties available.

AMARYLLIS BELLADONNA
Belladonna

Time to buy Bulbs, November–March. Mail order acceptable. Pot-grown, as available.

Where to find Bulbs, indoors on bulb display, loose or pre-packed. Pot-grown, outside in Perennials or Bulbs.

Size Bulbs, 8–9 in (20–23 cm) dia., or in pots.

Foliage Deciduous. Pot-grown, dark green in winter.

Bulbs Dry, firm and rot-free. Pots 4 in (10 cm) min. dia. Singly in pot.

Hints Any well-prepared soil. Planted in close proximity to wall. Scarce.
BULBS POISONOUS.

ANEMONE

Time to buy Corms, July–November, February–March. Mail order acceptable. Pot-grown, as available.

Where to find Corms, indoors on bulb display, pre-packed or loose. Pot-grown, outside in Alpines or Bulbs.

Size Corms, 2 in (50 cm) min. dia., or in pots.

Foliage Deciduous. Pot-grown, dark green.

Corms Dry, firm and rot-free. White mould-like markings are natural. Cut and divided corms standard practice. Pots 3 in (8 cm) min. dia. Three per pot.

Hints Any well-prepared soil. Soak for thirty-six hours in water before planting. Add a tablespoon of paraffin to water if rodents are a problem. Specific colour may be scare. Corms look dry and dead.

Most widely available *Anemone blanda*. *A. b.* 'Blue Shades'. *A. b.* 'Pink Star'. *A. b.* 'White'., *A.* 'De Caen'. *A. fulgens. A.* 'St Bridgid'.

ARUM ITALICUM
Arum Lily

Time to buy Bulbs, October–November. Mail order acceptable. Pot-grown, as available.

Where to find Bulbs, indoors on bulb display, loose or pre-packed. Pot-grown, outside in Perennials or Bulbs.

Size Bulbs, 6 in (15 cm) dia., or in pots.

Foliage Deciduous. Pot-grown, dark green, white markings.

Bulbs Dry, firm and rot-free. Pots 4 in (10 cm) min. dia., planted singly.

Hints Prepared moist soil, not alkaline, plus extra organic material, in light shade. May be scarce.

BRODIAEA LAXA 'QUEEN FABIOLA'

Time to buy Bulbs, August–October. Mail order acceptable. Pot-grown, as available.

Where to find Bulbs, indoors on bulb display, pre-packed. Pot-grown, outside in Alpines or Bulbs.

Size Bulbs, 2 in (5 cm) dia., or in pots.

Foliage Deciduous. Pot-grown, mid green.

Bulbs Dry, firm and rot free. Pots 3 in (8 cm) min. dia. Three or five bulbs per pot.

Hints Any well-prepared soil. Hardiness suspect. Avoid bulbs which are soft.

BULBOCODIUM VERNUM

Time to buy Bulbs, September–November. Mail order acceptable. Pot-grown, as available.

Where to find Bulbs, indoors on bulb display, pre-packed. Pot-grown, outside in Alpines or Bulbs.

Size Bulbs, $2\frac{1}{2}$ in (6 cm) dia., or in pots.

Foliage Deciduous. Pot-grown, mid green.

Bulbs Dry, firm and rot-free. Pots 4 in (10 cm) min. dia. Three to five per pot.
Hints Any well-prepared soil. Hardiness suspect. Care needed in positioning. May be scarce.

CAMASSIA

Time to buy Bulbs, September–December. Mail order acceptable. Pot-grown, as available.
Where to find Bulbs, indoors on bulb display, loose or pre-packed. Pot-grown, outside in Perennials or Bulbs.
Size Bulbs, 4 in (10 cm) dia., or in pots.
Foliage Deciduous. Pot-grown, mid green. Yellowing from June.
Bulbs Dry, firm and rot-free. No sign of mildew. Pots 3 in (8 cm) min. dia. planted singly.
Hints Any well-prepared soil in partial shade. May be scarce.
Most widely available *Camassia cusickii. C. leichtlinii. C. l. alba.*

CHIONODOXA

Time to buy Bulbs indoors on bulb display, pre-packed. Pot-grown, outside in Alpines or Bulbs.
Size Bulbs, 2 in (5 cm) dia., or in pots.
Foliage Deciduous. Pot-grown, March–May, mid green.
Bulbs Dry, firm and rot-free. Pots, 3 in (8 cm) min. dia. Three bulbs per pot.
Hints Any well-prepared soil in light shade. May be scarce.
Most widely available *Chionodixa gigantea. C. luciliae. C. l. rosea. C.* 'Pink Giant'.

COLCHICUM

Autumn Crocus
Time to buy Corms, July–September. Mail order acceptable. Pot-grown, as available.
Where to find Corms, indoors on bulb display, loose. Pot-grown, outside in Alpines or Bulbs.
Size Corms, $5\frac{1}{2}$–$7\frac{1}{2}$ in (13–18 cm) dia., or in pots.

Foliage Deciduous. Pot-grown, mid green in winter.
Corms Dry, firm and rot-free. May show signs of flower. Pots 4 in (10 cm) min. dia., planted singly.
Hints Any well-prepared soil. Range of forms not always available. Can be confused with true autumn crocuses. *Crocus speciosus, C.* 'Zonatus'. CORMS POISONOUS: take care when handling.
Most widely available *Colchicum autumnale. C. a.* album. *C. a. major* ('Byzantium'). *C. giganteum. C.* 'Lilac Wonder'. *C. speciosum album. C.* 'Waterlily'.

CROCUS

Dutch Large Flowering Crocus
Time to buy Corms, August–November. Mail order acceptable. Pot-grown, as available.
Where to find Corms, indoors on bulb display, loose or pre-packed. Pot-grown, outside in Alpines or Bulbs.
Size Hybrid corms, $2\frac{3}{4}$–4 in (7–10 cm), species 2 in (5 cm), autumn flowering $2\frac{1}{2}$ in (6 cm) dia., or in pots.
Foliage Deciduous. Pot-grown, green in spring/summer.
Corms Dry, firm and rot-free. Pots 3 in (8 cm) min. dia. Three to five corms per pot.
Hints Any well-prepared soil. Wide range. if rodents are a problem, soak corms in a solution of one gallon water and one tablespoon of paraffin for twenty minutes. Can be planted when in flower.
Most widely available
HYBRIDS *Crocus* 'Joan of Arc'. *C.* 'Mammoth Yellow'. *C.* 'Remembrance'. *C.* 'Flower Record'. *C.* 'Pickwick'. *C.* 'Purpureus Grandiflorus'. *C.* 'Mixed'.
SPECIES *Crocus* 'Bluebird'. *C.* 'Blue Pearl'. *C.* 'Blue Peter. *C.* 'Cream Beauty'. *C.* 'E. A. Bowles'. *C.* 'E. P. Bowles'. *C.* 'Fuscotinctus'. *C.* 'Gold Bunch'. *C.* 'Gypsy Girl'. *C.* 'Herald'. *C.* 'Ladykiller'. *C.* 'Minimus'. *C.* 'Queen Lilliput'. *C.* 'Satur-

nus'. *C.* Snow Bunting. *C.* Zwannenburg Bronze.

AUTUMN FLOWERING *Crocus sativus* (Saffron Crocus). *C. speciosus. C. zonatus.*

CYCLAMEN (hardy)
Time to buy Tubers, August–October. Some forms in spring. Mail order acceptable. Pot-grown, as available.
Where to find Tubers, indoors on bulb display, loose or pre-packed. Pot-grown, outside in Alpines.
Size Tubers, 4–6 in. (10–15 cm) dia., or in pots.
Foliage Deciduous. Pot-grown, spring/summer dark green, white markings.
Tubers Dry, firm and rot-free. Pots 4 in (10 cm) min. dia., planted singly.
Hints Well-prepared neutral to acid soil, plus well-rooted leaf mould, in light shade. Plant just below or at surface level. May not be available due to crop failure or control by C. I. T. E. S., an international agreement for control of bulbs imported from the wild. Special care needed when planting. Pot-grown, less difficult.
Most widely available: *Cyclamen cilicium. C. coum. C. c. album. C. hederifolium* syn. *neapolitanum.*

ERANTHIS HYEMALIS
Winter Aconite
Time to buy Corms, August–November. Mail order acceptable. Pot-grown, as available or 'in the green'.
Where to find Corms, indoors on bulb display, loose, pre-packed or in bulk. Pot-grown, outside in Alpines or Bulbs. Bulbs lifted when in leaf and sold. 'In the green', outside on special display or dug to order.
Size Corms, 1½–2 in (4–5 cm) dia., in pots or 'in the green'.
Foliage Deciduous. Pot-grown, light to mid green, March–May. 'In the green' light green, rapidly turning yellow.
Corms Dry, firm and rot-free. Pots 3 in

(8 cm) min. dia. Three corms per pot. 'In the green' in ten's, bare-rooted.
Hints Any well-prepared soil, in sun or shade. Soak corms in a solution of one gallon of water to one tablespoon of paraffin for twenty-four hours, if rodents are a problem. Corms slow to establish. Large numbers required for good display.

ERYTHRONIUM
Dog's Tooth Violet
Time to buy Tubers, August–October. Mail order acceptable. Pot-grown, as available.
Where to find Tubers, indoors on bulb display, pre-packed. Pot-grown, outside in Perennials or Alpines.
Size Tubers, minimum 1½ in (4 cm) long, thickness of pencil, or in pots.
Foliage Deciduous. Pot-grown, mid green, spring/summer.
Tubers Packed in moist peat, firm and rot-free. Pots 4 in (10 cm) min. dia., plant singly.
Hints Well-prepared neutral to acid soil, plus extra organic material. Should be potted for minimum of one year in good quality potting compost before planting out. May be scarce.
Most widely available *Erythronium dens-canis. E.* 'Pagoda'. *E.* 'White Beauty'.

FREESIA
Time to buy Bulbs, September–December, March–May. Mail order acceptable. Pot-grown, as available.
Where to find Bulbs, indoors on bulb display, loose or pre-packed. Pot-grown, outside in Perennials, Alpines or Bulbs.
Size Bulbs, 2 in (5 cm) min. dia., or in pots.
Foliage Deciduous. Pot-grown, light green, spring/summer.
Bulbs Dry, firm, rot-free and aphid-free. Pots 4 in (10 cm) min. dia. Three to five bulbs per pot.
Hints Any well-prepared soil. Pot-grown,

good quality potting compost. Deteriorate quickly, inspect thoroughly before purchasing.

FRITILLARIA IMPERALIS
The Crown Imperial
FRITILLARIA PERSICA
Persian Fritillaria
Time to buy Corms, September–November. Mail order acceptable. Pot-grown, as available.
Where to find Corms, indoors on bulb display, loose. Pot-grown, outside in Perennials or Bulbs.
Size Corms, *Fritillaria imperalis*, 6 in (15 cm), *F. persica*, 8 in (20 cm) dia., or in pots.
Foliage Deciduous. Pot-grown, March–May, mid green.
Corms Dry, firm and rot-free. Scales breaking from outer edges. Pots 4 in (10 cm) min. dia. One per pot.
Hints Any well-prepared soil. Mark planting position, if spiked by fork they bleed to death. Store in wood wool or similar dry material to prevent bruising.
Most widely available *Fritillaria imperalis* 'Aurora'. *F. i.* 'Lutea'. *F. i.* 'Rubra'. *F. persica*.

FRITILLARIA MELEAGRIS
Snake's Head Fritillary, Snake's Head Lily
Time to buy Corms, September–November. Mail order acceptable. Pot-grown, as available.
Where to find Corms, indoors on bulb display, loose or pre-packed. Pot-grown, outside in Alpines or Bulbs.
Size Corms, 2½ in (6 cm) min. dia., or in pots.
Foliage Deciduous. Pot-grown, mid green, March-May.
Corms Dry, firm and rot-free. Pots 4 in (10 cm) min. dia.
Hints Any well-prepared soil. Good in alkaline soils. Best grown in grass.

Obtain from horticulturally grown sources or from imports under C. I. T. E. S., an international agreement for control of bulbs imported from the wild.
Most widely available *Fritillaria meleagris alba* (syn. 'Aphrodite') ('White Snake's Head Fritillary').

GALANTHUS
Snowdrop
Time to buy Bulbs, September–November. Mail order acceptable. Pot-grown, as available. 'In the green' from open ground and should be immediately replanted.
Where to find Bulbs, indoors on bulb display; loose, in bulk or pre-packed. Pot-grown, outside in Alpines or Bulbs. 'In the green' in tens on special display.
Size Bulbs, 1½–2 in (4–5 cm) dia. 'In the green', 2 in (5 cm) dia., with green foliage, or in pots.
Foliage Deciduous. Pot-grown, mid green March–May. 'In the green', mid green, may look dejected and limp.
Bulbs Dry, firm and rot-free. 'In the green', kept moist. Pots 4 in (10 cm) min. dia., five bulbs per pot.
Hints Any well-prepared soil. Soak for twenty minutes in a solution of one gallon of water and one tablespoon of paraffin if rodents are a problem. Plant in clumps of minimum ten bulbs, 18 in (50 cm) apart. Bulbs of French origin can be difficult to establish. For preference plant 'in the green' or from pot. Some forms may be scarce.
Most widely available *Galanthus atkinsii. G. elwesii. G. nivalis. G. n.* 'Floreplena'.

GERANIUM TUBEROSUM
Tuberous Rooted Geranium
Time to buy Tubers, September–November. Mail order acceptable.
Where to find Tubers, outside in Bulbs, loose or pre-packed.

26. A sunny patio planting at Leckhampstead House, nr. Newbury, Berks.

27. One of the perennial borders in mid-summer at Hazelby House, nr. Newbury, Berks.

28. *Liatris spicata* with its summer spiky flowers.

29. *Eryngium bourgatii*. Blue star-like
flowers shown off against its grey foliage.

30. White African Lily (*Agapanthus
campanulatus* 'Alba'). A handsome
addition to any planting.

31. *Gentiana sino-ornata*, truly one of the most vivid of all blue-flowering alpines.

32. Edelweiss (*Leontopodium alpinum*) with its fascinating felt-like flowers.

33. *Acaena buchananii*. A most attractive grey, creeping carpet with brown burrs as seed heads.

34. Larkspur (*Consolida ambigua*). One of the easiest of the hardy annuals to create a cottage-garden effect.

35. *Lavatera trimestris* 'Silver Cup'. Flowers carried all summer in great profusion on this hardy annual.

36. Poached Egg Plant (*Limnanthes douglasii*). Summer flowering makes this hardy annual a favourite for any garden.

37. Ornamental Cabbage (*Brassica oleracea varacephala*). A good winter biennial for tubs and winter bedding.

38. Universal Winter-flowering Pansy (*Viola × wittrockiana*). For winter-long colour in all but the coldest of weather.

39. Double Ornamental Daisy (*Bellis perennis* 'Tom Thumb'). Well-established biennial for spring and summer colour.

40. Wallflower (*Cheiranthus cheiri* 'Persian Carpet'). A most attractive mixture of pastel and semi-pastel colourings.

41. *Viola cornuta* 'Prince John'. A biennial *Viola* which can become a permanent friend in the garden.

42. Forget-me-Not (*Myosotis alpestris*). Useful for adding to other spring-flowering plants, particularly bulbs.

43. *Cineraria maritima.* A grey-leaved 'spot' plant for summer bedding schemes.

44. *Rudbeckia* 'Marmalade'. Half-hardy bedding plant for startling colour in late summer and early autumn.

45. Painted Tongue (*Salpiglossus sinuata*). Annual bedding plant worthy of more attention and wider planting in gardens.

46. *Dianthus* 'Baby Doll'. Red-eyed white flowers, contrasting against its grey background foliage.

47. The Livingstone Daisy (*Mesembryanthemum crystallinum*). Succulent plant for attractive summer bedding.

48. Tobacco Plant (*Nicotiana* 'Domino Scarlet'). One of the finest coloured strains of flowering Tobacco Plants.

Size Tubers, 1½–2 in (4–5 cm) long, thickness of drinking straw.
Foliage Deciduous.
Tubers Stored in moist peat, firm and rot-free.
Hints Well-prepared soil, plus extra organic material. May be scarce.

HIPPEASTRUM
Amaryllis

Time to buy Bulbs, November–March. Mail order acceptable. Pot-grown, as available. For use only as house plants for conservatory or greenhouse.
Where to find Bulbs, indoors on bulb display, loose or pre-packed with container and potting compost. Pot-grown, indoors in House Plants.
Size Bulbs, 12 in (30 cm) min. dia., or in pots.
Foliage Deciduous. Pot-grown, dark green, January–May.
Bulbs Dry, firm and rot-free. Pots 5 in (12 cm) min. dia.
Hints Always plant in pots, using good quality peat-based potting compost. Keep moist and in sunny position. Not hardy. Must be kept under cover through winter and spring. May not be named.
Most widely available *Hippeastrum* 'Apple Blossom'. *H.* 'Cinderella'. *H.* 'Daydream'. *H.* 'Dazzler'. *H.* 'Masai'. *H.* 'Minerva'. *H.* 'Orange Sovereign'. *H.* 'Red Lion'. *H.* 'Scarlet Glow'. *H.* 'Telstar'.

HYACINTHOIDES HISPANICA syn. *Scilla campanulata*
Spanish Bluebell

Time to buy Bulbs, September–November. Mail order acceptable. Pot-grown, as available.
Where to find Bulbs, indoors on bulb display, loose, pre-packed or in bulk. Pot-grown, outside in Bulbs or Perennials.
Size Bulbs, 4 in (10 cm) min. or in pots.
Foliage, Deciduous. Pot-grown, dark green.

Bulbs Dry, firm and rot-free. Pots 4 in (10 cm) min. dia.
Hints Any well-prepared soil. Can become invasive. Offered mixed rather than single colours.
Range of colours Blue. Pink. White. Mixed.

HYACINTHOIDES NON SCRIPTA
syn. *Scilla nutans* and *Endymion non scripta*
Bluebell, English Bluebell

Time to buy Bulbs, September–November. 'In the green', following flowering to April. Mail order acceptable. Pot-grown, as available.
Where to find Bulbs, indoors on bulb display, loose, pre-packed or in bulk. 'In the green', lifted to order.
Size Bulbs or 'in the green', 1½ in (4 cm) dia. or in pots.
Foliage Deciduous. 'In the green', dark green, limp and dejected.
Bulbs Dry, firm and rot-free. 'In the green', moist and firm. Pots 4 in (10 cm) min. dia. Five bulbs per pot.
Hints Any well-prepared soil in shade. Should be produced horticulturally and not lifted from the wild. Large numbers required to achieve effect of bluebell wood.

DUTCH HYACINTHS
Time to buy Bulbs, August–September. Sixteen weeks prior to flowering time for forcing. Mail order acceptable. Pot or bowl-grown, December–April.
Where to find Bulbs, indoors on bulb display, loose or pre-packed. Pre-grown, pot or bowls in House Plants.
Size Prepared, 6½–7 in (16–17 cm) or 7–7½ in (17–18 cm) dia. Unprepared, 5½–6 in. (13–15 cm) dia., or pot or bowl-grown.
Foliage Deciduous. Pot-grown, mid green.
Bulbs Dry, firm and rot-free.
Hints Planted in bowls or in individual

3–4 in (8–10 cm) pots, using prepared bulb fibre. Use unprepared bulbs for planting outside. Wear gloves when handling prepared hyacinths as a natural acid from their flesh can cause irritation. Wide range, specific requirements may have to be sought from a number of outlets.

Most widely available

PREPARED FOR EARLY FLOWERING 'Anne Marie'. 'Ben Nevis'. 'Blue Orchid'. 'Blue Star'. 'City of Haarlem'. 'Delft Blue'. 'Holly Hock'. 'Jan Bos'. 'King Codro'. 'Ostara'. 'Pink Pearl Rosette'. 'White Pearl'.

UNPREPARED FOR POT OR GARDEN The above plus – 'Amethyst'. 'Amsterdam'. 'Bismark'. 'Blue Giant'. 'Blue Jacket'. 'Blue Magic'. 'Blushing Dolly'. 'Carnegie'. 'City of Bradfrd'. 'Distinction'. 'Fondant'. 'Gipsy Queen'. 'Lady Derb'. 'L'innocence'. 'Mulberry Rose'. 'Peter Stuyvesant'. 'Queen of the Pinks'. 'Violet Pearl'.

MULTIFLOWERED HYACINTHS

Time to buy Bulbs, September–November, Mail order acceptable. Pot-grown, as available.

Where to find Bulbs, indoors on bulb display, loose or pre-packed. Pot grown, indoors in House Plants.

Size Bulbs, 5½–6 in (14–15 cm) dia, or in pots.

Foliage Deciduous. Pot-grown, mid green.

Bulbs Dry, firm and rot-free. Pots 3 in (8 cm) min. dia.

Hints Plant in pots 3–4 in (8–10 cm) dia. using bulb fibre. Plant shallow. Not planted in open ground. May be scarce.

Range of colours Pink. Deep Pink. White. Blue.

ROMAN HYACINTH

Time to buy Bulbs, September–November, loose or pre-packed.

Size Bulbs, 5½–6 in (14–15 cm) dia.

Foliage Deciduous.

Bulbs Dry, firm and rot-free.

Hints Pot-grown, in pots 3–4 in (8–10 cm) dia. using bulb fibre. Plant shallow. Not planted in open ground. May be scarce.

Range of colours Blue. Pink. White.

IPHEION

Time to buy Bulbs, October–November or May. Mail order acceptable. Pot-grown, as available.

Where to find Bulbs, indoors on bulb display, pre-packed. Pot-grown, outside in Alpines or Bulbs.

Size Bulbs, 2 in (5 cm) min. dia., or in pots.

Foliage Deciduous. Pot-grown, mid green, May–July.

Bulbs Dry, firm and rot-free. Pots 3 in (8 cm) min. dia. Three to five bulbs per pot.

Hints Well-prepared, light, warm, dry soil in sunny position. Hardiness suspect and careful positioning required. May be scarce.

DUTCH IRIS

Time to buy Bulbs, September–November, April–May. Mail order acceptable. Pot-grown, as available.

Where to find Bulbs, indoors on bulb display, loose or pre-packed. Pot-grown, outside in Perennials or Bulbs.

Size Bulbs, 2 in (5 cm) min. dia., or in pots.

Foliage Deciduous. Pot-grown, dark green, May–August.

Bulbs Dry, firm and rot-free. Pots 4 in (10 cm) min. dia. Three to five bulbs per pot.

Hints Any well-prepared soil. Not always named. Offered mixed, but in the author's opinion straight colours preferred. One of the most economic of bulbs.

Most widely available Iris 'Golden Harvest'. I. H. C. Van Vliet'. I. 'Bronze Queen'. I. 'Purple Sensation'. I. 'White Excelsior'. I. 'Mixed'.

IRIS SPECIES (dwarf early flowering)
Time to buy Bulbs, September–November. Mail order acceptable. Pot-grown, as available.
Where to find Bulbs, indoors on bulb display, loose or pre-packed. Pot-grown, outside in Alpines or Bulbs.
Size Bulbs, 2 in (5 cm) min. dia., or in pots.
Foliage Deciduous. Pot-grown, dark green, March–May.
Bulbs Dry, firm and rot-free, showing no signs of attack by aphid. Pots 3 in (8 cm) min. dia. Minimum three bulbs per pot.
Hints Any well-prepared soil. Wide range. Offered mixed, but in the author's opinion straight colours preferred.
Most widely available *Iris danfordiae*. *I. histroides*. *I. reticulata*. *I. r.* 'Cantab'. *I. r.* 'Major Gordon'. *I. r.* 'Harmony'. *I. r.* 'Hercules'. *I. r.* 'Joyce'. *I. r.* 'J. S. Dijt'. *I. r.* 'Mixed'.

IRIS TUBEROSA
Tuberous-Rooted Iris
Time to buy, Tubers, March–May. Mail order acceptable. Pot-grown, as available.
Where to find Tubers, indoors on bulb display, pre-packed. Pot-grown, outside in Perennials, Alpines or Bulbs.
Size Bulbs, minimum 2 in (5 cm) long, thickness of pencil, or in pots.
Foliage Deciduous. Pot-grown, dark green, April–July.
Tubers Stored in moist peat, firm, rot-free. Pots 4 in (10 cm) min. dia. One per pot.
Hints Well-prepared moist, well drained soil, plus extra organic material. Often stored incorrectly, being too dry. Purchase early. May be scarce.

IXIA
African Corn Lily
Time to buy Bulbs, August–September, April–May. Mail order acceptable. Pot-grown, as available.
Where to find Bulbs, indoors on bulb display, pre-packed. Pot-grown, outside in Alpines or Bulbs.
Size Bulbs, 2 in (5 cm) min. dia., or in pots.
Foliage Deciduous. Pot-grown, mid green, May–August.
Bulbs Dry, firm and rot-free. Pots 3 in (8 cm) min. dia. Minimum three bulbs per pot.
Hints Well-prepared, well-drained soil in dry, warm position. Hardiness suspect. Avoid soft bulbs. Named varieties or specific colours scarce. Offered mixed, but in the author's opinion straight colours preferred.
Most widely available *Ixia* 'Bluebird'. *I.* 'Castor'. *I.* 'Hogarth'. *I.* 'Mabel'. *I.* 'Marquette'. *I.* 'Rose Emperor'. *I.* 'Venus'. *I.* 'Mixture'.

IXIOLORION PALLASII
Time to buy Bulbs, August–April. Mail order acceptable. Pot-grown, as available.
Where to find Bulbs, indoors on bulbs display, pre-packed. Pot-grown, outside in Alpines or Bulbs.
Size Bulbs, 1½ in (4 cm) dia., or in pots.
Foliage Deciduous. Pot-grown, dark green, April–July.
Bulbs Dry, firm and rot-free. Pots 3 in (8 cm) min. dia. Minimum three bulbs per pot.
Hints Well-prepared, well-drained, light, warm soil and position, plus extra organic material. Hardiness suspect. Requires careful positioning.

LEUCOJEUM
Snowflake
Time to buy Bulbs, August–October. Mail order acceptable. Pot-grown, as available.
Where to find Bulbs, indoors on bulb display, loose or pre-packed. Pot-grown, outside in Perennials, Alpines or Bulbs.
Size Bulbs, 3 in (8 cm) min. dia., or in pots.

Foliage Deciduous. Pot-grown, light to mid green, March–July.

Bulbs Dry, firm and rot-free. Pots 4 in (10 cm) min. dia. Minimum three bulbs per pot.

Hints Any well-prepared soil. Plant in clumps of minimum five bulbs. Apart from *Leucojeum aestivum*, other forms may be scarce.

Most widely available *Leucojeum aestivum* (Summer Snowflake). *L. a.* 'Gravetye Giant'. *L. vernum* (Spring Snowflake).

LILIUM
Lily

Time to buy Bulbs, October–December, March–April. Mail order acceptable. Pot-grown, as available.

Where to find Bulbs, indoors on bulb display, loose or pre-packed. Pot-grown, outside in Perennials or Bulbs.

Size Bulbs, $7\frac{1}{2}$–$8\frac{1}{2}$ in (18–22 cm) dia., or in pots.

Foliage Deciduous. Pot-grown, mid green June–August.

Bulbs Dry, firm and rot-free. Pots 5 in (12 cm) min. dia. One to three bulbs per pot.

Hints Any well-prepared soil. Grit sand under each bulb will avoid rotting. Avoid soft bulbs if purchased in spring. Specific forms may need searching for.

Most widely available

LARGE FLOWERING FORMS *Lilium* 'African Queen'. *L.* 'Bright Star'. *L.* 'Casablanca'. *L.* 'Connecticut King'. *L.* 'Elfin Sun'. *L.* 'Enchantment'. *L.* 'Fireking'. *L.* 'Golden Splendour'. *L.* 'King Pete'. *L.* 'Milano'. *L.* 'Monte Negro'. *L.* 'Olivia'. *L.* 'Omega'. *L.* 'Pink Perfection'. *L.* 'Royal Gold'.

SPECIES *Lilium candidum* (Madonna Lily). *L. citronella. L. hansonii. L. henryii. L. longiflorum. L. martagon. L. m. album* (Turk's Cap Lily). *L. nepalense. L. regale. L. r. album. L. speciosum* 'Rubrum'. *L. tenuifolium. L. tigrinum splendens* (Tiger Lily).

MUSCARI
Grape Hyacinth

Time to buy Bulbs, August–October. Mail order acceptable. Pot-grown, as available.

Where to find Bulbs, indoors on bulb display, loose or pre-packed. Pot-grown, outside in Alpines or Bulbs.

Size Bulbs, $2\frac{3}{4}$–3 in (7–8 cm) min. dia., or in pots.

Foliage Deciduous. Pot-grown, dark green, March–May.

Bulbs Dry, firm and rot-free. Pots 3 in (8 cm) min. dia. Three to five bulbs per pot.

Hints Any well-prepared soil. *Muscari armeniacum* may become invasive. Some forms scarce.

Most widely available *Muscari armeniacum. Muscari* 'Blue Spike'. *M. botryoides alba. M. plumosa.*

NARCISSUS
Daffodil

Time to buy Bulbs, September–November. Mail order acceptable. Pot-grown, as available.

Where to find Bulbs, indoors on bulb display, sold loose, by the purchaser filling a bag or container, pre-packed or twenty-five kilo sacks. Pot-grown, outside in Bulbs, predominantly in spring.

Size BULBS Trumpet 5–6 in (12–15 cm), large and small cupped 5–$5\frac{3}{4}$ in (12–14 cm), double 5–6 in (12–15 cm), dwarf and species 2–4 in (5–10 cm), orchid flowering 5–$5\frac{3}{4}$ in (12–14 cm), pheasant eye types 4–5 in (10–12 cm) dia.

Foliage Deciduous. Pot-grown, mid green, March–May.

Bulbs Dry, firm and rot-free. Pots 4 in. (10 cm) min. dia. for dwarf and species. Trumpet, large and small cupped, orchid, double and for pots, 5 in (12 cm) min. dia. All, minimum three bulbs per pot.

Hints Any well-prepared soil. For container-grown, use good quality potting compost. Wide range. Beware of special offers' sold late autumn. Buy from reputable source to ensure correct naming.

Most widely available

TRUMPET *Narcissus* 'Dutch Master'. *N.* 'Golden Harvest'. *N.* 'King Alfred'. *N.* 'Magnet'. *N.* 'Mount Hood'. *N.* 'Unsurpassable'.

LARGE CUPPED *Narcissus* 'Carbineer'. *N.* 'Carlton'. *N.* 'Flower Record'. *N.* 'Fortune'. *N.* 'Gigantic Star'. *N.* 'Ice Follies'. *N.* 'Salome'. *N.* 'Scarlet Elegance'. *N.* 'Sempre Avanti'.

SMALL CUPPED *Narcissus* 'Aflame.' *N.* 'Barrett Browning'. *N.* 'Birma'. *N.* 'Verger'.

DOUBLE *Narcissus* 'Cheerfulness'. *N.* 'Flower Drift'. *N.* 'Golden Ducat'. *N.* 'Mary Copeland'. *N.* 'Sir Winston Churchill'. *N.* 'Texas'. *N.* 'White Lion'. *N.* 'Yellow Cheerfulness'.

DWARF OR SPECIES *Narcissus* 'April Tears'. *N.* 'Baby Moon'. *N.* 'February Gold'. *N.* 'February Silver'. *N.* 'Garden Princess'. *N.* 'Jack Snipe'. *N.* 'Jenny'. *N.* *lobularis*. *N.* 'March Sunshine'. *N.* 'Midget'. *N.* 'Minnow'. *N.* 'Peeping Tom'. *N.* 'Rippling Waters'. *N.* 'Silver Chimes'. *N.* 'Suzy'. *N.* 'Tete à Tete'. *N.* 'Thalia'. *N.* *triandrus albus* (Angels Tears). *N.* 'Waterperry'.

ORCHID FLOWERING (SPLIT CORONA) *Narcissus* 'Baccarat'. *N.* 'Cassata'. *N.* 'Orangery'. *N.* 'Palmares'. *N.* 'Parisienne'.

PHEASANT EYE *Narcissus* 'Actaea'.

NARCISSI FOR BOWLS *Narcissus* 'Chinese Sacred Lily'. *N.* 'Grand Soleil D'Or'. *N.* 'Paperwhite'.

NERINE

Time to buy Bulbs, September–October, March–April. Mail order acceptable. Pot-grown, as available.
Where to find Bulbs, indoors on bulb display, loose or pre-packed. Pot-grown, outside in Perennials, Alpines or Bulbs.
Size Bulbs, 2¾–3 in (7–8 cm) min. dia., or in pots.
Foliage Deciduous. Pot-grown, dark green, December–March.
Bulbs Dry, firm and rot-free. Pots 4 in (10 cm) min. dia. Single bulb per pot.
Hints Any well-prepared soil. Plant near to fence or wall. *Nerine bowdenii* the only fully hardy form. Other forms need winter protection and best grown in pots under cover. Pot-grown, often look insipid and unhealthy.
Most widely available *Nerine bowdenii*. *N.* 'Pink Trumpet'.

ORNITHOGALUM
Star of Bethlehem
Time to buy Bulbs, August–October. Mail order acceptable. Pot-grown, as available.
Where to find Bulbs, indoors on bulb display, loose or pre-packed. Pot-grown, outside in Alpines or Bulbs.
Size Bulbs, 2 in (5 cm) dia., or in pots.
Foliage Deciduous. Pot-grown, sparse, dark green, March–May.
Bulbs Dry, firm and rot-free. Pots 4 in (10 cm) min. dia. Three to five bulbs per pot.
Hints Any well-prepared, well-drained soil. Allow adequate space.
Most widely available *Ornithogalum nutans*. *O. umbellatum*.

OXALIS
Time to buy Bulbs, August–October. Mail order acceptable. Pot-grown, as available.
Where to find Bulbs, indoors on bulb display, loose or pre-packed. Pot-grown, outside in Alpines or Bulbs.
Size Bulbs, 2½ in (6 cm) min. dia. or in pots.
Foliage Deciduous. Pot-grown, mid green, August.
Bulbs Dry, firm and rot-free. *Oxalis adenophylla* covered in long, brown, dry, root-like hairs. Pots 4 in (10 cm) min. dia. One to three bulbs per pot.
Hints Any well-prepared soil, plus extra organic material. Correct soil conditions important. *Oxalis* 'Iron Cross' grown in pots under protection.
Most widely available *Oxalis adenophylla*. *O. deppei*. *O.* 'Iron Cross'.

PUSCHKINIA
Time to buy Bulbs, August–October. Mail order acceptable. Pot-grown, as available.
Where to find Bulbs, indoors on bulb display, loose or pre-packed. Pot-grown, outside in Alpines or Bulbs.
Size Bulbs, 1½ in (4 cm) min. dia., or in pots.
Foliage Deciduous. Pot-grown, dark green, March–May.
Bulbs Dry, firm and rot free. Pots 3 in (8 cm) min. dia. Minimum five bulbs per pot.
Hints Any well-prepared soil, except extremely wet. Needs planting in large numbers to achieve good effect.
Most widely available *Puschkinia libanotica. P. l.* 'Alba'.

RANUNCULUS
Time to buy Tubers, August–October, March–May. Mail order acceptable. Pot-grown, as available.
Where to find Tubers, indoors on bulb display, loose or pre-packed. Pot-grown, outside in Alpines or Bulbs.
Size Tubers, 2 in (5 cm) min. dia., or in pots.
Foliage Deciduous. Pot-grown, mid green, April–June.
Tubers Dry, firm and rot-free. pots 4 in (10 cm) min. dia. Minimum three tubers per pot.
Hints Any well-prepared soil. Soak tubers in water for 24 hours prior to planting. If rodents are a problem, add one tablespoon of paraffin to one gallon of water and soak for twenty minutes. Can be difficult to establish.

SCILLA
Siberian Squill, Spring Squill
Time to buy Bulbs, August–November. Mail order acceptable. Pot-grown, as available.
Where to find Bulbs, indoors on bulb display, loose or pre-packed. Pot-grown, outside in Alpines or Bulbs.

Size Bulbs, 2¾–3 in (7–8 cm) min. dia., or in pots.
Foliage Deciduous. Pot-grown, dark green March–May.
Bulbs Dry, firm and rot-free. Pots 4 in (10 cm) min. dia. Minimum three bulbs per pot.
Hints Any well-prepared soil. *Scilla sibirica* can become invasive if planted in confined space. Give adequate space to develop.
Most widely available *Scilla sibirica* 'Alba'. *S. s.* 'Spring Beauty'. *S. tubergeniana.*

SPARAXIS TRICOLOUR
African Harlequin Flower
Time to buy Bulbs, August–October, March–April. Mail order is acceptable. Pot-grown, as available.
Where to find Bulbs, indoors on bulb display, loose or pre-packed. Pot-grown, outside in Alpines or Bulbs.
Size Bulbs, 2 in (5 cm) min. dia., or in pots.
Foliage Deciduous. Pot-grown, mid green, April–June.
Bulbs Dry, firm and rot-free. Pots 4 in (10 cm) min. dia. Minimum three bulbs per pot.
Hints Well-prepared, well-drained, warm, open soil in sunny position. If held over Christmas for spring purchasing may dehydrate. Only mixed colours offered.

STERNBERGIA LUTEA
Time to buy Bulbs, August–October. Mail order acceptable. Pot-grown, as available.
Where to find Bulbs, indoors on bulb display, loose or pre-packed. Pot-grown, outside in Alpines or Bulbs.
Size Bulbs, 2½ in (6 cm) dia., or in pots.
Foliage Deciduous, Pot-grown, dark green December–March.
Bulbs Dry, firm and rot-free. Pots 3 in (8 cm) min. dia. Single bulb per pot.

Hints Well-prepared, dry, well drained soil in sunny position. Any build-up of moisture in winter leads to rotting. May be scarce. Care must be taken with planting position.

TRILLIUM
Wake Robin
Time to buy Tubers, September–October. Mail order acceptable. Pot-grown, as available.
Where to find Not stocked as dormant tubers in garden centres. Pot-grown, tubers, outside in Alpines or Shade-loving Plants.
Size Tubers, mail order, minimum 2 in (5 cm) long, or in pots.
Foliage Deciduous. Pot-grown, mid to dark green, March–May.
Tubers Dry, firm and rot-free. Pots 5 in (12 cm) min. dia. One tuber per pot.
Hints Any well-prepared soil, plus extra organic material, in shade. Once planted do not disturb. Soil and aspect important. May be scarce.
Most widely available Trillium erectum. T. e. album. T. grandiflorum. T. luteum.

TRITELIA
Time to buy Bulbs, September–October. Mail order acceptable. Pot-grown, as available.
Where to find Bulbs, indoors on bulb display, loose or pre-packed. Pot-grown, outside in Alpines or Bulbs.
Size Bulbs, 2 in (5 cm) min. dia., or in pots.
Foliage Deciduous. Pot-grown, dark green March–April.
Bulbs Dry, firm and rot-free. Pots 4 in (10 cm) min. dia. Minimum three bulbs per pot.
Hints Well-prepared, well-drained, warm, open soil, plus extra organic material, in sunny position. May be scarce.
Most widely available Tritelia uniflora. T. 'Queen Fabiola'.

TULIPA
Tulip
Time to buy Bulbs, October–November. Mail order acceptable. Pot-grown, as available.
Where to find Bulbs, indoors on bulb display, sold loose by the purchaser filling a bag or container provided, pre-packed or in bulk. Pot-grown, outside in Perennials, Alpines or Bulbs.
Size All forms, except species, 5–6 in (12–15 cm) min. dia. Species 2½–3½ in (6–9 cm) min. dia., or in pots.
Foliage Deciduous. Pot-grown, mid green, April–May.
Bulbs Dry, firm and rot free. Pots 4 in (10 cm) min. dia. Minimum three bulbs per pot.
Hints Any well-prepared soil. In wet conditions, place a small amount of bulb fibre under each bulb. Dwarf forms better in windy or exposed areas. Container-grown, use good quality potting compost. Wide range. Specific forms may have to be sought from a number of outlets.
Most widely available
SINGLE EARLY Tulipa 'Apricot Beauty'. T. 'Bellona'. T. 'Brilliant Star'. T. 'Flair'. T. 'General De Wet'. T. 'Kiezerskroon'. T. 'Princess Irene'.
DOUBLE EARLY Tulipa 'Electra'. T. 'Mr van der Hoef'. T. 'Orange Nassau'. T. 'Peach Blossom'. T. 'Schoonoord'. T. 'Willemsoord'.
TRIUMPH Tulipa 'Athleet'. T. 'Aureola'. T. 'Cassini'. T. 'Douglas Bader'. T. 'Garden Party'. T. 'Lustige Witwe'. T. 'Orange Wonder'. T. 'Page Polka'. T. 'Sunray'.
DARWIN HYBRID Tulipa 'Apeldoorn'. T. 'A. Elite'. T. 'Elizabeth Arden'. T. 'Golden Apeldoorn'. T. 'Gudoshnik'. T. 'Jewel of Spring'. T. 'Orangezon'.
LATE SINGLE Tulipa 'Clara Butt'. T. 'Golden Harvest'. T. Halcro'. T. 'Picture'. T. 'Queen of Night'. T. 'Shirley'. T. 'Sorbet'.
LILY-FLOWERED Tulipa 'Aladdin'. T. 'Bal-

lade'. *T.* 'Burgundy'. *T.* 'China Pink'. *T.* 'Maytime'. *T.* 'Red Shine'. *T.* 'West Point'. *T.* 'White Triumphator'.

FRINGED *Tulipa* 'Bell Flower'. *T.* 'Blue Heron'. *T.* 'Burgundy Lace'. *T.* 'Fringed Beauty'. *T.* 'Maja'.

VIRIDIFLORA *Tulipa* 'Artist'. *T.* 'Dancing Show'. *T.* 'Doll's Minuet'. *T.* 'Green Eyes'. *T.* 'Greenland'. *T.* 'Hollywood'. *T.* 'Pimpernel'. *T.* 'Susan Oliver'.

REMBRANDT *Tulipa* 'Cordell Hull'.

PARROT *Tulipa* 'Black Parrot'. *T.* 'Blue Parrot'. *T.* 'Estella Rijnveld'. *T.* 'Fantasy'. *T.* 'Flaming Parrot'. *T.* 'Karel Doorman'. *T.* 'Orange Favourite'. *T.* 'Texas Gold'. *T.* 'White Parrot'.

LATE DOUBLE *Tulipa* 'Allegretto'. *T.* 'Gold Medal'. *T.* 'May Wonder'. *T.* 'Mount Tacoma'. *T.* 'Miranda'.

DWARF – KAUFMANNIANA *Tulipa* 'Cho-pin'. *T.* 'Early Harvest'. *T.* 'Fair Lady'. *T.* 'Fashion'. *T.* 'Gaiety'. *T.* 'Gluck'. *T.* 'Heart's Delight'. *T.* 'Jeantime'. *T.* 'Scarlet Baby'. *T.* 'Shakespeare'. *T.* 'Stresa'. *T.* 'The First'.

DWARF – FOSTERIANA *Tulipa* 'Dandela'. *T.* 'Concerto'. *T.* 'Grand Prix'. *T.* 'Hit Parade'. *T.* 'Orange Emperor'. *T.* 'Princeps'. *T.* 'Red Emperor'. *T.* 'White Emperor'. *T.* Zombie'.

DWARF – GRIEGII *Tulipa* 'Ali Baba'. *T.* 'Cape Cod'. *T.* 'Easter Surprise'. *T.* 'Jockey Cap'. *T.* 'Lady Diana'. *T.* 'Orange Elite'. *T.* 'Pandour'. *T.* 'Queen Ingrid'. *T.* 'Red Riding Hood'. *T.* 'Sweet Lady'. *T.* 'Yellow Dawn'. *T.* 'Zampa'.

SPECIES *Tulipa* 'Acuminata'. *T. linifolia.* *T.* 'Marjoletti'. *T. praestans* var. 'Tubergens'. *T. pulchella. T. stellata. T. tarda. T. turkestanica. T. urmiensis.*

Spring/Summer-Planted Bulbs Corms, Rhizomes and Tubers

The range of material in this group is very diverse, and covers subjects as wide as tubers (Dahlias), corms (Begonias), rhizomes (Lily of the Valley, Convallaria) and bulbs (Chincherinchee, Ornithogalum) and they are often displayed in nurseries and garden centres together.

The interest and colour that they add to the summer planting cannot be overstated. Species such as Dahlias, and Begonias and to a lesser extent Gladiolus and Gloxinia can become enthusiasts' plants and those who grow them must be aware that they may also become addicted.

The not so well-known bulbs such as Crinum, Crocosmia and Acidanthera should not be overlooked; however, some caution is required regarding soil and aspect.

Some tubers, such as Canna offer additions to the summer bedding displays. On the whole they grow in most soils but need good drainage and sunny aspects.

The range is ever-increasing and you may have to shop around for certain species. Some are available both in the autumn and spring planting periods; however, care must be taken to ensure that correct over-winter storage has been used and to make sure they are not soft, dehydrated or showing any signs of rot. The following list covers those bulbs, corms and tubers which are sold both in the spring and autumn: Allium, Anemone, Freesia, Galanthus, Galtonia, Ixia, Lilium, Nerine, Ranunculus, Sparaxis, Trillium, Triteleia.

All will need good soil preparation when grown in the garden, digging to a depth of at least 9 in (23 cm) with organic material added.

If planting in containers, use a good quality potting compost.

ACIDANTHERA MURIELLE BICOLOR
Peacock Orchid
Time to buy Bulbs, January–April. Mail order acceptable. Pot-grown, as available.
Where to find Bulbs, indoors on bulb display, loose or pre-packed. Pot-grown, outside in Perennials or Bulbs.
Size 2½–3 in (6–8 cm) dia., or in pots.

Foliage Deciduous. Pot-grown, spring/summer, mid green. Yellowing towards autumn.
Bulbs Dry, firm and rot-free. Pots 4 in (10 cm) min. dia. Maximum three bulbs per pot.
Hints Well-prepared dry, warm, neutral to acid soil. Hardiness suspect. Needs careful positioning.

BEGONIAS
Time to buy Corms, March–May. Mail order acceptable. Pot-grown, May–June. May be found as fully grown house plants.
Where to find Corms, indoors on spring bulb display, loose or pre-packed. Pot-grown, outside in Summer Bedding.
Size Corms, double, pendula and frimbriata, 1–2½ in (3–6 cm) dia. Corms maxima, double-flowered pendula and non-stop. 1½–2 in (4–5 cm) dia. Others 1½–2½ in (4–6 cm) dia., or in pots.
Foliage Deciduous. Spring/summer, dark or purple green.
Corms Dry, firm and rot-free. Pots, 3½ in (9 cm) min. dia. One corm per pot. Grown as house-plants, which can be planted out, pots 4–5 in (10–12 cm).
Hints Any well-prepared soil, plus extra organic material. Containers, good quality potting compost. Start dormant corms in pots before planting out. Corms take 8 weeks to shoot. Pot-grown, avoid planting until spring frosts have finished. Avoid any showing signs of mildew. Must be stored in frost-free environment.
Most widely available
DOUBLE, PENDULA, FRIMBRIATA, MAXIMA, SENSATION AND NON-STOP BEGONIAS Crimson, orange, pink, white, yellow.
OTHER BEGONIAS *Begonia* 'Bouton de Rose'. *B.* 'Cameliaflora'. *B.* 'Marmorata'. *B.* 'Marginata Crispa' (yellow). *B.* 'Marginata Crispa' (white).

CALLA AETHIOPICA syn.
Zantendeschia
Arum Lily
Time to buy Root rhizomes, February–April. Mail order acceptable. Pot-grown, April–June.
Where to find Root rhizomes, indoors on spring bulb display, loose or pre-packed. Pot-grown, outside in Summer Bedding.
Size Root rhizomes, min. 2 in (5 cm) long.
Foliage Deciduous. Spring/summer, green or purple-green.

Root rhizomes Dry, firm and rot-free. Pots 5 in (12 cm) min. dia. with one per pot.
Hints Organic and moist well-prepared soil. Must not dry out. May be scarce.
Most widely available *Calla* 'Black-Eyed Beauty'. *C.* 'Bridal Blush'. *C.* 'Cameo'. *C.* 'Harvest Moon'. *C.* 'Lavender Petit'. *C.* 'Mauron Daisy'. *C.* 'Shell Pink'.

CANNA
Indian Lily
Time to buy Root rhizomes, February–April. Mail order acceptable. Pot-grown, April–June.
Where to find Root rhizomes, indoors on Spring Bulb display, loose or pre-packed. Pot-grown, outside in Summer Bedding.
Size Root rhizomes, 2–3 in (5–8 cm) long. 1 in (3 cm) min. dia., or in pots.
Foliage Deciduous. Spring/summer, green or purple-green.
Root rhizomes Dry, firm and rot-free. Pots 5 in (12 cm) min. dia. with one root rhizome.
Hints Planted in pots in good quality potting compost, kept under protection, planted when spring frosts have finished. May be scarce. Store in cool, frost and rodent-free environment. Not hardy.
Most widely available *Canna indica* 'Black Knight'. *C. i* 'Lucifer'. *C. i* 'Orchid'. *C. i* 'Picasso'. *C. i* 'The President'. *C. i* 'Wyoming'. *C. i* 'Yellow Humbert'.

CONVALLARIA
Lily of the Valley
Time to buy Root rhizomes ('pips'), February–March. Mail order acceptable. Pot-grown, as available.
Where to find Pips outside, covered with moist peat, with overhead protection. Pot-grown, outside in Perennials or Alpines.
Size Pips, 8–10 in (20–25 cm) long. Single bud at top, or in pots.
Foliage Deciduous. Spring/summer, mid green.
Root rhizomes Pips moist and firm. Pots

3 in (8 cm) min. dia. Normally singly.
Hints Any well-prepared soil, plus extra organic material. Shady, moist situation, with no disturbance from other cultivation operations. Pot-grown pips rarely look healthy.
Most widely available *Convallaria majalis. C. rosea.*

CRINUM
Elephant Lily
Time to buy Bulbs, March–April. Mail order acceptable. Pot-grown, as available.
Where to find Bulbs, indoors on spring bulb display, loose or pre-packed. Pot-grown, in Perennials or Bulbs.
Size Minimum 8 in (20 cm) dia. and 15 in (40 cm) length, or in pots.
Foliage Deciduous. May–September, mid green.
Bulbs Dry, firm and rot-free. Surface may be greasy. Pots 5 in (12 cm) min. dia.
Hints Any well-prepared soil, plus extra organic material. May be scarce. Research overall size.
Most widely available *Crinum × powelli. C. p. alba.*

CROCOSMIA
Montbretia
Time to buy Bulbous rhizomes, March–May. Mail order acceptable. Pot-grown, as available.
Where to find Bulbous rhizomes, indoors on bulb display, pre-packed. Pot-grown, outside in Perennials.
Size 4–5 in (10–12 cm) dia., or in pots.
Foliage Deciduous. May–October, light green. Yellowing from July.
Rhizomes Dry, firm and rot-free. Pots 4 in (10 cm) min. dia. Three per pot.
Hints Any well-prepared soil, plus extra organic material. *Crocosmia masonarum* is the most widely offered. Can become invasive. Research overall size.
Most widely available *Crocosmia* 'Ci-tronella'. *C.* 'Emily McKenzie'. *C.* 'Lucifer'. *C. masonarum.*

DAHLIAS
Time to buy, Tubers, March–May. Mail order acceptable. Pot-grown or one-year cuttings, May–June.
Where to find Tubers, indoors on spring bulb display, loose or pre-packed. Pot-grown or one-year cuttings, outside under limited cover in Summer Bedding.
Size Tubers, 2 in (5 cm) long min. and ½ in (1 cm) min. dia. Each clump minimum two tubers, or in pot.
Foliage Deciduous. Pot-grown or cuttings, mid green.
Tubers Dry, firm and rot-free. No signs of white fungus. Pot-grown or one-year cuttings, pots 4 in (10 cm) min. dia.
Hints Any well-prepared soil, plus extra organic material. Do not plant until spring frosts have finished. Copious supplies of water needed. Wide range. Tubers should be stored in cool, dry, frost and rodent-free environment. Rooted cuttings not always offered.
Most widely available
CACTUS 'Alfred Grille', 'Bach'. 'Berger's Record'. 'Couleur Spectacle'. 'Gold Crown'. 'Good Earth'. 'Helga'. 'Herbert Smith'. 'Ludwig Helfert'. 'My Love'. 'Orfeo'. 'Popular Guest'. 'Purple Gem'. 'Vulcan'. 'Vuurvogel'.
DECORATIVE 'Arabian Night'. 'Diamond'. 'Duet'. 'Edinburgh'. 'Feu Celeste'. 'Garden Wonder'. 'Gerrie Hoek'. 'Glory of Heemstede'. 'Golden Emblem'. 'Kelvin Floodlight'. 'Lavender Perfection'. 'Majuba'. 'Procyon'. 'Rosella'. 'Thomas Edison'.
POMPON 'Brilliant Eye'. 'New Baby'. 'Potgieter'. 'Stolze Von Berlin'. 'White Aster'.
DWARF BEDDING – BALL 'Bantling'. 'Deepest Yellow'. 'Peter'. 'Red Cap'. 'Warmunda'. 'Fascination'.
DWARF BEDDING – BORDER 'Bonnie Esperance'. 'Little Tiger'. 'Musette'. 'Park Princess'. 'Red Pigmy'.

DWARF AND BEDDING 'Chessy'. 'G. F. Hemerik'. 'Honey'. 'Reddy'.

ANEMONE FLOWERED 'Honey'. 'Siemen Doorenbosch'.

EUCOMIS BICOLOR
Pineapple Plant
Time to buy Bulbs, February–April. Mail order acceptable.
Where to find Indoors on spring bulb display, pre-packed.
Size 6 in (15 cm) min. dia.
Foliage Deciduous.
Bulbs Dry, firm and rot-free.
Hints Any well-prepared soil, plus extra organic material. Container-grown, good quality potting compost. Widely available. Not hardy. Grow in pots initially and plant when spring frosts have finished.

GALTONIA CANDICANS
Autumn Hyacinth
Time to buy Bulbs, February–March. Mail order acceptable. Pot-grown, as available.
Where to find Bulbs, indoors on spring bulb display, loose or pre-packed, normally in three's. Pot-grown, outside in Perennials.
Size Bulbs, $6\frac{1}{2}$–$7\frac{1}{2}$ in (16–18 cm) dia., or in pots.
Foliage Deciduous. Pot-grown, mid green July–December. Foliage yellowing from October.
Bulbs Dry, firm and rot-free. Pots 4 in (10 cm) min. dia. One bulb per pot.
Hints Any well-prepared soil. Worth planting for its flowers. Bulbs large.

GLADIOLI
Gladiolus
Time to buy Corms, February–May. Mail order acceptable. *Gladioli nana* only, pot-grown as available.
Where to find Corms, indoors on bulb display, loose by number or pre-packed. *Gladioli nana*, pot-grown, outside in Alpines or Perennials.

Size Corms, Primulinus and Butterfly, 4–5 in (10–12 cm) dia. Large flowering, $5\frac{1}{2}$ in (13 cm) dia. *Gladioli nana*, $2\frac{3}{4}$ in (7–8 cm) dia., or in pots.
Foliage Deciduous. *Gladioli nana*, pot-grown, green May–August. Yellowing from September.
Corms Dry, firm and rot-free. *Gladioli nana* pots 4 in (10 cm) min. dia., three corms per pot.
Hints Any well-prepared soil, plus extra organic material. All forms except *Gladioli nana* lifted in autumn, stored over winter. Wide range. All forms except *Gladioli nana* will require caning.
Most widely available
PRIMULINUS FORMS *Gladioli primulinus* 'Leonore'. *G. p.* 'Perky'. *G. p.* 'Robin'. *G. p.* 'Sabu'. *G. p.* 'White City'. *G. p.* 'Mixed'.
BUTTERFLY FORMS *Gladioli* 'Dancing Doll'. *G.* 'Jackpot'. *G.* 'Jupiter'. *G.* 'Little Green Jade'. *G.* 'Skipper'. *G.* 'Wisecrack'. *G.* 'Mixed'.
LARGE FLOWERING FORMS *Gladioli* 'Ben Trovato'. *G.* 'Blue Conqueror'. *G.* 'Fidelio'. *G.* 'Flowersong'. *G.* 'Hunting Song'. *G.* Mary Housley'. *G.* 'Nova Lux'. *G.* 'Oscar'. *G.* 'Peter Pears'. *G.* 'Praha'. *G.* 'Snowprincess'. *G.* 'Traderhorn'. *G.* 'Wind Song'. *G.* 'Woodpecker'. *G.* 'Mixed'.
NANUS (DWARF) FORMS *Gladioli nana* 'Amanda'. *G. n.* 'Charm'. *G. n.* 'Elvira'. *G. n.* 'Nymph'. *G. n.* 'Robinetta'. *G. n.* 'The Bridge'. *G. n.* 'Mixed'.

GLOXINIA
Time to buy Corms, February–April. Mail order acceptable. Pot-grown, April–July.
Where to find Corms, indoors on spring bulb display, loose or pre-packed. Pot-grown, outside under limited cover, in Summer Bedding or indoors in House Plants.
Size Corms, $2\frac{1}{2}$–3 in (6–8 cm) dia., or in pots.
Foliage Deciduous. Pot-grown, dark green, April–September.

Corms Dry, firm and rot-free. Pots 5 in (12 cm) min. dia. singly.

Hints Well-prepared soil, plus sedge peat. Best container-grown. For outside use, start corms in pots first and plant out when spring frosts have finished. Not winter hardy. Dislikes storage. Purchase early and store in dark, frost and rodent-free environment.

Most widely available Gloxinia 'Blanche De Meru'. G. 'Etoile De Feu'. G. 'Holly-wood'. G. 'Kaiser Friedrich'. G. 'Kaiser Wilhelm'. G. 'Mont Blanc'. G. 'Tigrina Red'.

ORNITHOGALUM THYRSOIDES
Chincherinchee

Time to buy Bulbs, February–March. Mail order acceptable. Pot-grown, as available.

Where to find Bulbs, indoors on spring bulb display, loose or pre-packed. Pot-grown, outside in Perennials or Alpines.

Size Bulbs, 2–2½ in (5–6 cm) dia., or in pots.

Foliage Deciduous. Pot-grown, mid-green May–August. Yellowing from July.

Bulbs Dry, firm and rot-free. Pots 4 in (10 cm) min. dia. Three bulbs per pot min.

Hints Any well-prepared soil, plus extra organic material. One of the most attractive of scented summer bulbs.

PLEIONE FORMOSANUM
Garden Orchid

Time to buy Root tubers, February–April. Mail order acceptable. Pot-grown, as available.

Where to find Root tubers, indoors on spring bulb display, pre-packed. Pot-grown, outside in Alpines.

Size Root tubers, minimum 1 in (3 cm) long, pencil-thick, or in pots.

Foliage Deciduous. Pot-grown, spring/summer, mid to dark green.

Tubers Dry, firm and rot-free. Pots 3 in (8 cm) min. dia. One tuber per pot.

Hints Best grown in containers, flowered under protection or outside only in summer. Not hardy. Careful winter protection needed. Tubers purchased as soon as available and potted up.

SCHIZOSTYLIS
Kaffir Lily

Time to buy Bulbs, February–April. Mail order acceptable. Pot-grown, as available.

Where to find Bulbs, indoors on bulb display, loose or pre-packed. Pot-grown, outside in Perennials or Bulbs.

Size Bulbs, 2½–3 in (6–8 cm) dia., or in pots.

Foliage Deciduous. Pot-grown, dark green, April–September. Yellowing from September.

Bulbs Dry, firm and rot-free. Pots 5 in (12 cm) min. dia. Minimum three bulbs per pot.

Hints Any well-prepared soil in sunny position. May be scarce. Offered as perennials and the best form in which to purchase.

Most widely available Schizostylis coccinea. S. 'Mrs Hegarty'. S. 'Viscountess Byng'.

TIGRIDIA
Mexican Shell Flower

Time to buy Bulbs, February–April. Mail order acceptable. Pot-grown, as available.

Where to find Bulbs, indoors on bulb display, pre-packed. Pot-grown, outside in Perennials, Alpines or Bulbs.

Size Bulbs, 3 in (8 cm) dia., or in pots.

Foliage Deciduous. Pot-grown, spring/summer, mid green. Yellowing September.

Bulbs Dry, firm and rot-free. Pots 4 in (10 cm) min. dia. Minimum three bulbs per pot.

Hints Well-prepared warm, well-drained soil in sunny position. Hardiness suspect. Needs careful positioning. May be scarce.

TUBEROSE HYMENOCALLIS NARCISSIFLORA syn. *Hymenocallis calathina*, syn. *Ismene*, syn. *Ismene andreana*, syn. *Ismene quitoensis*, syn. *Leptochiton quitoensis*

Peruvian Daffodil or Peruvian Narcissus

Time to buy Bulbs, February–April. Mail order acceptable.

Where to find Indoors in bulb display.

Size Bulbs, 2½–3 in (6–8 cm) dia.

Foliage Deciduous.

Bulbs Dry, firm and rot-free.

Hints Well-prepared soil in sheltered position. Container-grown, good potting compost. Best grown in pots and kept under cover in winter. Rarely winter hardy. May be scarce.

ZEPHYRANTHES ROBUSTUS

Time to buy Bulbs, February–April. Mail order acceptable. Pot-grown as available.

Where to find Bulbs, indoors on bulb display, pre-packed. Pot-grown outside in Perennials or Alpines.

Size Bulbs, 2½–3 in (6–8 cm) dia., or in pots.

Foliage Deciduous. Pot-grown, mid green, June–September.

Bulbs Dry, firm and rot-free. Pots 5 in (12 cm) min. dia. Minimum three bulbs per pot.

Hints Any well-prepared soil in warm, sheltered, sunny position. Hardiness suspect. May be scarce.

Biennials

Biennials cover two specific sectors of plants that are purchased and planted at approximately the same time. First are the winter-flowering bedding, plants such as Wallflowers, Polyanthus, Winter Primroses and Pansies. Second are those that flower in the early and mid summer, such as Foxgloves, Canterbury Bells and Hollyhocks.

Biennials are one of the most often overlooked of all plant groups. They are raised from seed, sown in early to mid summer either in the soil or in trays; then, in both cases, the ensuing plants are planted in their flowering position in autumn for flowering in the following spring or summer.

The need to purchase and plant in the autumn, when winter seems to be approaching, is often a deterrent. You may fear the effects of winter cold, frost and snow but in actual fact these plants are able to withstand all of these conditions. They might look a little limp when first planted (particularly Wallflowers) and they may look frosted and uncomfortable during the winter, but once the spring warms up, root-systems which they made after planting force them into growth, and an abundant display of flowers will follow.

Many biennials reflect the old cottage gardens, particularly plants such as Foxgloves, Hollyhocks and Canterbury Bells which are being more widely used today to remind us of those bygone years.

Once flowered, they die, and that is the end of their life-cycle; but amongst them are some of the most vivid and bright of all the spring colours and some of the most elegant and artistic flowers of the early summer.

As with all plants, soil preparation is important, both in the seed bed and in the final position: a depth of preparation in excess of 9 in (23 cm) is not a luxury. For seed raising in trays, use a good quality seed compost.

CHERIANTHUS ALLIONII
Wallflowers (bedding)
Time to buy Bare-rooted, freshly lifted September.
Where to find In Biennials or Winter Bedding.
Size Bare-rooted, min. 6 in (15 cm) long, bundles in ten's. Tray-grown 3–4 in (8–10 cm) high.
Foliage Evergreen. Mid green. Avoid plants showing yellowing. Tray-grown, mid green.
Roots Bare-rooted, good fibrous root system. Tray-grown, established.
Hints Any well-prepared soil. Do not plant after November.
Most widely available Cherianthus × allionii 'Blood Red'. C. a. 'Cloth of Gold'. C. a. 'Eastern Queen'. C. a. 'Fair Lady Mixed'. C. a. 'Fire King'. C. a. 'Golden

Bedder'. *C. a.* 'Ivory White'. *C. a.* 'Persian Carpet'. *C. a.* 'Tom Thumb Mixed'. *C. a.* 'Vulcan'.

BIENNIALS (spring and summer flowering)
Time to buy Root clumps, tray-grown, August–October. Pot-grown, August–April.
Where to find Outside in Biennials or Winter Bedding.
Size August–October, 2 in (5 cm) min. height. Spring, 4 in (10 cm) min.
Foliage Evergreen. Mid green.
Roots Root clumps, good fibrous root system. Pots 3 in (8 cm) min. dia.
Hints Any well-prepared soil. Offered January–February when conditions are unsuitable. Avoid plants that have been lifted for some time.
Most widely available *Althaea* (Hollyhock). *Aquilegia* (Columbine. Monk's Cap. Lady's Bonnet). *Campanula medium* (Canterbury Bell). *Dianthus barbatus* (Sweet William). *Digitalis* (Foxglove). *Primula vulgaris* (Primrose). *Verbascum bombyciferum* (Giant Mullein). *Viola × wittrockiana* (Spring-flowering Pansy). *Viola × wittrockiana* (Summer Flowering Pansy).

BIENNIALS (winter and spring flowering)
Time to buy Root clumps or box-grown, August–April, except January. Seed from May.
Where to find Outside in Winter Bedding or Biennials. Seed indoors on seed racks.
Size Root clumps, pot or box-grown. August–September, 2 in (5 cm) min. height. Spring, 4 in (10 cm) min. Seed in packets.
Foliage Evergreen. Mid green.
Roots Root clumps, good fibrous root system. Pots 3 in (8 cm) min. dia.
Hints Any well-prepared soil. Root clumps, August–December for preference. Container-grown use good quality potting compost.
Most widely available *Bellis perennis* (Double Daisy). *Brassica* (Ornamental Cabbage). *Cherianthus* (Wallflower) – see separate entry. *Cherianthus × allionii* (Siberian Wallflower). *Myosotis alpestris* (Forget-me-Not). *Primula auricula*. *Primula variabilis* (Polyanthus). *Primula vulgaris* hybrids (Ornamental Primrose). *Viola cornuta*. *Viola × wittrockiana* (Winter Flowering Pansy).

Summer Bedding

The range of new forms of bedding plants seems endless with increased colour, sizes and performance. Even the packaging they are presented in is constantly changing. The old seed trays can still be found, but rigid and flimsy plastic, polystyrene and even paper trays are becoming more common.

Trays are sectioned with various numbers and sizes of compartments. A recent innovation is plugs, where small plants, such as *Begonia semperflorens*, are grown in individual holes in a large tray, ready for growing-on.

Plants are offered for sale at different ages, from seedlings and plugs to finished trays or pot-grown plants but almost all are not frost hardy and must be kept under protection until all fear of frost has passed, Antirrhinums, Mesembryanthemums, Lobelia and Allysum are exceptions and can be planted from mid April onwards.

Some forms will be grown in trays, others in pots with an amount of overlap in between. The following entries attempt to define the most suitable methods for each form.

These plants are frequently used in traditional bedding schemes but spot-planting and infilling in newly planted shrub and mixed borders is another worthwhile use. That they are also ideal for use in tubs, window boxes and hanging baskets, goes without saying.

Comparing the price of the units is not always simple in garden centres. You need to count how many plants you are buying and note the size of the plant you are getting for your money. You should shop around. Never, never, go into a garden centre and split a tray, unless it clearly indicates that this is acceptable, likewise, never take individual plants out of full trays.

Information regarding individual plants can sometimes be difficult to obtain. The range of varieties is ever-changing. It is often a good idea to consult the supplying garden centre for information regarding an individual variety. If they are not in a position to give the information at once, they can at least contact their supplier for the answer.

Planning a display and obtaining the chosen material can be difficult. There are still some nurseries and garden centres which will take orders, and hold plants until you are ready for planting, but these are decreasing. It is a case of going to the garden centre, seeing what is ready from mid April onwards and buying as seen; remembering that some, such as Zinnia's, will not be available until well into June.

Plants in trays may be better value, but from June onwards, more and more plants will be pot-grown. For instant effect, they can be purchased well into August and still give good results.

If you require maximum effect and growth from bedding plants, preparation of the soil is important and digging to a depth of 9 in (23 cm) and incorporating adequate organic material is a must. Feeding them regularly through the summer with a liquid fertilizer will keep the new growth and flowers always coming.

When bedding plants are grown in containers, hanging baskets or window boxes, use a good quality potting compost and provide good drainage, regular watering and feeding.

SUMMER BEDDING (spring planted and offered in individual pots)
Time to buy Pot-grown, May, when fear of frost has passed.
Where to find Outside in Bedding or under limited cover.
Size 2–12 in (5–30 cm) depending on type.
Foliage Fresh, well coloured.
Roots Pots 3 in (8 cm) min. dia.
Hints Any well-prepared soil, plus extra organic material. Hanging baskets or containers, use good quality potting compost. Wide range. Information labels limited. Research overall size.
Most widely available Amaranthus. Begonia. Brassica (Ornamental Cabbage). Calceolaria. Calendula. Campanula (bedding forms). Celosia. Cineraria (bedding forms). Coleus. Cordyline. Dahlia (bedding forms). Fuchsia. Gazania. Geranium. Gerbera. Helichrysum. Heliotropium. Impatiens (Busy Lizzie). *Impatiens* 'New Guinea Strain'. Ipomoea. Kochia (Burning Bush). Lavatera. Lobelia. Nasturtium. *Parthenium* 'Aureum'. Ricinus. Rudbeckia (annual forms). Salpiglossis. Salvia. Sanvitalia. Schizanthus. Stocks (Dwarf Ten Week). *Thunbergia.* Thymophylla. Torenia. Vinca (bedding forms). Viola (bedding forms). Zinnia.

Range ever-increasing, and the above is a general selection.

SUMMER BEDDING (normally offered in trays or multi-unit containers)
Time to buy Trays, strips or multi-unit containers, May–June, when fear of frost has passed. (Antirrhinum, Lobelia and Mesembryanthemum can tolerate limited frost.)
Where to find Outside in Bedding.
Foliage Avoid drawn, weak or dehydrated plants.
Roots Trays contain 20–40 plants. Number, and size of tray will vary. New tray systems arrive every year.
Hints Any well-prepared soil, plus extra organic material. Hanging baskets and containers, use good quality potting compost. Often sold before hardened off. Wide range available. Use pot-grown, June onwards. Not always labelled clearly.
Most widely available Ageratum. Alyssum. Antirrhinum. Aster. Begonia. Candytuft. Carnation. Chrysanthemum. Dahlia. Dianthus. Godetia. Marigold. Mesembryanthemum. Mimulus. Nemesia. Nicotiana. Pansy. Petunia. *Phlox drummondii.* Sweet Pea. Tagetes. Verbena.
Wide range available: above is a general selection.

Flower and Grass Seed

Many plants can be sold as hardy annuals, where the seed is purchased from mid-winter onwards and sown, as per directions on the packet, directly into its flowering position in the garden. A hardy annual germinates, is thinned, grows and flowers, re-seeds itself *in situ* for the following year, then dies at the first frost to be replaced by the new seedlings in the following spring.

Some forms can become invasive, although it is a very nice invasive effect to have, and the plants are relatively easy to control simply by physically removing.

They can be planted in planned borders where hardy annuals are used solely for design reasons, but they also make very good in-fillers, particularly in newly planted shrub or mixed borders. Some forms can be encouraged to become 'wild'.

Few other 'plants' sold at garden centres carry as much instruction on the packet as hardy annuals and this should always be read and adhered to, in particular instruction on soil preparation.

Lawn seed is included in this section. There is a wide range available. Care should be taken to select exactly the right seed for the desired effect as should the correct preparation and sowing season which is indicated on the packet.

HARDY ANNUALS

Time to buy Seeds in packets, January onwards. Follow instructions on packet. Also grown as summer bedding plants in trays and pots, when frosts have finished.

Where to find Seed, indoors on seed racks. Tray or pot-grown, with Summer Bedding.

Size Seed in packets. Box or pot-grown 1½– 3½ in (4–9 cm) tall. Trays contain twenty– forty plants. Pots, 3 in (8 cm) min. dia.

Foliage Tray or pot-grown, mid green. No damage or wilting.

Hints Any well-prepared soil. Sowing details as packet instructions. Seed sown directly will need thinning. Sow in narrow drills or broadcast. With latter, sow some in short lines so seedlings can be identified. Some can become evasive.

Most widely available Acroclinium*. Ageratum*. Alyssum*. Antirrhinum*. Calendula*. *Campanula carpatica**. Candytuft. Clarkia. Clary. Cornflower. Eschscholzia. Godetia. Larkspur. Lavatera. Limnanthes (Poached Egg Plant). Linaria (Toadflax). Linum (Flax). Nasturtium. Nigella (Love-in-a-Mist). Phlox*. Scabious. Stock. Sunflower.

Collections of more than one species may be offered: a good purchase as long as space is available.

*May benefit from being grown under protection.

GRASS SEED

Time to buy Pre-packed in advance of recommended sowing time.

Where to find Inside, normally adjacent to seed display or lawn care products.

Size Sold by weight, 500 g, 1 kg, 2 kg, 10 kg, or 25 kg.

Lawn types Offered with or without rye grass. Mixtures with rye grass for play areas, sports fields and rough grass. Without rye grass for bowling greens, golf greens, prestige grass areas, lesser prestige and general purpose areas. Special mixtures for shady conditions and kits for repairing lawns. Descriptions and usages on package. Rye least expensive.

Hints Well-prepared by deep digging and soil raked to fine seed sowing bed (tilth). Sow April–June or August–September, at $1\frac{1}{2}$–2 oz. per square yard (45–60 g per square metre).

Vegetables

It is hard to prove that vegetables grown in one's own garden are any better or any less expensive than those purchased from the supermarket but there is certainly a possibility of more flavour from fresher material which is known to be organically grown, and the satisfaction of self-sufficiency is always a reward.

In the main, vegetables are either grown directly from seed in pots or trays, or bare-rooted pre-grown plants. Onions, potatoes and artichokes are normally grown from dry bulbs or tubers. It is embarrassing for a new gardener to ask for a vegetable in the wrong season and conditions: the following entries attempt to alleviate this problem.

Seed has instructions on the packet and is available from mid-winter. Be careful to prepare soil and sow as per instructions. Any deviation may lead to disappointment.

Pre-packed potatoes, onions and so on also carry information regarding their cultivation needs. Cabbage plants are sold bare-rooted in bundles and do not need protection other than the prevention of drying out.

Non-hardy plants, such as tomatoes, mushrooms, marrows, and cucumbers must be planted outside after all danger of spring frosts has passed. Some, however, can be grown in heated or unheated greenhouses and this can bring the crop forward. Many vegetables can also be grown under the protection of frames and cloches, again extending the season.

Soil preparation, plant rotation, specific feeding needs and requirements of each of the crops should be taken into account and referred to. The tendency, particularly with seeds, is to purchase too many, either of varieties or quantity. Careful pre-planning saves wasted expenditure.

ASPARAGUS OFFICINALIS
Time to buy Pot-grown, March–June. Bare-rooted root tubers and pre-packs March–April. Do not purchase outside of this period. Should not be lifted more than twenty-one days before purchase.
Where to find Pot-grown and bare-rooted, outside in Vegetables. Pre-packs under limited cover.
Size Bare-rooted and pre-packs, 4 in (10 cm) long, minimum two-years-old.

Foliage Deciduous. Pot-grown, mid green, soft frond-like.
Roots Stored in moist organic compost. Pots 4 in (10 cm) min. dia.
Hints Any soil. Preparation important – take reference. Avoid one-year-old plants. Short planting season.
Most widely available Asparagus officinalis 'Connover's Colossal'. A. o. 'Martha Washington'. A. o. 'Sutton's Perfection'.

AUBERGINE
Egg Plant

Time to buy Seed, not later than February. Pot-grown, for greenhouse March–April. For outside when frosts have finished.

Where to find Indoors on vegetable seed rack or outside under limited cover in Vegetables.

Size Seeds. Pot-grown, 2–4 in (5–10 cm) high.

Foliage Pot-grown, mid green, fleshy, lush.

Roots Pots 3 in (8 cm) min. dia.

Hints Ideal for pots and growbags, both indoors and outside. To grow in heated greenhouse, plant March; unheated greenhouse from April; outside when frosts have finished. All will need caning. Use good quality potting compost. Check base of stem for root rot (botrytis). Often not labelled with variety.

Most widely available Aubergine 'Black Prince'. A. 'Dusky'. A. 'Large-fruited Slice-Rite No. 23', A. 'Long Purple'. A. 'Moneymaker'. A. 'Rima'.

BORECOLE
Time to buy Seed in packets from January.

Where to find Indoors on seed racks.

Size Seed in packets.

Hints Sown directly into any well-prepared soil as instructions on packet. Early-sown can fail in wet spring.

Most widely available 'Dwarf Green Curled'. 'Fribor'. 'Pentland Brig'. 'Tall Green Curled'. 'Thousand Head'.

BEANS
Time to buy Seed, from January. Tray or pot-grown when frosts have finished. Broad Beans, pot-grown from April, or sown, October–March.

Where to find Indoors on seed racks. Tray or pot-grown, outside under limited cover.

Size Seed in packets. Trays and pots, 4 in (10 cm) high. Trays up to forty plants. Three plants per pot.

Foliage Trays or pot-grown, mid to dark green, clean, fresh and fleshy.

Roots Pots 3 in (8 cm) min. dia.

Hints As instructions on packet in any well-prepared soil, plus extra organic material. Soak seeds in water for twelve hours before sowing. Runner beans need staking. Dwarf, broad and runner beans need control for black fly from an early stage. Protection from small rodents may be needed. May not be named. Short planting season.

Most widely available

BROAD BEANS 'Aquadulce'. 'Colossal'. 'Giant Exhibition Longpod'. 'Hylon'. 'Imperial White Long Pod'. 'Imperial White Windsor'. 'Masterpiece Green Long Pot'. 'Meteor'. 'Red Epicure'. 'Reina Blanca'. 'The Sutton' (Dwarf). 'Witkiem Major'.

FRENCH BEANS (Kidney Beans) 'Blue Lake'. 'Garrafal Oro'. 'Hunter'. 'Kinghorn Wax'. 'Masterpiece'. 'Purple Queen'. 'Purple Podded'. 'Sigmacropper'. 'Sprite'. 'Tendercrop'. 'Tendergreen'. 'The Prince'.

RUNNER BEANS 'Achievement'. 'Best of All'. 'Butter'. 'Bokkie'. 'Crusader'. 'Enorma'. 'Erecta'. 'Goliath'. 'Kelvedon Marvel'. 'Gower Emperor'. 'Mergoles'. 'Painted Lady'. 'Polestar'. 'Prizewinner'. 'Purple Podded'. 'Red Knight'. 'Scarlet Emperor'. 'Stringline'. 'Sunset'. 'White Achievement'.

RUNNER BEANS (STRINGLESS) 'Butler'. 'Mergoles'. 'Pickwick'. 'Polestar'.

SCARLET RUNNER 'Multiflorus'.

BEETS and similar root crops
Time to buy Seed in packets from January.

Where to find Indoors on seed racks.

Size Seed in packets.

Hints Sown directly into well-prepared soil as instructions on packet. Early sown first crops can fail in wet spring.

Most widely available
BEETROOT 'Boltardy'. 'Burpees Golden'. 'Cylindra'. 'Detroit'. 'Globe' (Suttons). 'Monoder'. 'Monogram'. 'Cheltenham Greentop' (Suttons). 'Forono'. 'Regala'.
CELERIAC 'Iram'. 'Tellus'.
KOHL RABI 'Rowel'. 'Purple Vienna'. 'White Vienna'.

BRASSICAS
Time to buy Seed in packets. Bare-rooted, March–April or August–September. Tray and pot-grown, April or September.
Where to find Seed, indoors on seed rack. Pot-grown, outside in Vegetables. Bare-rooted outside stored in peat.
Size Seed, in packets. Trays, thirty to forty plants. Bare-rooted bundles of ten not more than 5 in (12 cm) long.
Foliage Mid green. Rigid and firm. Bare-rooted look weak.
Roots Pots 3 in (8 cm) min. dia. Bare-rooted, inspect for club root (small gnarled lumps on roots).
Hints As per instructions on packet in any well-prepared soil, plus extra organic material. Use rotation plan. Bare-rooted should not have been lifted for more than seven days. May not be named. Broccoli, Cauliflower and Brussels Sprouts get mixed up.
Most widely available
BROCCOLI *Calabrese*: 'Autumn Spear'. 'Corvet'. 'Emperor'. 'Express Corona'. 'Green Duke'. 'Mercedes'. 'Romaniso'. 'Royal Banquet'. 'Top Star'. *Sprouting*: 'Early White Sprouting'. 'Improved White Sprouting'. 'Nine Star Perennial'. 'Purple Sprouting'.
BRUSSELS SPROUTS 'Bedford'. 'Fillbasket'. 'Bedford Winter Harvest'. 'Citadel'. 'Early Half Tall'. 'Fortress'. 'Groninger Stiekema'. 'Mallard'. 'Peer Gynt'. 'Pegasus'. 'Roger'. 'Roodnerg Early Button'. 'Tardis'. 'Wellington'. 'Widgeon'.
CABBAGE *Spring Sowing*: 'Celtic'. 'Christmas'. 'Drumhead'. 'Golden Acre May Express' (Suttons). 'Golden Acre Primo'.

'Hawke'. 'Hispi'. 'Histanda'. 'Holland Late Winter'. 'June Star' (Suttons). 'Marner Allfruh'. 'Mercury'. 'Minicole'. 'Red Drumhead'. 'Winnigstadt' (Suttons Selection). *Autumn Sowing*: 'April'. 'Autumn Pride'. 'Durham Early'. 'Offenham 1 Spring Bounty' (Suttons). 'Pixie'. 'Spring Hero'. 'Wheeler's Imperial'. Savoy: 'Aquarius'. 'Best of All'. 'Celtic'. 'Icebridge'. 'Ice Queen'. 'Lucetta'. 'Ormskirk Rearguard' (Suttons). 'Ormskirk'. 'Ormskirk Late'. 'Savoy King'. 'Winter King'. CAULIFLOWER *Early*: 'All the Year Round'. 'Alpha Polaris' (Suttons). 'Andes'. 'Snowball' (Suttons). 'Snow Crown'. *Spring Sowing*: 'Autumn Giant Superlative Protecting'. 'Flora Blanca'. Australian: 'Barrier Reef'. 'Brisbane'. 'Wallaby'. *Late Summer and Autumn*: 'Autumn Glory'. 'Canberra'. 'Dok Elgon'. 'Mill Reef'. 'Royal Purple'. 'White Rock'. 'White Summer'. Winter: 'Angers No. 1 Superb Early White'. 'Angers No. 2 Westmarsh Early'. 'Snow White' (Suttons). *Extra Hardy*: 'Asmer Pinnacle'. 'English Winter Reading Giant'. 'Walcheren Winter Birchington'. 'Walcheren Winter Thanet'.

CAPSICUMS
Peppers
Time to buy Seed, January–February. Pre-grown, to grow under protection March–April. Outside when frosts over.
Where to find Indoors on seed racks.
Size Seed in packets. Plants 2–4 in (5–10 cm).
Foliage Pre-grown, mid green, fleshy and lush.
Roots Pots 3 in (8 cm) min. dia.
Hints Well-prepared soil when frosts have finished. Good for growbags or pots indoors and outside. Heated greenhouse, plant March; unheated greenhouse, April. All need caning. Check base of stem for root rot (botrytis). Not named. Avoid plants over 4 in (10 cm).
Most widely available 'Ace'. 'Californian Wonder'. 'Canape'. 'Early Prolific'.

'Gypsy'. 'Hot Gold Spike'. 'Luteus'. 'Midnight Beauty'. 'Edskin'. 'Red Chilli'. 'Salad Festival'. 'Worldbeater'.

CARROTS
Time to buy Seed, from January.
Where to find Indoors on seed rack.
Size Seed in packets.
Hints Sow directly into well-prepared soil as per instructions on packet. Soil preparation important.
Most widely available
EARLY 'Amsterdam Forcing Amstel'. 'Amsterdam Sweetheart'. 'Chantenay Red Cored'. 'Early Nantes'. 'Early Scarlet Horn'. 'Nantes' (Champion Scarlet Horn). 'Nandor'. 'Nantes Express'. 'Nanthya'. 'Panther'. 'Tiana'.
MAINCROP 'Autumn King' (Early Giant). 'Autumn King Vita Longa'. 'Beacon'. 'Favourite'. 'Fedora'. 'James' Scarlet Intermediate'. 'New Red Intermediate'. 'St Valery'.

CELERY
Time to buy Seed, tray and pot-grown, April–June.
Where to find Indoors on seed racks.
Size Seed in packets. Tray-grown thirty to forty plants.
Hints For seed, follow instructions on packet. Well-prepared soil for young plants. Trench preparation is important for trench varieties. Use rotation plan.
Most widely available
SELF-BLANCHING: 'American Green Greensnap'. 'Golden Self-Blanching'. 'Ivory Tower'. 'Lathom Self-Blanching'. TRENCH: 'Giant Pink Unrivalled'. 'Giant Red'. 'Solid White'.

CELTUCE
Time to buy Seed, in packets from January.
Where to find Indoors on seed rack.
Size Seed in packets.
Hints Sown directly into any well-

prepared soil as per instructions on packet. Not well known.

CHICORY
Time to buy Seed, in packets from January. Pre-packed roots from March.
Where to find Indoors on seed rack.
Size Seed in packets. Pre-packed roots, min. 3 in (8 cm) long, in peat.
Hints Sown directly into soil as instructions on packet. Pre-packed roots into well-prepared soil. Avoid pre-packed with premature growth.
Most widely available 'Crystal Head'. 'Normato'. 'Sugar Loaf' ('Pain de Sucre'). 'Witloof' ('Brussels Chicory').

CHINESE CABBAGE
Time to buy Seed, in packets from January.
Where to find Indoors on seed rack.
Size Seed in packets.
Hints Sown directly into any well-prepared soil as instructions on packet. Not well known.
Most widely available 'China Pride'. 'Green Rocket'. 'Kasumi'. 'Pe-Tsai'. 'Sampan'.

COURGETTES
Time to buy Seed, in packets from January. Pot-grown, under protection March–May.
Where to find Seed, indoors on seed rack. Pot-grown under overhead protection.
Size Seed in packets. Pot-grown, 2–4 in (5–10 cm) high.
Foliage Dark green, firm and rigid.
Roots Pots 3 in (8 cm) min. dia.
Hints Any well-prepared soil, plus extra organic material. Follow instructions on packet. Pot-grown, avoid planting until spring frosts have finished. Pot-grown not named.
Most widely available 'All Green Bush'. 'Chefini'. 'Burpee Golden Zucchini'. 'Gold Rush'. 'Green Bush F1 hybrid'.

CRESS
Time to buy Seed in packets from January.
Where to find Indoors on seed rack.
Size Seed in packets.
Hints Sown directly into well-prepared soil as instructions on packet. Regular sowings of small amounts is best.
Most widely available 'American Salad'. 'Curled Cress'. 'Fine Curled'.

CUCUMBER and GHERKINS
Time to buy Seed, from February. Pot-grown, for indoors, March–April, outside when spring frosts have finished.
Where to find Seed, indoors on seed rack. Pot-grown under limited cover.
Size Seed, in packets. Pot-grown, 2–4 in (5–10 cm) high.
Foliage Dark green, firm and rigid.
Roots Pots 3 in (8 cm) min. dia.
Hints Follow instructions on packet. Well-prepared soil, plus extra organic material. Container-grown use good quality potting compost. Pot-grown not named.
Most widely available
GLASSHOUSE OR FRAME *All Female Flower Types:* 'Diana'. 'Femspot'. 'King George'. 'Landora'. 'Monique'. 'Petita'. 'Perpinex'. Male and Female: 'Sigmadew'. 'Telegraph'. 'Telegraph Improved' (Suttons).
RIDGE (OUTDOOR) 'Burpless Tasty Green'. 'Bush Champion'. 'Crystal Apple'. 'King of the Ridge'. 'Long Green'. 'Tokyo Slicer'. GHERKIN 'Gherkin Conda'. 'Venlo Pickling'.

ENDIVE
Time to buy Seed, in packets from January
Where to find Indoors on seed rack.
Size Seed in packets.
Hints Sown directly into well-prepared soil as instructions on packet. Not widely grown.
Most widely available 'Batavian Green'. 'Golda'. 'Green Curled'. 'Moss Curled'.

LEAF BEET
Time to buy Seed, from January.
Where to find Indoors on seed rack.
Size Seed in packets.
Hints Sown directly into well-prepared soil as instructions on packet.
Most widely available 'Rhubarb Chard'. 'Silver Sea Kale' (Swiss Chard).

LEEKS
Time to buy Seed, in packets. Tray and pot-grown, April or September. Bare-rooted, March–April, August–September.
Where to find Seed, indoors on seed rack. Tray and pot-grown, under limited protection. Bare-rooted, in bundles in moist peat.
Size Tray-grown thirty to forty plants. Pots, 3 in (8 cm) min. dia. Bare-rooted 4–6 in (10–15 cm) long.
Foliage Mid-green, firm and rigid. Bare-rooted may look weak.
Hints Seed, follow instructions on packet. Young plants, well-prepared soil, plus extra organic material. Use rotation plan. Avoid plants lifted for more than seven days. May not be named.
Most widely available 'Albinstar'. 'Autumn Mammoth Early Market'. 'Blue Solaise'. 'Gennevilliers Splendid'. 'Giant Winter Catalina'. 'Giant Winter Royal Favourite'. 'King Richard'. 'Lyon Prizetaker'. 'Mammoth Blanch'. 'Mammoth Pot Leek'. 'Musselburgh'. 'Winter Leek'. 'Yates Empire'.

LETTUCE
Time to buy Seed, in packets. Tray or pot-grown, April or September.
Where to find Seed indoors on seed rack. Tray or pot-grown outside in Vegetables.
Size Seed in packets. Tray or pot-grown, 2–3 in (5–8 cm) high. Trays contain thirty to forty plants.
Foliage Mid to light green, firm and rigid.
Hints Seed, follow instructions on packet. Plants, well-prepared soil. Not always named.

Most widely available

SPRING AND SUMMER SOWING OUTDOORS
Butterhead varieties: 'All Year Round'.
'Avondefiance'. 'Continuity'. 'Dolly'. 'Fortune'. 'Hilde 11'. 'Imperial Winter'.
'Musette'. 'Novita'. 'Sigmaball'. 'Sigmahead'. 'Tom Thumb'. 'Unrivalled'.
PICKLING 'Lollo Rosea'. 'Red Salad Bowl'.
'Salad Bowl'. 'Salad Bowl Mixed'.
ICEBERG AND CRISP HEARTED 'Great
Lakes'. 'Lakeland'. 'Lake Nyah'. 'Malika'.
'Saladin'. 'Tires'. 'Webb's Wonderful'.
'Wiundemere'.
FOR CULTURE UNDER GLASS OR IN FRAME
'Cynthia' (Butterhead). 'Dandie'. 'Diamant'. 'Kwiek'. 'Marmer'. 'May Queen'.
AUTUMN SOWING TO MATURE IN SPRING
'Arctic King'. 'Valdor'.
COS 'Buttercrunch'. 'Little Gem'. 'Lobjoits
Green Cos'. 'Padox'. 'Winter Density'.

MARROWS

Time to buy Seed, from March. Pot-grown,
from April, when frosts have finished.
Where to find Seed, indoors on seed
rack. Pot-grown under limited protection.
Size Seed in packets. Pot-grown, 2–4 in
(5–10 cm) high.
Foliage Dark green, firm and rigid.
Roots Pots 3 in (8 cm) min. dia.
Hints Follow instructions on seed packet.
Well-prepared soil, plus extra organic
material. Pot-grown not named. Offered
before spring frosts have finished.
Most widely available
BUSH 'Early Gem'. 'Eldorado'. 'Green
Bush Smallpak'. 'Tiger Cross'. 'Tender
and True'. 'Zucchini'.
TRAILING 'Long Green'. 'Long Green
Striped'. 'Table Dainty'.
UNUSUAL 'Custard Yellow'. 'Vegetable
Spaghetti'.

MELON

Time to buy Seed, from March. Pot-grown
from May.
Where to find Seed, indoors on seed rack.
Pot-grown under limited protection.

Size Seed in packets. Pot-grown, 2–4 in
(5–10 cm) high.
Foliage Dark green, firm and rigid.
Roots Pots 3 in (8 cm) min. dia.
Hints Follow instructions on seed packet.
Well-prepared soil, plus extra organic
material. Pot-grown not named. Offered
before spring frosts have finished.
Most widely available 'Bleinheim
Orange Superlative'. 'Emerald Gem'.
'Hero of Lockinge'. 'Charantais'. 'Early
Sweet'. 'Ogen'. 'Sweetheart'.

MUSHROOMS

Time to buy Mushroom spawn, as available.
Where to find Indoors, pre-packed boxes
of straight spawn or with planting
medium and container.
Size Amounts manageable for production.
Foliage None.
Roots Spawn moist but not wet.
Hints Dark, dank growing area. Follow
instructions on container. May not be
available in garden centres all the time.
Adequate growing conditions may not be
available.
Most widely available 'Darlington's
Pelletized Spawn'. 'Darlington's Grain
Spawn'.

MUSTARD

Time to buy Seed, in packets from
January.
Where to find Indoors on seed rack.
Size Seed in packets.
Hints Sow seed as instructions on
packet. Avoid over-sowing at one time.
Most widely available 'Chinese Mustard'. 'Green-in-Snow'. 'Fine White.'
'White'.

ONIONS (culinary)

Time to buy Seed in packets, December–
January. Onion sets, March–April for
spring planting, October for autumn.

Where to find Seed, indoors on seed racks. Onion sets on special display in $\frac{1}{2}$ lb (227 g) or 1 lb (454 g) bags.
Size Onion sets firm, disease-free, $\frac{1}{2}$ in (1 cm) long and in diameter.
Foliage No foliage.
Roots Sets dry, firm with no signs of root or shoot growth.
Hints Any well-prepared soil. Not planted soon enough. After April all supplies sold. Short planting season.
Most widely available
KEEPING ONIONS 'Ailsa Craig'. 'Bedfordshire Champion'. 'Brunswick'. 'Hygro'. 'Mammoth Improved'. 'Mammoth Red'. 'North Holland Blood Red'. 'Reliance'. 'Rijnsburger'. 'Rijnsburger Jumbo'.
JAPANESE 'Express Yellow O-X'. 'Extra Early Kaizuka'. 'Senshyu Semi Globe Yellow'.
PICKLING 'Aviv'. 'Paris Silverskin'.
WELSH 'Giant Perennial'.
SETS 'Rocardo'. 'Sturon'. 'Stuttgarter Giant'. 'Unwin's Autumn Planting'.

PAK CHOI
Time to buy Seed, in packets from January.
Where to find Indoors on seed rack.
Size Seed in packets.
Hints Sow directly into well-prepared soil as instructions on packet. Not widely known.
Most widely available 'Chinese Pak Choi'. 'Joi Choi'.

PARSNIP
Time to buy Seed, in packets from January.
Where to find Indoors on seed rack.
Size Seed in packets.
Hints Sow directly into well-prepared soil as instructions on packet. Requires depth of soil to encourage good root.
Most widely available 'Avonresister'. 'Exhibition Long'. 'Improved Hollow Crowned'. 'Tender and True'. 'The Student'. 'White Gem'.

PEAS
Time to buy Seeds, March–April.
Where to find Indoors on seed rack.
Size Seed in packets.
Hints Sow directly into well-prepared soil as instructions on packet. Soak peas in solution of 3 fl. oz. (0.1 l) paraffin to 2 pints (1 l) of water for twelve hours as a deterrent from rodents. Avoid sowing out of season. Medium and tall growing will need pea sticks, netting or similar support.
Most widely available
EARLY 'Early Onward'. 'Feltham First'. 'Holiday'. 'Hurst Beagle'. 'Kelvedon Wonder'. 'Little Marvel'. 'Meteor'. 'Pilot'. 'Sweetness'.
SECOND-EARLY AND MAINCROP 'Achievement'. 'Alderman'. 'Hurst Green Shaft'. 'Lord Chancellor'. 'Onward'. 'Senator'. 'Show Perfection'. 'Sleaford Three Kings'.
OTHER VARIETIES *Snap and Sugar Peas*: 'Edula Oregon Sugar Pod'. 'Sugarbon'. 'Sugar Dwarf'. 'Sweetgreen'. *Petits Pois*: 'Waverex'.

POTATO
Time to buy Tubers for under cover, March. March–April for outside.
Where to find Indoors, close to seed rack. Normally pre-packed in 1.25 lbs (1 kilo), 3.75 lbs (3 kilo), 7.5 lbs (6 kilo), 12.5 lbs (10 kilo) or 31.25 lbs (25 kilo) nets.
Size Tubers 1–1$\frac{1}{2}$ in (3–4 cm) length and dia.
Roots Tubers firm, rot-free, showing only short shoots not more than $\frac{1}{4}$ in (5 mm) long.
Hints Any well-prepared soil. Use crop rotation. Often not purchased soon enough. Sprouted by standing tubers upright in trays in light, frost-free area.
Most widely available
FIRST EARLIES 'Arran Pilot'. 'Concorde'. 'Dunluce'. 'Foremost'. 'Homeguard'. 'Lola'. 'Maris Bard'. 'Pentland Javelin'. 'Rubinia'.

SECOND EARLY 'Kondor'. 'Marfona'. 'Nadine'. 'Ratte'.

MAIN CROP 'Arran Banner'. 'Arran Consul'. 'Cara'. 'Desiree'. 'King Edward'. 'Kirsty'. 'Majestic'. 'Pentland Crown'. 'Romano'.

SALAD 'Pink Fir Apple'.

PUMPKIN
Time to buy Seed in packets, April. Pot-grown, May.
Where to find Seed, indoors on seed rack. Pot-grown under limited protection.
Size Seed in packets. Pot-grown, 2–4 in (5–10 cm) high.
Foliage Dark green, firm and rigid.
Roots Pots 3 in (8 cm) min. dia.
Hints Follow instructions on packet. Well-prepared soil, plus extra organic material. Not always named. Offered before spring frosts have finished.
Most widely available 'Atlantic Giant'. 'Hundredweight'. 'Hubbard Squash Golden'. 'Jackpot'. 'Mammoth Ornamental'. 'Table Ace'.

RADICCHIO
Time to buy Seed in packets, from January.
Where to find Indoors on seed rack.
Size Seed in packets.
Hints Sown directly into well-prepared soil as instructions on packet. Becoming more widely known.

RADISH
Time to buy Seed, in packets from January.
Where to find Indoors on seed rack.
Size Seed in packets.
Hints Sown directly into well-prepared soil as per instructions on packet. Often over-sown.
Most widely available
SUMMER 'Cherry Belle'. 'Crystal Ball'. 'French Breakfast Crimson'. 'Globe Varieties' (Turnip) mixed. 'Long White Icicle'. 'Prinz Robin' (Red Prince). 'Saxa Short Top Forcing'. 'Scarlet Globe'. 'Sparkler'.

WINTER 'Black Spanish Round'. 'Chinese Rose'. 'Mino Early'.

SALSIFY
Time to buy Seed, in packets from January.
Where to find Indoors on seed rack.
Size Seed in packets.
Hints Sown directly into well-prepared soil as instructions on packet. Not widely planted.
Most widely available 'Giant'. 'Mammoth'.

SCORONERA
Time to buy Seed, in packets from January.
Where to find Indoors on seed rack.
Size Seed in packets.
Hints Sown directly into well-prepared soil as instructions on packet. Becoming more widely known.
Most widely available 'Long John'. 'Russian Giant'.

SPINACH
Time to buy Seed, in packets from January.
Where to find Indoors on seed rack.
Size Seed in packets.
Hints Sown directly into well-prepared soil as instructions on packet. Requires fertile soil.
Most widely available 'Cabellero'. 'Long Standing Round'. 'Monarch Long Standing'. 'New Zealand'. 'Norvak'. 'Perpetual Spinach' (Leaf Beet). 'Sigmaleaf'.

SPRING ONIONS
Time to buy Seed, in packets from January.
Where to find Indoors on seed rack.
Size Seed in packets.
Hints Sow directly into well-prepared soil as instructions on packet. Avoid over-sowing.
Most widely available 'Ishikura'. 'White Lisbon'. 'White Lisbon' (Winter Hardy).

SWEDE
Time to buy Seed, in packets from January.
Where to find Indoors on seed rack.
Size Seed in packets.
Hints Sown directly into well-prepared soil as instructions on packet. Requires deep soil or will fail.
Most widely available 'Best of All'. 'Marian'. 'Sutton's Western Perfection'.

SWEET CORN
Time to buy Seed, in packets from February. Trays from April.
Where to find Indoors on seed rack. Trays outside under limited cover.
Size Seed in packets. Tray-grown thirty–forty plants.
Hints Sown directly into well-prepared soil as instructions on packet, or plant out tray-grown when spring frosts have finished.
Most widely available 'Canle'. 'Earlibelle'. 'Early Xtra Sweet'. 'First of All'. 'Kelvedon Glory'. 'Sundance'.

TOMATO
Time to buy Seed, no later than February. Pot-grown, for indoors March–April, outside when spring frosts have finished.
Where to find Indoors on seed rack. Pot-grown, indoors March or May under limited protection.
Size Seed in packets. Plants 2–6 in (5–15 cm) high.
Foliage Mid green, fleshy and lush.
Roots Pots 3 in (8 cm) min. dia.
Hints For use in growbags or pots, indoors and outside. Heated greenhouses, plant in March, unheated, in April, and outside when spring frosts have finished. All need canes. Check base of stem for root rot (botrytis). Offered unnamed. Avoid long and leggy plants.
Most widely available
GREENHOUSE 'Big Boy'. 'Counter'. 'Dona'. 'Eurocross BB'. 'Grenadier'. 'Ida'. 'Rootstock KNVF'. 'Seville Cross'. 'Shirley'.
GREENHOUSE OR OUTDOOR 'Ailsa Craig'. 'Ailsa Craig Leader'. 'Alicante'. 'Beef Steak Marglobe'. 'Best of All'. 'Gardener's Delight'. 'Golden Sunrise'. 'Harbinger' (Suttons). 'Marmande'. 'Moneymaker'. 'Sioux'. 'Stoner's Exhibition'. 'Sweet 100'.
OUTDOOR 'French Cross'. 'Histon Early'. 'Red Alert'. 'Roma'. 'Ronaclave'. 'Sigmabush'. 'The Amateur'. 'Tornado'. 'Yellow Perfection'.
PATIO VARIETIES 'Pixie Hybrid'. 'Tiny Tim'. 'Totem'.
UNUSUAL VARIETIES 'Mixed Ornamental'. 'Tigerella'.

TURNIP
Time to buy Seed, in packets from January.
Where to find Indoors on seed rack.
Size Seed in packets.
Hints Sown directly into well-prepared soil as instructions on packet.
Most widely available 'Golden Ball'. 'Green Globe'. 'Manchester Market'. (Green Top Stone). 'Purple Top Milan'. 'Snowball Early White Stone'. 'Veitch's Red Globe'.

Aquatic Plants

Aquatic plants' need for water makes them one of the most unattractive-looking of all plants purchased from nurseries and garden centres. They need the water and final planting position to mature and evolve, and they will look very uninteresting, often with little or no sign of growth, and what growth there is looking weak and insipid.

There is the additional problem that they are stored in troughs of water and so access to them can be a messy business, but the nursery or garden centre staff will always help.

There is a wide range of forms, but careful research needs to be done to make sure that they do not become invasive. The size of pond or pool that is available for their planting needs to be taken into account.

The planting depth is important and you should try to adhere to those recommended.

There is a fine line between Aquatic or Marginal plants, and many Perennials straddle both areas. There are also perennial plants which give an aquatic feeling and don't necessarily need very moist soil.

As well as being ornate, many aquatic plants are used to aerate the water. It is important to have the right number of plants per volume of water for this purpose.

Many nurseries and garden centres now stock aquatic plants, but ordering mail-order is an acceptable method of purchase. The plants that arrive will look very indifferent in appearance but will grow rapidly once planted.

With perennial plants that are grown in proximity to water gardens, care must be taken to make sure that they represent value for money compared to those that are sold for aquatic purposes. Often one can find larger plants that on a price ratio basis are better value amongst the perennials, rather than amongst the aquatic material.

True aquatic plants which are used as marginals, floaters or for deep-water planting must be transported in water and planted as soon as possible. You need to make sure that adequate material, such as planting baskets and planting soil, is available to do the job immediately. Of course, the pond or pool must be finished and in a condition ready to receive the various material chosen for it.

FLOATING DEEP MARGINALS
Time to buy Pot-grown, April–September. Bare-rooted, April–May.
Where to find Outside in Aquatic Plant Tanks, submerged in water.
Size Height and spread not important.
Foliage Green or variegated. May look insipid and weak.
Roots Pots 4 in (10 cm) min. dia. Bare-rooted, clumps kept wet.
Hints Allow to float on surface of water. May have to be purchased mail order.
Most widely available *Azolla caroliniana* (Fairy Moss). *Eichornia crassipes* (Water Hyacinth) *Hydrocharis morsus ranae* (Frogbit). *Lemna gibba* (Thick Duckweed). *Lemna minor* (Common Duckweed). *Lemna polyrrhiza* (Greater Duckweed). *Lemna trisuica* (Ivy-leaved Duckweed). *Pistia stratiotes* (Water Lettuce). *Stratiotes aloides* (Water Soldier or Water Cactus). *Trapa natans* (Water Chestnut).

MARGINALS and DEEP MARGINALS
Time to buy Pot-grown, April–September. Bare-rooted, April–May. Mail order acceptable.
Where to find Outside in Aquatic Plant Tanks, submerged in water.
Size Height not important.
Foliage Green or variegated. May look insipid and weak.
Roots Pots 4 in (10 cm) min. dia. Bare-rooted, clumps kept wet.
Hints Planted in baskets at appropriate depth or into permanently wet soil. Soil should contain large amount of organic material. Wide range, may have to be sought from specialist nurseries. Research overall size.
Most widely available
MARGINALS Figures in brackets denote planting depth.
Acorus (Sweet-scented Rush) – (3–5 in/ 8–12 cm).

Alisma – (3–6 in/8–15 cm).
Butomus umbellatus (Flowering Rush) – (3–5 in/8–12 cm).
Calla palustris (Bog Arum) – (2–4 in/5–10 cm).
Caltha palustris (Marsh Marigold or Kingcup) – (1–3 in/3–8 cm).
Caltha polypetala (Giant Marigold) – (3–5 in/8–12 cm).
Cotula coronopifolia (Golden Buttons) – (up to 5 in/12 cm).
Cyperus (Ornamental Rush) – (2–5 in/5–12 cm).
Eriophorum angustifolium (Cotton Grass) – (up to 2 in/5 cm).
Glyceria spectabilis variegatus – (2–5 in/ 5–12 cm).
Houttuynia – (2–4 in/5–10 cm).
Iris kaempferi – (4 in/10 cm).
Iris laevigata – (2–4 in/5–10 cm).
Iris pseudacorus – (3–5 in/8–12 cm).
Iris versicolor – (2–4 in/5–10 cm).
Juncus ensifolius – (up to 3 in/8 cm).
Lobelia cardinalis – (2–3 in/5–8 cm).
Lysichitum – (4 in/10 cm).
Mentha squatica – (up to 3 in/8 cm).
Menyanthes trioliata – (2–4 in/5–10 cm).
Mimulus (Musk) – (1–4 in/3–10 cm).
Myosotis palustris (Water Forget-me-Not) – (up to 3 in/8 cm).
Myriophyllum proserpinacoides (Parrot's Feather) – (3–6 in/8–15 cm).
Peltranda – (3–5 in/8–12 cm).
Pontederia cordata (Pickerel) – (3–5 in/ 12 cm).
Ranunculus – (1–5 in/3–12 cm).
Sagittaria (Arrowhead) – (3–6 in/8–15 cm).
Saururus cernuus (Swamp Lily) – (up to 2 in/5 cm).
Scirpus zebrinus (Zebra Rush) – (3–5 in/ 8–12 cm).
Sisyrinchum boriale – (up to 1 in/3 cm).
Sparganium ramosum (Burr-reed) – (3–5 in/8–12 cm).
Typha (Reedmace) – (1–5 in/3–12 cm).
Veronica beccabunga (Brooklime) – (up to 4 in/10 cm).

DEEP MARGINALS

Aponogeton distacyus (Water Hawthorn) – (6–18 in/15–50 cm).

Aponogeton kraussianus – (12–18 in/30–50 cm).

Hottonia palustris (Water Violet) – (6–12 in/15–30 cm).

Orontium aquaticum (Golden Club) – (3–12 in/8–30 cm).

Villarsia 'Bennettii' – (4–18 in/10–50 cm).

Zantedeschia aethiopica (Arum Lily) – (6 in/15 cm).

NYMPHAEAS
Water Lilies

Time to buy Pot-grown, April–September. Bare-rooted, April–May. Mail order acceptable.

Where to find Outside in Aquatic Tank, submerged in water.

Size Pot-grown showing signs of growth, relatively small in spring.

Foliage Limited, particularly in spring. Looks insipid until established.

Roots Pots 4 in (10 cm) min. dia. Metal pins holding root rhizomes into pots. Bare-rooted, limited signs of growth.

Hints Purchased and transported in moist condition and planted as soon as possible. Aquatic baskets should be purchased when obtaining plants. Aquatic potting compost should be used. Do not plant into soil at base of pool. Research overall size. If planted in too small a pool, they will destroy all other plants. Specific forms from specialist nurseries.

Most widely available

VIGOROUS GROWING Planting depth 9–36 in (23 cm–1 m). *White: Nymphaeas alba.* Pink: N. 'Colossea'. N. × 'Marliacea Carnea'. *Red:* N. 'Conqueror'.

MEDIUM GROWING Planting depth 6–18 in (15–50 cm). *White:* N. 'Albatross'. N. × 'Marliacea Albida'. N. 'Odorata

Alba'. *Pink:* N. 'Amabilis'. N. 'American Star'. N. × 'Marliacea Rosea'. N. *odorata* 'Eugene De Land'. N. 'Rose Arey'. N. *tuberosa rosea. Red:* N. 'Attraction'. N. 'Rene Gerrard'. *Yellow:* N. × 'Marliacea Chromatella.'

SMALL GROWING Planting depth 6–12 in (15–30 cm). *White:* N. 'Odorata minor'. *Red:* 'Froebelii' *Yellow:* N. 'Odorata sulphurea'. Copper: N. 'Indiana'. N. 'Robinsonii'. N. 'Sioux'.

MINIATURE GROWING Planting depth 4–9 in (10–23 cm). *White:* N. *candida. Yellow:* N. *pygmaea* 'Helvola'.

OXYGENATING PLANTS

Time to buy Bunches of non-rooted or rooted material, April–September. Specific species may not be available.

Where to find Outside in Aquatic Tank, submerged in water.

Size Not important.

Foliage Bright green or variegated. May look insipid and weak.

Roots Pots 4 in (10 cm) min. dia. Bare-rooted clumps kept wet.

Hints Bunches inserted into soil at base of pond, or into baskets containing aquatic potting compost. One bunch per 2 sq. ft (80 sq. cm) of water surface. Look uninteresting but important to well-being of pond. May have to be sought from more than one outlet, possibly mail order.

Most widely available *Callitriche autumnalis. Ceratophyllum demersum* (Hornwort). *Eleocharis acicularis* (Hair Grass). *Elodea canadensis* (Anacharis). *Fontinalis antipyretica* (Willow Moss). *Lagarosiphon major* (*Elodea Crispa*). *Myriophyllum verticillatum* (Mifoil). *Potamogeton crispus. Ranunculus aquatilis* (Water Buttercup). *Tillaea recurva.*

House Plants

No other section of plants featured in this publication offers such a wide choice for the purchaser. Some forms are regularly available but others will have a seasonal trend and may only become available at certain times, for example, Hyacinths in the spring, Azaleas near Christmas.

Many forms are not always available from every nursery and garden centre, but can be searched for and found in a wide range of sizes from small 'tots' which will be no more than 2 in (5 cm) tall to specimen plants many feet (centimetres) in height.

House plants cover a number of divisions, chiefly flowering, foliage, cacti, air plants and bonsai, all of which have their own characteristics and specifications.

Always inspect the plant being purchased. If in flower attempt to get in bud or in near bud. Check the foliage to make sure it's clean and not distressed in any way, and has no signs of mildew, insect infestation or damage.

Most house plants need to be grown under very controlled conditions of correct light, warmth, humidity and feeding programmes. This can make them difficult to maintain in normal household conditions: but there are a number of good inexpensive publications available, which will give good advice as to which ones are best in a particular position. It's worthwhile doing a little research to make sure the conditions you can provide are suitable for the plants you have chosen.

Eventually, all will need potting-up and when they do, check the type of soil in the pot, and try to mimic this when you choose your potting compost. Most garden centres will be able to help and give you an idea of which is the closest to those used by the grower.

Houseplants should always be stored under protection. It is best to always purchase from reputable nurseries and garden centres and try to avoid those offered in other retail outlets, particularly if they are kept outside. They may well look in good order when purchased, but there may be tissue damage caused by drafts or extremes of heat, cold, or wet which you will not see immediately, which will develop very quickly once they are in your home environment.

When transporting home from the nursery, never keep in the car or car-boot longer than is necessary.

BONSAI

Time to buy As required. Larger plants found pre-Christmas.

Where to find Plants for outside, under limited cover. For indoors, near House Plants.

Size Very much a personal choice regarding shape and size.

Foliage Evergreen, no signs of leaf or needle drop, except March–April. Deciduous, spring/summer green or coloured. Premature autumn colour and leaf drop.

Roots Grown in root container, which is shallow, saucer-like, either oblong, oval or square and glazed.

Hints Growing techniques are specific and reference should be taken. For wide selection may need to visit specialist grower. Important that species for outside are grown outside, and inside grown indoors.

Most widely available

FOR DISPLAY OUTDOORS Acer (Maple). Azalea. Buxus (Box). Carpinus (Hornbeam). Cotoneaster. Crataegus (Thorn). Fagus (Beech). Pyracantha (Firethorn). Zelkova (Elm).

CONIFERS Abies (Firs various). Chamaecyparis (False Cypress Various). *Ginkgo biloba* (Maidenhair Tree). Juniperus (Juniper Various). Larix (Larch). *Metasequoia glyptostroboides* (Prehistoric Dawn Redwood). Pinus (Pine Various). Taxodium (Swamp Cypress).

FOR DISPLAY INDOORS Bougainvillea. *Carmona microphylla* (Fukien Tea). Crassula (Jade Tree). *Cycas revoluta* (Cycad). Ficus (Fig Various). *Fortunella hindsii* (Dwarf Orange). Gardenia. Jacaranda. *Kadsura japonica* (Scarlet Kadsura). *Lagerstroemia indica* (Crab Myrtle). *Punica granatum* (Pomegranate). *Sageretia theezans* (Sageretta). *Schefflera actinophylla* (Umbrella Tree). *Serissa foetida* (Tree of a Thousand Stars).

CACTI

Time to buy As required. Large selections offered pre-Christmas, Easter and Mothering Sunday.

Where to find Indoors in House Plants.

Size 1–18 in (3–50 cm).

Foliage No actual foliage. Should show no signs of mealy bug (white clusters of cotton wool-like substance).

Roots Pots 2 in (5 cm) min. dia.

Hints Keep dry in winter. Water once or twice a week in late spring and summer, reducing in autumn. Specific reference required for individual species. Wide range. May be necessary to purchase from specialist grower or mail order.

Most widely available

THOSE REQUIRING AVERAGE TEMPERATURE OF 40°F (5°C) MIN. *Aloe aristata*. *Echeveria microcalyx*. Echinocereus. Graptopetalum. Helianthocereus. Lobivia. *Mamillaria gracilis* var. *pulchella*. Oreocereus. *Pachyphytum*. *Rebutia*. *Sedum pachyphyllum*.

THOSE REQUIRING AVERAGE TEMPERATURE OF 50°F (10°C) MIN. Acanthocalycium. Aporophyllum. *Borzicactus icosagonus*. Ceropegia. *Cleistocactus reae*. *Copiapoa humilis*. *Coryphantha nova*. *Echinocactus grusonii*. Echinocereus. Echinopsis. Espostea. Ferocactus. *Farileacatafracta*. Gymnocalcium. *Haageocereus aureispinus*. *Hamatocactus septispinus*. Lobivia. Mamillaria. *Matucana comacephala*. Neoporteria. Notocactus. Opuntia. Parodia. Pilosocereus. Rebutia. Rhipsalis. *Sedum morganianum*. Stenocactus. Trichocereus. *Weingartia hediniana*.

CONSERVATORY PLANTS

Time to buy As required. Ensure correct conditions can be maintained.

Where to find Indoors in House or Conservatory Plants.

Size Price dictated by size. 12 in–10 ft (30 cm–3 m).

Foliage Majority evergreen. No signs of yellowing or browning. Deciduous, premature autumn colour and leaf drop.

Roots Pots 5 in (12 cm) min. dia.

Hints Can be planted into soil in beds, which have been excavated to depth of 2 ft (60 cm) min. and infilled with good potting compost. Container-grown should have largest practicable container and good quality potting compost used. Reference regarding soil needs. Regular feeding throughout their life with liquid fertilizer. Climbing plants will require wires. Selection of correct plants for environment important.

Plants which require, or adapt, or perform well in conservatory conditions:

Most widely available

THOSE REQUIRING AVERAGE TEMPERATURE OF NOT LESS THAN 40°F (5°C): *Shrubs:* Abutilon. Acacia (Wattle). Callistemon (Bottle Brush). Camellia. Cassia. Cestrum. Erica, tender forms. Grevillea (Silk Oak). Rhododendron, tender forms. *Climbers:* Clianthus (Parrot's Bill). Jasminum, tender forms (Jasmine).

THOSE REQUIRING AN AVERAGE TEMPERATURE OF NOT LESS THAN 50°F (10°C) *Shrubs:* Aphelandra (Zebra Plant). Bouvardia. Brunsfelsia. Citrus (Calamondin). Clivia. Cymbidium (Orchid). Datura (Angel's Trumpets). Ferns. Hisbiscus (Shrubby Mallow). Lantana. Nerium (Oleander). Palms. Punica (Pomegranate). Sparmannia (African Hemp). Tibouchina (Glory Bush). Yucca. *Climbers:* Bougainvillea (Paper Flower). Hoya (Wax Flower). Lapageria (Chilean Bellflower). Mandevilla (Chilean Jasmine). Passiflora, tender forms (Passion Flower).

THOSE REQUIRING AN AVERAGE TEMPERATURE OF NOT LESS THAN 60°F (15°C) *Shrubs:* Crossandra. Gardenia (Cape Jasmine). Jacobina. *Climbers:* Allamanda. Clerodendron. Dipladenia (Pink Allamanda). Stephanotis (Madagascar).

Above are the structural shrubs and climbers that are suitable. Bulbs grown in pots, hardy and half-hardy annuals can also be considered.

FLOWERING HOUSE PLANTS (pre-grown)

Time to buy All year round. Some may only be available at specific times.

Where to find In House Plants.

Size Wide range of sizes.

Foliage Avoid those showing damage, browning of edges or yellowing (except for variegated forms), mildew, green fly, white fly and scale.

Roots Pots 2–20 in (5–55 cm). Normally plastic pots. If in clay pots, when potting up use larger size clay pot.

Flower Purchase in bud or just opening.

Hints Feed regularly with general liquid fertilizer and water as required. Keep away from windows in winter. Wide range with many new forms. Protection required when transporting in autumn, winter and early spring.

Most widely available

SUITABLE FOR SHADY POSITIONS *Aechmea fasciata* (Urn Plant). *Aeschynanthus lobbianus* (Lipstick Vine). *Ananas cosmosus* (Pineapple). Anthurium *Ardisia crenata* (Coral Berry). *Azalea indica* (Azalea). Begonia. *Brunsfelsia calycina* (Yesterday, Today and Tomorrow). Cineraria. *Clerodendrum thomsoniae* (Glory Bower). *Columnea* (Goldfish Plant). *Cyclamen persicum* (Cyclamen). Diplandenia. *Duchesnea indica* (Indian Strawberry). *Eucharis grandiflora* (Amazon Lily). *Fuchsia.* *Guzmania* (Scarlet Star). Hyacinthus (Hyacinth). *Hydrangea macrophylla* (Hydrangea Mop-headed and Lace-cap). *Hypocyrta glabra* (Clog Plant). Impatiens (Busy Lizzie). *Jacobinia carnea* (King's Crown). *Pachystachys lutea* (Lollipop Plant). *Smithiana hybrida* (Wax Flower). *Streptocarpus hybrida* (Cape Primrose). Tillandsia. Tulipa (Tulip). Vriesea.

SUITABLE FOR NORMAL ROOM LIGHT Abutilon. *Acalypha hispida* (Chenille Plant). *Achimenes hybrida* (Cupid's Bower). *Aphelandra squarrosa* (Zebra Plant). Browallia (Bush Violet). *Campanula isophylla* (Italian Bellflower). *Capsicum annuum*

(Christmas Pepper). Cestrum (Jessamine). Chrysanthemum (Pot Chrysanthemum). *Clivia Miniata* (Kaffir Lily). *Crossandra undulifolia* (Firecracker Plant). *Cuphea ignea* (Cigar Plant). Dianthus. Episcia. Erica (Tender Heathers). *Exacum affine* (Arabian Violet). *Gardenia jasminoides* (Gardenia). *Gerbera jamesonii* (Barbeton Daisy). *Gloriosa rothschildiana* (Glory Lily). Gloxinia. *Haemanthus katharinae* (Blood Lily). *Hippeastrum hybrida* (Amaryllis). *Hoya carnosa* (Wax Plant). *Ixora coccinea* (Flame of the Woods). Jasminum (Jasmine). *Kalanchoe blossfeldiana* (Flaming Katy). *Kohleria eriantha*. *Lachenalia aloides* (Cape Cowslip). *Manettia inflata* (Firecracker Plant). *Nertera depressa* (Bead Plant). Orchid. *Pittosporum tobira* (Mock Orange). *Plumbago auriculata* (Cape Leadwort). Poinsettia. *Punica granatum nana* (Dwarf Pomegranate). Rechsteineria (Cardinal Flower). *Rochea coccinea* (Crassula). *Ruellia makoyana* (Monkey Plant). Saintpaulia (African Violet). *Salpiglossis sinuata* (Painted Tongue). *Sanchezia nobilis* (Sanchezia). *Schizanthus hybrida* (Poor Man's Orchid). Solanum. *Sparmannia africana* (House Lime). *Streptosolen jamesonii* (Marmalade Bush). *Thunbergia alata* (Black-eyed Susan). *Vallota speciosa* (Scarborough Lily). *Zantedeschia aethiopica* (Calla Lily).

SUITABLE FOR FULL SUN *Acacia armata* (Kangaroo Thorn). *Agapanthus africanus* (Blue African Lily). *Beloperone guttata* (Shrimp Plant). *Bouganvillea glabra* (Paper Flower). *Calistemon citrus* (Bottlebrush Plant). Celosia. Citrus (Orange or Lemon). *Clianthus formosus* (Glory Pea). *Euphorbia milii* (Crown of Thorns). *Heliotropium hybridum* (Heliotrope). *Hibiscus rosa-sinensis* (Rose of China). *Lantana camara* (Yellow Sage). *Nerine flexuosa* (Nerine). Nerium Oleander (Oleander). *Passiflora caerulea* (Passion Flower). *Pelargonium* (Geranium. Primula. Rosa (Miniature Rose). *Stapelia*

variegata (Carrion Flower). *Strelitzia reginae* (Bird of Paradise).

FOLIAGE HOUSE PLANTS
(pre-grown)

Time to buy All year round. Some may only be available at specific times.

Where to find In House Plants.

Size Wide range of sizes.

Foliage Avoid those showing damage, browning of edges, mildew, green fly, white fly or scale.

Roots Pots 2–20 in (5–55 cm) dia. Normally sold in plastic pots. If in clay pots, when potting-up, use larger size clay pot.

Hints Feed regularly with liquid fertilizer. Water as required. Keep away from windows in winter. Wide range with many new forms. Protection required when transporting in autumn, winter and early spring.

Most widely available

SUITABLE FOR SHADY POSITIONS *Acorus gramineus variegatus* (Sweet Flag). Adiantum (Maidenhair Fern). Aglaonema (Chinese Evergreen). *Araucaria heterophylla* (Norfolk Island Pine). Asparagus (Asparagus Fern). *Aspidistra elatior* (Cast Iron Plant). *Asplenium* 'Nidus' (Bird's Nest Fern). Begonia. *Blechnum Gibbum* (Blechnum). *Breynia nivosa roseopicta* (Leaf Flower). Caladium. Calathea. *Callisia elegans* (Striped Inch Plant). Chamaedorea (Reed Palm). *Chlorophytum comosum* (Spider Plant). *Chrysalidocarpus lutescens* (Areca Palm). *Cissus antartica* (Kangaroo Vine). *C. discolor* (Begonia Vine). Cocos (Coconut Palm). *Coffea arabica* (Coffee Tree). Coleus. *Ctenanthe oppenheimiana tricolor* (Never Never Plant). *Cycas revoluta* (Sago Palm). *Cyrtomium falcatum* (Cyrtomium). Dieffenbachia (Dumb Cane). *Dizgotheca elegantissima* (False Aralia). Dracaena. *Fatshedera* 'Lizei' (Ivy Tree). *Fatsia japonica* (Castor Oil Plant). Ficua (Fig). Fittonia (Snakeskin Plant). Hedera (Ivy). *Helxine soleirolii* (Mind Your Own

Business). Howea (Kentia Palm). Maranta (Prayer Plant). *Monstera deliciosa* (Swiss Cheese Plant). *Neanthe Bella* (Parlour Palm). *Nephrolepis exaltata bostoniensis* (Boston Fern). *Ophiopogon jaburan* (White Lily Turf). *Oplismenus hirtellus* (Basket Grass). *Pandanus veitchii* (Screw Pine). Pellaea. Pellionia. Peperomia. Philodendron. Phoenix (Date Palm). *Phyllitis scolopendrium* (Hart's Tongue Fern). Pilea. *Piper crocatum* (Ornamental Pepper). *Platycerium bifurcatum* (Staghorn Fern). Plectranthus (Swedish Ivy). *Pleomele reflexa variegata* (Song of India). *Polypodium aureum* (Hare's Foot Fern). Polyscias. *Polystichum tsussimense* (Tsusina Holly Fern). Pteris. *Rhoeo discolor* (Boat Lily). Rhoicissus. *Saxifraga sarmentosa* (Mother of Thousands). *Schefflera actinophylla* (Umbrella Tree). *Scindapsus aureus* (Devil's Ivy). Selaginella (Creeping Moss). *Sonerila margaritacea* (Frosted Sonerila). *Syngonium podophyllum* (Goosefoot Plant). *Tetrastigma voinierianum* (Chestnut Vine). *Tolmiea menziesii* (Piggyback Plant).

SUITABLE FOR NORMAL ROOM LIGHT *Abutilon striatum thompsonii* (Spotted Flowering Maple). *Acalypha wilkesiana* (Copper Leaf). *Beaucarnea recurvata* (Pony Tail Plant). *Caryota mitis* (Fishtail Plant). *Chamaerops humilis* (European Fan Palm). *Codiaeum variegatum pictum* (Croton). *Cordyline australis* (Cabbage Tree). *C. terminalis* (Ti Plant). *Cryptanthus* (Earth Star). *Cyanotis kewensis* (Teddy Bear Vine). Cyperus (Umbrella Plant). *Grevillea robusta* (Silk Oak). *Gynura sarmentosa* (Velvet Plant). *Heptapleurum arboricola* (Parasol Plant). *Hypoestes sanguinolenta* (Freckle Face). *Livistone chinensis* (Chinese Fan Palm). *Mikania ternata* (Plush Vine). *Mimosa pudica* (Sensitive Plant). Pelargonium (Scented-leaved Geranium). *Podocarpus*

macrophyllus (Buddhist Pine). *Radermachera danielle* (Radermachera). *Rhapis excelsa* (Littel Lady Palm). Sanseviera (Mother-in-Law's Tongue). *Senecio macroglossus* (Cape Ivy). *Setcreasea purpurea* (Purple Heart). *Strobilanthes dyeranus* (Persian Shield). Tradescantia (Wandering Jew). *Washington Filifera* (Desert Fan Palm). *Zebrina pendula* (Zebrina).

SUITABLE FOR FULL SUN *Aeonium arboreum* (Aeonium). Agave (Century Plant). Aloe. *Bryophyllum daigremontianum* (Devil's Backbone). *Ceropegia woodii* (Rosary Vine). *Coleus blumei* (Flame Nettle). Cotyledon. Echeveria. Euphorbia. *Faucaria tigrina* (Tiger Jaws). Haworthia. Iresin. *Kalanchoe tomentosa* (Panda Plant). *Kleinia articulata* (Candle Plant). Lithops (Living Stones). *Pachyphytum oviferum* (Sugar Almond Plant). *Pedilanthus tithymaloides* (Jacob's Ladder). Sedum. Sempervivum (Houseleek). *Senecio rowleyanus* (String of Pearls). *Yucca elephantipes* (Spineless Yucca).

TILLANDSIA
Air Plants
Time to buy As and when required. Available all year round.
Where to find Special display indoors in House Plants.
Size 2–6 in (5–15 cm). Numerous aerial shoots. Offered loose or with ornamentation, normally shell or driftwood.
Foliage None. Stems grey to grey-green.
Roots No roots.
Hints Light, airy environment, not overdry. Tolerates central heating if air moisture is present. Temperature 60°F (15°C) min. Avoid plants over-priced, advisable for economy to make up own display arrangement rather than purchase.
Most widely available *Tillandsia argentea. T. caput-medusae. T. ionantha. T. juncea.*

Wild Flowers

The words 'wild flowers' conjures up images of a meadow in the spring, perfume, the humming of the bees and other insects as one lays in the long grass. It's not quite so simple to create the effect in your garden. Wild flowers are just the same as any other plant and adherence to the correct methods of sowing and growing are important.

Many wild flowers have to be grown as small pot-grown plants and then planted into their final areas. As with all plants, wild plants need specific conditions and you may not be able to provide all these within your garden. It may be a case of trial and error, sowing one to five species in year one, seeing which ones do best and then sowing new ones to replace those that have done poorly. No collection of wild seed will grow in all conditions, due to their individual requirements of soil, climate and aspect.

Some wild flowers will be annual or biennial, and the conditions that you are able to offer may not be suitable for the overwintering of the seed in the soil. If a particular form is required annually, you may well have to re-sow each year.

A wild garden when established can be one of the most attractive of all garden features. However, be aware of the fact that many wild flowers will become invasive and may well encroach out of their intended area.

WILD FLOWERS (bare-rooted or pot-grown as perennial plants)
Time to buy February–April
Where to find Outside in Perennials or Wild Plants. Also Alpines, Herbs, Fruit and Bulbs.
Size Pot-grown or bare-rooted, varying height of summer growth.
Foliage Deciduous and evergreen. Normally green and fresh.
Roots Pots 3 in (8 cm) min. dia. Bare-rooted, good fibrous root system.
Hints Well-prepared soil. Research specific needs. Wide range. May need to be sought from more than one outlet.
Most widely available Agrimony (*Agrimonia eupatoria*). Alexander's or Black Lovage (*Levisticum*). Bedstraw, Lady's (*Galium verum*). Bellflower, Clustered (*Campanula glomerata*). Betony (*Stachys officinalis*). Bird's-Foot Trefoil (*Lotus corniculatus*). Bugle (*Ajuga reptans*). Burnet, Salad or Lesser (*Sanguisorba*). Buttercup, Meadow (*Ranunculus*). Campion, Red (*Melandrium rubrum*). Celandine, Lesser (*Ranunculus ficaria*). Chamomile, Corn (*Anthemis arvensis*). Chicory, Wild (*Cichorium intybus*). Columbine (Aquilegia) Corncockle (*Agrostemma githago*). Cornflower (*Centaurea cyanus*). Cowslip (*Primula veris*). Cranesbill, Meadow (*Geranium pratensis*). Daisy, Ox-eye (*Chrysanthemum leucanthemum*). Dog-

Violet Common (*Viola riviniana*). Elecampane (*Inula helenium*). Everlasting Pea, Narrow-leaved(*Lathyrussylvestris*).Feverfew (*Chrysanthemum parthenium*). Flax (*Linum usitatissimum*). Forget-me-Not, Field (*Myosotis arvensis*). Foxglove (*Digitalis prupurea*). Gentian, Spring (*Gentiana verna*). Globeflower (Trollius). Goat's Head or Wild Salsify (*Aruncus dioicus*). Grass-of-Parnassus (*Parnassia palustris*). Harebell (*Campanula rotundifolia*). Horned-Poppy, Yellow (*Glaucium flavum*). Hounds-Tongue (*Cynoglossum officinale*). Iris, Yellow (*Iris pseudoacorus*). Knapweed, Common or Hardheads (*Centaurea nigra*). Knapweed, Greater (*Centaurea scabiosa*). Lady's Smock or Cuckooflower (*Cardamine pratensis*). Mallow, Common (*Malva sylvestris*). Mallow, Musk (*Malva moschata*). Marigold, Corn (*Chrysanthemum segetum*). Marjoram, Wild (*Origanum vulgare*). Marsh-Marigold or Kingcup (*Caltha palustris*). Meadowsweet (*Filipendula ulmaria*). Monkeyflower (Mimulus). Mullein, Dark (*Verbascum nigrum*). Mullein, Great or Aaron's Rod (*Verbascum thapsus*). Oxlip (*Primula elatior*). Pansy, Wild or Heartsease (*Viola tricolor*). Pimpernel, Scarlet (*Anagallis arvensis*). Pink Maiden (*Dianthus deltoides*). Poppy, Field or Common (*Papa ver rhoeas*). Poppy, Welsh (*Meconopsis cambrica*). Primrose (*Primula vulgaris*). Primrose, Bird's-Eye (*Primula farinosa*). Purple-Loosestrife (*Lythrum salicaria*). Ragged-Robin (*Lychnis flos-cuculi*). Rampion, Round-Headed (*Physeteuma orbiculare*). Saxifrage, Meadow (Saxifraga). Scabious, Devil's Bit (*Succisa pratensis*). Scabious (*Knautia arvensis*). Soapwort (*Saponaria officinalis*). Stitchwort, Greater (*Stellaria holostea*). Strawberry, Wild (*Fragaria vesca*). Tansy (*Tanacetum vulgare*). Teasel (*Dipsacus fullonum*). Thrift or Sea-Pink (*Armeria maritima*).Thyme, Wild (*Thymus serpyllum*). Toadflax, Common (*Linaria vulgaris*). Toadflax, Ivy-leaved

(*Cymbalaria muralis*). Tormentil (*Potentilla erecta*). Valerian, Common (*Valeriana officinalis*). Violet, Sweet (*Viola odorata*). Viper's-Bugloss (*Echium vulgare*). Wallflower, Wild (*Cherianthus allowi*). Woad (*Isatis tinctoria*). Yarrow (*Achillea millefolium*). Yellow-Rattle or Hay-Rattle (*Rhinanthus mirror*).

WILD FLOWERS (from seed, bulbs and corms)
Time to buy Seed, December–May. Mail order acceptable.
Where to find Indoors on seed rack.
Seed Packets stored dry and unsealed.
Hints Follow instructions on packet. Wide range. May need to be purchased from specialist seed source.
Most widely available Bird's-Foot Trefoil (*Lotus corniculatus*). Common Forget-me-Not (*Myosotis arvensis*). Common Knapweed or Hardhead (*Centaurea nigra*). Common Mallow (*Malva sylvestris*). Corn Chamomile (*Anthemis arvensis*). Corncockle (*Agrostemma githago*). Cornflower (*Centaurea cyanus*). Corn Marigold (*Chrysanthemum segetum*). Cowslip (*Primula veris*). Feverfew (*Chrysanthemum parthenium*). Field Poppy (*Papaver rhoeas*). Foxglove (*Digitalis purpurea*). Greater Knapweed (*Centaurea scabiosa*). Harebell (*Campanula rotundifolia*). Ivy-leaved Toadflax (*Cymbalaria muralis*). Lady's Bedstraw (*Galium verum*). Lady's Smock or Cuckoo Flower (*Cardamine pratensis*). Meadow Cranesbill (*Geranium pratense*). Mullein (Verbascum). Muskmallow (*Malva moschata*). Narrow-leaved Everlasting Pea (*Lathyrus sylvestris*). Ox-Eye Daisy (*Chrysanthemum leucanthemum*). Oxlip (*Primula elatior*). Primrose (*Primula vulgaris*). Ragged Robin (*Lychnis flos-cuculi*). Red Campion (*Melandrium rubrum*). Scarlet Pimpernel (*Anagallis arvensis*). Spring Gentian (*Gentiana verna*). Sweet Violet (*Viola odorata*). Teasle (*Dipsacus fullonum*). Tormentil (*Potentilla erecta*).

Welsh Poppy (*Meconopsis cambrica*). Wild Pansy or Heartsease (*Viola tricolor*). Wild Strawberry (*Fragaria vesca*). Wild Wallflower (*Cherianthus allowi*). Yarrow (*Achillea millefolium*).

BULBS AND CORMS Aconite, Winter. Bluebell (*Hyacinthoides non-scripta*). Meadow Buttercup (*Ranunculus acris*). Snake's-Head (*Fritillaria meleagris*). Snowdrop (Galanthus).

Where to See Plants Growing

Many nurseries, garden centres and private gardens open to the public will have specimen plants growing within their grounds. In addition, the following offer good collections.

The Royal Horticultural Society Gardens at:
  Wisley, Surrey;
  Pershore Agricultural College, Worcester.
  Rosemoor Gardens, Devon.
  Wakehurst Place, Sussex.
  Northern Horticultural Society Gardens, Harlow Carr, Harrogate, Yorkshire.
Bath Botanical Gardens.
Bedgebury National Pinetum, Sussex. (Conifers)
The Birmingham Botanical Gardens.
Bristol University Botanic Gardens.
Brogdale Trust, Faversham, Kent. (Fruit)
Burford House Gardens, Tenby Wells, Worcester.
Barnsley House, Barnsley, Gloucestershire.
Cambridge University Botanic Gardens.
Capel Manor, Waltham Cross, Middlesex.
Chelsea Physics Gardens, London.
Dundee University Botanical Garden.
Edinburgh Botanical Gardens.
Fletcher Moss Botanic Gardens, Manchester.
Glasgow Botanic Gardens.
Hillier Arboretum, Winchester.
Hull University Botanic Garden.

Hume's South London Botanical Institute Botanic Garden.
Leicester University Botanic Garden.
Liverpool University Botanic Garden.
Mottisfort Abbey, Romsey, Hants. (Roses)
Oxford University Botanical Gardens.
Probus Gardens, Truro, Cornwall.
Queen Mary's Rose Garden, Regents Park, London. (Roses)
Royal Botanic Gardens at Kew.
Saville Gardens, Windsor.
Sheffield Botanic Gardens.
Southampton University Botanic Gardens.
St Andrews University Botanic Gardens.
The Gardens of the Rose, St Albans. (Roses)
University College of Swansea Botanic Gardens.
Waterperry Gardens, Oxford.
Westonbirt Arboretum, Wiltshire.
Winkworth Arboretum, Guildford, Surrey.
Younger Botanic Gardens, Argyll, Scotland.

Also, The National Collections of Hardy Plants, administered by the National Council for Conservation of Plants and Gardens.

Glossary

Acid (as in soil) Term applied to soils with a pH of 6 or below, usually containing no free lime. Important in relation to acid-loving plants. See **pH**, and **Soil testing**.

Alkaline (as in soil) Term applied to soils with a pH of 7 or above, commonly but not exclusively associated with chalk or limestone soils. See **pH**.

Bare-rooted Description of a plant grown and dug from soil then sold without soil around roots.

Blackfly Small sucking insect attacking young parts of plants, damaging the tissue.

British Standards Standards set by the British Standards Institute and used by wholesale, retail and landscape sections of horticulture to specify plant size.

Bud Early stage of a new shoot or flower. The term refers to obvious growth bud and also to incipient swelling.

Budding Propagation method where a single bud from a selected parent is inserted into selected understock.

Bush Classification of shrub or small tree where branches grow from soil level or on a small 2 ft (60 cm) high stem.

Cane Length of bamboo used for support and training in the first years of establishment.

Canker Airborne fungus which enters through damaged stems and girdles the stem cutting off growth system with fatal results.

Cold wind Winds lower temperature than normal, causing a wind-chill factor, damaging certain susceptible plants.

Conservatory A construction with glazed areas used to display plants and not normally for propagation or growing.

Conservatory plants Plants for conservatory use.

Coral spot Fungus which attacks dead wood and then spreads into healthy tissue. Seen as small, coral pink spots. Cut-out once identified.

Cordons Classification and method of growing where a single stem with short side branches is growing and secured to a support at an angle of 35°. Maintained as such by annual pruning.

Cuttings Method of propagation where plants are produced by a small selected section of a parent, induced to form roots.

Deciduous Annual loss of all foliage to be regenerated in following spring e.g. *Acer palmatum* 'Dissectum' in Shrubs.

Defoliated Plants which have lost their leaves due to natural, climatic, or cultivation causes.

Die-back Where twigs, branches and stems become brittle, dark brown or black in colour. Affected shoots must be removed back to healthy tissue. Die-back occurs due to winter frost, summer drought or mechanical root damage.

Division Propagation method where root-clumps are divided into segments to form new plants as in *Rudbeckia* in 'Perennials'.

Dutch Elm Disease A virus spread by the Dutch Elm Beetle.

Drought Lack of rain causing soil to dry out in summer. Planting at this time is extremely dangerous, due to dehydration.

Espalier See **Horizontal-trained**.

Evergreen Retaining foliage throughout the year, except for small proportion which is unobtrusively shed, i.e. *Ilex aquifolium* (Holly). (See 'Shrubs').

Fan-training Classification or method of training; branches radiate from the base or trunk in a fan shape. Support is required and annual pruning: e.g. *Prunus domestica* Plum Victoria (see 'Fruit').

Feathered tree Classification of size and shape of young tree which has in excess of three side branches, distributed the length of the stem. Some trees are maintained in this form for life e.g. *Betula pendula* (see 'Trees') or further trained by removal of the lower branches to form bushes, half-standard or standard trees, as in *Fagus sylvatica* (Beech) (see 'Trees').

Fibrous root-system Root-system with small branching roots and rootlets.

Fire blight Fungus visible from July to September. Plant looks as if burnt. Cannot be controlled: remove affected plant and destroy.

Forestry outlets Growers of plants that are used for forestry.

Forms A word to describe varieties, cultivars and specific species of plants.

Fruits Edible, poisonous or ornamental fruits containing seeds of plants e.g. *Mespilus germanica*, *Medlar*. (See 'Fruit').

Garden centres Retail outlets for purchasing plants and other garden requirements.

Grafting Propagation method in which a section of stem from a selected plant is grafted on to an understock.

Greenfly Small sucking green or grey insect which attacks plant tissue.

Greenhouse Glazed construction in which plants are propagated and grown for production, protection or display.

Ground cover Low-growing plants forming a low carpet of growth e.g. *Lonicera pileata* (see 'Shrubs').

Grow *in situ* Plants grown from a small size in their final planting position e.g. *Davidia involucrata* (see 'Trees').

Half-standard trees Tree classification with a pre-trained stem or trunk 3 ft (1 m) and not more than 5 ft (1.5 m) or of a specific nominated height with branch system above. The height of stem or trunk does not extend once trees are planted and selection of the right height for position required is important.

Hardy Description of a plant able to withstand normally experienced winter frosts and cold.

Hardwood cuttings Propagation method by taking section of stem 8–12 in (20–30 cm) long of last year's growth and inserting into prepared soil.

Hedging Planting in a single or double line to form a barrier or screen.

Heeling in Process of storing bare-rooted plants from October–March prior to purchase. Roots are covered with soil or peat to prevent them drying out.

Horizontal-trained (espalier) Many wall-trained trees, shrubs and climbers are trained into a horizontal tiered shape to show off their beauty to the full and also to aid ripening of fruit. Support is required to maintain this shaping.

In the green Selected species of bulbs that transplant successfully when lifted and planted in leaf.

Invasive Some shrubs, perennials, plants and bulbs can, if conditions suit them, become a nuisance by spreading aggressively and occupying more spece than is required.

Kept under protection Vulnerable plants

are kept under protection until such times as planting can be done safely.

Layering Propagation method where a young shoot is laid horizontally and covered with soil until rooted.

Layers Plants produced by layering.

Leader Central, leading shoot of a tree, shrub or conifer.

Leaf canker Fungus disease that eats into the leaf tissue and disfigures it.

Leaf scorch Discoloration and shrivelling of foliage due to cold winds or strong sunlight.

Leaves Energy-producing part of a plant, carried on the branches.

Leg Short trunk or stem from which branches emerge as in *Ribes grossularia* (Gooseberry) (see 'Fruit').

Maiden trees (maidens) Classification of two-year-old tree, limited or few side branches.

Mail order Method of ordering and transporting plants from reputable nurseries. Charge made for postage and packing.

Mildew Airborne fungus producing a white, downy coating over leaves, flowers and fruits. High humidity and warmth will encourage it particularly from July onwards. Good cultivation and a systemic fungicide will keep under control.

Mop-headed Classification of tree or shrub which is grafted on to a short stem e.g. *Wisteria* as standard (see 'Trees').

Moss peat Dry peat. See **Peat**.

Mulch 2–3 in (5–8 cm) deep layer of organic material applied to the soil surface in autumn and winter. Retains moisture and keeps down weeds.

Multi-stemmed Classification or growing shape of trees and shrubs, both young and mature.

Neutral Measure of pH on the acidity–alkalinity scale of pH 6.5.

Nurseries Either wholesale or retail production units where a wider range of plant material may be found.

One-year grafts Classification of young plants produced by the propagation method of grafting. See **Grafting**.

Organic material Decayed or partially decayed vegetable or animal material such as garden compost, well-rotted farmyard manure, spent mushroom compost or peats that are used to improve the soil structure.

Ornamental specimens Plants of all types that are grown for their ornamental shape, flower or foliage effect.

Outside Area of a nursery or garden centre where plants are kept without protection.

Peat Organic material in condition of partial decay, forming naturally in waterlogged areas and used to improve soil texture. See **Moss Peat** and **Sedge Peat**.

pH Scale of measurement used to determine the amount of acidity and alkalinity in the soil using a soil-testing kit. A numeric scale pH of 6 or under as acid, 6.5 as neutral, 7 or above as alkaline. Chalk or limestone tends to be alkaline. The determining factor is not the actual mineral composition but the origin of the soil water.

Planting Replacing of plant into soil following transplanting.

Plants Word used to describe all growing, live vegetable material, of whatever type, also more specifically to describe plants with no woody stem.

Pleaching Method of training trees to grow horizontally to form a hedge on stilts. Usually *Lilia* (Lime), *Carpinus* (Hornbeam) or *Salix* (Willow).

Pollination Transference of pollen from one plant to another to produce fertilization of its fruit.

Pollinator Tree or shrub planted for the purpose of supplying pollen from itself to another selected plant of close relationship to help in fertilization of the fruit.

Pots Containers of various types and materials used for growing of plants.

Pre-packed Presentation method where roots are contained within moist peat and plant packed in a clear plastic sleeve with a pictorial and/or written description.

Propagation Method used to multiply any given parent plant such as budding, cuttings, grafting, layering or seed-sowing.

Protection Usually from wind or cold, but sometimes from rodents and birds. Also, areas in garden centres or nurseries where plants are protected from the effects of adverse weather.

Root-balled Description of a plant dug from the soil in which it was grown, with an ample ball of soil surrounding its roots. Should be enclosed in hessian sacking to prevent root disturbance during transportation.

Root clumps Description of plant material where no apparent stems, branches etc, are above ground and only the root remains.

Root system System that anchors the plant, stores food and acts as a transport system to transfer moisture and plant nutrients to other parts of the plant from the soil.

Root-wrapped Process where bare-rooted plants have roots wrapped in peat and a plastic outer covering to maintain moisture and protect from frost.

Rust Airborne fungus disease producing a red, rust-like coating on the leaves and stems. Good cultivation methods or a systemic fungicide will control.

Scab Airborne fungus producing grey-brown lesions on leaves and fruit, particularly in *Malus pumila* (Apple) varieties. A systematic fungicide will control.

Season The correct time for any operation or possible plant performance.

Sedge peat Peat sold in a wet condition. See **Peat**.

Semi-evergreen Normally evergreen, but likely to shed some or all leaves in unusually cold weather to which the plant is not accustomed.

Semi-mature trees Classification of trees, shrubs and conifers that are offered for sale as heavy standards or extra-heavy standards from specialist nurseries.

Shrub Woody plant with a growth pattern of stems branching from or near its base.

Side branches or branches Shoots emerging from the main stem, normally at a specified height and number.

Silver-leaf fungus Fungus apparent as a silver sheen on leaves of *Prunus* from late spring. No effective treatment and the tree should be destroyed.

Single shoots Classification where plants with only one shoot or stem are purchased.

Slow-growing A specified plant markedly slower-growing than other principal forms within its group.

Soil testing By using a chemical or electrical soil-testing kit to determine the pH, value of the soil. See **pH**, **Acid**, **Alkaline** or **Neutral** soil.

Soil types Various types of soil that are available applying to garden or potting soils.

Specialist nurseries Nurseries that specialize in one or limited specific groups of plants and can be contacted and consulted for a particular requirement.

Specimen plant A plant planted singly for display in an area able to exploit its full growth potential.

Stake and ties Securing of a plant to prevent wind damage.

Standard trees Classification applied and maintained for a tree with a clear stem of 5 ft (1.5 m) minimum and not more than 8 ft (2.5 m) or as specified.

Sub-shrub Woody plant producing stem growth which dies back in winter.

Subsoil Layer of soil directly below the uppermost layer (topsoil), generally having a poor composition and containing fewer plant foods.

Substitutions Sometimes a different variety is offered for the one required. Care should be taken before accepting substitutes as they may not always have the same habit or characteristics or produce the same display and attraction as the original choice.

Sucker Growth on a plant arising from an underground root, or bud. In some plants this is a natural method of growing, but suckers produced from grafted plants are always undesirable and should be removed.

Sun scorch Damage to leaves in the form of browning, mottling and shrivelling, caused by exposure to strong sunlight.

Support Any form of support used to keep the plant upright or to support a trained shape.

Tender Description of a plant liable to frost or cold in winter and early spring.

Timber Trees grown to produce useable

timber for commercial use. See *Populus* in 'Trees'.

Topsoil Uppermost layer of soil which has a good workable texture and contains a high proportion of plant foods.

Topworking Description of a propagation method by grafting using an understock with height as required.

Trees Wood plant typically producing a single stem (trunk) below a canopy of branches.

Trunk Single upright section of growth in trees that supports the upper canopy of branches.

Understock Selected seedling or specially grown young plant used as the rooted base on to which the techniques of budding and grafting are carried out.

Universal pollinator Plant that will pollinate a number of others, e.g. as in *Malus pumila* (Apple). (See 'Fruit').

Variety Term specifying a naturally occurring variant of a plant, but also used loosely to describe any variant closely related to a particular form. In this publication the word 'form' has been used to cover this term, with the exception of fruit and vegetables.

Vegetative propagation Methods of producing new plants from existing specimens, e.g. by budding, cuttings, division, grafting or layering rather than from seed.

Vine system System of plant training used on some climbers were individual stems are trained by tying to horizontal fixed wires and removing any surplus growth in early spring not required to cover the intended area. Horizontal wires should not be more than 18 in (50 cm) apart.

Wall specimens Shrub, tree or other

plant which specifically allows itself, by its growth nature, to be trained against a wall for support or protection, often in a fan-trained shape.

Waterlogged Ground containing excessive water.

Well-established Plant that has been allowed to build up a good root-system within its pot, prior to being offered for sale.

Well-prepared Good preparation of soil, prior to planting.

Whips Classification of plant up to one-year-old with a single stem and no branches.

Whitefly Small sap sucking insect which hides on the undersides of leaves and causes leaf damage, use a systemic insecticide to control.

Willow scab Fungus attacking willows, in particular *Salix chrysocoma* (Golden Weeping Willow). Difficult to control, remove damaged growth and spray with a systemic fungicide.

Wind protection Normally netting erected, particularly through winter, on the exposed windward side of plants.

Wind scorch Damage to leaves caused by wind when water vapour is too rapidly lost from the leaves.

Index

To aid reference, the index has been divided into sections corresponding to the various sections in the main body of the text.

Where specific species have been entered in detail within the text, these are listed here, and where a number of species have been grouped together, the broader groups are listed.

As with all of the text, all plant names and groups are given as they are most commonly found in garden centres. Use the text index in conjunction with your garden centre or nursery layout to link the species you find to the information you want.

Once you have located the group entry you require, you will find it expands to cover most of the commonly found forms available through garden centres and nurseries.

Index

FOR THE BEST IN PAPERBACKS, LOOK FOR THE

In every corner of the world, on every subject under the sun, Penguin represents quality and variety – the very best in publishing today.

For complete information about books available from Penguin – including Puffins, Penguin Classics and Arkana – and how to order them, write to us at the appropriate address below. Please note that for copyright reasons the selection of books varies from country to country.

In the United Kingdom: Please write to *Dept E.P., Penguin Books Ltd, Harmondsworth, Middlesex, UB7 0DA.*

If you have any difficulty in obtaining a title, please send your order with the correct money, plus ten per cent for postage and packaging, to *PO Box No 11, West Drayton, Middlesex*

In the United States: Please write to *Dept BA, Penguin, 299 Murray Hill Parkway, East Rutherford, New Jersey 07073*

In Canada: Please write to *Penguin Books Canada Ltd, 2801 John Street, Markham, Ontario L3R 1B4*

In Australia: Please write to the *Marketing Department, Penguin Books Australia Ltd, P.O. Box 257, Ringwood, Victoria 3134*

In New Zealand: Please write to the *Marketing Department, Penguin Books (NZ) Ltd, Private Bag, Takapuna, Auckland 9*

In India: Please write to *Penguin Overseas Ltd, 706 Eros Apartments, 56 Nehru Place, New Delhi, 110019*

In the Netherlands: Please write to *Penguin Books Netherlands B.V., Postbus 195, NL–1380AD Weesp*

In West Germany: Please write to *Penguin Books Ltd, Friedrichstrasse 10–12, D–6000 Frankfurt/Main 1*

In Spain: Please write to *Alhambra Longman S.A., Fernandez de la Hoz 9, E–28010 Madrid*

In Italy: Please write to *Penguin Italia s.r.l., Via Como 4, I-20096 Pioltello (Milano)*

In France: Please write to *Penguin Books Ltd, 39 Rue de Montmorency, F-75003 Paris*

In Japan: Please write to *Longman Penguin Japan Co Ltd, Yamaguchi Building, 2–12–9 Kanda Jimbocho, Chiyoda-Ku, Tokyo 101*